THE MAGE

The Mage

Book 2 of the Acacia Chronicles

Julie H. Peralta

PALMETTO
PUBLISHING
Charleston, SC
www.PalmettoPublishing.com

Copyright © 2024 by Julie H. Peralta

All rights reserved

No portion of this book may be reproduced, stored in a retrieval system, or transmitted in any form by any means–electronic, mechanical, photocopy, recording, or other–except for brief quotations in printed reviews, without prior permission of the author.

Paperback ISBN: 979-8-8229-4463-3
eBook ISBN: 979-8-8229-4464-0

Contents

Chapter 1—Contact 1
Chapter 2—Injured 9
Chapter 3—Surprises 19
Chapter 4—The Village 31
Chapter 5—DaiSur 43
Chapter 6—The Order of the Mages 57
Chapter 7—Fractured 70
Chapter 8—A Difficult Journey 82
Chapter 9—The Temple of Anaia 93
Chapter 10—Aistra 109
Chapter 11—Resolutions 119
Chapter 12—The Meeting 131
Chapter 13—Information 145
Chapter 14—The Note 158
Chapter 15—The Morning 171
Chapter 16—Plans 185
Chapter 17—Departure 201
Chapter 18—First Contact 213

Chapter 19—A New Plan 222
Chapter 20—Going West.. 234
Chapter 21—Dreams.. 245
Chapter 22—The Blue Stone 256
Chapter 23—To Divide 266
Chapter 24—The Emissaries 283
Chapter 25—And Conquer.. 293
Chapter 26—The Mage's Army.. 305
Chapter 27—The Rogue Mage... 318
Chapter 28—The Strategy 331
Chapter 29—Evasion 338
Chapter 30—Reunion.. 349
Chapter 31—Exchanges 361
Chapter 32—Return to the Temple... 372
Chapter 33—The Diviners and the Martial Artists 385
Chapter 34—Explanations 404
Chapter 35—Family 415
Epilogue 429
About the Author.. 433

Dedication

To Alisia Peralta Pendygraft for your continued encouragement, commitment, and support.
Without you, this would not have been possible.

Thank you.

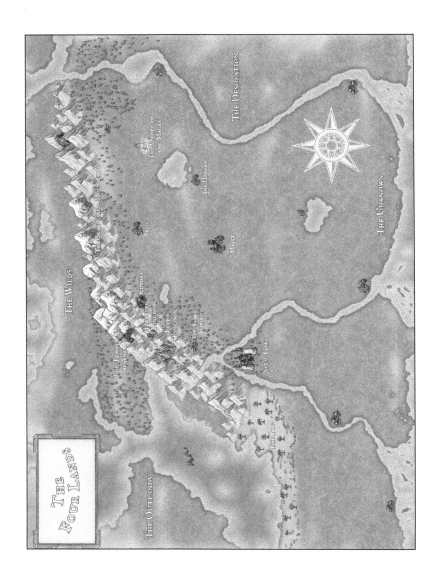

Chapter 1–Contact

Alia walked down the streets of Miast. It was very early, the sun had just begun to peep over the horizon, and she was exhausted. She had been out all night with a patient who had a very difficult childbirth. So difficult, in fact, that Alia was on the verge of calling Sairima for help. But then the baby came, and everything was fine.

It had been nearly a year since her marriage to Shao, and the two of them were deliriously happy. Alia had never dreamed that life could be so perfect. There was only one black cloud that hung in the sky for them, and that was the *vision* that their friend, the diviner, Zimpf had seen shortly after their marriage. It was a *vision* of the mage, Marek, who had mesmerized Alia last year and stolen the powerful, magical Orb of Ahi from her. Then he had bewitched and kidnapped an elven princess and led Alia and the princess into near death by a group of orcs. Granted, he did help them defeat the orcs in the end. But everyone believed he had died.

Alia and Shao, along with her twin sister Sh'ron and her brother-in-law, the warrior, Chhdar, Shao's sister, the healer, Sairima, and, of course, Zimpf, had discussed the vision in detail. They decided that the best way to handle things was to go about their lives as normally as possible and to prepare for any adversity. To that end, Shao had been training Alia, and sometimes Sh'ron, in the martial arts. Alia had gotten pretty good, although she would never be on the same level as Shao; no one would ever be as good as Shao.

Aside from learning how to defend herself without her sword, Shao, had taught her how to be hyperaware of her surroundings—for example, how to know when she was being followed.

And Alia was certainly being followed. The footsteps behind her walked when she walked and they turned where she turned; the steps quickened when her steps quickened.

Tired of the cat and mouse game, Alia decided to end it. She turned down the nearest street then swiftly and silently ducked into an embrasure. The figure, clothed in a cloak with the hood pulled up, fell for the trick, rushing past her. Alia stepped out behind the footpad, grabbed the cloak, and pulled the person bodily onto the ground, stepping onto the assailant's neck and pinning the stalker to the ground.

"Alia!" a familiar voice gasped.

It was Medjii, one of the elders from the Order of the Mages.

"What are you doing?" Alia demanded. "You scared me half to death!"

"You didn't do me any good either," Medjii accused. "Do you mind getting off my throat?"

"Sorry," Alia said. She lifted her foot then extended her hand to help the older woman rise. Alia also handed Medjii the satchel she had dropped.

"Thank you," the older mage said politely.

Alia stood, her arms crossed over her chest and her foot tapping impatiently on the ground. "Do you want to explain why you were creeping around behind me?"

"I needed to talk to you," Medjii answered, rubbing her neck.

"You could have just come to the house," Alia invited.

"I couldn't," said Medjii. "I need to talk to you without alerting Shao."

"No," Alia said firmly.

"But I really think—"

"No," Alia interrupted.

"I demand that you—" Medjii started to insist.

"No," Alia persisted. "Anything you say to me I will share with him. So, you may as well give up all the clandestine secrecy."

Medjii stared at the young woman's resolve then finally relented. "Let's go see Shao then."

They walked silently side by side; just before they turned the last corner by Alia's house, Medjii tried once again to detain the young woman. But Alia slipped easily through the mage's grasp, turned the corner, and was gone from her view.

The older woman sighed, clutched her satchel closer to her chest, and followed.

As soon as Alia rounded the corner, she saw Shao standing in front of their house, waiting for her.

Alia had long suspected that Shao followed her on these late-night medical runs, but she could never catch him at it. His casual reaction at seeing Medjii follow Alia around the corner served to solidify her suspicions.

"Hello Medjii," he greeted her. "It's nice of you to visit."

"Shao," she replied, unconsciously rubbing her neck again.

"Come in," he invited, glancing nonchalantly at the bruise starting to form on the older woman's throat. "Breakfast is almost ready."

He directed her to the dining room and turned to greet Alia with a knowing smile and a kiss.

"How was the delivery?" he asked. He then whispered in his soft voice, "I have summoned the others."

Alia smiled up at him and nodded.

Clearly, they agreed. Whatever Medjii had come to say, she would be forced to reveal it to all of them.

Within moments of breakfast being served, Zimpf suddenly appeared, letting himself in through the back door.

"I smell breakfast!" he announced, sauntering in the dining room and carrying an empty plate from the kitchen. He seated himself, then looked over at Medjii in feigned surprise.

"Medjii!" he exclaimed. "When did you get here? Shao and Alia didn't tell me they had company."

Medjii looked at him with a deadpan expression. "Sure," she said tonelessly. Then, she looked at Shao. Shaking her head, she muttered, "I should have known."

Just as Zimpf finished filling his plate with food, there was a polite knock at the front door.

"I wonder who that could be?" Medjii asked sarcastically.

"It's Chhdar and Sh'ron," Zimpf announced. Everyone turned to look at him. "No, I didn't *see*," he told them, looking around at the sudden silence. "Well, I meant I didn't *see* them like that. But I did see them walking up the street toward your house," he explained.

Alia got up, let them in, and handed them plates.

The couple, though solemn, looked very happy together.

Sh'ron looked curiously at Medjii's neck, started to say something, and then swallowed her words as Alia gave a quick shake of her head.

After everyone had eaten, Alia started the unofficial meeting rather abruptly.

"Okay, Medjii," she said. "What's going on? Why did you show up here suddenly and demand to talk to me alone?"

Medjii was silent for so long that Alia began to think she wasn't going to talk.

Finally, she leaned down, picked up her bag, and pulled out a curious-looking, oddly shaped black canister. She set the item down carefully in the middle of the table.

"Before we address this," she announced, indicating the canister, "I have something to tell you."

The room was silent as everyone waited for her to continue.

Looking around, she finally uttered the words they had been dreading: "Marek is alive."

No one spoke. Instead, the friends looked back and forth at each other.

"You're not surprised," Medjii stated.

"No," said Shao.

"Why?"

"We let Zimpf *vision* us last year," Alia explained. "Shao and I saw him then."

"Why would you do that?" Medjii asked, looking back and forth between them and Zimpf. "Were you looking for something specific in your future? Were you trying to *see* Marek?"

No one answered.

"So, what does he want?" Shao wanted to know.

"Is he after us?" Sh'ron asked. "Is he angry because we left him?"

"How could he even survive?" Chhdar questioned. "We saw where he had been standing. It looked like he had been buried under feet of lava. Plus, he had an orc arrow buried in his chest."

Medjii looked from one person to the next, finally focusing on Chhdar. "He survived because he is a mage." Then she held up her hand before anyone could say anything. "We at the Order of the Mages vastly underestimated his abilities. It seems that his mentor taught him much more than we presumed. My best guess is that he performed a dasima, or transportation spell, which allowed him to be conveyed to another location. He probably had been practicing it for weeks, maybe even months."

"Where do you think he went?" Alia asked. But before Medjii answered, Alia knew. She and Sh'ron looked at each other, then whispered together, "home."

"Yes," Medjii admitted. "He went home."

Everyone turned to stare at her.

"He summoned me using magic. I went to him and found him badly injured. Once he recovered, we spoke at length," she acknowledged. "He is after something…" She paused then continued to speak, although Alia thought she seemed to be struggling to say the words. "He would not tell me, and I could not ferret it out." Medjii drew a deep breath, swallowed hard, and stopped. She put her hand over her eyes then fought to look up. She clenched her jaws hard and looked down again. After a moment, she seemed to gain control and choked out, "he is afraid."

"Of what?" Alia asked.

"Of you all," she continued. "He thinks that the five of you will try to stop him."

They sat in shocked silence for several moments.

"Stop him?" Shao questioned.

Medjii nodded then began to shake, her face turning an alarming shade of red.

"No!" she gasped in agony. "I cannot do this!"

Alia stood and ran to the shuddering woman's side. But Medjii jerked out of her chair then raked her fingernails in deep grooves down her face. They instantly filled with rivulets of blood.

Grabbing both sides of her head, her eyes began to bulge dangerously. "I gave it to him," she screeched. "I gave him the Aghara! Stop him!" she gutturalized. Then, lurching toward the table in a sudden, jerky movement, Medjii grabbed the black object sitting placidly on the table. She pulled it up against her stomach with clawlike hands.

Zimpf jumped to his feet and began screaming, "Out! Now! Everyone out!" Then he began pulling people out of their chairs and shoving them toward the front door.

Everything happened in a flash.

But Alia saw it in slow motion.

Medjii, gibbering insanely, twisted the container open.

Chhdar grabbed Sh'ron and sprinted with her out the front door.

The object in Medjii's hands began to smoke.

Zimpf shouted.

Alia met Shao's eyes.

Medjii's object flashed a spark.

Shao picked up Alia and threw her to the front door.

The spark grew into a volatile flash.

Alia fell hard against Zimpf; they both fell to the ground outside.

The room exploded into light and fire.

Marek spent several weeks recovering from his burns, from the arrow injury, and from the damage the Orb of Ahi had inflicted. According to Medjii, had the orb not been destroyed, he would never have survived. He spent his days quietly reading and studying the books about the history of the Order of the Mages that he had pressed upon Medjii to bring. She had refused at first, but Marek, if nothing else, was charming and charismatic. Finally, she relented, seeing no harm in his request.

It was in those books that the young mage found what he was seeking: a way to exact revenge upon those who he perceived had wronged him.

He spent the evenings with Medjii and a woman named DaiSur, who he knew had encouraged his master to apprentice him—a woman he had once worked for.

It only took a few evenings of friendly camaraderie to dupe the two women into believing he had changed, that he wanted nothing more than peace and solitude, that his master had lied and tricked him into doing what he now knew to be evil.

Then he began the insidious whispering, the unremitted mesmerizing, and the deceitful compelling to sway the vulnerable women until they had no choice but to obey his commands.

Medjii left for the headquarters of the Order of the Mages and then returned with the desired magical object. Shortly thereafter, he dismissed DaiSur and sent Medjii on what would turn out to be her last task.

Chapter 2–Injured

Alia rolled quickly to her feet and turned to check on Shao. He wasn't behind her. She scanned the yard quickly; he wasn't there. She couldn't find him.

He's still inside! she thought in horror. She sprinted to the front door, screaming for her husband. "Shao! Shao!"

But Zimpf stopped her from running back inside her burning home. He grabbed her arm, but she twisted loose skillfully.

"Shao!" she shrieked again, still running for the door.

Again, Zimpf stopped her by grabbing her around the waist.

Alia fought back, kicking, biting, scratching. Finally, she wrenched her way free.

Then Chhdar was there. He detained her by the simple expedient of picking her up from behind and holding her while she fought viciously to free herself and save her husband. The big man's arms corded with effort, but he was unmovable.

Suddenly the door was kicked violently open from inside, and

Shao, carrying the unconscious Medjii, stumbled out, crossed the porch, and sank onto the lawn, gently laying her on the grass.

Alia instantly collapsed, weeping in relief.

Shao calmly walked over to the big warrior and held out his arms.

Wordlessly, Chhdar handed Alia to him and went to wrap his arms around Sh'ron.

By now, a crowd had begun to gather around the burning house.

Shao set Alia on her feet and held her while she sobbed hysterically.

Sh'ron watched for a moment to make sure her twin was not hurt, then she looked down the street to see Sairima sprinting toward them. It was easy to see by her athleticism that she and Shao were siblings. Sairima had brought with her several healers-in-training and aids. But the tall woman was far outpacing her medical staff.

When she made it to the burning home, she took a quick look around, assessed the situation, and immediately took charge. She sent a townsman to organize a bucket brigade to put out the fire. At the same time, she knelt by Medjii, examined her professionally, then sent her to the hospital on a litter she had her staff bring. Finally, she demanded that everyone who had been in the house present themselves to the hospital. "Now!"

Almost like a line of abashed school children, they followed Sairima to the big house.

In the hospital wing, Sairima attempted to send them to separate examination rooms. But Alia refused to leave Shao, then Sh'ron refused to be separated from Chhdar. The healer finally relented and allowed each couple to wait together.

Alia and Shao were ushered into a large room near Sairima's office. Alia tried to be the healer for which she was being trained; she failed miserably.

She had Shao sit on the examination table, but her hands were shaking so hard that she couldn't complete the physical. So, she turned away from him to gather what Sairima would need to treat the martial artist. But she was crying so hard that she couldn't see to gather the bandages and salve. Instead, she stood with her back to Shao, sobbing quietly and shaking visibly.

Shao slid agilely off the table, turned Alia to face him, then held her tightly while she wept against his chest. They were still holding each other when Sairima entered the room.

Sairima made Shao sit back on the examination table and ordered Alia to sit in a nearby chair. Shao had a nasty cut above his right eyebrow, the left side of his face was slightly burned, blisters had formed on his right hand, and his clothes and hair were singed. There were no other injuries.

Sairima wordlessly stitched up the cut above his eye, applied a salve to his face and hand, then wrapped his right hand in a light cotton material.

Then she demanded they trade places so she could check Alia. Aside from a couple of bumps and bruises from Shao throwing her out the door and her collision with Zimpf, Alia was unharmed.

Finally, Sairima sat to talk to them.

"What happened?" she questioned.

Alia told the story, starting with her meeting Medjii that morning as she was walking home after delivering the baby.

"I heard you did a good job with a very difficult delivery," Sairima congratulated her.

"Thank you," Alia said quietly. Sairima did not give compliments easily, and Alia was surprised to get one.

"How are the others?" Alia asked.

"Your sister and brother-in-law were completely unharmed. They were only worried about you two. Zimpf was not burned. But he suffered a myriad of scrapes, scratches, and contusions," she said, looking at Alia. "Did you do that?"

Alia looked at the floor and nodded. "I owe him an apology," she muttered ashamedly.

"I'm sure he will forgive you." Sairima told her.

"He will," Shao agreed. "But you are never going to live this down," he teased her.

Alia smiled slightly. She still had tears running down her face, but she had calmed down somewhat.

"What about Medjii?" Shao asked, just as Alia started to ask the same question.

Sairima's face grew serious. "She is not likely to survive; she was very badly burned. Whatever that device was which she brought into your house did enormous damage. It is my opinion that had she not cradled it against her body like she did, you would all be dead."

Alia, her eyes wide in shock, looked at Shao. She was remembering how Medjii had pressed the black canister against her stomach just before Zimpf ordered everyone out.

"That is enough talking for now," Sairima told them. "You both need some rest." She handed Alia a bag of herbs and gave instructions for making a calming tea. "This will help you both to sleep, and it will also provide some pain relief for you," she said, looking at Shao.

"Also, I have received word that it was only your dining room that was damaged. I have taken the liberty of having some of your things brought here and placed in the suite on the top floor. Workmen will begin fixing your house tomorrow. It will take about two weeks to complete," Sairima stated matter-of-factly. "During that time, you will be relieved of your duties," she added, looking at Alia.

"Now go to bed," she ordered them. "I want you to rest for a while. You can discuss this with everyone tomorrow. I have already arranged for breakfast to be sent to your suite in the morning."

Shao held out his good hand and helped Alia stand. With their arms around each other, they walked up the stairs.

Alia had never been in the suite to which Sairima directed them. But she was enchanted by the simple aesthetics of the room. It was tastefully decorated with soft, muted colors and pastoral paintings. There was a huge sitting room large enough to seat at least a couple dozen people, a separate dining area with a table for twenty, a bathroom with a tub big enough to swim in, an enormous bed, and a closet already filled with their clothes.

She helped Shao undress, take a quick sponge bath, and get settled in the massive bed. Then she took a bath, put on her night clothes, fixed their tea, and climbed in bed beside him. They quickly fell asleep.

Alia woke up in the middle of the afternoon. Shao was still asleep. While he slept, she took the opportunity to examine his wounds. The cut above his right eye was sewn up perfectly with small, even stitches. Alia was sure he wouldn't even have a scar. His face was burned red on one side, but there was no sign of blistering; she thought it would heal quickly. His right hand was bandaged. She decided she would look at it in the morning. As she was checking him, she realized that the corners of his mouth had turned up in a slight smile.

"How long have you been awake?" she asked.

"For a while," he told her.

"How are you feeling?" Alia questioned him.

"You're almost a healer now," Shao smiled proudly. "You tell me."

Alia looked at him seriously. "I was so scared," she confessed.

"I'm fine," he told her. "To be honest, I'm very tired of just lying around. Why don't we grab some food from the kitchen and take a walk?"

So they packed some food and walked out to the grounds, eventually making their way to the hidden garden that Shao had made for Alia. They sat and talked quietly until dusk and then walked slowly back to the big house, where Alia made them some more of the potent tea Sairima had sent. They retired early.

The next morning, Shao, responding to a summons from Sairima, went down to the hospital wing to have his hand reexamined while Alia waited for their guests. Sh'ron and Chhdar arrived early so the sisters could talk. Chhdar was nibbling on some of the breakfast food that had just been delivered and Alia and her twin were sitting on the sofa talking quietly when Zimpf limped into the room.

The diviner's injuries were much more severe than Sairima had led Alia to believe. Poor Zimpf came limping in, leaning heavily on a cane. His right pant leg had been split up to his thigh to allow room for the massive bandage encircling his badly swollen knee. Alia could see the grimace of pain on the diviner's face each time he attempted to take a step. Zimpf's arms, especially his right arm, were a mass of bruises, and his face was also badly contused. He sported a spectacular black eye on his right side, the bridge of his nose revealed what was almost certainly a bad break, and three massive gouges made their way from his left temple through his patched left eye and across his face, stopping just above his right shoulder.

Alia dropped the water glass she had been holding and ran to the badly injured man.

"Oh no!" she shrieked, rushing to the severely injured man.

"Oh, Zimpf! Did I do all that? I am so sorry!"

Alia put one arm around his waist, and Sh'ron, who had followed, ran to his other side to help the limping man make his way painfully to a comfortable chair. Once he was seated, Alia had Chhdar pull up a small table while she ran into the bedroom to get a pillow to elevate Zimpf's leg. Together, she and Sh'ron gently lifted the man's damaged limb until it was comfortably situated. Then, Chhdar fixed the battered diviner a massive plate of food.

The entire time, Alia was apologizing profusely.

Just as Zimpf began to eat, Shao came back into the room with his hand newly wrapped.

He stood staring at Zimpf's extensive injuries with a quizzical look and a smirk playing around the edges of his lips.

"Did Alia do that much damage to you?" he questioned, looking at his wife proudly.

"Shao!" Alia said his name in shock. "It's not funny!"

"It's fine, Alia," Zimpf moaned in pain. "It's not your fault," he forgave her magnanimously.

Shao nodded and made his way stealthily across the room. "Let me help you, my friend," he said softly. Then, unpredictably, the martial artist struck at his friend like a black-footed cat.

Zimpf was yanked forcefully from his seat, twisted vigorously, flipped upside down, then propelled violently across the room and over a sofa. Almost as an afterthought, Shao threw the cane which made a solid "bonking" sound as it made contact with Zimpf's head.

It happened so fast that Alia didn't even have time to scream.

"Ouch," Zimpf said lightly.

Then he jumped up effortlessly, eyepatch gone, his bandage puddled around his ankle, and the bruises and gouges smeared.

"Ta-da!" Zimpf shouted exuberantly while performing an awkward tap dance. "I'm cured!"

Alia looked at the man in stunned surprise. Then, she turned to Shao, who held up his hands. Smeared all over his good left hand and his bandaged right hand, she could see the makeup which Zimpf had used to create his "injuries."

The twins looked at each other, then at Shao and Chhdar, and finally, Zimpf, who was grinning from ear to ear, his dimples springing to life. Then they began to laugh.

"I thought you were really, really hurt," Alia said to him when she finally caught her breath.

Then she looked at Shao. "My heart nearly stopped when you tossed your injured friend across the room."

Shao was still laughing. "Well, he did deserve it. Didn't you?" he asked Zimpf.

"No, not really," Zimpf chortled. "I did sustain some serious injuries," he said, pointing at three barely visible scratches across his face and nodding his head seriously. "And I have a bruise." He pointed to a light purple spot on his left wrist.

"I'm just embarrassed." Alia confessed, burying her hands in her face. "I spent a whole year training, and that's the worst I could do."

Shao walked across the room and raised Alia's chin up with his index finger. "Don't think like that," he gently admonished her. "You are good. It's just that Zimpf has been trained to break all of the holds I taught you and to avoid all of the punches you delivered."

"I had to learn those," Zimpf protested. "You used me as a punching bag too many times at school."

Just then, there was a soft knocking at the door, and Sairima entered. She looked curiously at Zimpf. "What happened to you?" she asked, indicating the makeup smeared all over the man's face and arms.

No one answered.

"Sit down," she told them. "Except for you," she indicated Zimpf. "Go wash off that ridiculous makeup. And be quick about it!"

Zimpf ran.

By the time he returned, everyone was seated at the dining room table with Sairima at the head.

"I have news," she told them in a businesslike tone. "Medjii passed away this morning."

Everyone gasped.

Alia looked down and began to cry. Sh'ron echoed her. Shao, Chhdar, and Zimpf looked silently at the table.

"She didn't really have a chance," Sairima continued. "She absorbed most of the energy from that container into her own body. I'm sorry," she said. "I thought you should know before you started your meeting."

Sairima looked at the five of them. "I sent for Ciern yesterday. Amicu and Mama should be here sometime today." She smiled girlishly when she said Amicu's name.

Then she stood abruptly. "I must be going; I have patients to attend to." And with that, she retreated purposefully, shutting the door silently behind her.

They heard the lock click loudly in the doorknob. It sounded like a warning.

Marek studied the Aghara, trying desperately to unlock its secrets. He knew that vessel contained the essence of great power, power which would imbue him with complete and total control over the thoughts and actions of others.

So, he went to work. First, he needed to unlock the mysteries sealed inside the lidded vase, then he would have to learn how to control them.

Chapter 3–Surprises

"When do we leave?" Zimpf asked of the group sitting quietly around the table.

"I say as soon as possible," Sh'ron asserted.

"I agree," Chhdar rumbled in his deep voice. "We can't let that mage get away with the cold-blooded murder of one of our friends," he stated firmly.

Everyone looked at Shao to see what he would say. He sat silently, looking at the floor for several moments before finally looking up. "Where do you propose we go?" he asked Zimpf. "Do you *see* something?"

The diviner opened his mouth and closed it several times without responding.

"Shao?" Alia asked quietly.

"Amicu will be here in a few hours. I think we should wait and discuss things with him," Shao responded thoughtfully. "He is probably the best tactician in the Four Lands. We would be wise to confer with him before we make any decisions."

"Shao is right about Amicu," Zimpf agreed.

One by one, the others nodded.

"I also think that we need to be very careful," Shao said in a deadly tone. "We have to remember that this attack was directed at the five of us, not at Medjii. Marek could have set up a number of assassination attempts in order to defeat us."

"What do you recommend we do then?" Chhdar asked with his arm wrapped protectively around Sh'ron.

"I think there are some things we can do to protect ourselves," Shao answered. "First, there is always safety in numbers. No one is to go out alone, for any reason. I would like to see all of you move to the Big House here. Second, be aware of anything that is odd or different. If there is a staff member you don't recognize, or if anyone seems like they don't belong or seems nervous, report it to me immediately. Finally, trust your instincts. If something feels the least bit off, get help immediately." Shao looked at each of them intensely, his eyes resting on Alia.

They all nodded grimly.

"Chhdar and I will set up the school so that it runs itself," Sh'ron announced. "We'll leave now and be back by lunchtime. Do you think that will be okay?" she said, asking Shao's permission.

He nodded. "Go now and come back to this room as quickly as possible."

The couple moved purposefully out the door.

"Let's go get your things," Shao told Zimpf while reaching for Alia's hand.

The three of them followed Chhdar and Sh'ron out into the hallway.

They had to pass Alia and Shao's home to get to Zimpf's house. As they neared it, Shao stopped, looking at the front door thoughtfully.

"Did anyone get the bag that Medjii was carrying?" he asked. Then, without waiting for an answer, he went up the stairs and opened the door. He turned to look at Alia and Zimpf. "Come on. I meant what I said about no one being alone."

"I didn't expect you to be worried about going anywhere by yourself," Zimpf remarked snidely as he entered the house ahead of Shao.

"I wasn't worried about me," Shao told him.

"Oh, I see," Zimpf said, glancing quickly at Alia.

"I wasn't worried about her either," Shao teased.

"Well, if you're going to be *that* way about it," Zimpf groused, marching into the house with his face set and his back stiff in aggravation.

Alia and Shao laughed.

The house was surprisingly undamaged except for the dining room, which would need extensive repairs. They located Medjii's bag then quickly went to Zimpf's house, which was a couple of blocks away. It only took the diviner a short while to gather his things.

They hurried back to the big house.

As soon as they entered, they were greeted enthusiastically by Amicu and his mother who insisted on being called Mama. Amicu had been a classmate at the Temple of Anaia with Shao and Zimpf. The Temple, a specialty school located high up in the Skarsgaard Mountains, was designed to train the most talented youth in the Four Lands in a wide variety of disciplines. Amicu's specialty had been tactics since he and his parents lived in a village close to the mountains which was a dangerous area prone to orc attacks.

Mama was delighted to see them and demanded that they come with her into the huge dining room for a snack and to chat.

Amicu excused himself, promising to meet them shortly. Then, before anyone could stop him, he darted out the door to look for Sairima. He and the healer had met the year before at Alia and Shao's wedding. They had an almost instant connection and had been dating long distance ever since.

Alia, Shao, Zimpf, and Mama moved to the dining room. They selected a light lunch and sat at a large, round table. Almost as soon as they got comfortable, Sh'ron and Chhdar joined them. The group talked and laughed as Mama told them stories about life in Selo.

"How long will you all be visiting?" Sh'ron asked politely.

"Well, we will just have to see what happens," Mama smirked mysteriously.

Zimpf's eyes immediately went blank for a moment, then he winked at Mama. She grinned in return.

Just then, Amicu and Sairima came into the room, holding hands and smiling. "We thought we would find you all here," Amicu told them. "Sairima and I would like to see if you all would like to join us for a dinner party tonight?"

Everyone agreed and started talking at once—all except Shao, who looked at Amicu gravely. Almost imperceptibly, he tilted his head at the door. Amicu nodded once.

After lunch, Mama went with Sairima to make her rounds at the hospital, and Amicu convened with the others in Alia and Shao's room on the top floor. They told him everything that had happened, and he listened to the entire story without asking any questions. Finally, Shao fell silent; Amicu sat, thinking quietly.

"You sure know how to ruin a man's day," he said unhappily,

looking at the floor.

"We had to include you in on all the fun, oh mighty tactician," Zimpf replied in a mocking tone.

"Shut up, Zimpf," Amicu told him.

Zimpf opened his mouth to reply, but Shao kicked him under the table.

"Ow!" he complained.

"I wish Ciern were here. I would love to hear his opinion," Amicu said wistfully.

"He should be on his way," Shao told him.

"Did you send for him?" Amicu looked up curiously.

"Sairima did," Shao answered. "She sent a fast messenger to him the morning of the explosion."

"She's quite a woman, isn't she?" Amicu bragged proudly.

"Yeah, but she's scary," Zimpf announced, looking around the room for support.

Amicu leaned over quickly and smacked Zimpf solidly.

"Ow!" the diviner complained again, rubbing the back of his head.

"Do you have the bag that Medjii carried?" Amicu asked.

Shao got up and retrieved the bag from the bedroom where he had hidden it that morning.

Amicu pulled everything out of Medjii's bag, and they examined each article thoroughly but didn't find anything of interest.

"I wish Ciern was here," Amicu said again. "He's the strategist."

"I have a question," Chhdar asked Amicu. "You are a tactician and Ciern is a strategist, is that correct?"

"Yes," Amicu confirmed.

"I have always wondered, what is the difference?" the big warrior asked.

Amicu smiled, pleased at the question. "I studied tactics, or the art of understanding your enemies, and Ciern studied strategy, or the art of preparing for war. It's kind of like I'm on offense and he's on defense."

"Together the two of them are almost unstoppable," Shao bragged.

"Talk about unstoppable," Amicu laughed. "You should have seen some of the things Shao did at school."

"What about me?" Zimpf protested. "I believe we were a team."

"Sure," Amicu replied facetiously, winking outrageously behind Zimpf's back.

Everyone laughed.

"It's getting late," Amicu said then. "I most certainly do not want to be late for the dinner party tonight. Why don't we stop now and plan to meet here in the morning?"

With that, he left, and everyone except Alia and Shao followed him out.

The dinner party started just as the sun was beginning to set. Sairima had ordered that one large, round table be placed outside on the patio. There were screens of draperies arranged around the square to form a large, curtained room, which diffused the lit candles into a soft golden glow. The dinner consisted of several courses, each more delicious than the last. The party was a welcome respite after the stress of the last two days, and Alia thoroughly enjoyed herself. Shao, Amicu, and Zimpf told story after story of their days at Temple, and their antics had everyone crying from laughing so hard. The evening was so enjoyable that Alia never wanted it to end. Finally, though, the last plate was taken away and the laughter died down.

Sairima, who had to get up early to attend to her patients, stood up first to signal that the evening was over. Before she could say anything or even turn away, Amicu stood up, blocking her exit.

"Sairima," he said, taking both of her hands in his. "It is always an absolute joy to be with you. When I leave here, I spend all of my time thinking about us and planning my next visit when we can be together again."

Sairima looked at him, her eyes growing larger and larger.

Amicu continued. "I love you," he told her while dropping down on one knee and presenting her with a ring. "Please say that you will be my wife."

For the first time since Alia had met her, Sairima didn't say anything. But she nodded her head as her eyes filled with tears. Finally, she choked out a whispered, "Yes."

The room erupted in cheers and applause as the newly engaged couple kissed.

"I knew she would say yes," Zimpf said in a whispered aside to Mama.

"Well done!" a new voice congratulated them from a corner of the curtained room.

Everyone turned at the same time.

It was Ciern. He was another graduate of the Temple of Anaia. He, as the prince to the elven people, had studied strategy in order to fully understand all of the techniques involved in protecting his people.

He walked over to Amicu, shook his hand, and then politely kissed Sairima on the cheek. "Congratulations," he told them quite calmly while everyone else was talking at once.

"Ciern?"

"How did you get here so quickly?"

"We weren't expecting you for at least a week!"

Ciern turned to his friends and smiled broadly. "Calm down," he laughed. "Give a man a chance." He pulled up a chair from the corner and sat down. "I'll tell you what happened if you feed me," he promised.

At once, Sairima sent a server to bring Ciern dinner. He talked as he ate. "I was at one of our outposts doing inspections when Sairima's urgent message arrived. I sent word to my father and left immediately. I have been traveling almost nonstop since yesterday." He looked around at them, noting Shao's burned face and bandaged hand and Zimpf's scratches.

"So," he said casually, "what did I miss?"

"It was Medjii," Shao answered. "She set off an explosive device that would have killed all of us had Zimpf not warned us at the last instant."

"At the last instant?" Ciern looked penetratingly at Zimpf.

"If I may," Sairima interjected. "It is late, and we are all tired. Why don't you all discuss this in the morning? I will have breakfast sent up to Shao and Alia's room."

With that, Sairima rose to leave, and Amicu followed her. Everyone else filed out quietly.

Once they were in their room, Alia turned to Shao. "I have been meaning to ask you a question. But I didn't want to ask in front of Zimpf."

"Yes," Shao answered, walking over to hold her in his arms.

"Why couldn't Zimpf *see* what Medjii was going to do before she set off that device?"

"Because the future is fluid," Shao answered, kissing the top of

Alia's head.

She smiled up at him. "What do you mean?"

"Zimpf can't tell you what someone is going to do until they decide to do it." Shao smiled down at her.

"So, Medjii didn't plan on killing us initially," Alia said shrewdly.

Shao pulled back and looked at her seriously. "I think that's a question we need to bring up tomorrow."

The next morning dawned bright and clear. Alia and Shao were both up early. Shao went down to the hospital so that Sairima could look at his hand again, and Alia stayed to set everything up for their guests.

Sh'ron and Chhdar arrived just as Shao left so that the twins would have time to talk before the others arrived. They had barely stepped inside when a commotion exploded out in the hallway. All three fighters were under arms, and they raced, swords drawn to the melee.

At the end of the hallway, just at the top of the stairs, Shao was fighting off three assailants simultaneously. Before the ruffians could even hope to reach him, the martial artist had sidestepped a knife thrust from a skinny, long-haired man, grasped his arm firmly, then twisted and embedded the knife deep in the attacker's stomach. Shao pushed the knife downward, curving as he slashed. The man crumpled to the ground, his entrails gushing onto the floor ahead of him.

Meanwhile, the second attacker, a young, heavyset, blond-haired man, threw a long silver cord over Shao's chest and pulled it taut, obviously hoping to restrain the martial artist, but Shao crossed his arms over the cord, turned, and bent over quickly, flipping the man over. He landed jarringly on his feet then turned to face Shao, a long-bladed hunting knife in one hand. Before he could even think how to use it, the martial artist had already placed one hand on either side of the man's head and twisted quickly, breaking his neck. The man crashed to the ground, dead.

The third assailant, a boy too young to grow a beard, had backed into a corner, his eyes wide with fright at the sudden awful violence Shao had unleashed.

"Please, please," the young man kept repeating. He had thrown down his knife and was almost crying in fright.

Chhdar, almost too big to be real, advanced on the blithering man-child and placed his sword firmly against the boy's throat. Alia could see a small rivulet of blood cascade down his chest.

"Talk!" the big warrior commanded in a threatening tone.

Just then, Zimpf came running up the stairs, his bow notched and drawn.

"I was asleep," he panted, "and when I woke up, I *saw...*" He trailed off. "Well dang," he said. "I'm too late."

A few moments later, Amicu and Ciern came bounding up the stairs, Amicu with his sword drawn and Ciern with an arrow notched in readiness. They stopped to stare at the destruction.

"What happened?" Ciern asked.

"I was on my way to see Sairima when I found myself surrounded. They tried to attack from everywhere at once," Shao told him.

"We were in the suite," Chhdar volunteered, still pressing his sword against the young man's throat. "When we heard the commotion, we came running to help, but Shao had already put down two of his attackers."

"You mean five of his attackers," Amicu corrected, looking down the staircase.

"Six!" Alia gasped, her eyes wide in shock. "You fought off six men at once!"

Shao turned to look at her, one eyebrow raised quizzically. He grinned boyishly.

"What about this fellow?" Amicu said of the ruffian who was still being held by Chhdar.

Ciern studied the sobbing young man before answering. "Zimpf," he ordered.

The diviner walked to the attacker and looked him full in the face.

"Excuse me," he said politely before touching the boy's forehead with an index finger. The young man collapsed to the floor.

"Excuse me?" Shao laughed incredulously. "Excuse me??"

"There's no need to be uncivil," Zimpf replied loftily.

By now, a crowd had gathered. Shao looked at the servants milling around the carnage and selected two men. "Clean this up," he ordered authoritatively. "Take the bodies to Sairima in the hospital and tell her I want to see her as soon as she has completed her examination."

The men immediately went to work.

"What about this fellow?" Zimpf asked, indicating the sleeping boy.

"Bring him," Ciern ordered gruffly.

Zimpf and Chhdar each took one of the ruffian's legs and dragged him unceremoniously down the hallway, his head bouncing and banging on the wooden floor.

Through trial, error, and a plethora of attempts, Marek finally accomplished half of his goal; he discovered how to extract some of the contents of the Aghara. Learning how to dominate the power within, however,

would prove to be much more challenging.

The removal of the mist like substance was surprisingly simple. His master had taught him a basic spell to extricate liquid from the earth so that he could always have access to fresh water. The incantation worked unbelievably well. The only problem was that Marek wasn't a very strong mage with routine spells; his strength lay solely in destruction. It took an inordinately long time to master the spell, and he was only able to withdraw about a thimble full of the noxious, green substance, which could best be described as a liquid gas.

Marek was studying how best to utilize this substance when he received a message from DaiSur informing him of Medjii's death. He shrugged his shoulders unconcernedly and wondered idly if she had hired the assassins he ordered.

Chapter 4 – The Village

They tied up the young ruffian and dumped him in a corner of Alia and Shao's suite.

"Do we need to wake him up?" Chhdar asked.

"No," Zimpf answered, kneeling in front of the unconscious young man. Then he reached out to place his hands on either side of the boy's head. "I can read his thoughts, just like I did with Alia in the elven capital that time Marek altered her mind."

Alia looked at him sharply then glanced at Shao.

Shao winked at her.

Zimpf grew silent, his head bowed and his eyes closed. After a few minutes, he looked up.

"Nothing," he said in a disappointed tone. "All he knows is that he was offered a lot of money to help capture what he believed to be a thief. He had no knowledge of the plan to kill Shao. The man who paid him now lies dead in the hospital downstairs."

"Let's get him out of here," Ciern told them.

Amicu stepped outside and spoke with one of the men still cleaning up the carnage.

"I sent someone to get the constable," he informed them. "This kid was baldly misled, but I am sure that we can all agree that we don't want him sneaking around behind us."

"Hey!" Zimpf protested indignantly. "I could *see* for him, you know."

"You didn't *see* the first time," Shao murmured quietly to Alia. She giggled.

Zimpf looked at them but didn't say anything.

It only took a few minutes for the constable to arrive with his men and haul the prisoner to jail.

Breakfast arrived almost as soon as they left. Once it was served, the group of seven sat down to eat.

Ciern started the meeting by asking what had happened, then he sat listening to the story attentively.

Only after everyone fell silent did Ciern speak. "Medjii said that she gave Marek the Aghara. Did she say what that was?"

"No," Shao answered. "When I was carrying her out of the house, I asked, but she was almost totally senseless by then. I had hoped that Sairima could help her, but…"

"In the elven language, 'Aghara' translates to 'chaos.'" Ciern mused. "But why would someone want chaos?"

"Do you think it was Marek?" Shao asked.

Ciern nodded thoughtfully. "It's very possible," he acceded. "But we shouldn't be focused solely on Marek. He could be a pawn, like with the Orb, or he could be controlled by another. But if that is so, who would control him, and why?"

"Somehow you all—well, we all," he amended, including himself and Amicu, "have made a very powerful enemy."

"Why us?" Alia wanted to know. "We would have been happy to live our lives here in Miast." She looked at Shao, her heart in her eyes.

"If it is Marek, he knows that we won't stand around and watch the world burn. He knows that we are the only group with enough talent and power to thwart his plan," Amicu suggested. "Maybe what he wants to do is stop us before he gets started."

"Either that or he's after me," Alia suggested. "When Medjii first approached me, she insisted on speaking to me alone. She insisted that Shao not be told about her visit."

Both Ciern and Amicu looked at her sharply.

"Perhaps," Ciern finally said, then he was quiet, pensive. When he looked up, his face was troubled. "We have more questions than answers," he mused thoughtfully.

Amicu nodded in agreement.

"Ciern?" Shao asked.

The elven prince looked up and then began firing off questions without waiting for answers. "Why would Medjii agree to meet with Marek? What did she and the mage discuss? Why did Medjii want to talk to Alia alone? What is the 'Aghara'? How did Marek convince Medjii to get it for him? Why does Marek want it? Is he acting alone? And the most important question is this: Is he targeting all of you?" Then his eyes met Shao's. "Or is he only targeting Alia and the rest of us just got in the way?"

The room went deadly silent.

Alia could see Shao's jaws clench and his eyes tighten in anger. At the same time, he reached down and took her hand, gently holding it in both of his hands.

"Why would he target me?" Alia asked nervously.

"If that's what he was doing, then we need to find out why," Amicu answered.

"I know where we need to start looking for answers," Shao said quietly, looking at Alia.

"Home," Alia and Sh'ron said at the same time.

Chhdar nodded in agreement.

"Let's get packed today," Ciern told them. "We'll leave first thing in the morning."

"My new fiancée is not going to like this," Amicu said gloomily.

"She is *really* scary," Zimpf asserted again. "I'm glad I won't be around when you tell her."

"Tell me what?" Sairima demanded, stepping into the room and staring menacingly at Zimpf.

"Why didn't I *see* the future before I opened my mouth?" he moaned sadly. Then he was silent.

Sairima continued into the dining room, pulled out a chair, and sat beside Amicu. He smiled and gave her a quick kiss.

Zimpf remained silent.

"I don't have much to tell you about the dead men downstairs," Sairima reported. "Other than that Shao did a very thorough job of dispatching them."

"Good," Alia whispered to her husband.

He squeezed her hand.

"I can tell you that they are not from here," Sairima continued. "I had our staff attempt to identify them. No one recognized them."

"That's what I expected," Amicu said. "They were probably sent here as backup in case Medjii failed."

Sairima looked at the group, focusing on Amicu and then Shao. "When are you leaving?" she asked.

"In the morning," Shao told her. Then he looked around the table at the rest of the group. No one said anything.

Sairima sat silently, thinking. "I will arrange to have food and clothing packed for everyone, and I will have the grooms attend to everyone's horses," she said in a businesslike tone.

Amicu smiled at her. "Thank you," he whispered.

"I would like to talk to some of you today," she announced. "Amicu, can I see you this evening after dinner?" she asked softly.

He nodded.

"Shao and Alia, I want you both to come to my office just before dinner," she told them. "Zimpf, you will come to my office now," she ordered.

Zimpf groaned then saw Sairima staring intently at him. He nodded bravely and stood to follow the healer. Alia thought he looked a little pale.

The meeting ended as everyone left to prepare for the journey.

Alia walked their guests to the door and promised that she and Shao would meet everyone for dinner in the dining room that evening. Once everyone had left, she closed the door and locked it firmly. Then she wedged a chair under the doorknob. When she turned, Shao was standing in the middle of the room smiling, one eyebrow raised questioningly.

"Do you remember that night two days before our wedding?" she asked.

He nodded seriously. "The binding ritual."

"I want to do it again today. Right now," Alia said, blushing.

They spent the remainder of the day laying atop the bed, laughing, kissing, and talking to each other.

"Were you really surprised that I took out six men this morning?"

Shao asked at one point.

She smiled. "I am happy that you took out six men this morning," she responded gratefully, leaning up to give him a kiss.

"I'm always a little bit afraid that at some point I'm going to scare you away," Shao admitted.

Alia laughed lightly, then saw the slightly worried frown between his eyebrows.

"It's too late for that." She smiled, kissing the frown. "Can I ask you a serious question?" Alia asked then.

"Of course," Shao answered anxiously.

"Why is Zimpf so afraid of Sairima?"

Shao burst out laughing. "Do you remember what Zimpf did to you the first time you met him?"

"How could I ever forget? He stole my clothes while I was bathing, and I walked into camp wrapped in poison weed vines." Alia blushed; the memory still embarrassed her.

Shao smiled at the recollection of watching her march into camp barely decent and wrapped in the worst foliage known to mankind. "I thought you were the most beautiful woman I had ever seen," he told her, "and at the same time, I felt pity for you."

Alia blushed, the color deepening to a dusky rose.

"Anyway," Shao continued, "what Zimpf did to Sairima was worse."

"Worse than stealing clothes?" Alia asked.

"Worse than having to walk into camp wearing poisoned weed," Shao answered.

Alia looked at him, her eyes growing wide in sudden understanding.

"Sairima and a couple of her friends had gone riding near a

stream just west of town. They found a swimming hole, and since it was a very hot day, they decided to take a quick dip to cool off. They didn't want to get their clothes wet, so…" Shao trailed off.

"So they took them off, and Zimpf stole them," Alia commented drily.

"Their clothes, their shoes, their horses, everything. Those girls had to walk three miles back to town. They created quite a stir when they returned," Shao told her, shaking his head.

Alia looked at Shao, her eyes wide and the palm of her left hand pressed over her open mouth.

"Well, you know how Sairima does not like embarrassment," Shao said. "She gave Zimpf quite a dressing down. She had already started studying to be a healer, and she told him if he ever played a prank on her again that she would 'accidentally' put him to sleep, and then she would start to remove body parts."

Alia started laughing.

"He took her threat very seriously," Shao said, laughing with her.

"Do you know what else Sairima doesn't like?" Alia said, looking at the sun as it was starting to sink.

"Tardiness," Shao answered. "I guess we had better get down to her office."

As they walked hand-in-hand down the hallway, Alia felt like her head was on a swivel. She was trying to look everywhere for hidden attackers. She wore her sword unbuckled in its scabbard, and she could sense Shao's tense alertness. But they did not encounter anyone in that entire wing of the house. It was completely deserted. When they reached the bottom of the last set of stairs, they learned why. A set of pocket doors that Alia had never even noticed were pulled shut. In front of the door, a set of armed guards stood on either side.

"Sairima," Shao muttered as they proceeded down to the healer's office.

Shao's sister was waiting impatiently for them when they arrived. She was all business as she directed them to an examination room, where she unwrapped Shao's burned hand, applied more salve, and then rewrapped it. The healer checked his face, which had faded from a bright red to a dull pink. Then, Sairima checked his stitches and applied a different salve.

"You're approved to travel," she said permissively.

Shao didn't answer.

Then Sairima addressed Alia. "Apply the burn salve and change the dressing on Shao's hand every other day until the blisters are completely healed. You can remove the stitches in five days."

"Yes, Healer," Alia said respectfully.

"Now, Alia," Sairima continued, "I have something for you." Then she handed the young woman a bag.

Alia looked up in surprise; it was a medical bag. She stared at her sister-in-law, unable even to speak. Only healers or advanced healers-in-training were allowed to carry medical bags.

"Don't get too excited," Sairima informed her seriously. "You are not a healer. I just thought that someone with medical training should have supplies on this trip. You are advanced enough that you will be able to handle all but the most serious cases. Besides," Sairima continued, "I wanted to give my first medical bag to someone I could trust."

Alia finally managed to respond. "Thank you," she whispered in awe.

Sairima smiled. "Just be sure you bring my brother and my fiancé back safely," she ordered firmly.

Alia was so touched by Sairima's confidence in her that she could only nod. Then she glanced over at Shao, who was looking at her proudly.

"Sairima?" Shao asked then. "What did Zimpf tell you?"

She smiled. "That you all will return safely."

Alia and Shao left to go to dinner, leaving Sairima to attend to another patient.

"Why did you ask about Zimpf?" Alia asked. "He admitted that he always lies to her about the long-term future."

"He tells her what she wants to hear so that she won't have to stay behind and wonder about our safety." Shao paused. "Knowing Sairima, she would probably go quietly insane."

"So the reason Zimpf lies to her is to protect her peace of mind?"

"Believe me, the alternative would be much worse," Shao chuckled. "She would either insist on coming with us or she would make the lives of the hospital workers unbearable."

Alia nodded, she know how intense Sairima could be when she was worried.

They were a quiet group at dinner that night. Finally, Mama broke the ice. "Shao?" she asked quietly. "Is the person causing these problems the same one who is responsible for the attack on Selo?"

"We think so, Mama," he replied.

She nodded. "You know what to do when you find him?" she asked.

"Yes, Mama," he said confidently, holding up a rather large wooden spoon. The table erupted in laughter. All except Sairima, who looked at Shao and then Mama quizzically.

"I'll explain it to you later," Amicu laughed.

They ended the night early and then were up before the sun rose the next morning. Just as it was beginning to get light, they rode out of the stables and through the newly opened city gates. The group traveled at a mile-eating canter, stopping to camp late each night and rising early each morning.

Finally, after a week of hard riding, they topped the hill that led to the twins' small village. As Shao, who rode rearguard, crested the knoll, he stopped and sat, silently staring below. He whistled sharply; everyone turned and drew near the martial artist. He and Ciern exchanged a long, troubled look.

Alia saw their faces and turned to look. The little town was quiet. Too quiet. There were no people. No one was working in the fields. No smoke rose from the chimneys. No children played in the streets.

"What?" asked Chhdar. "I don't see anything." Then he paused. "I—I don't see anything at all," he stammered.

"So, what do we do?" Sh'ron asked.

"Zimpf," Ciern told the diviner. "Have a look."

But Zimpf was already sitting perfectly still while staring with unseeing eyes at the little hamlet below. After several moments, he looked over at Alia and Sh'ron.

"They're gone," he said simply. "Everyone is gone. The whole place is abandoned."

"But where did they go?" Alia asked worriedly.

"I don't know," Zimpf answered. "I don't even know if they are dead or alive. I can only tell you that they have been gone for a long time. I can sense no trace of any people."

"Do you sense any danger?" Amicu questioned.

Zimpf shook his head slightly then continued to scrutinize the village below.

Ciern and Amicu looked at each other and then at Shao.

"Zimpf," Shao asked carefully, "can you tell us if it's safe for us to enter the village?"

Zimpf looked at him, troubled. "We need to," he whispered.

"Why?" Shao asked.

Zimpf turned to look at his friend, for the first time looking away from the town.

"Because there is a message for us."

"From whom?" Amicu asked.

But Zimpf couldn't answer.

So they rode down the hill and into the eerily silent village together.

At first, they tried knocking on some of the doors and calling out for people. But the village remained silent. Finally, they made their way to the twins' house. Everything was just as they had left it more than a year ago when they came to get Alia's wedding dress.

"Why don't we check Marek's old house?" Alia suggested.

Then she led them down a small path to the very edge of town. At the end of the road sat a small, mean-looking hut. The windows were shuttered, but the door stood wide open. They crowded into the squalid, dirt-covered living area. There, in the middle of the room, stood a small, well-polished table with a note neatly folded on the top. There were two words written in cursive.

"To Alia"

Marek knew he would have to be careful with the limited contents of the Aghara. He also knew that he would have to gain power before he used any of the potent liquid gas. Unsure how to utilize the miniscule

amount of the substance, he decided that he would use his senses to explore the components inside of the vessel using a technique his master had taught him.

"Never smell any unknown substance," the old mage had lectured. "Always hold it up close to your nose, then waft the scent toward you."

So, very carefully, Marek poured a miniscule amount of the thick, noxious fluid into a small glass vial. Then he secured the top in the vase and held up the tiny vial, studying it carefully.

Very gently, he fanned a trace amount of the gaseous liquid toward himself.

He was not expecting what would happen next.

The thick green liquid did not drift smoothly toward him as it should have.

Instead, it exploded forcefully, hitting him full in the face and wrapping itself around his head as though it was a snake!

Marek found himself being hurled violently backward; he hit the wall so hard that he left a head-sized indentation. For a moment, he couldn't catch his breath, and at the same time, he could feel an ice-cold substance burning its way down his throat and into his lungs. He looked in horror at the vial, which was still clutched firmly in his right hand.

It was empty.

Chapter 5 – DaiSur

Alia reached out to pick up the note.

"No!" Zimpf screamed.

The next thing Alia knew, she had been pushed so hard that she fell sideways, tripped over her own feet, and tumbled into Amicu with such force that he plunged to the ground. As he fell, he managed to twist and throw Alia to Shao, who caught her deftly but then hooked the heel of his boot in the uneven flooring and toppled backward, landing hard with Alia on top of him. They lay together silently for a moment. Alia waiting for Zimpf to fill the room with his infectious laughter. But the room remained silent. She looked down at Shao's stunned face, rolled onto the floor, and stood up quickly, offering her hand to her husband. When they turned to look at Zimpf, he was frozen in stasis, his eyes wide and unseeing.

Everyone remained silent, staring at Zimpf. Finally, he blinked once, then twice, tears filling his eyes. He looked at Shao.

"I can hear them," he said in a low voice. "The people. They were crying."

"Did he kill them?" Shao asked softly.

"I don't know," Zimpf answered. "The memory is garbled, undecipherable."

"Zimpf?" Alia wanted to know. "Is it tied to this?" She indicated the untouched note in Marek's spidery handwriting.

"It doesn't seem to be," he answered. "The vision of the people who lived in this little hamlet stems from being this close to such strong emotions. The note is separate, but it exudes evil. Vicious evil." Zimpf paused, trying to pull himself together enough to explain. "Being virtually on top of Marek's force gives me fleeting bursts of his depravity." Then he turned toward the door. "We need to get out of here," he said forcefully.

"What about the note?" Alia asked.

"Find something with which to pick it up and to carry it," he ordered. "But do not touch it with your bare hands!" Then he pushed his way past them.

Alia noticed that he was very pale, and his hands were shaking. She followed him outside, accompanied by Shao.

A few minutes later, the others joined them.

"We found some tongs that we used to lift the note, and we put it in this," Ciern reported, holding up a saddlebag. "It belonged to Airafae," he reported angrily.

"Let's go," Zimpf demanded. "Now!" He was already mounted.

The others also mounted and followed Zimpf as he galloped out of the village and out of the area. He finally slowed his lathered horse to a canter then a walk after a couple of miles. By then the sun had started to sink toward the horizon behind them.

"We're far enough away," he told them. "Why don't we find a

place to camp before it gets dark, and then we'll talk about what I saw? Besides," he said, trying to be his normal, jovial self, "I have no idea where we're going."

The others chuckled lightly at his last statement.

They only traveled a little way before finding a camping spot. It was in a small copse of trees with a stream nearby. As usual, everyone helped to set up camp. Sh'ron and Chhdar tended the horses, Ciern started a fire, Zimpf and Amicu set up the tents, and Alia and Shao foraged for fresh food to supplement their dried meat.

Alia was very quiet as they gathered fresh vegetables, and Shao kept looking at her, waiting for her to talk, but she remained withdrawn.

As they were walking back, side by side, he suddenly stopped. "Do you want to talk about it?" Shao asked quietly.

Alia shook her head.

"Let's see what Zimpf has to say," Shao suggested, looking over at Alia.

She stood silently, staring at the ground.

Shao waited patiently. Finally, he stepped in front of her and gently laid his hand on the right side of her face. "We'll figure it out," he whispered into her left ear.

Alia looked at her husband and nodded gratefully. They went back to camp and prepared dinner for everyone.

After everyone had eaten, they sat around the campfire waiting for Zimpf to start talking. Finally, he looked at each member of the group.

"I know you want me to tell you what happened," he said, addressing everyone, "but I can't, because I don't know. I don't understand it myself."

"Just tell us what you can," Ciern encouraged him.

Zimpf nodded reluctantly. "It started with the village. I could sense nothing. Nothing," he repeated uneasily. "When I visit places, the dwellings leave…memories. I have an impression of not only the people who live there, but their sense of self, their emotions. Even if a spot has been abandoned for years, I can still *feel* the memories. But that village was…empty, barren, devoid." Zimpf shuddered, looking at them with panicked eyes. "Then, when we went into the mage's house and Alia reached out to pick up the note, I had a violent sensation of pure evil." He turned to look at Alia. "I'm sorry I pushed you so hard," he apologized. "But I couldn't allow you to touch such a vile object."

Alia shuddered, remembering how the note seemed to call to her.

Zimpf continued, "Then my mind was assaulted by image after image of devastation, pain, death. And behind those visions was etched the face of Marek."

No one said anything for several moments.

"These images you saw," Amicu asked, "were they the past or the future?"

"I don't know, maybe some of both," Zimpf told him.

But Shao had seen Zimpf cut his eyes toward Alia. "Were we in your visions?" he probed, staring at his friend intensely.

Zimpf nodded. "We were all in his vision, except for Amicu. That's why I think some of the images were in the past. Marek never met Amicu, and if what I saw foretold the future, then Amicu would have been included."

"That makes sense," Ciern agreed.

"So, what now?" Sh'ron asked. "Where do we go?"

"That's the question," Amicu said. "Where do we go?"

After much discussion, the group finally agreed that the logical place to go for answers would be the Order of the Mages.

They turned in early except for Alia and Shao, who volunteered to take the first shift on guard duty.

"Zimpf is really upset," Alia noted after everyone else had retired to their tents. "He didn't make one comment about us doing guard duty alone."

"Give him a day or two." Shao smiled. "He'll be back to normal soon enough, and then you'll miss the quiet Zimpf."

Alia smiled wistfully. "I guess so. But it's almost depressing when he's so solemn."

"Speaking of being solemn," Shao said, taking Alia's hand and holding it against his chest. "How are you feeling?"

Alia sat brooding silently as she stared into the fire.

Shao began to think that she wasn't going to answer. He wrapped his arm around her shoulders and pulled her closer.

Finally, she began to talk. She told him about how she and Marek had grown up together, how he was her closest friend, her greatest ally except for her twin. How the three of them were virtually inseparable. Then she looked up at Shao, her eyes troubled. "I just can't understand how I could grow up with evil and not see it."

Shao considered his answer carefully before responding. "People aren't always what they seem to be," he told her. "Sometimes the person most willing to hold his hand out to help others is the one with the most to hide."

Alia thought about Shao's answer, then turned to face him. "That's very profound."

"You don't have to look so surprised," he teased.

Alia smiled. "Thank you," she said simply. Then she reached up to kiss him, but they were rudely interrupted.

"You are supposed to be on guard duty!" Zimpf complained loudly.

"Finally!" Shao jumped up, grabbed Alia's hand, and pulled her toward the tent, laughing. "I thought he was never going to get up to relieve us," he protested loudly.

"Hmph!" Zimpf complained.

The next morning dawned bright and clear. They rose early, ate quickly, and were on the road before the sun finished climbing beyond the horizon. They had a long trip ahead of them to the Order of the Mages. According to Zimpf, they would be traveling for just over two weeks.

Zimpf and Ciern took the lead, followed by Chhdar and Sh'ron. Alia, Shao, and Amicu rode as the rearguard.

"Um, why are we following Zimpf?" Amicu asked curiously. "As I recall, he has the worst sense of direction of anyone I have ever met."

Shao and Alia exchanged a quick glance. "It's because he has a map to the location of the Order of the Mages embedded in his head," Shao told him. "Medjii gave it to him when we went in search of Marek after he stole the Orb."

They traveled easily for the next week, avoiding small villages and towns in their rush to arrive at their destination. But early on the morning of the eighth day, a small town appeared on the horizon. Zimpf pulled his horse to a stop, carefully studying the horizon ahead of them.

"Zimpf?" Amicu questioned, pulling his horse up beside the diviner.

"I don't know," Zimpf answered. "Something or someone is… calling."

"Should we investigate, or should we avoid the area completely?" Amicu wanted to know.

Ciern looked at Amicu and then at Zimpf. "I don't think we should parade into a potential trap," Ciern told them.

"It's not a trap." Zimpf frowned. "It's more like someone is waiting for us."

"Do you sense danger?" Shao asked in his quiet voice.

Zimpf shook his head. "It feels more like an invitation."

"I don't like this," Ciern told them. "If we look at this from a strategist's point of view, walking into unanticipated dangers in an unknown town makes us extremely vulnerable."

Zimpf looked at him with a hurt expression on his face. "I told you, there is no danger," he said in a disappointed voice.

Amicu was looking back and forth between Zimpf and Ciern. "From a tactician's point of view, I agree with Ciern; this is the perfect setup for an ambush."

Zimpf started to protest, but Amicu held up his hand. "However," he continued, "Zimpf possesses a remarkable talent for discernment. I think we should trust him."

"I agree with Amicu," Shao agreed. "But I think that we should split up, just in case there are any problems."

Zimpf opened his mouth to protest and then realized that he was outvoted. "Fine," he told the group. "But you're going to see that I'm right," he said in a snippy tone.

After much discussion, it was agreed that Shao, Alia, and Zimpf would enter the town and Sh'ron, Chhdar, Amicu, and Ciern would wait for them about a mile on the other side. The group would meet up by the time the sun reached its zenith.

"If you're not back in time, we're coming in after you," Ciern told Shao firmly. "Leave the usual trail," he commanded. Then he spurred his horse to the northeast. The others followed.

Alia, Shao, and Zimpf walked their mounts slowly into the small town. Alia felt nervous, but as soon as they entered the town, she somehow knew that everything would be fine. A sense of peace and tranquility enveloped her. She looked at Shao in confusion.

He was riding warily, his eyes looking everywhere in his search for hidden dangers. Alia could see him surreptitiously dropping pebbles as a trail for Ciern.

"Relax," Zimpf whispered to him.

They had ridden perhaps halfway into town when a heavily veiled person walked into the middle of the street and held up a gloved hand, palm out. The horses stopped immediately. The figure pointed to their right then began walking in that direction, clearly expecting the trio to follow. After a quick glance at Zimpf, who nodded, they followed.

The shrouded figure stopped at the side door of a large wooden structure and waited for them to dismount. Then, she walked wordlessly inside. Zimpf followed unhesitatingly. Alia looked over at Shao; they entered together.

Initially the dimness of the room made it difficult to see anything, but after a few moments, Alia's eyes adjusted.

The enigmatic person turned to face them while at the same time pulling off her cloak and veil. Alia suppressed a start of surprise. It was a strikingly beautiful younger-looking woman.

"Where are your companions?" she asked conversationally.

"Who are you?" Alia started to ask. But before she could open her mouth, Shao tapped her lightly on the arm. She looked over, shocked to see that both he and Zimpf were bowing almost to the ground before the unnamed woman. Alia bowed in confusion.

"Arise," the woman commanded. "We shall not stand on ceremony here."

Shao and Zimpf stood to face the woman, who was smiling gently. She kissed them courteously on each cheek, then she turned to Alia and nodded her head respectfully.

"Welcome, Alia," she said formally.

"Alia," Shao introduced the stranger in a courtly manner. "This is DaiSur. She is the special envoy to the leaders of all the peoples of the Four Lands."

Alia nodded politely, although she was still very bewildered.

"Please, be seated," DaiSur insisted.

They turned to a large table where Zimpf quickly pulled out the chair at the head of the table and held it for DaiSur.

Once everyone was seated, she asked again, "Where are your companions?"

"They're waiting for us on the east side of this town," Shao answered.

DaiSur tapped the table with her fingernail, and instantly, a serving man appeared from the next room. "Give my guests here something to drink. Have lunch prepared for eight. And send someone to fetch my other guests from the east side of town." Then she looked at Shao. "Give him your token."

Shao instantly reached into his pack and handed the man a small silver coin.

Within moments, a second servant entered the room, bringing an assortment of beverages.

While they waited for Sh'ron, Chhdar, Ciern, and Amicu, DaiSur passed the time by politely asking questions. She inquired about the wedding and about Sairima's recent engagement to Amicu. She asked Alia about her training as a healer. The woman seemed to know everything.

Then she turned to Zimpf. "So you haven't married yet?" she probed.

Alia saw the quick play of emotions race across Zimpf's face: surprise, anger, loss, sorrow, and resignation.

Just then, the others came into the room.

Both Ciern and Amicu immediately bowed formally; Sh'ron and Chhdar bowed politely.

"Come. Be seated," DaiSur commanded. Then she said to the serving man who had accompanied them, "lunch will be served now."

Immediately, servants appeared from a door in the back and placed dishes of food before the group. Then they disappeared almost instantly.

"We will discuss current events while we dine," DaiSur announced. Then she continued, "I am aware of the events surrounding the Orb of Ahi. Both King Ganayt of the Dwarven People and King Elator of the Elven Kingdom sent me dispatches. I am also aware of the death of Medjii and the attempts on your lives. What I want to know is, what has happened since you left Miast?" She looked firmly at Ciern for the answer.

He told her everything.

Then she looked studiously at Zimpf. "Will you share the images with me?"

She phrased it like a question, but Alia thought it sounded more like a command.

Reluctantly, Zimpf got up and made his way around the table. DaiSur pushed her chair back, and Zimpf knelt respectfully before her. With a practiced hand, he reached out and gently laid both of his hands on either side of her head. He closed his eyes, and she followed suit. After a few moments, he dropped his hands.

"Let me see the letter," she ordered peremptorily.

Ciern handed her Alia's saddlebag. "Zimpf warned us not to touch it."

DaiSur waved away the warning, opened the saddlebag, and dropped the note onto the table. She looked at Alia after seeing her name scrawled across the top. "Zimpf didn't allow you to open this?" she mused.

Alia shook her head.

DaiSur tapped on the table with a fingernail, and a servant immediately appeared at her side. She spoke to him in such a low tone that Alia could not hear what was said. The servant left the room and returned rapidly, carrying a silvery-looking piece of material. DaiSur deftly wrapped the note in the material, being extremely careful not to touch the letter. Then she picked it up and offered it to Zimpf.

He held out his hand reluctantly.

DaiSur smiled slightly. "It is now safe to touch," she told him.

Zimpf put the wrapped note back into the saddlebag.

"Take the note to the Order of the Mages," she commanded. "Give it to Sorgin and tell him I am calling a council at Asath Tesai immediately. If you fail in that quest"—DaiSur stopped to look directly at Zimpf—"then the note must be taken to Aistra. You know where to find her."

Zimpf jumped noticeably at the name. His face drained of all color and his eyes filled with tears. Alia could see his lips tremble.

DaiSur looked at Zimpf, who was staring at the table. Her face was full of sympathy, but when she spoke, there was no compassion in her tone. "You will have to deal with this, Zimpf," she said harshly to the diviner.

He didn't respond.

Then DaiSur looked at the group gathered around her table. "Once you have delivered the note, then by my command, you will report to the elven kingdom. This must be stopped," she said to them ominously. "If we fail, the rogue mage, Marek, will destroy our world."

When Marek was finally able to sit up, he knew that he had been subtly changed. He felt…stronger, wiser, more cunning. He could see more clearly, think more lucidly, sense more intensely.

Suddenly, he knew what he needed to do.

Without even considering it, he went out into the small hamlet in search of his first victim. It turned out to be an old man who had been friends with Marek's father.

"Marek?" the old man questioned in a thin, quavering voice. "Is that you?"

Marek didn't answer. Instead, he just stood there and studied the old man speculatively.

"What happened to you? Where are Alia and Sh'ron? Where is that warrior who went with you? What was his name? Chabar? Where did you all go to anyway?"

The old man continued on, asking one inane question after another until Marek couldn't stand it anymore. Without even thinking about it, the mage placed his hand on the man's cheek and whispered one word.

"Leave."

Instantly, he felt a sort of tingling power race down his arm all the way to the tips of his fingers and enter the old man.

His father's friend immediately stopped talking, then, without question, he turned and walked away. No one in that little hamlet ever saw or spoke to him again.

Marek stared at his hand, first in shock and then in rising excitement.

The Aghara gave him power over others.

In the following days, he continued to experiment with his newfound discovery. He learned that all he had to do was order someone to perform a task, any task, then touch their face. Suddenly, their eyes would glaze over, and they would obey, instantly, eagerly, willingly.

It was almost a week later when he received a note from DaiSur that Alia and her friends had left Miast and appeared to be traveling in his direction.

He thought seriously of using his new powers on the people he saw as the ones who had scorned him. After all, it was their fault the volcano had erupted; it was their fault he had been caught in the explosion; it was their fault he had been hurt. They were the ones who had abandoned him and left him for dead. The fact that Marek had betrayed them, had kidnapped the princess, had stolen the Orb of Ahi, and had designed the plan to blow up the volcano did not seem to have occurred to him.

So, Marek called the few dozen people in the community together. At first, they didn't want to talk to him, but he convinced first one and then another until everyone was standing in a circle holding hands. He silently joined the circle, taking a spot between the oldest and youngest residents. He wasn't sure if he could alter people's minds this way, but he needed to try.

The Mage began to speak softly, urgently, convincingly. And one after another, they began to cry, a small refinement he added. Almost *as soon he released the circle of people, they departed, never to return.*

Marek watched them leave with a sly smile then turned to leave a note for his old comrades in arms.

Chapter 6 – The Order of the Mages

They were a somber group when they filed out of the wooden structure after meeting with DaiSur. No one said anything as they mounted their horses and rode quietly out of town. They remained silent until later that evening after they had set up camp and finished eating.

Finally, Alia could stand it no longer, and she knew that Sh'ron and Chhdar felt the same way.

Turning to Shao, Alia finally asked, "Will you please explain everything to us? Who exactly was that woman? How does she know everything? Why are we doing her bidding?"

Shao, Ciern, Amicu, and Zimpf looked back and forth, each waiting for the other to begin.

Finally, Ciern spoke. "Perhaps it will be easier if we tell you a little more about the school we attended together. Not just the fun, silly antics where we didn't get caught. But the purpose of the school itself," he said soberly. "As you well know, we were trained at the Temple of Anaia. The Temple is in one the crests high up in the Skarsgaard Mountains. It is a difficult, dangerous trip that not many will even attempt." He paused.

Amicu took up the story. "When you arrive at the temple, you are tested to see if you are suitable for acceptance. The tests are… arduous. Not many applicants are accepted. Once admitted, life for the pupils is difficult. We were expected to attend classes, learn lessons, do chores, and excel in our instructions. Failure was met with harsh punishment."

Alia looked at Shao in admiration. She had no idea how difficult his years of training had been. He met her gaze and winked. Then he continued the story.

"The philosophy behind the school justifies the unforgiving nature of the curriculum," he said as he looked at the horror-stricken faces of Alia, Sh'ron, and Chhdar. "The things we learn mean life or death to the people we interact with. I am a martial arts master. I protect and defend those who may not be able to protect themselves. Ciern graduated in strategy and defense because one day he will be king and must know how to defend his subjects. Amicu studied tactics because his home is on the edge of the Wilds. He must be able to understand his foes to protect his people. Zimpf majored in divination. His area of study is a specialty which encompasses the understanding of all peoples—their past, present, and future. He can ferret out secrets, spy on enemies, and scrutinize intentions."

"DaiSur also attended the Temple of Anaia," Ciern told them, "although she was about four years ahead of us. She is highly intelligent and very well trained. She studied everything, knows everything we know: martial arts, strategy, tactics, and even divination."

"But I'm better," Zimpf interrupted.

Ciern ignored him. "She also studied with the mages. There is literally nothing that the woman cannot do. Her father was an envoy to all the peoples. She inherited her position from him when he passed away a couple of years ago."

"What exactly does an envoy do?" Chhdar wanted to know.

"What DaiSur does is work with the kings and advisors of all the people in the Four Lands," Amicu answered his question. "She collects reports from all over our world, analyzes them, then sends out intelligence briefings to all of the leaders. Her organization of information is what keeps our lands peaceful."

"The fact that she's concerned with this issue involving Marek is evidence of the seriousness of the problem," Shao told them.

They sat quietly for a while, thinking. Finally, as Sh'ron reminded them, it was late, and they needed to get up and start riding early if they intended to get to the compound of the Order of the Mages within the week.

Everyone went to their tents except for Alia and Shao, who always took the first watch. Once everyone had retired, they did a perimeter check then sat before the fire.

Alia kept sneaking quick looks at her husband. She had been more and more horrified at the stories about his school. She could not have imagined being sixteen years old and living away from home in such a harsh environment.

As always, Shao was aware of her surreptitious looks. But he sat silently, holding her hand and pretending to look at the fire.

Finally, Alia saw the corners of his mouth start to turn up in a hidden smile.

"You saw me looking, didn't you?" she demanded.

He nodded, smiling. "Did you have some more questions, or

do you just want to continue to stare?" he teased.

Alia laughed. "I was just thinking that it must have been very difficult for you to be in such an unforgiving environment, so far from home, all alone."

"I wasn't alone," he told her. "Zimpf was with me."

"Darned skippy!" they heard Zimpf shout from his tent.

Alia continued as though she hadn't heard. "How long were you in school?"

"Six years," Shao answered.

"But it seemed like a lot longer!" Zimpf interjected.

Shao continued, ignoring his friend. "For the first two years, all acolytes are required to take basic courses. We all took strategy and defense, tactics, martial arts, and divination."

"You all flunked divination miserably!" Zimpf announced loudly.

Shao's jaws clenched briefly in irritation, but he persisted in his story. "We also spent hours learning self-defense and weapons mastery. We were expected to excel at archery—"

"But I'm the best!" Ciern claimed.

"And swordsmanship," Shao struggled to finish.

"I'm the finest swordsman!" Amicu proclaimed.

"And knife-throwing and hand-to-hand combat," Shao rushed to explain, before saying loudly, "Which they were all terrible at doing!"

"Hey! I was pretty good!" Ciern disagreed.

"I always beat you, Ciern!" Amicu declared.

"I beat Shao…once!" Zimpf announced.

"Only because you cheated," Shao growled.

"That is enough!" Sh'ron shouted from her tent. "Some of us are trying to sleep. And if you all don't settle down, I'm going to get Mama's wooden spoon from Shao's backpack and beat you all with it!"

The camp suddenly went silent.

Alia and Shao looked at each other and laughed.

Later, after they had been relieved and were laying in their tent, Alia asked Shao, "Was it terribly difficult? School, I mean. Not just the classes but being away from home."

"It was at first, but once Zimpf and I made friends, it became easier."

Alia leaned over and kissed her husband. "I am more and more amazed by the person you are. I love you more and more each day," she admitted shyly.

Shao smiled and blushed slightly. Then he wrapped his arms around her and pulled her closer so that her head rested on his shoulder.

"Can I ask a question?" Alia plunged on without waiting for an answer. "I've noticed that when Ciern is around, you all seem to defer to him. Why?"

"He was the captain of our dorm," Shao told her. "He outranked us. I guess old habits die hard," he said with a smile.

"Can I ask you one more question?" Alia wanted to know.

"Just one?" Shao asked.

"Who is Aistra, and what is she to Zimpf?"

"That's two questions," Shao said before falling quiet. When he spoke, it was not the answer that Alia expected. "We all vowed to Zimpf to never discuss her with anyone," he told Alia.

"Okay," she whispered.

"Are you angry with me?" Shao looked at her worriedly.

"No, of course not. You can't break a promise, especially to Zimpf. He would know immediately," she pointed out.

"I will tell you this much," Shao confessed. "If we have to deliver that note to her, then everything will become clear."

Alia had a strong suspicion about the connection between Aistra and Zimpf. And she hoped with everything she had that Zimpf would not have to face the woman again.

They were up early the next morning. According to Zimpf, they still had about six days before they made it to the compound that housed the Order of the Mages. They rode hard, stopping late and starting out early each day. On the evening of the fourth day, Zimpf announced that, barring any *unseeable* circumstance, they would make it to the compound late on the following day. They were all relieved and were looking forward to a solid meal and a soft bed.

Just before they stopped to camp that night, Zimpf suddenly pulled his horse to an abrupt stop, his eyes wide and far away. Everyone halted, waiting for the diviner.

"Marek has been here very recently," he said, looking at Shao.

"Has he hurt anyone?" Shao asked quietly.

"No," Zimpf replied. "At least not yet. All I can *see* is him loitering here. He was staring into the trees that lined the left side of the road. Then he moved on."

"Did you get any sense of what he was doing or where he was going?" Amicu asked.

Zimpf shook his head. "No; he has gotten better at hiding his mind from me. Although I could sense a feeling of great anger. I need to stop for a minute. I have to try to *see!*" Zimpf said in frustration.

With that, they all dismounted. Zimpf took a red silk scarf from his saddlebag and sat on the ground, his back resting against one of the trees. He wrapped the scarf around his head, completely covering his eyes, and sat very still, his face buried in his hands.

"This could take a while," Shao told them.

"Why don't we go ahead and set up camp now and then we can leave early in the morning?" Ciern suggested.

Amicu stayed by Zimpf while the rest of them moved deeper into the woods to set up camp and start dinner.

It was perhaps half an hour later when Zimpf and Amicu joined them. Zimpf was clearly upset.

"Nothing," he said. "The future is too fluid. Marek hasn't made any plans."

"Is it possible that he was just passing through?" Chhdar asked.

"Maybe," Zimpf answered. "But I have a bad feeling."

Shao, Ciern, and Amicu shared quick glances. They had all learned to respect Zimpf's feelings.

"We'll set up double watches tonight," Ciern decided.

Alia, Shao, Sh'ron, and Chhdar took the first watch. Nothing happened, although it was very quiet. Too quiet. Alia began to feel uneasy. The horses seemed skittish, and a sense of impending doom permeated the air. Zimpf, Amicu, and Ciern joined them on watch a couple of hours before they were expected.

"There is an unwieldy sense of *wrong* surrounding us," Zimpf muttered to no one in particular.

They built up the fire and sat with their backs to it, studying the nearby trees. It was just before dawn when they were attacked.

"There!" Zimpf pointed. "And there, and there, and there," he said, his voice sounding more and more alarmed. Slinking toward them, their bellies low and positioned to attack, was an entire sneak of mongers.

Mongers were small, vicious creatures about as big as a medium-sized dog; they had claws and catlike features.

Alia and Sh'ron exchanged horrified looks; a sneak of mongers had killed their parents.

Everyone stood with their backs to the fire, prepared to fight. Zimpf and Ciern began shooting arrow after arrow into their ranks, dropping them by the dozens. Meanwhile, Shao, who had a stack of poisoned shuriken ready, began throwing the sharpened weapons with deadly accuracy.

Finally, a monger larger and braver than the rest launched himself straight at Alia, who immediately sliced his head off. Then other mongers began to hurl themselves toward the group of fighters. Alia, Sh'ron, and Chhdar fought together as a group, chopping, stabbing, and eviscerating any creature that came close to them.

Ciern and Zimpf, back-to-back, fired arrows without ceasing at the periphery of the attacking animals.

Amicu stood alone, his back to the flames. He still had his sword, but he was hurling flaming sticks into the dry tender surrounding the campsite. He had already started a blazing inferno that had begun to drive the weaker creatures back into the woods.

But it was Shao who was the definition of devastation to the mongers. He was everywhere at once. He threw shurikens; he killed creature after creature with deadly speed using an evil-looking knife; he fought with his bare hands and his feet. He stabbed, and ripped, and gouged.

Finally, due to the sheer violence of the warriors, the mongers turned tail and ran howling into the blazing forest.

"Get the horses!" Ciern commanded. "Leave everything else. We can reoutfit with the mages."

They all mounted in the early morning light and galloped toward the compound that housed the Order of the Mages.

After several miles, Zimpf reined in his lathered horse, dropping from a gallop to a canter, to a trot, and finally, to a walk. He held up a clenched fist, indicating to the others to stop.

"Can you *feel* that?" Zimpf asked inquisitively.

Alia listened intensely. She didn't hear or see anything out of the ordinary. She looked at Sh'ron, who shook her head, then she looked at Chhdar, who was looking back at her with one eyebrow raised questioningly. Then she glanced at Shao, who winked.

"I don't hear anything but birds chirping," Chhdar said.

"Exactly," Zimpf said with a smile. "Chirping birds means no mongers."

They all began to relax slightly.

"How far is it to the Order of the Mages?" Amicu asked.

"Just a couple of hours," Zimpf told him. "Do you all want to take a break, or should we push on?"

"I need to take a break," Amicu announced, unexpectedly climbing down off his horse. He stood holding on to the saddle horn for a moment, then called softly, "Alia."

She took one look at the violently trembling tactician and ran toward him. "Shao!" she screamed.

The martial artist, who was standing closest to the suffering man, turned and caught him before he fell.

They could all see the blood pouring from Amicu's chest.

Alia laid the injured man on the ground, quickly assessed him, then immediately began issuing orders in crisp, even tones. She called for her medical bag then cut away the shirt he had been wearing. Raked from his upper left chest all the way down to his right hip were four long gouges where he had taken a swipe from a monger. The wounds were deep, but thankfully, not life-threatening.

She put a salve on the open wounds to fight infection and to numb the area. Then Alia stitched up the deepest of the scratches with the tiny, even stitches that Sairima had taught her. Finally, she covered the cuts with lambswool and bound the injury to prevent further damage and to speed healing. Once she was finished, she gave Amicu a drink from a potion bottle which she carried in her medical bag to ease the pain once the numbing solution wore off.

They went ahead and ate a quick lunch while they were stopped. Afterward, Amicu claimed that he was feeling well enough to travel. Alia finally agreed to allow him to continue the journey but insisted that they travel slowly so as not to aggravate his injuries.

Everyone was so concerned about getting Amicu up on his horse that only Shao noticed Zimpf standing frozen in the middle of the road, his eyes glazed.

Shao went to his side and touched him lightly. "Zimpf?" he said softly. "Brother?"

After several tense moments, Zimpf answered, his eyes still glazed and tears streaming down his face. "We're too late," he said.

"Too late for what?" Shao asked softly.

"The mages," Zimpf answered, staring blankly toward the west.

"Zimpf?" Shao asked. "What do you *see*?"

But Zimpf didn't answer. He finally looked directly at Shao. "We need to go," was all he said.

Shao nodded in agreement, and together, the two of them led the others to the compound of the Order of the Mages.

When they arrived at the tag end of the day, the vision Zimpf had seen was more horrific than any of them could have imagined.

The huge entrance gates were splintered into tiny shreds. The hall, which seemed as though it had grown out of the very stones of the earth itself, was obliterated. All the outbuildings, the classrooms, the dorms, even the hospital wing, had been razed to the ground. There was nothing left. Nothing. The compound was totally and utterly annihilated.

Laid out on the ground against what was left of the exterior fence were dozens upon dozens of dead bodies. There was perhaps a score of mages working to extract the remainder of the casualties of Marek's rage from the crumbled remains of the buildings.

The group entered the devastation solemnly and immediately went to work. Shao, Ciern, Chhdar, and Zimpf began searching for victims, both dead and alive. Alia and Sh'ron, with Amicu's help, set up a triage area so Alia could begin treating the survivors. They worked late into the night, providing what aid and comfort they could.

As the sun broke over the horizon the next day, Alia was still hard at work. She had been up all night long caring for the wounded and the dying. She had removed shrapnel, stitched up lacerations, straightened and bound broken bones, and even performed minor surgery. The healer-in-training bolstered the despairing, calmed the weeping, and comforted the dying.

Finally, she reached the last patient in a long line of patients. As she leaned down to examine him, she gasped in surprise.

"Ch'vin," Alia called the young man's name softly. Tears began to pour down her face.

The badly injured man looked at her, blinking rapidly as he tried to focus his swollen eyes.

Alia took his left hand in hers and held it gently. "Do you remember me?" she asked softly. "You stole my horses once and we fought."

"You mean you paddled my bottom with the flat of your sword."

He tried to smile, but the pain overwhelmed him. He groaned then gasped for breath. "I...I...deserved it."

He licked his lips, then continued. "Is...is Sh'ron...here too?" he panted between waves of pain.

"Get Sh'ron! Now!" Alia hissed over her shoulder to Shao. But he was already sprinting away.

Within moments, the two of them returned.

Sh'ron looked at Alia; the healer shook her head sadly.

"Ch'vin?" the swordswoman whispered. She knelt down beside the young mage.

He reached for her hand, and she gave it to him. With her free hand, she pushed his hair out of his face.

He smiled weakly; his eyes fluttered open.

"I...I...wanted to...to see...you," he gasped. His voice had grown low and weak.

"Don't go," Sh'ron pleaded. "Look, I still have the gift you gave me." She reached into one pocket and pulled out an oval rock. It had been polished until the red stone glowed like it held a spark within.

Ch'vin smiled weakly. "I...love..." He paused, drew in a hitching breath, released it, then nothing.

His chest didn't rise again.

Sh'ron buried her face in her hands and sobbed.

Suddenly, Chhdar was there. He lifted his wife in his arms and cradled her gently as he carried her back to their tents. She clung to him like a brokenhearted child.

Shao watched as Alia covered the young mage's face with a tattered blanket then bent her head, too broken to even cry.

It seemed like Ch'vin's death represented the sum and total of all the horror inflicted by one man.

Marek abandoned the small, derelict cottage that had once been his home shortly after leaving his "surprise" for Alia and her friends.

What he didn't see was the agent that DaiSur had sent to keep an eye on him. Almost as soon as he stepped foot inside the old hut, the man fled on a fast horse, making his way directly to DaiSur with an alarming report.

By the time the mage emerged, the observer was long gone.

Marek mounted the black stallion that DaiSur had given him. His goal was to deprive everyone who had ever thwarted him of everyone and everything they valued.

He was nearing his next target—those who had attempted to hinder his goals—when he began to sense that he was being followed. But he could not perceive who or what pursued him. He was not a diviner. The mage did, however, know a permanent way to discourage those shadowing him. So, using a spell his master had taught him, Marek summoned a sneak of mongers and ordered them to dismember the next group that traveled down the road. He didn't know if it was DaiSur and her retainers, Alia and her friends, or some innocent travelers. It didn't matter.

He left the ambush to the mongers and rode away with an uncaring shrug.

Once he made it to the Order of the Mages, he administered what he considered to be a barely suitable punishment.

Chapter 7 – Fractured

Alia finally wept. She sat on the ground and cried for the loss of life and for her inability to save the victims of Marek's evil. Suddenly, she felt Shao's arms envelop her, and she leaned heavily against him, drawing comfort and peace from his strength.

He wiped the tears from her face and kissed her forehead softly. "Come with me," he told her. "You have helped all of the patients who needed treatment. You must rest."

Alia looked around to see that he was right. The long line of injured people was gone. She allowed Shao to lead her to the shelters that the mages had set up for them, where she nodded over her breakfast and then collapsed on the blankets in the corner. Shao gently pulled an extra blanket over her shoulders.

Alia awoke early in the afternoon with the sun streaming onto her face. Shao lay quietly beside her. At first, she thought he was asleep, but when she rolled over to look at him, she saw that he was looking back at her and smiling.

"How are you feeling?" he asked.

"Better," she told him. "But I need to get up and check on my patients."

"I'll help you," he offered.

"You can't help with my first patient," she said firmly.

"Why?" he wanted to know. "I've assisted Sairima lots of times."

"Because." Alia smiled. "You are my first patient."

"Me? I'm not hurt," he protested.

"You were," she answered. "I need to check your hand, and I believe it's time for those stitches to come out."

"Then I will lay right here and be a very good patient," he told her. "But only if you pay me first."

"Pay you?" Alia asked, confused.

"Yes." Shao smiled. "It will cost you one kiss."

Smiling shyly, Alia kissed him. First, she checked his hand, which was free of all blisters and seemed to have healed completely. Then, she began to gently remove the tiny, even stitches that Sairima had so carefully sewn into the gash above his eyebrow.

As she was working, Shao watched her every move intently. Once the last stitch was removed, he took her hand, kissed it, and whispered, "I am more and more amazed by the person you are. I love you so much."

Alia blushed.

"Do you mind if I ask you a question?" he asked.

"Of course not," she replied, frowning as she removed the sutures.

"Who was that young man that you called Sh'ron to see yesterday?"

Alia looked sadly at the tent flaps for a moment, then sighed heavily. "A few years ago, Sh'ron and I were sent to get the healer. A man in our little hamlet was badly injured in a farm accident, and the caregiver did not have the skill to treat him. One night, while Sh'ron and I were sleeping, he snuck into our camp and stole our horses. We tracked him to his house, and when I demanded the return of my animals, he refused. He was rude and hateful and belligerent. When he attacked me with his sword, I had to defend myself."

"But you didn't hurt him," Shao surmised.

"Just his dignity." She smiled at the memory.

"By giving him a smack bottom with the flat of your sword?"

Alia laughed. "I also nicked his shoulder, just a little bit."

"Is that when he surrendered?" Shao grinned back at her.

"No." She started to chuckle. "He cried for his mama."

Shao threw his head back and roared.

"I can hear you all laughing," Zimpf announced. Then he continued in a more subdued voice, "I have lunch ready if anyone is hungry."

"Zimpf cooked?" Alia asked in surprise.

Shao laughed. "He's actually a pretty good cook."

"Yeah, if he didn't poison us," Alia muttered.

"I heard that!" Zimpf protested.

When they walked outside, everyone else was there as well. Once they finished eating, Alia had Amicu sit on a nearby log to examine him. The scratches from the monger were still red and angry-looking. But they did not seem to be infected. She applied a healing salve, rewrapped his injury, and demanded that he take it easy until she gave him permission to do otherwise.

"If you don't listen to me," she threatened, "when we get back to Miast, I'll tell Sairima how you disobeyed my orders."

"I wouldn't move an inch," Zimpf warned him. "It's not worth it to make Sairima angry."

"Angry at you," Shao muttered under his breath.

Alia giggled.

Zimpf looked back and forth between the couple, but both Shao and Alia looked back with innocent expressions.

"Hmph!" Zimpf grumbled under his breath.

Alia, Shao, and Sh'ron spent the rest of the afternoon checking on Alia's patients and making them as comfortable as possible. They discovered that two of the wounded were healers who were not severely hurt and would be up and able to tend to the injured in a couple of days.

At dinner that night, Shao delivered the news that Sorgin was one of the fatalities of the blast.

"We are going to have to continue our journey," he said, looking in concern at Zimpf. "DaiSur commanded us to take Marek's note to Aistra."

Zimpf didn't say anything. He just stared hard at the ground.

But Alia could see his eyes glistening with tears. She looked at Shao, who nodded toward Sh'ron and Chhdar then tilted his head toward the injured.

Alia stood up. "Sh'ron, Chhdar?" she asked politely. "Will you two help me with my rounds?"

The couple immediately got up and walked with her to the other end of the compound. One of the buildings, which had not been badly damaged, was now being used as a temporary hospital; the few surviving mages had been housed there. As they walked away, Alia glanced back to see that Shao and Ciern had seated themselves on either side of the diviner, and Amicu was seated in front of him. Shao had wrapped one arm around his friend's shoulders and was talking quietly to him.

Sh'ron looked back as well, then turned to Alia. "What's that all about?"

"I don't know for sure, because Shao wouldn't tell me," Alia answered.

"Shao wouldn't tell you?" Chhdar said in surprise.

"He said they had all made a vow to Zimpf never to discuss Aistra. Ever."

"We don't need Shao to tell us anything anyway," Sh'ron said. "It's pretty clear that she absolutely broke that poor man's heart."

Alia and Chhdar both nodded in agreement.

"I think it's going to be a rough trip for him," Chhdar said sadly. "It must really be hard to love someone that much and not have that love returned." Then he leaned over and hugged Sh'ron lightly, kissing her on the top of her head.

Alia smiled. Sometimes Chhdar's compassion surprised her. He was such a huge man and lethal warrior that it was easy to forget how thoughtful he could be. It was touching to see them so happy together.

In the makeshift hospital, Alia was surprised to see one of the healers up and moving around. She allowed Alia to give her a physical and then they spent time checking on the progress of each patient.

"You are a natural healer," she told Alia.

"I'm only a healer-in-training," Alia answered, but she was pleased by the compliment.

"When will you all need to leave?" the woman asked curiously.

"We'll probably stay for another day at least. We were attacked by an entire sneak of mongers a day before we arrived, and one member of our party suffered some injuries. I would like to give him another day before deciding if he is fit to travel.

"Mongers?" The healer gasped. "They are very rarely seen around here, and I have never heard of a group of them attacking. They are typically solitary animals."

Alia didn't answer, but she had a strong suspicion of who had incited them to attack.

Shao met them as they were walking back to the tents. "When do you think we will be able to leave?" he asked Alia.

"How about the day after tomorrow? I would like to give Amicu one more day before we begin traveling."

Shao nodded his agreement. "The next leg of the journey will be easy, but the final leg will be extremely difficult," he told them.

"Where do we have to go to find this Aistra?" Sh'ron asked.

"The Temple of Anaia."

Alia, Sh'ron, and Chhdar all stopped in shock.

"We're going to Selo first," Shao was saying as he continued walking. When no one answered, he realized that the others had stopped. He turned back to look at them, one eyebrow raised questioningly.

"The Temple of Anaia?" Alia said incredulously.

"I'm afraid so," Shao answered. Then he continued, "We're going to go to Selo next to get outfitted again. We can be there within a week; we'll leave for the Temple from there."

"How long will it take us to arrive at our destination once we leave Selo?" Chhdar wanted to know.

Shao thought for a few moments, considering everything. "Maybe two weeks," he mused. "If we don't have any problems."

When they got back to the tents, Zimpf had already retired for the night. The rest of them sat up late, making plans for the next leg of the journey.

The next morning, both Shao and Ciern went with Alia to check on her patients. When they walked into the building where the patients were housed, the healer that Alia had met the day before was waiting for them.

"Some of us are having a quick breakfast meeting, and we would like to invite you to join us," she said, smiling.

"We would be honored," Shao replied.

"I have already sent someone to invite your friends," she said. "Follow me please," she told them.

They all met under a huge, undamaged tree located in the back corner of the fenced property. A large table had been set up, and there were four other mages there in addition to Amicu, Zimpf, Sh'ron and Chhdar. The table had a variety of food, which they served themselves.

After everyone finished with breakfast, the healer called the meeting to order.

"First, I would like to thank Alia and all of her friends for helping us in one of our blackest hours," she said.

Everyone applauded, looking at Alia.

She blushed rosily.

"We have finished our count. There were 326 souls in the compound, 287 mages." The healer paused, then continued quietly. "We lost 271 people; 253 mages." There were gasps of horror, angry mutterings, and cries of loss. "We all know that the rogue mage, Marek, was responsible. Many witnesses saw him destroy the gate and decimate the buildings within using evil magic of some kind."

"He has the Aghara," Ciern told them.

The healer's eyes grew wide with shock. "How do you know this?" she asked.

Ciern nodded to Shao, who told them of the visit by Medjii and what all had happened. He ended by telling them that they had been sent by DaiSur to invite Sorgin to a meeting at Asath Tesai. He did not tell them about the note.

The healer nodded. "We have sent out an alert to all mages to return immediately. We have been attacked and must prepare for war if need be. We will select a representative from our number to attend DaiSur's conference."

"Thank you," Ciern said simply.

"No," the healer said, "thank you. I understand that you all must continue your journey in the morning. We have stores of food and supplies that were untouched. Please take what you need."

Then she looked at Alia. "Do you need anything for your medical bag?"

Alia nodded.

"Let's replenish your bag now," the healer said, "then we'll make rounds."

The rest of them spent the remainder of the day procuring supplies and packing for the trip to Selo. They took only enough food to last them while they were traveling.

The next day dawned bright and clear. Alia and her friends were up early, packed, and mounted. They were a somber group as they left the shattered and fragmented home of the mages and turned toward Amicu's hometown of Selo.

Thankfully, this leg of the journey proved uneventful. It only took them five days to reach Selo, because they rode late into each night and were back on the road as soon as the sun rose each morning. They spoke rarely, partly because of the horrors they had seen at the home of the mages and partly because they were exhausted from riding so hard.

It was with enormous relief when they finally rode up to Amicu's home late one afternoon. Grooms met them in front of the house and took their tired horses to the stables in the back. Upon entering the home, the group was met by a servant, who immediately took charge of their well-being since Mama was still in Miast with Sairima. "Dinner will be served in an hour," the servant, who escorted them to their quarters, informed them.

Alia and Shao's suite was beautiful. It had a sitting area and a huge bedroom with an attached bath. The tub was full of hot, soapy water.

Alia looked at Shao with a huge smile on her face. They had been traveling so hard that Alia felt like the smell of her horse would never dissipate from her skin. The hot, soapy water was the most inviting thing she had seen in days.

Shao smiled at Alia's excitement. "Go ahead," he told her, "I can wait." Then he stretched out on the bed to rest while she bathed.

Although Alia wanted to soak forever, she bathed quickly, washed her hair, and dressed. Then she waited patiently for Shao. Once he was dressed, they walked down to the dining room to meet the others.

It was nice to sit at a table, relax, and eat deliciously prepared food that someone else had cooked. They were a happy, jovial group who gathered that evening, and they all laughed and told stories while they ate—all, that is, except for one.

Zimpf sat quietly at the end of the table, his eyes downcast and his face inconsolable. As soon as he finished eating, he got up and quietly left the room. Alia looked at Shao, who watched Zimpf slide unnoticed from the room.

The next morning, Alia rose early. Just as she softly opened the door, Shao stopped her. "Where are you going so early?"

"I'm going to find Zimpf," she told him decisively.

"Do you want me to come with you?" he asked.

"No. I am going to bully my way in to see him as a healer. And if he tries to resist, I'm going to threaten to tell on him to Sairima," Alia said menacingly.

"Yeah, I don't want to get in the middle of that." Shao laughed. "I'll…I'll just meet you in the dining room for breakfast."

Alia marched resolutely to Zimpf's room and knocked solidly on the door. He didn't answer, so she knocked again, this time demanding that he open the door.

After several moments, he pulled the door open and stepped back to let her inside.

"What is going on?" he demanded crossly. "Why did you see fit to barge your way into my room while I was sleeping?"

"You've slept long enough," Alia said heartlessly. "Sit down," she ordered. "I have been charged with the health and well-being of this group by Sairima herself. So, by her orders, I am going to take care of you."

Zimpf opened his mouth, but before he could say anything, Alia continued, "Do you *want* me to tell Sairima that you refused treatment?"

He turned to the couch in his sitting room and plopped down ungratefully.

Alia started by following the protocol for a regular physical. She looked into his eyes and mouth, she felt his forehead for fever, she listened to his heart and lungs, she watched him breath and she felt his pulse. She knew his "illness" was not physical, she just needed a starting point.

Once she was finished, Alia sat down beside him while he pouted;

his body curled into the very corner of the sofa and his arms crossed tightly over his chest.

She silently waited.

Zimpf continued to mope, but he began to sneak furtive looks at her.

Alia remained silent.

He looked at her and then looked away several times.

She stayed quiet.

Zimpf turned to stare openly.

Alia continued to look off into the distance. But she reached out and took his hand, holding it gently.

Zimpf began to cry.

She pulled the weeping man toward her and wrapped her arms around his shoulders.

He clung to her fiercely, laid his head on her shoulder, and sobbed brokenheartedly, his whole body shaking in despair.

Alia held him until his outburst of grief had run its course. Then he began to talk. He told her all about Aistra—everything. He admitted his mistakes, acknowledged his feelings, confessed his fears. He described his hopes, dreams, and sorrows. Then he told her about his loss, anger, grief, and resignation.

Alia listened quietly without comment, judgment, or advice.

Zimpf fell silent, staring at nothing. Finally, he looked at her gratefully, tears still in his eyes. "Thank you for listening to me," he said sincerely.

She leaned in to hug him gently and then kissed him lightly on his forehead. "No one should carry such a heavy load alone," Alia asserted. "I don't have an answer for you concerning this woman. Only you can decide if you want to accompany us to the Temple to face her again. But no matter what happens, I can promise you this: you will not be alone."

"Thank you," Zimpf said simply.

"Now," Alia invited, "would you like to escort me to breakfast?"

"I would," Zimpf told her. "But only under one condition."

"What?" Alia asked, confused.

"That you don't tell Shao about that kiss on my forehead," Zimpf teased. "I don't need him to be mad at me again." He shuddered in mock fear.

They laughed, then together, they made their way to the dining room to join the others.

Marek left the devastated headquarters of the Order of the Mages with a satisfied smirk on his face. He had hoped to raze the building to the ground and simultaneously annihilate its occupants using only the small boost of power from the Aghara. But there still seemed to be a limit to his abilities. Nonetheless, he had done so much damage that it would take many, many years to rebuild.

He felt very proud of himself as he rode to the west, seeking the help he knew he would need in order to implement the next phase of his plan.

Chapter 8–A Difficult Journey

Everyone was quiet when Alia and Zimpf joined them for breakfast that morning. Once they started chatting, Alia had a strong suspicion that Shao had carefully contrived the conversation.

Sh'ron, who was seated by Zimpf, started by asking him about divination. What all could he *see*? How did his *visions* work? What was scrying? How did he learn he could *see*? Zimpf was in his element; his favorite subject was divination.

Once that conversation had run its course, Ciern started talking about his bow. "It just seems off," he complained. "I'm not shooting as well as I did. Maybe I need to restring it," he mused. "Zimpf, you're a bowman. What do you think?" he asked. The two of them spent some time talking about bows and what could be wrong. Finally, they agreed to go outside of Selo that morning to do some shooting.

Then Amicu started. "I must do some things around the house this morning, but I need to go to the market this afternoon. We need to get an idea of what all we'll need on the journey. Do you want to come with me, Shao?" he asked politely.

"No, I'm sorry, Alia and I have plans," he declined.

Alia looked at him in surprise, and he winked at her.

"Sh'ron, Chhdar? What about you two?"

"No," they said at the same time and then laughed. "My horse drew up lame just before we got to town," Sh'ron said. "We need to go down and talk to the groom to see what needs to be done."

Alia raised one eyebrow at her questioningly. She knew there was nothing wrong with Sh'ron's horse.

"That leaves you two," Amicu told Ciern and Zimpf. "I need help this afternoon and you two just volunteered."

"Sure, why not," Ciern acceded for both of them.

Zimpf didn't answer, but he did look at Alia with a sad smile.

After they had eaten breakfast, Shao stood up and offered Alia his hand. "Let's go," he said. Then, without waiting for an answer, he led her out back, stopping only long enough to pick up a picnic basket that was sitting by the door. The two of them walked hand-in-hand to the secret garden that Papa had built for Mama and then quietly slid through the hidden entrance. The garden was breathtaking, but Alia would always favor the one that Shao had created for her.

"So, what was that all about?" Alia asked, referring to the others' treatment of Zimpf.

"When I got to the dining room, I told everyone that you were meeting with Zimpf. We—well Sh'ron actually—decided that we needed to do something to make him feel important."

"I would say it worked." Alia smiled.

Shao grew serious. "Did he tell you everything?"

Alia nodded. "He's been grieving for a long time, and now he's forced to face her again. It has been incredibly difficult for him."

"What do you recommend?" Shao asked as they sat on a bench facing a small pool.

"Lots of attention. The more we keep Zimpf occupied and involved, and the more he knows he is not alone, the easier it will be for him," Alia answered.

"No matter what happens?" Shao asked.

"No matter what happens," Alia answered.

"Now I have a question for you," Alia said, then she plowed on without waiting for an answer. "You said we had plans today. What exactly are our plans?"

Shao smiled at her. "This," he said, gesturing at the garden. "We haven't had a moment when we were truly alone since we left Miast. Our plans are to sit here, talk, and"—he leaned over and kissed her—"kiss," he said. Then he wrapped his arm around her shoulders and pulled her close. They stayed like that for the remainder of the afternoon, enjoying each other's company.

They heard the dinner bell ring just as the sun began to sink, so they made their way back to the dining room to meet their friends. At dinner, the talk centered around the preparations for their trip. Alia was pleased to notice that everyone was still paying extra attention to Zimpf.

The preparation for the trip took almost a week. Some of the cold weather supplies had to be sent for, and it was agreed that the horses needed time to rest from being pushed so hard. Also, it was Alia's firm opinion that Amicu needed time to recuperate from the monger attack.

Two days before they were scheduled to leave, Alia took time to check on both of her patients. That morning, she went to Zimpf's room before breakfast. She and Shao had been visiting with him each morning since she had first examined him. But that day, she went alone. Zimpf seemed happy to see her. They sat together on the sofa and chatted for a while before she finally asked him directly.

"How are you really feeling, Zimpf?"

He was quiet for a moment before answering seriously. "Scared. I'm scared to see her again."

"What are you afraid of?" Alia asked gently.

"Everything," he answered, staring off into the distance as he remembered the pain, the heartbreak, and the struggle.

Alia nodded. "Just remember that you will not shoulder this alone. No matter what happens, we will be there to help you."

Zimpf looked at her with a wan smile. "Thank you," he said simply.

After breakfast, she asked Amicu to visit the rooms where she and Shao were staying so she could examine him. "Your wounds have almost healed," she told him. "I think we can take these stitches out now." She went to work removing the tiny, even sutures that Sairima had taught her to sew. Afterward, she applied some healing salve and sent the man on his way.

Shao had watched her working the entire time with a look of wonder.

"What?" she said, smiling at her husband.

"I just love watching you work." He grinned back at her.

They spent the rest of the morning going over their supplies and checking to see if they needed anything. Then, in the afternoon, they accompanied Sh'ron, Chhdar, and Zimpf to the marketplace to obtain the last few missing items.

The next day, they packed, then Alia, with Shao and Sh'ron's help, made some of the medicines they might need on the journey.

Finally, the day came for their departure. They all met for a good breakfast and then left before the sun was up.

The first week of the trip was uneventful. It reminded Alia of their trip to the elven capital. They traveled on well-used streets that narrowed down to village roads then to country lanes, which dwindled into desolate trails and finally faded altogether.

As they traveled into the mountains, they climbed higher and higher. Alia had not been sure what to expect, although she imagined that they would be riding upward toward steep peaks. Instead, they followed a series of switchbacks. They would ride for a few miles east then make a U-turn and travel west, climbing upward with each turn. The trees gradually changed from broad-leafed deciduous to spiky-needled conifers, and it seemed like each morning was colder than the last. The sky remained a brilliant azure, clean and cloudless. When they camped each night, the stars hung so low in the sky that Alia felt like she could reach out and take one. And each morning when they awoke, the views of the land around them took her breath away. She hadn't realized how exquisitely beautiful the world could be.

The second week of their journey to the Temple of Anaia proved more difficult. They had just finished another switchback and had planned on crossing a bridge to the other side of the peak they had been climbing. But when they got to the bridge, they were surprised to find it destroyed. They could clearly see a portion of it still clinging to the mountain pass on the other side, but this side of the bridge was shattered.

Shao, Amicu, Ciern, and Zimpf discussed what to do at length and finally decided to continue climbing upward in search of a second bridge that they hoped would still be serviceable.

It grew colder and colder the higher they climbed, and the cool, clear weather that they had experienced gradually changed to rain, then ice, then snow, making the footing for the horses difficult and dangerous. They were forced to slow their pace down to a crawl.

One morning, a couple of days after finding the broken bridge, Alia woke early and quietly left the tent to start the campfire.

But sitting before a blazing fire that had been built atop the previous night's pit was a thin, old man with bushy eyebrows and a long, white beard. He was cooking a stew over the fire using one of their pots.

Alia froze then quietly slipped back inside the tent. Shao looked up at her curiously; she laid her forefinger on her pursed lips and nodded to the tent flap. Shao stepped quietly to the door and peered out at the old man. Then he turned to look at Alia with one eyebrow raised questioningly.

"I can see you two looking at me," the old man announced, staring directly at their tent. "You might as well come on out and let me get a look at you," he said conversationally.

Shao and Alia stepped out together and moved to sit on the other side of the fire from the man, who was staring at them with piercing brown eyes.

"I don't know you," he said to Alia. "But it seems like I should know who you are," he said, shifting his gaze to Shao.

"I am Shao, and this is my wife, Alia," Shao introduced them.

The old man nodded but didn't introduce himself.

"You trained at the temple," he stated. "I have heard of you."

"What can we help you with, YeYe?" Shao asked, using the elven word for a well-respected grandfather, then he bowed his head respectfully at the elderly man.

"It is I who have come to help you," the man said. Then he looked at Alia. "Would you please wake your friends so that I can speak to everyone?" he asked politely. Then he addressed Shao. "Will you please serve the breakfast meal that I have prepared?"

Alia and Shao both looked at each other then got up to do as the old man asked.

Several minutes later, they were all gathered around the fire the stranger had built and eating the stew he had prepared. Ciern had tried to get the man to talk, but he simply said, "We will eat first."

So, they ate in silence.

Finally, the old man set his plate down and looked at them seriously.

"I came to warn you," he told them seriously.

"Warn us about what?" Ciern asked.

"You are heading for trouble, Prince of the Elves," he answered.

"How do you know me?" Ciern demanded.

"The same way I know the martial arts master, the diviner, and the leader of men," he said, looking at Shao, Zimpf, and Amicu in turn.

"Were you at the Temple?" Amicu asked.

"No, but I know those who attend."

"What is this warning you came to give us, YeYe?" Ciern asked again, addressing him the same way Shao addressed him earlier.

"I came to warn you of the taotie."

Shao, Ciern, Zimpf, and Amicu looked back and forth at each other anxiously.

Although she had never heard the word, Alia knew it was bad because she could see the tenseness in Shao's face as his jaws clenched and unclenched in apprehension.

"Excuse me," Sh'ron asked politely before either Alia or Chhdar could speak, "but what exactly is a 'taotie'?"

No one spoke for a few moments. Finally, the old man began to explain.

"The broken bridge that turned you back and sent you in this direction was a ploy set by the beast. He is luring you into a trap to slay you all and then devour each of you in turn."

"Can we get back down?" Shao asked.

"No, he has blocked all other ways off the mountain. The only way to escape is through his territory."

"What do you recommend we do?" Amicu asked.

Before the old man answered, Chhdar echoed Sh'ron's question. "What exactly is a taotie?"

Shao looked directly at Alia as he answered. "It's like an orc, only bigger and smarter."

"We're in for a fight," Zimpf told them. "A bad one."

"So, what do we do?" Alia asked.

"We fight," Shao said, looking at the stranger.

"No," the old man answered, looking at each of them in turn. "We plan."

Sometime later, the group began their trek to the very heart of the monster's lair.

The strange, old man who refused to disclose his name but accepted the honorary title of YeYe walked in the front of the group beside Zimpf. The two of them were scouting for the monster—YeYe with his eyes and Zimpf with his mind. They were followed by Ciern with his bow at the ready and Amicu, who had unsheathed his sword. Alia and Sh'ron came next, swords drawn as well. Chhdar with his sword and Shao with a stack of poison-tipped shuriken walked rearguard. The horses trailed behind.

They only walked for perhaps a mile when Zimpf gasped and pointed at a ridge high up to their right. Standing there was the most fearsome beast Alia had ever seen. She did not know such monsters existed. Her mouth went dry in sudden fear, and her heart began to race.

The taotie was huge, fully eight feet tall with gray leathery skin covering a heavily muscled frame. It had protruding brow ridges and deep-sunk eyes that glittered with malicious intelligence. The ears of the monster were small and catlike and flattened against his skull in anger. He had a jutting lower mandible with tusks projecting upward. The beast carried a huge, spiked club, and as soon as it saw them looking, it raised its weapon and bellowed a growling challenge. Then it leaped from the ridge, landing softly on the trail behind them.

Alia knew that if YeYe had not prepared them and Zimpf had not warned them, it would have slaughtered them from behind.

But as it was, they were ready.

Everyone turned toward the taotie, prepared to put their plan into action. Chhdar ducked to give Shao more room to begin his deadly barrage. His aim was unerring, and soon, the monster was bleeding from dozens of star-shaped barbs. One of them had embedded itself in his hand, causing him to drop the club. Then, Chhdar moved in, with Alia and Sh'ron flanking him. They began their attack by stabbing and slicing with their swords and then rapidly retreating, but the creature was much quicker than they anticipated. He wheeled swiftly and connected a strong backhand blow to Chhdar's chest, knocking him backward. The beast, seeing an advantage, stalked the massive warrior, but the rain of arrows from Zimpf and Ciern drove him back. Shao grabbed the fallen man and pulled him up and out of the way while Chhdar shook his head groggily. Then the taotie barreled his way through the defenders in a single-minded attempt to exterminate Ciern and Zimpf and their onslaught of arrows. His unanticipated attack slammed both Alia and Sh'ron to the ground. Alia stood shakily. Sh'ron didn't get up.

"Watch him!" Zimpf yelled, anticipating the taotie's movements at the same time he began to retreat.

Zimpf and Ciern continued their barrage. Amicu, his sword point held low and dangerous stabbed the creature from the side, then dove to his right just as the taotie rammed him. The enraged beast turned toward Amicu, but Shao was there with his evil-looking knife.

The martial artist had slipped silently behind the attacker, neatly hamstrung the animal, rolled to his feet with catlike grace, and then darted out of the way.

The taotie raised his muzzle in an earsplitting roar of fury.

"Down!" the old man abruptly screamed in a voice too loud to be believed. The group instantly lunged in all directions, covering their eyes as they had been instructed. There was a loud pop, a screeching cry, and a wave of heat. Then silence.

Alia looked up, and the taotie was dead, his skin completely burned from his frame so that only his bones were visible.

Then Shao was beside her, helping her up. "Are you hurt?" he asked, a frown between his eyebrows as he checked her for injuries.

"I'm fine," she answered, although her wrist was in agony. "Check the others," she told him as she moved painfully toward her twin.

Shao checked each of their friends then turned to look for the old man who had saved their lives. "Thank you," he started to say, but then froze in astonishment.

The old man had vanished.

Marek arrived in Kuthra two weeks later on a horse nearly dead from hard riding. The first two men he encountered tried to waylay him; his response was quick and brutal. He merely waved one hand at them, and both fell instantly to the ground, groaning in unimaginable pain with blood streaming heavily from their eyes.

After that, no one came near him.

He rented a room located above a squalid tavern in the seediest part of town, where he let it be known that he was looking for strong men to escort him high into the Skarsgaard Mountains.

Within a day, he had several applicants.

He chose the three biggest and strongest men, who no doubt thought they would take the job then murder the skinny mage in some desolate spot high up in the peaks.

But by the time they left the next morning, the men were totally devoted to Marek, each vowing to kill or die to protect their new master.

The rogue mage smiled maliciously to himself as they set out together. He had once again used the Aghara to dominate the will of others—others who were not likely to survive the next portion of the trip.

Chapter 9 – The Temple of Anaia

Although Shao looked all around the attack site, and Zimpf tried to *see* the old man, the search was futile. It was as though the stranger had never existed. They finally decided to move to a more suitable camping spot so Alia could tend to their injuries. Zimpf and Amicu went back for the horses and Shao helped Chhdar and Ciern to their feet while Alia checked Sh'ron. Once Zimpf and Amicu returned, they mounted and rode slowly up the path, Shao carrying the unconscious Sh'ron. Chhdar had demanded to carry his wife, but Alia flat-out refused the request.

"I suspect you have some cracked ribs, and I will not allow you to injure yourself further. You shouldn't even be on that horse," she told him crisply, her face pale.

So at Alia's insistence, they all rode at a slow, cautious pace until they found a suitable camping spot. Zimpf dismounted first and took Sh'ron from Shao, allowing him to dismount. Shao turned to assist Chhdar, who groaned with pain as he twisted out of the saddle.

Meanwhile Amicu went to aid Ciern, who had grown noticeably pale. Shao turned to ask Alia what she needed first. That's when he realized that she was still atop her horse, her face pale as she swayed dangerously in her saddle.

"Alia!" he cried as he struggled to reach her. "I am sorry. I…I didn't realize." He berated himself for not paying more attention to her.

But Amicu, who was standing next to her, deftly caught Alia as she toppled from her horse.

"Give her to me!" Shao demanded. "Get some blankets."

Amicu immediately handed Alia to her husband then hurried to gather several blankets and place them on the ground. Shao laid Alia down, and Zimpf laid Sh'ron beside her sister.

"Start a fire," Shao ordered. "And somebody get me Alia's medical bag."

Zimpf ran for the bag while Amicu started a fire with the flint, steel, and tinder he always carried. Ciern had sunk down on the ground beside the twins while Chhdar leaned painfully against his horse and watched Shao.

"I need water and a pan," Shao announced.

Zimpf dropped the medical bag and rushed to the pack horse to get a pan and a water skin.

"Rag," Shao demanded, holding out his hand while he stared intensely at Alia's face.

Amicu handed him a rag; Zimpf leaned over and poured cold water on it. Very gently, Shao wiped Alia's face.

At the same time, Zimpf laid his hand on the unconscious woman's forehead.

She regained consciousness almost immediately.

The first thing she saw was Shao's frantically worried face.

"Alia!" he exclaimed. "Are you okay? Of course you're not okay," he said, answering his own question.

"Help me sit up," she told him.

Shao and Zimpf both helped her to sit upright.

Once she was up, she looked at Shao's troubled face. "I really am fine," she told him. "I injured my left wrist when the taotie knocked me aside, and the pain finally got to me."

Shao immediately raised her wrist while supporting her hand and arm so she could see it better. Alia winced noticeably as she tried to examine her own injury.

"Where is my bag?" she asked.

Zimpf handed it to her.

She directed Shao to make a tea that would alleviate pain. She drank some, then gave some to both Ciern and Chhdar. There was plenty left for Sh'ron.

"Let me attend to my wrist, and then I want to examine every one of you," she insisted.

"Aaannd she's back!" Zimpf exclaimed.

"Zimpf," Shao said firmly. "Go gather some firewood and start cooking dinner."

Amicu chuckled as Zimpf scampered away.

As soon as the pain began to fade, Alia began to work. She examined her hand, wrist, and arm with help from Shao. After several moments and a variety of tests, she looked up and smiled. "I don't feel any breaks," she told him. "It's badly sprained though. It needs to be wrapped, and I think it would be a good idea if I splint it at least until we get to the temple."

Shao helped her wrap and splint her injury then kissed it gently.

But he still frowned.

"Again with the smooching?" she heard Zimpf complain.

"I'm feeling better," Alia said suddenly. "I need to check you all, and I think I would like to start with you," she demanded of Zimpf.

She turned to wink at Shao, but he didn't smile back at her. He was quiet, solemn.

"On second thought," she said, looking at her husband who was staring at the ground like an abashed schoolboy, "I think I will start with you instead."

As they started to walk away for some privacy, they heard Zimpf chanting in a sing-song voice, "Shhaaoo's in troouuble, Shhaaoo's in troouuble."

Alia turned, fixing him with a steely glare and pointing one finger threateningly. "You're next."

Zimpf was instantly quiet. He swallowed his laughter and nodded, his eyes wide. As she turned to lead Shao away, she heard Amicu and Ciern laughing.

Once they were alone, Alia faced Shao and waited patiently for him to speak. Finally, he took her good hand in his. "I am so sorry," he began, but Alia stopped him.

"No Shao," she answered defiantly.

He looked up at her, confused and hurt.

Alia licked her lips nervously and continued. "I am the one who is sorry. You asked me if I was hurt, and I told you I was fine. You had no way of knowing." Then, because everything seemed to crash in on her all at once, her eyes filled with tears, and she looked at the ground so he wouldn't see her cry. "I feel like I let you down. I told you I would never lie to you but…but…I did." She choked back her tears. "I didn't do it on purpose. My wrist did hurt, but…I…I…

thought I was okay."

Shao leaned in and hugged her tightly, being careful of her injury. He could feel her shaking.

"Shhh," he said in a comforting tone. "Shhh, Alia, it's okay."

They stood together quietly for several minutes while Shao comforted Alia.

Finally, she pulled herself together. "I'm sorr—"

But Shao interrupted her by placing his finger on her lips, then he smiled at her. "You're okay now; that's all that matters." Then he leaned in and kissed her. "Come on," he told her. "We should get back so you can check the others."

Back at camp, Zimpf and Amicu had pulled up some logs for them to sit on, the tents had been erected, the horses were picketed, and dinner was cooking.

Alia, with Shao working beside her, began her examinations. She started with Sh'ron while Chhdar hovered over them. Finally, she looked up at him in relief. "It is as I thought when I looked at her earlier. She is fine, just unconscious. She should wake up soon and will probably have a blinding headache. I'll give her something for the pain and something to help her sleep through the night. By tomorrow, she'll be back to normal."

Then she checked each of the others. Chhdar had a couple of broken ribs, which Alia bound tightly. Ciern had a burn on his right shoulder and arm, the result of being so close to the old man's spell. Alia applied a burn cream to ease the pain. He also had some deep contusions but was otherwise fine. Amicu and Zimpf both had some minor cuts and bruises; Shao was unharmed.

They retired as soon as Sh'ron regained consciousness, was treated, and had eaten her dinner.

They rose early the next morning, and the bedraggled group continued their journey as though nothing had happened.

It was another three days before they saw the Temple of Anaia. They turned yet another switchback, and suddenly, there it was. It was perched snugly between the two highest mountain peaks.

Alia thought the building itself was alien-looking; the edges of the roof flared up to the height of the top of the temple. The entire roof was covered in overlapping tiles with ornate animal statues perched across the peak. Alia could make out a dragon at the highest point. The front of the building was painted red and was lined with small, round windows. A long flight of stairs made their way elegantly up to the double front door. The landscaping was flawless with meandering pathways, perfectly trimmed lawns, and ornately shaped shrubs. Interspersed throughout the grounds were splashing fountains. The entire temple exuded a feeling of peace and tranquility.

Three of the graduates looked at each other and then at the temple in excitement.

"It feels like coming home, doesn't it?" Ciern asked.

The others smiled and nodded, all except for Zimpf.

Alia had noticed that the closer they got to the temple, the more Zimpf drew in on himself. She happened to be near him when they stopped. She leaned over quietly and touched his arm. He looked at her with tears standing in his eyes.

"I'm here for you. We all are," she mouthed and gestured at the others.

He nodded firmly once, blinked away the tears, then stared bravely at the building.

It only took a couple of hours for them to reach the grounds of the temple. They passed under a huge arch which served as a gated entrance that was connected to the tall fencing surrounding the temple.

Once inside, Ciern instructed them to dismount and walk their horses along the gravel drive leading to the stairs.

They had only gone a few yards when they were suddenly and viciously attacked.

Shao, who was in front, ran to meet the five assailants, who came sprinting down the lawn. They all wore black, loose-fitting clothes with black scarves tied across their faces.

Alia immediately reached for her sword with her right hand, but Ciern gently grabbed her arm, holding her back. She twisted in an attempt to free herself, but Ciern hissed, "No! You'll only throw him off balance if you interfere." Then he pointed at Shao with his chin. "Watch," he told her with an eager smile on his face.

Alia turned, her bandaged hand rising involuntarily to her open mouth in awe. She had seen Shao fight before. But this…this was poetry in motion.

Shao took on each attacker individually, and at the same time, he fought them all at once. The first man that reached Shao jumped up, swinging his leg out to kick him, but Shao turned sideways, effortlessly hitting the man's foot, pushing him off balance, turning, and kicking the man's feet out from under him. He went down, hard. Two more attackers were there simultaneously. Shao jumped high in the air, kicking first one assailant in the face and then immediately afterward kicking the second one full in the chest with his other foot. Both men fell heavily to the ground. The next foe tried to punch him, but Shao twisted, grabbed the man's wrist, turned quickly, and tripped him with one foot hooked behind the man's ankle. Then Shao elbowed him in the stomach. The man collapsed, gasping for air. The final attacker grabbed Shao from behind, but he elbowed the man hard in his chest, causing him to lose his grip. Shao then reached back, grabbed the attacker by his head, bent over quickly, and flipped him brutally. He didn't get up either.

There was a vast silence.

Alia noticed that Shao wasn't even breathing hard.

Then a man dressed similarly to the attackers walked out of the temple, down the long flight of stairs, and across the lawn to stand before Shao. He raised his right hand in a fist and then covered it with his left hand, bowing respectfully. Shao also covered his right fist with his left hand and bowed in return.

Ciern, Zimpf, and Amicu applauded.

Alia, Sh'ron, and Chhdar exchanged confused glances.

Shao looked at his friends with a big smile on his face.

The strange man turned to eye everyone seriously.

"Ciern, Amicu, Zimpf," he said, nodding to each of them in turn. They bowed politely, each covering their right fist with their left hand.

"Welcome back. Have you brought me some new recruits?" he asked, looking at Alia, Sh'ron, and Chhdar.

"No, Sifu," Shao told him, moving to stand beside Alia. "This is my wife, Alia," he announced proudly.

The stranger looked at her piercingly. "As was foretold," he said with a sideways glance at Zimpf.

"This is Sh'ron and Chhdar." Shao introduced them. They both nodded politely.

"This man is my Sifu," Shao announced respectfully. "He taught me everything I know. You may also call him Sifu." The martial arts instructor at the Temple of Anaia was of average height and weight, he had black hair that was gray at the temples, and almond-shaped brown eyes. He was soft-spoken and introspective.

"You were ever an apt pupil," he replied nonchalantly.

But Alia could see the pride in the teacher for a student who excelled.

"Come," Sifu said, "let's go to the dining room. You all need food." Then, he looked pointedly at their injuries. "And a healer," he added.

"What about the attackers?" Alia whispered to Shao with a worried frown.

"Sifu?" Shao asked, looking at the men he had defeated.

"They need to learn their lessons more thoroughly," he said clinically. "Perhaps some students in this group should take note of what happens to those who do not excel," he glared at Zimpf.

Amicu and Ciern both chuckled until he turned a baleful eye on them as well.

"Yes, Sifu," the three men muttered in unison.

They left their horses with grooms before climbing the flight of stairs leading to the temple. Once inside, Alia was surprised to see that the temple was a large, ornate room with a vaulted ceiling held up by red-painted columns. The columns were covered in gold writing in a language she didn't recognize. The room itself was bare, and their footsteps echoed hollowly as they passed through.

On the back side of the temple, there was a maze of long, low buildings. Sifu took them outside, across a paved courtyard, and straight into what turned out to be the dining room. There was a buffet all along one wall with plates and utensils stacked nearby.

Once they had served themselves and were seated at a table, Sifu turned to Shao. "Why have you returned? What news do you have of the outside world?"

Shao looked around the room at the other students and teachers gathered there. "May we speak privately this evening?"

Sifu looked surprised, but he nodded politely.

After they had eaten, he showed them to their rooms then left after telling Shao, "come to my quarters when the dinner bell rings. I will arrange to have food delivered to us."

Then he spoke to the entire group. "Please stay in your rooms until after the healer has had a chance to examine each of you. After that, I'm sure one of our former students would be delighted to give you a tour." Then, he turned and walked away.

Alia and Shao's room was plain but meticulously clean. It consisted of one room with a bed, table, and two chairs, and it had an attached bathroom.

"It's not very luxurious, I'm afraid," Shao told her.

Alia went to sit on the bed. The mattress was quite hard, and she made a face.

"Not comfortable?" Shao asked.

Alia patted the bed beside her. "It's fine, as long as you're with me." She smiled.

Shao sat beside her and then leaned back, stretching his long frame on the bed and pulling Alia down beside him.

"What was that attack all about when we first arrived?" Alia wanted to know.

Shao chuckled. "It was Sifu's way of welcoming me back."

Alia looked at him in surprise. "That's a pretty harsh welcome home. What if you had lost?" she fretted.

He didn't answer.

Alia glanced over, thinking that maybe he had fallen asleep. But he was studying her with one eyebrow raised sardonically.

"Oh," she said. Then she felt her face grow hot as her cheeks flushed with embarrassment.

Shao burst out laughing. "You are absolutely irresistible when you blush like that," he told her.

Just then, there was a polite knock at the door.

Shao opened it and admitted an older man carrying a medical bag. He checked Alia's wrist and agreed with her assessment of a bad sprain.

"Are you the healer?" he asked her, glancing at her medical bag.

"Healer-in-training," she answered.

"You're very talented. I checked the big warrior with the broken ribs and the elven prince with the burns. There was nothing else I could do for them because of your treatment," he complimented her.

"Thank you," Alia said.

"Who is training you?" he inquired.

"Sairima of Miast."

The healer jumped as though someone had slapped him. "That explains it," he said. Then he packed his bag and left without looking back.

Alia and Shao looked at each other for a long moment before bursting into laughter.

"Would you like to take a tour?" Shao invited her.

"I thought you would never ask," Alia said excitedly. "Can we see if Sh'ron and Chhdar want to go too?"

The four of them spent the afternoon touring the compound. Shao showed them the temple again, explaining the gold writing on the columns.

Alia was surprised that Shao spoke the strange language, although she knew she shouldn't have been. It seemed like there was nothing her husband could not do.

They toured the training grounds, where Alia could see dozens of young men and women practicing martial arts. Shao showed them the classroom and dormitories. Then they walked over the grounds, following the winding paths while he explained the meanings behind the numerous fountains that adorned the grounds.

"I don't understand," Chhdar confessed. "This place is beautiful and peaceful, yet they train for war. Why?"

"It is because there can be no light without darkness," Shao answered, almost automatically, it seemed.

"Is that from Sifu?" Alia asked curiously.

"Yes, it is." Shao turned to smile at her. Then he looked at Chhdar. "To answer your question, we train for war to prevent it. If we can stop evil before it grows, there would be no war."

Chhdar frowned, thinking over the alien concept.

Just then, the dinner bell rang, and Shao led them to Sifu's quarters. The others had already arrived and were seated around the table, talking over old times and laughing over old pranks. All except for Zimpf.

Alia immediately saw that he had retreated into a corner and withdrawn into himself. He was very pale and was shaking visibly. There was a polite knock at the door just then, and she saw him jump nervously, his eyes wide and panicked.

But it was only some of the staff bringing dinner.

Everyone began to serve them themselves, still chatting amiably. No one except Alia seemed to have noticed Zimpf. Alia touched Shao's arm and cut her eyes at the diviner. He nodded. He had noticed.

Of course, he noticed, Alia thought.

One other person had noticed as well. Sifu had seen Alia watching Zimpf. He leaned over quietly and whispered so low that she knew no one else could hear him, "I will take care of our friend." Then he continued entertaining his guests as though he had never spoken.

After they had eaten, Sifu began the meeting. "What is happening in the world?"

Shao told him everything from the time Alia was presented with the Orb of Ahi by a dying mage until they arrived at the Temple that very afternoon.

Sifu listened intently until the story was finished. "Even we here at the Temple of Anaia have heard of the rogue mage, Marek," he told them. "If DaiSur has involved herself personally, then the situation is dire indeed. Also, there is the attack on the Order of the Mages that must be answered for."

They all nodded in agreement.

"Do you all have any idea what is in this note he left for Alia?" he asked.

No one answered him.

"Zimpf," he said, turning to the diviner. "What do you *see*?"

Zimpf looked up from his misery. "Nothing, Sifu," he answered quietly. "I *see* nothing."

"Perhaps, my child," Sifu said kindly, "you should see with your heart and not your head." He looked over and nodded at the darkest corner of the room, where a young woman with short, blond hair stood silently.

"Aistra!" Zimpf gasped.

Marek led his new retainers far up into the Skarsgaard Mountains, acting on an idea he had gotten from DaiSur.

The mage had begun to formulate his plan during one of the many long evenings he had spent with the envoy and Medjii during his recovery period. DaiSur had foolishly told what she most certainly thought was an innocent story about the Vheral people who lived in the far north and how she alone had prevented their planned southern invasion, which would have resulted in the defeat of the entirety of the southern nations.

Hearing about the wild men to the north gave Marek an idea. Since he used a transportation spell to escape the erupting volcano set off by the Orb of Ahi, he had been seeking some way to wreak vengeance on those he blamed for hurting and then abandoning him. The stories of the power trapped within the Aghara along with the certain knowledge of a leaderless army just to the north presented a tempting resolution—a way to get even.

Artfully, he plied his guests with question after question, stopping occasionally to falsely congratulate DaiSur on her cunning resolution to an almost unsolvable situation.

Neither of the two women were aware of his duplicity. He had completely convinced them of his redemption and thus his desire to aid others in their times of need.

Marek had always been considered charming and charismatic. The truth was, however, that he was exceptionally talented at reading people. He had to be. He grew up with an angry, uncaring father who blamed him for the death of his mother. So the mage had learned to study his father's expressions and actions as he looked for those minute danger signals that indicated anger.

The first person—aside from the indifferent father—that he consciously began practicing his manipulation skills on was Alia. Within a couple of weeks, he could read both her and her twin, Sh'ron, like a book. A frown meant no, one raised eyebrow was a question, both raised eyebrows was a challenge, eyes wide open meant yes.

His talent for observation and the ensuing manipulation skills worked just as well on Medjii and DaiSur as it had on his peers. He beguiled them during those evening conversations into telling him everything they knew about the Vheral people in the far north—their lifestyles, their battle tactics. DaiSur even told him about her travels through the mountains and the dangers encountered within.

Once the mage and his new servants were nearly to the peak of the huge mountain range, he established a defensive strategy. He was well aware of the taotie who lurked at this elevation, so he sent one man nearly a mile ahead to act as lookout and another at least a mile behind to act as rearguard, knowing full well that one of them would most certainly be the first to fall victim to the vicious creature.

He was right.

Three days later, they heard an agonizing scream of excruciating, unbearable pain and it was all the worse because it was interspersed with cries for help that seemed to go on and on.

The servant nearest Marek took that first running step toward the echoing shrieks.

"Berk!"

But the name died on his lips as the rogue mage shushed him with a single, whispered word.

"Silence!"

The man immediately froze.

When the servant riding rearguard caught up with them several moments later, they hadn't moved. Instead, they stood motionless, listening to the agonizing cries of the slowly dying man along with the audible *sounds of the feeding taotie.*

Finally, after what seemed like forever, the sounds died away, and Marek allowed them to continue. They had been traveling on foot, leading their horses up the narrow path lined with steep cliffs on one side and precipitous crevasses on the other. Because of the necessity for slow going, it was nearly an hour later before they came upon the brutal attack site. The area was bathed in blood, and the walls of the rock face were covered in a wide arc of fine droplets, evidence that the taotie had aggressively shaken its prey.

Further up, swaying dangerously over a deep mountain chasm, was a narrow bridge. Fresh blood streaked its way across the thin wooden planks.

Without a word, Marek pulled out the silver knife he kept strapped to his wrist, bent down, and cut the ropes holding the bridge aloft.

It swung hard, slammed into the other side with a vast clattering, then hung there uselessly.

Later that night as they camped in a tiny embrasure just off the trail, the rearguard dared to ask his first question.

"Why didn't you try to save Berk?"

At first, Marek didn't answer. He hadn't known the man's name; he hadn't bothered to learn any of the men's names. He hadn't expected any of them to live this long.

Finally, he looked up at the two servants, who both stared at him with accusing eyes.

"Did you want to die too?" he asked callously.

Chapter 10–Aistra

Alia looked back and forth between Zimpf and the strange woman who had so devastated his life. She could see Zimpf's face as it registered somewhere between abject terror and absolute adoration. It finally settled into an expression of such hopelessness that Alia was touched to the quick by it.

Then she looked at the woman who had emerged from her place of concealment in the corner. She was very young. She walked toward Zimpf, her eyes absorbed in his. Her expression was one of serious resolve, which was unusual in one so young. She reminded Alia of Sairima when she was working with a particularly difficult case and was determined to succeed.

The room went deathly quiet.

"This portion of the meeting is over," Sifu announced. "You are excused," he said dismissively. "I expect you to return here for breakfast tomorrow."

Everyone stood to leave, including Zimpf, who was still staring at Aistra.

Sifu picked up Zimpf's right hand and held it gently but firmly in both of his own hands. He was not going to allow the diviner to leave.

"Except for you, child. You will stay."

Alia looked at Zimpf as they left; he looked like a man ready to bolt.

They were a quiet bunch as they filed solemnly out the door and down the pathway to their quarters.

Once they were in their room, Alia turned to Shao. "Did you know she was in the room?" she asked incredulously.

"Yes," he answered. "I was trained to be vigilant of my surroundings."

"I thought I was getting to be pretty good with you teaching me," she moaned hopelessly. "But I guess not, because I had no idea she was there."

Shao smiled at her. "I would have been surprised if you had. I knew she was there because I saw Sifu glance in that corner," he admitted.

"She was so invisible," Alia marveled. "Why didn't Zimpf *see* her?"

"That is one of her talents," Shao answered. "Aistra has a number of talents."

"Like what?" Alia asked, puzzled.

"Sit down," Shao told her, "and I'll try to explain."

They sat together on the bed and held hands as Shao talked.

"Those of us who are accepted here either have a job to do—like Ciern, who will be a king, or Amicu, who is expected to lead—or we have a talent, like my athleticism or Zimpf's divination. Even then, it is difficult to be accepted. The rules also stipulate that a student must be at least sixteen years old before they can be admitted because of the harsh nature of the instruction. But Aistra was already a student here when Zimpf and I arrived. She couldn't have been much older than twelve or so. The story was that her parents left her at the front gate alone because she exhibited some rather peculiar traits that, quite frankly, scared them."

"How sad," Alia murmured. "That must have been frightening for her. I can't begin to imagine how terrified I would have been if my parents had abandoned me that young."

Shao nodded in agreement.

"Anyway," he continued. "The instructors here discovered she was a polyimpano."

"A what?" Alia said.

"A polyimpano. It means that she has many talents, though they are not as defined as someone with only one talent."

Alia looked at him in confusion. "What exactly does that mean?" she questioned.

Shao laid back on the bed and pulled Alia with him, cradling her head on his chest.

"Zimpf has the talent of discernment. He is what is described as a true diviner. He *knows* how people feel, he *sees* their past and present, and he *visions* their future. Aistra can discern, but she can only *sense* how people feel. She only has part of his talent. She has parts of many other talents as well."

"Like what?" Alia asked.

"She can make herself unnoticeable, for one thing. That's why no one saw her sitting in the corner during the meeting."

"No one but you," Alia pointed out.

Shao smiled and then continued. "She can speak every language in the Four Lands. And she's a strong mage."

"Can she fight like you?" Alia wanted to know.

"No one can fight like me," he smiled at her.

"What about Sifu?" she teased.

Shao was quiet for a moment before speaking. "No," he answered with both pride and regret. "The day I defeated Sifu is the day I was told I was finished with my lessons. There was nothing left for him to teach me."

Alia raised up to study his face. "Did you not want to leave?"

"This had become my home," he said simply. Then he kissed the top of her head. "But it worked out, because if I had stayed, I would never have met you."

They continued talking late into the night, not even realizing when they fell asleep.

They woke early the next morning, got dressed, and waited for the breakfast bell to ring so they could continue the meeting with Sifu.

Alia was very quiet. She was thinking about Aistra and Zimpf.

"Why so glum?" Shao asked in his soft voice.

"I was thinking about Zimpf," Alia told him. "Are you able to tell me how it started?"

Shao didn't answer for a moment, then finally, he shrugged. "When we were accepted, we were both sixteen. Aistra was already here; she was only twelve. We sort of took her in as a little sister. She and Zimpf were especially close because of their talents. They complimented each other. When he was sixteen and she was twelve it was such a sibling relationship, but as they grew, their relationship grew as well. When we graduated, he was almost twenty-three and she was nineteen. By then, they were inseparable. He wanted her to leave with us, he had asked for her hand…" Shao trailed off thoughtfully.

"She said no," Alia said sadly.

"She said yes," Shao answered. "But then, the morning we were all supposed to leave, Zimpf arrived late at the front gate without Aistra. He refused to tell us what had happened, and he made us swear to never mention her name again. He was absolutely inconsolable for months."

"He told me about leaving her behind, but he didn't tell me why either," Alia admitted.

"At the time, I couldn't understand his devastation," Shao admitted. "But after thinking I had lost you…" he paused, looking seriously at Alia.

Just then, the breakfast bell rang.

"Before we go, can I ask one question?" Then Alia plowed on. "When you all left here, where did you go?"

"We went with Ciern to visit the elven kingdom." Shao smiled at her. "I believe I told you the rest of that story. That's where Sairima came to look for me and where she bullied the elves into training her."

The breakfast bell rang a second time, so they hurried to Sifu's quarters. Everyone else was seated around the table eating when they arrived.

Sifu didn't say anything, but he looked at Shao disapprovingly. Shao bowed respectfully, holding his right hand out in a fist and covering it with his left palm.

"I'm sorry Sifu," he apologized. "I will manage my time more efficiently."

Sifu bowed his head in acceptance.

Alia, however, was searching the room for Zimpf. She finally saw him curled up and sleeping in the same chair he had occupied the night before. Aistra was seated in an adjoining chair. Her head was bowed, and her eyes were shiny with tears as she watched him sleep.

"Shall we begin?" Sifu announced, kicking Zimpf's chair to wake him.

Zimpf raised his head wearily then stretched and yawned. He was very pale, but he had lost the look of hopelessness that had been etched on his face the evening before. He glanced over at Aistra and gave her a cautious smile. She looked down at her hands, and when she raised her face back up to look at him, she no longer cried.

They both moved to the table and sat down.

Alia noticed that though they sat beside each other, they were careful not to touch. It was as though an invisible fence had been erected between them.

Surprisingly, Sh'ron started the meeting.

"Sifu," she said politely. "When we were traveling, the bridge we wanted to cross was destroyed, and we were forced to take a different route. A couple of days later, a strange old man appeared at our campsite and told us that a taotie was stalking us. He helped us to defeat the monster, but he disappeared as soon as the creature was destroyed. Can you tell us anything about him?"

"You all were blessed beyond measure," Sifu smiled at them. "You were visited by a Zduhac."

No one said anything.

"What exactly is that?" Sh'ron finally asked in a puzzled voice.

"A Zduhac is a spirit creature that lives in the mountains and aids travelers," he explained. "They appear as humans to give warnings, and if needed, will aid them with magic. It is said they disappear once their magic is used."

"He died?" Chhdar blurted in horror.

"No, child," Sifu answered with a slight smile. "Zduhacs regenerate with their magic. It's akin to you getting tired and resting."

They all looked back and forth at each other, surprised and pleased.

"Now," Sifu said. "Let's get started with this meeting. We have some decisions to make." Then he turned to Zimpf. "Do you have that letter?"

Zimpf nodded, got up, and went to get his saddlebag, which he had brought to the meeting the night before.

Alia noticed that when he arose from his chair, he did so by turning his back to Aistra.

He retrieved the note, which was still sealed in the wrapping in which DaiSur had encased it and laid it gently on the table.

"And it was addressed to you?" he said to Alia.

"Yes, Sifu," she answered.

He nodded. "DaiSur sent you to find Sorgin of the Order of the Mages, and if you were unsuccessful, you were to come here to find Aistra."

"That is correct, Sifu," Ciern asserted.

"Well, my dear, I guess it is your turn. Do not open it," he warned Aistra. "Just tell us what you sense."

Everyone watched as Aistra reached out to touch the wrapping on the note. Just before her fingers brushed it, she snatched her hand back as though it had been burned.

"Evil!" she gasped. "Great evil!" Her eyes went wide with terror.

"Zimpf!" Shao said sharply, standing quickly as the diviner stiffened in an almost comatose state.

Alia could see Zimpf's eyes moving back and forth rapidly behind his closed lids.

As fast as Shao moved, Aistra was quicker. In a movement born of pure fear, she grabbed his chair with his inert body still sitting there and turned it to face her. Placing her hands on either side of Zimpf's face, she leaned in until her forehead was touching his. Then she began to speak to him. Alia couldn't hear what she was saying, but the tone of her voice was low and musical. After several moments, Zimpf began to blink, then he opened his eyes. Aistra pulled away from him, but not before wiping the tears gently from his cheeks.

Zimpf looked at her gratefully, but his face was very pale, and he was gasping for breath.

While Aistra and Sifu were attending to Zimpf, Alia sent Chhdar to get her medical bag. While he was gone, she poured hot water from a breakfast kettle into a mug. Chhdar was back quickly. Alia selected the herbs from her bag for a calming tea, fixed Zimpf a cup, and then wordlessly handed it to him.

"Thank you," he told her, swallowing the tea in one long gulp. Then he sat quietly for a few moments, trying to collect his thoughts. "I'm feeling better now," he said. Finally, he looked at Aistra. "Thank you."

She looked down, but Alia could see the beginning of a smile playing around the corners of her mouth.

Everyone returned to their seats.

Alia noticed that the invisible wall between Zimpf and Aistra seemed to have dissipated. She wondered if they were unconsciously holding hands under the table.

"What did you *see*?" Sifu asked Zimpf.

"The same as before," he admitted, looking at all of them. "I *saw* the people of Alia and Sh'ron's village crying. I *sensed* despair, and hopelessness, and loss. My mind was *assaulted* by pain. And behind those visions was etched the face of Marek." Then he looked up at Sifu. "He must be stopped," Zimpf asserted forcefully. "According to Medjii, he has the Aghara, and—"

He was interrupted by Aistra, who hissed, "The Aghara! He has the Aghara?"

"Yes," Shao confirmed. "We believe he somehow mesmerized Medjii into stealing it for him."

Aistra buried her face in her hands in defeat.

"Aistra?" Sifu asked. "I am unfamiliar with the objects of the mages. Can you explain to us what this Aghara is?"

She was silent for several moments.

Finally, Zimpf broke through to her. "Aistra?" he said her name softly. "Will you explain this to us?"

Squaring her shoulders, she looked at the people sitting around the table. Then she began to talk. "The Aghara is an object of ancient evil from the earliest days of the mages. Back before the organization of the Four Lands, hundreds of years ago, the world was in absolute anarchy. Men, elves, dwarves, and all the forces of chaos, including orcs, fought for power—for the control of our world. It was a time of great turmoil where malevolence reigned supreme. The evilest among the wicked held the most power, which they used to crush their enemies with ruthless abandon. They viciously destroyed millions in their quest for power. The diviners went to the mages and explained that they could *see* the destruction of our world. So, in an attempt to save it, the mages created the Aghara. Then the two groups invited the leaders of that violent, bloody world to meet with them to discuss peace terms. The leaders came not for peace but because each hoped to bend the mages' will to their own, which would give them even greater power. The Aghara was unleashed during that titanic meeting, absorbing greed and evil from the hearts of those who attended." Aistra fell silent.

"So, if the Aghara is ever unsealed, then evil and greed would permeate the world, and it would fall to chaos," Ciern finished the thought.

Aistra nodded.

"Why would Marek want chaos?" Chhdar asked.

But Alia knew. "He doesn't want chaos," she said. "He wants power."

They were in the mountains for over a month. By the time they reached the Wilds to the far north, there was only Marek and one remaining servant, a man who said his name was Kamet.

The other servant, the one who had asked the mage why he didn't try to save Berk, had foolishly plummeted to his death a few days after the taotie attack. He had not been watching his footing, had stepped too close to the edge of the trail, and had fallen cleanly over the edge.

Marek had watched silently as the man fell screaming to his death, shrugged his shoulders apathetically, then continued walking as though nothing had happened.

Chapter 11–Resolutions

"So let me get this straight," said Amicu. "All we need to do is find a missing rogue mage and retrieve a magical object from him that he wants to use to destroy the world. Have I got that right?"

"We have to get you away from Zimpf," Shao commented dryly. "You're starting to sound just like him."

"Hey!" Zimpf protested. "I'm sitting right here."

Everyone laughed. Alia was pleased to see Zimpf complain. It was the first Zimpf-like statement he had made in days.

"Aistra, do you know how to destroy the Aghara?" Shao asked.

"No," she answered. "That knowledge has been lost in antiquity."

"My people may have the answer," Ciern told them. "We have kept the histories of the Four Lands dating back to ancient times."

"So we leave for Asath Tesai, just like DaiSur ordered," Amicu stated.

"When do we leave?" Aistra asked.

Zimpf looked at her in surprise. "You want to come with us?"

She looked at the others gathered around the table. "Will you allow me?" she asked softly.

They all looked back and forth at each other except for Alia. She was looking at Zimpf, who was staring down at the table. When no one said anything, he looked up and locked eyes with Alia. Finally, he acquiesced with a single nod of his head.

"Of course," Alia invited warmly.

They decided to leave in three days. That would give them time to gather supplies and tend to the horses. They would meet again in two days to finalize the plan for their trip.

They began to file out.

Alia noticed that Zimpf made a hasty exit and that Aistra sadly watched him leave. Then, with her head hanging low, she walked out and turned in a different direction from the diviner.

Shao had been speaking with Sifu while the others left, and Alia waited for him. When he joined her, he wore a smile tight with excitement and carried some clothes that Alia had not seen.

"Sifu has asked me to practice forms with him and then to help teach this afternoon," he told her. "Would you like to watch us?" he invited her.

"Sure!" she answered excitedly. "I would love to."

They went back to their quarters, where Shao changed into some of the loose-fitting clothing similar to what their attackers had worn the day before. Then they walked out to an area that Shao called the practice arena. There was a large, flat space in the center with several seats situated around the perimeter. Alia sat down and leaned forward, excited to watch her husband.

Shao and Sifu met in the middle. They both did the ritual bow and then began.

Alia was mesmerized. She had never seen such a display of elegant athleticism. They began by weaving their hands in a sinuous pattern and then swayed with their bodies while their feet stepped artfully toward and away from each other gracefully. Then the pace picked up to short, quick, explosive movements. They backed away and came together in crushing step maneuvers, moving forward aggressively, throwing distinctive blocks and chain punches, which culminated in foot sweeps, as well as high-flying tornado-like kicks. Then they slowed, coming together and falling apart again powerfully, demonstrating the agility and flexibility of their art.

When they were finished, Shao glanced at Alia and saw her wide-eyed amazement. Smiling, he walked over to her.

"Did you enjoy that?" he asked.

"I have never seen anything more amazing in my whole life!" she blurted in astonishment.

Shao laughed. "Do you mind if I work with Sifu and some of his students?" he asked, indicating a small crowd that had started to form. "Besides, I think someone wants to talk to you." Then without waiting to explain, he walked back to Sifu, who had begun to order his students into columns and rows.

Alia looked around but didn't see anyone. She sat back down. The lessons began, and Alia watched Shao intently as he worked with the students, demonstrating forms for them and correcting their stances.

"He is the best that this temple has ever seen or ever will see," said a low, musical voice.

Alia jumped slightly; she had not seen anyone approach. She looked over to see Aistra sitting beside her.

"Can you fight like Shao?" Alia asked conversationally.

"Not like Shao, no. No one can fight like Shao," she said.

Alia smiled with pride at her husband.

"How long have you two been together?" Aistra asked curiously.

"We met almost two years ago. We've been married for just over a year."

"You're well suited to each other."

"Thank you," Alia answered. "We just kind of clicked."

"Zimpf and I clicked," Aistra confessed.

Alia didn't answer. Instead, she turned to look steadily at the young woman and waited for her disclose her mind.

After several moments, Aistra continued. "I understand you are the healer for the group."

Alia knew that was not what Aistra intended to say. But she nodded. "Actually, I'm still in training."

"Do you…fix everything?" Aistra asked, then she rushed on. "Physical and emotional?"

"I look after all of my patient's needs," Alia replied modestly, wondering where Aistra was going with her questions.

Aistra was quiet for several moments while Alia waited patiently.

"Can I ask you something?" the young woman finally ventured.

"Of course," Alia said, turning her full attention to Aistra and smiling.

"Zimpf is so angry with me. Do you think that…" She trailed off as her eyes filled with tears, which she tried desperately to blink away before they spilled over and ran down her cheeks.

Alia leaned over and wrapped a comforting arm around Aistra's shoulders. "Shao explained some of your talents. Can you tell me what you *sense* about Zimpf?"

"Not really," Aistra said sniffling. "It's just a welter of confused emotions."

"Zimpf is not really angry," Alia told her truthfully. "He is hurt, and sometimes, people express their hurt as anger. Why don't you give him some time to process his emotions?"

"Do you think…do you think I still have a chance with him?" she asked.

"I think there is always hope," Alia answered.

"Thank you, Alia," Aistra said with a sad smile. Then she stood up to leave.

"Aistra, would you like to stay and watch Shao with me?" Alia invited. "It looks like he'll be busy for a while. Then maybe we can eat dinner together."

"Thank you. I would like that," she answered softly.

By dinner that evening, the two women had formed a cautious friendship. They both walked with Shao to the cafeteria to meet their friends for dinner. Chhdar, Sh'ron, Amicu, and Ciern were already waiting for them. Both Chhdar and Sh'ron were welcoming of Aistra. Ciern, Amicu, and Shao treated her like a little sister, teasing and laughing at her. They were having such a good time that at first, no one saw Zimpf enter. He stood silently at the door, watching the group as they told stories and laughed. It was Aistra's sudden look of anxiety that alerted first Shao and then Alia.

They turned to see Zimpf staring at them with a look of betrayal. He turned to leave, his face set and his back straight. Before anyone could even say anything, Shao was out of his chair and across the room, tackling Zimpf to the floor and holding him down in a tight headlock. He had wrapped his hand across Zimpf's mouth and was frantically whispering something into his ear—something that caused the diviner to blush a bright red.

Just then, Sifu entered and looked at the two men disapprovingly.

"Since you are so anxious to fight, child," he said to Zimpf. "Perhaps you would like to spar with Shao tomorrow in a demonstration for the students."

Zimpf looked up in consternation. "No, Sifu," he declined, shaking his head in fear as Shao released him. He stood up, trying to regain his shattered dignity.

"Zimpf doesn't want to get his butt handed to him again," Amicu snickered under his breath as the others chuckled softly.

"Then come sit here," Sifu ordered Zimpf, indicating the seat by Aistra. "We shall dine like civilized humans."

Then Alia, answering Sifu's question, told the story of how they had met Shao and Zimpf. She told of the stolen clothes and of her poisoned weed covering. The group erupted with laughter at Alia's embarrassment. She laughed good-naturedly with them.

"Zimpf, I thought I told you to stop stealing clothes," Sifu admonished him.

"Do you have a habit of doing that?" Alia asked in exasperation. "Because I'm pretty sure Ciern's father said the exact same thing to you."

"He stole my clothes," Aistra announced suddenly. "I had to walk all the way back to Temple, past hundreds of students, while wearing only my shoes."

Zimpf burst out laughing.

For the first time, Alia saw them exchange a fond look of their shared history.

They all retired early that night. Everyone wanted to finish their preparations before lunch so they could watch Shao. He had agreed to spar with several of Sifu's top students the next afternoon.

Alia and Shao had just shut their door when they heard a quiet knock. It was Zimpf.

"May I come in?" he asked politely.

Alia and Shao exchanged a quick look. Zimpf was never that polite.

Shao stepped back and opened the door.

Zimpf slumped into the room and plopped himself down on one of the chairs. "I need help," he said without preamble.

Alia sat in the chair opposite of him; Shao sat on the bed.

"How can we help?" Alia asked, touching his arm comfortingly.

He looked at her and then at Shao. But when he began to talk, it was to the floor. "It's Aistra."

"Did something happen?" Shao asked in his quiet voice.

"No," Zimpf replied. "It's just that…" He hesitated then looked at Shao. "Do you remember how you felt when you thought you lost Alia?"

Shao nodded and then looked at Alia, his heart in his eyes.

"That's how I felt when Aistra stayed. Now I'm back, and she is here, and beautiful, and perfect. The passing of time has not diminished my connection to her. But, what if…" Zimpf hesitated. "What if the same thing happens?" He looked up at the two of them with tears in his eyes. "I cannot survive that again."

Alia picked up Zimpf's hand. "Close your eyes, diviner," she demanded.

He did as he was told.

"Use your talent. What do you *see*?"

Zimpf closed his eyes and Alia watched him searching, sensing, feeling.

"See if this helps," she whispered. And taking his hand, she laid his palm on her temple. "*See*, Zimpf," she ordered. "*See* through my eyes." Alia closed her eyes as images of Aistra filled her head—Aistra looking at Zimpf when she first emerged from the corner, Aistra working to pull Zimpf from his *vision* with love and determination carved into her face, Aistra watching him leave the room while she lingered alone, Aistra crying to Alia at the practice arena, Aistra's excitement at seeing Zimpf join them at dinner, her anxiety at the possibility of being rejected, and finally, the absolute joy on Aistra's face when Zimpf laughed with her.

Zimpf moaned softly and pulled his hand away. His face was wet with tears.

"Such love is worth the risk," Alia asserted. "Go to her, Zimpf. Talk to her. Let her *search* your past, let her *sense* your feelings, and let her *feel* your fears."

Zimpf looked first at Alia and then at Shao.

Shao nodded. "Go to her," he said softly.

Zimpf walked resolutely to the door. He opened it, then looked back at Alia. "Thank you," he said, and then he was gone.

Shao waited for maybe a minute, then with a wink at Alia, he slipped out the door as quiet as a cat and soundlessly followed his friend. He was back perhaps ten minutes later.

"They're talking," he smiled at Alia. "Well, not exactly talking. When I looked in on them, they were seated on her sofa with their hands on each other's faces sharing thoughts."

Alia burst out laughing. "I can't believe you spied on your friend like that."

"They should have shut the curtains," he smirked.

"Have you ever spied on me?" Alia asked curiously.

"Frequently," he admitted. "But only when you were out very

late on a medical call." Then he hesitated. "And one other time."

Alia smiled. "I suspected that you were following me in Miast," she confessed. "But I could never catch you at it. When was the 'one other time'?"

Shao grinned, remembering. "When we were traveling from Miast to the elven kingdom. You and Marek went for a walk; you told him that you liked me."

Alia's face burned red in embarrassment. "I can't believe you heard that."

"I had to follow you," Shao insisted. "The previous time you took a walk with him, you came back with bruised knuckles and a swollen hand."

"And he had a black eye," Alia reminded him.

"Yeah, I liked that part of it." Shao grinned. "Now I have a question for you. What did Zimpf *see* in your memory?"

"Aistra. He saw everything I had observed about her. My turn now," Alia said. "What did you say to Zimpf to make him turn so red after you tackled him?"

Shao laughed. "I told him to stop being such a baby and join us at the table like a man. Then I told him that if he continued to act like a child, I would treat him like one. I threatened to get Mama's wooden spoon and give him the smack bottom of a lifetime in front of everyone."

Alia howled with laughter.

They went to bed shortly after that.

The next morning, they were awake early. They packed their clothes and replenished their food supply for the upcoming journey. Luckily, the trip to the elven kingdom was only expected to take about a week. Then they visited with Sh'ron and Chhdar, and the four of them went over the supply list and examined the horses. At lunch, they all met Amicu and Ciern for one final check of everything needed for their trip.

"Has anybody seen Zimpf?" Chhdar asked. "He was supposed to meet us here."

Ciern and Amicu looked at each other and laughed.

"We saw him," Ciern admitted.

"With Aistra," Amicu tattled.

"They looked pretty friendly," Ciern snitched.

"Well, what do you know?" Alia asked in feigned surprise.

"What did you do?" Sh'ron asked her twin curiously.

Alia winked at her.

"I need to report to Sifu," Shao told them with an excited grin. "It's almost time to spar with his students."

Alia stood up to accompany him. "Does anyone want to come with me to watch?" she invited.

Within the hour, they were all sitting in the arena, waiting for the competition to begin. Apparently, everyone in the temple had heard about the exhibition, because it was crowded with onlookers.

Ciern and Amicu agreed that the entire school had turned out, something that neither graduate had ever seen happen.

Sifu and Shao walked out to the middle of the arena to thunderous applause. They faced each other. Each of them held up their right fists, covering it with their left hands, and bowed respectfully to each other.

Then they began to run the forms that Alia had seen earlier. It was breathtaking to see them come together and break apart in the ancient ritualistic dance of their craft. Some of the forms made it seem almost as if they were battling, and others they performed simultaneously in a ballet of synchronous athleticism. When they finished, the arena erupted in an explosion of applause. The martial artists bowed to each other and then to the crowd.

Then the sparring began. There was a line of nervous students prepared to compete with Shao, but after seeing the forms, Alia thought most of them looked green with fear. After the first four students were defeated in rapid succession, Shao called a halt to the rout. He suggested that the students spar with him en masse.

Although Alia knew how good Shao was—she had seen him demonstrate it multiple times, and she had been told repeatedly that he had no equal—it still made her nervous to see him fight against almost a dozen people all at once.

She need not have worried. Just as with the attackers upon their arrival, Shao fought them individually and all at the same time. He employed every form he had demonstrated earlier. He stepped artfully toward and away from his various attackers with quick, explosive movements. He turned sideways avoiding punches while delivering blows so quickly they were almost invisible. He tripped, kicked, and flipped his attackers. He put up blocks and threw chain punches, and he jumped into the air to deliver high-flying roundhouse kicks.

When it was over, he was the only one standing inside the arena. There was a moment of absolute silence where Sifu bowed to his former student in reverence.

The crowd remained soundless as each person echoed Sifu. In a noiseless wave, they bowed one by one toward Shao, their left hands covering their right fists with profound respect. Then they quietly drifted away until only Alia and Shao were left staring at each other across an empty field.

Marek bowed artfully toward the first group of Vherals that approached them. Then he held his right hand up, palm facing the Vherals in a gesture of peace, as DaiSur had told him.

"Who are you?" the leader asked suspiciously. He was a tall, thick-muscled, powerful-looking man with shaggy black hair and a thick, unruly-looking beard and mustache.

"My name does not matter. What I have come to offer is what is important," the mage answered softly.

"People from the south are not welcome here," the Vheral man declared harshly.

Marek didn't answer; he simply stared calmly, penetratingly, imperiously.

"Did you not hear me? I told you to leave my territory," the man threatened as he fingered the arrow he had already nocked onto his bowstring.

"I heard you," the mage replied.

With an evil grin, the bowman smoothly drew back his bow and aimed directly at the intruder.

Kamet, Marek's servant, pulled his horse directly in front of his master in an effort to protect him.

"Move!" Marek hissed, suddenly spurring his horse forward just as the arrow was released.

Before it had traveled even half the distance to him, Marek held up both hands, palms facing outward with his thumbs touching. He whispered a single word in the spidery language of magic, and the arrow erupted into flame, burning so hot and fast that it fell to the ground in ashes.

"Mage!" the belligerent leader gasped in astonishment.

Chapter 12 – The Meeting

The next morning, they met at the arch, which served as a gate to the temple. Everyone was there early except for Zimpf and Aistra. They waited for several minutes, but neither of them ever showed.

Finally, Shao said, "I'd better go check on them."

"I'll go with you," Alia told him.

They were all thinking approximately the same thing: that Aistra had changed her mind again and that either Zimpf was staying as well or that he was too broken to meet them.

As soon as Alia and Shao walked into the temple, they heard a sharp whistle from behind.

"That's Sh'ron," Alia said. They turned around to see their friends all looking at the top of the arch.

Standing on either side at the top were Zimpf and Aistra.

"Where are you going?" Zimpf called in a bantering tone. "You said to meet at the arch."

Shao stooped, picked up a rock, and hurled it at Zimpf so

quickly that Alia wasn't even sure it happened. Then it connected with a solid-sounding thump.

"Ow!" Zimpf complained, rubbing his shoulder.

"Shao!" Alia said, surprised. "You could have knocked him off the top of that thing!"

Shao laughed. "If I wanted to knock him off of the top, he would already be on the ground."

Alia shook her head and giggled. "How did they get up there?"

"It's not nearly as impressive as it looks." Shao answered. "There is a ladder on the other side."

By the time Alia and Shao walked back to the arch, Aistra and Zimpf were both on the ground. Just then, Sifu joined them.

"Haven't I told you not to climb up on the arch?" he rebuked Zimpf.

"Yes, Sifu. I'm sorry," Zimpf said with feigned sincerity.

"Aaannd heee's baaack!" Amicu announced.

Everyone laughed. Even Sifu smiled tolerantly.

"I have come to bring you these," Sifu said to the group. Then he handed each of them a small silver coin. "You can present them to any inn in the Four Lands and the innkeeper will see that you receive whatever you need—a place to sleep, food, clothes, medical help, or anything else."

Then he bowed to each of them. When he got to Shao, he bowed the deepest while covering his right fist with his left palm. "Be safe, my son," he said respectfully.

Then he turned and walked purposefully to the temple.

Mounting their horses, the group silently left the Temple of Anaia.

It would be just under a week before they arrived at the elven city of Asath Tesai. The first two days of their trip were mountainous and rough. The terrain was steep, and they frequently had to climb off their horses and lead them along narrow trails, whose edges dropped off into nothing far below. At one point they were forced to backtrack for several hours to forge a turbulent mountain stream. They were exhausted at the end of each day from the demanding landscape, so there was no friendly banter around a warm campfire. They merely set up their tents, ate a cold meal, climbed into their blankets, and fell asleep.

Alia began to wonder if Ciern had gravely underestimated the length of the trip. Then, about midmorning on the third day, they descended into a wooded valley teeming with deer, who gazed at them with open-eyed wonder. A clear, blue stream meandered its way lazily through the center.

They set up camp an hour or so before sunset so they could rest from the grueling descent. The plan was to get up early the next morning and try to make it to the elven stables, which were run by their friend Meyta. After that it would be a two-day journey to the capital.

As always, Sh'ron and Chhdar took care of the horses, Ciern and Amicu started a fire and gathered firewood, and Zimpf and Aistra erected the tents. Alia and Shao went to forage for edibles to supplement their travel rations.

They had just finished gathering some root vegetables and were walking back when Shao stopped. "Why is Zimpf looking for us?" he wondered.

Alia could hear Zimpf calling for them in a whispered voice.

"It sounds like Zimpf, but it doesn't sound *like* Zimpf," Alia replied in confusion.

"Let's give him something to see," Shao said, grabbing Alia and pulling her to him.

Then he proceeded to kiss her seriously, very seriously. Just as her knees were starting to buckle, she felt his lips tighten in a soundless laugh.

"What do you want, Zimpf?" Shao demanded between kisses. "We're busy."

"Um," Zimpf began with a nervous cough. "We, um, didn't mean to interrupt."

Stunned by his politeness, Alia and Shao pulled apart, and quickly turned to see both Zimpf and Aistra standing there.

Zimpf was staring at them with a mischievous grin. Aistra was blushing a deep red while looking at the ground. Shao smirked at Zimpf impudently.

Alia could understand Aistra's embarrassment. She too was blushing a rosy red. Kissing in public was the worst sort of manners, both in Miast and in the tiny hamlet where she was raised.

"Why are you bothering us?" Shao demanded.

"We wanted to talk to you two alone," Zimpf said seriously.

Alia and Shao exchanged a quick glance.

Aistra finally looked up. "We wanted to thank you. Both of you," she said sincerely.

Zimpf took Aistra's hand and then looked up at Alia gratefully. "After our conversation where you let me *see* Aistra through your eyes, I went to visit her, and we had a long conversation."

Aistra nodded. "I hurt Zimpf terribly before," she admitted mournfully. "I...I just didn't realize," she choked. She opened her mouth as though she wanted to explain but then seemed unable to speak. Tears welled up in her eyes, and her breathing became shaky.

Finally, she took a deep breath to steady herself, blinked away the tears, and looked up at Zimpf, in admiration.

"Anyway," Zimpf continued, wrapping one arm around her comfortingly and pulling her close. "We are together again. We wanted you to be the first to know."

Even though Alia and Shao already knew, it was wonderful to hear Zimpf confirm it to them.

Shao leaned in and hugged Zimpf while Alia hugged Aistra.

"My heart soars for you, brother," Shao whispered.

Then the four them walked together back to the campground where Alia and Shao cooked dinner.

After they ate, Zimpf stood and pulled Aistra up with him.

"I know you all have been talking about us behind our backs," he said accusingly while he stared furiously at each person in turn.

Everyone except for Alia and Shao froze in shock at Zimpf's irate tirade.

"Well, we have something to say!" he growled as he leveled an angry finger at them.

The group had gone deathly silent.

"We are back together again!" he suddenly shouted exuberantly. Then he laughed uproariously at their stunned faces and began pointing at each of them in turn, chanting, "I got you, and you, and you, and you."

First one and then another and finally everyone began to laugh and then gather around the couple to congratulate them. Despite the plan to retire early, they stayed up late, talking over old times and laughing.

They got up early the next morning and rode hard for the entire day, stopping only long enough to eat a quick lunch and to allow the horses to rest briefly. Just as the sun was beginning to set, Ciern stood up in his saddle and pointed.

Riding toward them was an elf.

"Meyta!" Ciern and Zimpf roared as they, along with Amicu, raced their horses toward the elf, shouting and laughing. By the time the others had caught up, they had all dismounted and were hugging and pounding each other on the back excitedly.

"Meyta," Shao grinned at the elf.

"Shao!" Meyta said enthusiastically. "Get down here and greet me properly," he demanded. Then, grinning from ear to ear, he hugged Shao while lifting him off the ground and then dropping him.

"Hello Alia," he greeted her. Then he looked at her and Shao. "Congratulations on your wedding," he said formally.

Then Meyta turned to greet Chhdar and Sh'ron. "Welcome back," he said. "Congratulations on your wedding as well," he told them seriously.

Then he looked at Aistra curiously.

"Meyta," Zimpf said formally to the elf, while at the same time taking Aistra's hand. "I would like you to meet Aistra."

Meyta's eyes widened in surprise. He looked at the two of them, his eyes dropping quickly to their linked hands. Then Meyta glanced at Shao with one eyebrow raised questioningly.

Shao responded with a quick nod.

"Welcome to the elven stables, Aistra," the elf said in a friendly tone.

Turning to the group, he bowed politely. "Please consider being our guests for the evening," Meyta said formally. Then he led them into a concealed back door and down into a round pavilion, where he showed them to their rooms.

"You will sleep here tonight, then tomorrow you can begin the trek to the capital. You will only need to take enough supplies for a two-day journey. Your horses and other belongings will arrive within a few days."

"Thank you," Ciern told him. "Have you heard anything from the city? Have there been any problems or threats?"

"No," Meyta replied. "DaiSur arrived a few days ago. She told us to be on the lookout for you and to send you straight to the capital upon your arrival," he reported seriously. "Other than the difficult terrain, you should have no problems. Now, I have duties to attend to. Meanwhile, please feel free to explore." He stood to leave, and Ciern and Amicu left with him.

Alia and Shao retired to their room to refresh themselves. They still had a little while before dinner, so Shao asked if she wanted to explore the elven stables again. They stopped by Sh'ron and Chhdar's room to invite them along as well.

Shao showed them the door that hid the caves from outsiders and the mechanism that locked it from intruders. He took them to the open pavilion behind the caves, where there was a crystal-clear waterfall and gardens of flowers, vegetables, and herbs. He pointed out the hidden back door they would use to leave the next day. Alia had fun; it was nice just being able to hang out with her family.

They met everyone for a cheerful dinner that night. As soon as they had finished eating, they decided to retire early. The plan was to be up and ready to leave before sunrise. As they began to file out of the room, Meyta touched Shao's arm, indicating for him and Alia both to stay.

"What happened with them?" He nodded toward Zimpf and Aistra's retreating backs. "When you all were here after the breakup, he was absolutely grief-stricken. I have never seen a man so broken. If you remember, he was even beyond our healer's reach. I don't think he would have survived if it hadn't been for Sairima."

"DaiSur sent us to the temple to get Aistra," Shao told him.

"How did they get back together though?" Meyta asked, burning with curiosity.

"Alia talked to him," Shao told him proudly.

"Actually, all I really did was let him *see* what I saw," she said modestly.

Meyta turned to look at her, then he bowed with profound respect.

They met in the dining room before the sun was up the next morning. While they ate, Meyta continued to look at Aistra and Zimpf incredulously and at Alia respectfully.

Finally, he took them out the back door, and they were on their way.

Alia remembered clearly how treacherous the route was to the elven capital. First, they had to climb a ladder cut out of the side of a vertical cliff face to leave the cavern system. Then they spent several hours traversing a very narrow trail that took them around to the peak of the cliff, where there were sinkholes scattered at random on the summit. From there, they had to wend their way down into the valley.

Once they reached the valley floor, they were forced to walk several miles northeast, parallel to a raging river, to reach the bridge which allowed them to cross. The crossing was a single-path rope bridge that swung and swayed dangerously, threatening to spill each of them hundreds of feet into the seething water below. Only one person could cross at a time; thankfully, they all made it safely to the other side.

By then it was nearly dusk, and they stopped for the night.

The next day was easier than the previous one. They walked down a hill into another valley and then back up to a bridge that sat several hundred yards away, swaying dangerously over a dry gorge.

Alia clearly remembered the crossing last time. The bridge had broken, and Shao had nearly died saving her life. Luckily, Zimpf had been able to rescue Shao from toppling backward into the abyss.

Ciern led them across the bridge and into a valley, where they followed the basin floor as it curved from east to west toward the home of the elven people. Finally, the route ended in a box canyon. At the edge of the canyon, they stopped. Ciern placed both of his hands on a promontory and leaned in until his lips nearly touched the rock. He spoke a few musical words in a low whisper, which unlocked the door into the elven city.

They walked through a tunnel, which opened to reveal a stunning view of the Asath Tesai.

Alia and Shao, holding hands, stopped with the others to admire the beauty of the city below. There were golden bridges spanning a blue river, which wound its way across the valley floor. The homes, which were every color and hue imaginable, were dug into the sides of the valley, looking like a profusion of flowers. There were towering waterfalls streaming from the valley sides to feed the stream. At the far end, where the valley rose into a peak, was the castle.

They would have liked to stay longer, but one of the men standing guard at the door said something in a low voice to Ciern. He looked at the man in surprise.

Then Ciern turned to the others. "We must hurry," he announced. "The meeting is ready to start. They are only waiting for us to arrive."

The group rapidly descended the stairs and climbed into the waiting carriages, which quickly conveyed them to the castle proper. They were greeted by the same fussy, old elf as the last time. He hustled them through the castle, across the throne room, and finally into the meeting room itself. The others were already waiting.

They trooped into the meeting dirty and road-weary and carrying their saddlebags.

King Elator rose to meet them, welcoming Ciern first with a hug. "My son," he said proudly. "Welcome home."

Then he greeted the rest of them in turn. "It is wonderful to see you all again," he said in a friendly tone. "And it is my pleasure to meet you, my dear," he said to Aistra. "As always, it is my command that we will not stand on ceremony."

Then he instructed everyone to take seats while he began the introductions. King Ganayt of the Dwarven Kingdom and his son Skala were in attendance. DaiSur was also there with a middle-aged man Alia didn't know. King Elator introduced him as Guiden.

"Please excuse the lack of hospitality," King Elator began. "But DaiSur and Guiden must leave in the morning.

"Let us begin," DaiSur ordered. "We will start with Alia and the Orb of Ahi."

Everyone turned to look at Alia. She told the story of finding the dying mage who gave her the Orb and Marek's offer of help to consult the elves. She described their meeting of Shao and Zimpf and their journey to Asath Tesai. Then Shao took over and told of Marek's kidnapping of Airafae and of her rescue. He told of their attempt to regain the Orb and of the abduction of Marek, Alia, and Airafae. Then Alia explained the orcs' plan to dominate the world.

Finally, she and Shao both told of the destruction of the orb, the demolition of the orcs' tunnels, and what they believed to be the demise of Marek.

Shao continued the story by telling of Medjii's visit, the strange explosive device, her death, and the note left for Alia. They finished by describing the attempted destruction of the Order of the Mages.

The room was silent when they finished with the story.

"It seems to me that this note may provide us with knowledge of the rogue mage's intentions," said Guiden. "Have you read it?"

"No," Zimpf told him. "There is something evil that lurks within those pages. Each time I come near to touching it, I have visions of horror and destruction."

"And you," DaiSur demanded of Aistra. "What do you sense?"

"The same, DaiSur," Aistra answered respectfully.

"Maybe we shouldn't open it then," King Elator suggested. "It sounds like it could be a trap of some kind. Either another explosive or maybe something to ensnare the mind."

DaiSur was quiet for a moment, thinking. Then she looked at the others in the room. "We do not have to decide immediately. I would counsel caution. Let us examine the exterior of the note first."

With that, Zimpf opened his saddlebag and retrieved the note, still in the protective covering DaiSur had provided. He laid it gently on the table and backed away as far as he could get.

DaiSur removed the wrapping, and both she and Guiden leaned in and studied the envelope. It seemed harmless, just an ordinary note with the name "Alia" scrawled across the front of it in Marek's spidery handwriting.

Being careful not to touch it, Guiden ran his hand over the top of the note. Immediately it began to glow with an unhealthy green radiance. He gasped softly and immediately drew away from the table, his eyes wide with fright.

"It's a good thing the diviner was with you," he announced. "This note is imbued with an ikibi spell. A rather nasty one from what I can tell."

"What's that?" Chhdar said, asking what everyone else was thinking.

"An ikibi spell is used to change someone utterly. If a person is kind and thoughtful, they will suddenly become mean and conceited," Guiden explained.

"Why would anyone create such a spell?" Amicu demanded. He sounded horrified.

"When the spell was developed, it was thought it could be used to rid the world of evil by changing the wicked. The problem was that the spell often killed those under its influence. I understand their deaths were particularly gruesome," Guiden told them.

"But that's not what I *saw* at all," Zimpf protested.

"No," Guiden agreed. "What you *saw* were parts of Marek's spirit. In order to cast an ikibi spell, the mage must imbue it with his own lifeblood."

"Is there any way to reverse the spell?" King Ganayt rumbled in his deep voice.

"Yes," the mage answered. "Someone must fight their way through the essence that Marek consigned within the spell."

"We will try to break the spell and open the note," DaiSur decided. "It will give us insight into the mage's mind."

The room went instantly quiet as everyone looked at each other.

The dwarven prince, Skala, cleared his throat and everyone turned to look at the reticent prince. "Obviously you expect Zimpf to complete this task; but what danger does he face?"

"We need the information," DaiSur insisted.

"At what cost?" Skala challenged.

"Zimpf?" DaiSur said. It was more of a challenge than a question

Zimpf cursed. "Somebody go get me that comfortable chaise lounge Alia used last time for her visioning."

"No, Zimpf! No!" Aistra objected.

But the king had already stepped outside to send a guard after the lounge chair.

"Aistra, it will be okay," Zimpf tried to soothe her.

"No." She looked at the people in the room. "When it happened at Temple, I almost couldn't get him back," she confessed, near hysterics.

"Aistra." Zimpf leaned toward her, placing his hands on the sides of her temples and whispering in a voice so low that no one could hear what he was saying.

Aistra froze, her eyes lost in Zimpf's face.

When he finally lowered his hands, she nodded. But her face bore the expression of an indomitable will.

Zimpf climbed ruefully onto the chaise lounge that had been carried into the room by two guards. Aistra sat on one side of the diviner, and Alia insisted on occupying the other side. Shao sat with her.

Guiden brought the tainted letter in its wrapping to Zimpf. "Once it is unwrapped, all you have to do is run your hand over the top. But do not touch the envelope," he warned.

Zimpf nodded then nervously ran his hand carefully above the unwrapped letter.

Marek spent the next few weeks ingratiating himself into Vheral society. Clearly the family group the belligerent man saw fit to take him to had never met a mage; they were awed by what he could do. The fact that Marek could not create but only destroy didn't seem to register with them. The mage also had another valuable ability that helped to cement his place in society. His old master had insisted that he study and understand the various properties and uses of a variety of plants. So, Marek suddenly found himself acting as the de facto healer for the family, a position that Marek initially found absurd but which he later discovered to be a useful way to dispose of anyone who opposed him.

His talents, combined with his ability to charm, soon had the group wholly under his command.

And as the family traveled to various locations in search of food, they inevitably met with and absorbed other groups into their own. And everyone was skillfully manipulated into accepting Marek's command.

Chapter 13–Information

Instantly Zimpf was unconscious. Although his eyes were closed, Alia could see the movement behind the lids. They dashed and darted right and left furiously. Zimpf began to shake his head from side to side. "No!" he screamed in horror. He threw his hands up in front of his face to ward off whatever terrors he was seeing.

Aistra immediately reached to help him, but DaiSur was there. She grabbed Aistra's wrist in an iron grip and refused to release the young woman despite her struggles. "Leave him!" she commanded in a towering voice.

But Aistra continued to struggle.

Zimpf screeched. It was a primal roar of unimaginable loss and anger. "No!" Then he began to claw ineffectively at the empty air, fighting, tearing, scratching.

Aistra fought DaiSur harder. But the older woman refused to relent.

Zimpf writhed as though enduring agonizing pain. His breathing became labored, and his chest heaved with effort. He began to pant and finally to cried out in great, braying sobs.

Alia reached up to wipe his face and found her wrists gripped tightly by Guiden. "No," he stopped her. "You cannot touch him lest you be pulled into the spell."

So she was forced to watch the struggling man vacillate between abject horror and unbearable pain.

It seemed to take forever, but Zimpf finally broke through the nightmare that was Marek.

Very slowly, he ceased struggling, his tears dried on his face, and his eyes fluttered, opened, then closed, again and again.

DaiSur released Aistra.

The young woman climbed completely on top of the diviner, straddled him, and laid her hands on the sides of his face. She leaned in until her forehead was touching his and began whispering inaudibly.

Although she could barely hear the whispers, Alia thought Aistra was saying Zimpf's name, talking to him, calling him back. Her face grew pale with the effort.

Zimpf blinked his eyes again and finally opened them, but his gaze was glassy and far away. Aistra pulled her forehead back, frowning at him. Then she placed her hands on his temples and closed her eyes, her face filled with an inhuman concentration. She squinched her eyes shut and began to sweat; her face slowly drained of all color.

Suddenly there was an audible pop, and Zimpf opened his eyes. He looked at Aistra, smiled weakly, and immediately lost consciousness. Aistra's head drooped as she toppled to the floor. She would have hit the ground had Shao not been sitting there to catch her.

The martial artist lifted the unconscious young woman in his arms and turned to face King Elator, looking at him questioningly.

"This meeting is adjourned for now," the king announced in a shaking voice as he gazed back and forth between Zimpf and Aistra.

"No," DaiSur disagreed. "You all heard the pop of the spell as it broke. We must continue," she ordered. Then she looked at Shao. "Just put her beside the diviner."

King Elator glared angrily at DaiSur with all the authority of his station. "I said, this meeting is at an end for now. My order stands."

"Haven't you done enough damage?" Skala growled at the special envoy.

King Ganayt spoke scathingly to DaiSur at almost the same time, "you will respect the elven king's order."

DaiSur didn't reply, but she glared the dwarves as though her face was carved in stone.

King Elator turned to Ciern. "Show them to their rooms in the west wing." Then he looked at Alia. "Do you need me to send a healer?"

"No, Your Majesty," Alia replied gratefully. Then she looked around the room.

"Chhdar, will you please carry Zimpf? And Sh'ron, will you bring my medical bag? I will need your help."

As they all filed out past the fuming DaiSur, Alia heard Amicu.

"Well, I'm not staying in here alone with them," he muttered, and without another word, he picked up the letter, still in its protective wrapping, and followed them from the room.

As soon as they left the meeting chamber, Ciern stopped to say something to one of the guards, who then sprinted away. By the time they reached the west wing, the same fussy, old elf was waiting for them. He escorted them up the stairs and down the hallway, stopping to open the door to a well-appointed room. Chhdar carried Zimpf through a sitting room and into a bedroom, where he gently laid the diviner on the bed.

"Sh'ron? Chhdar? Will you accompany Shao and stay with him and Aistra until I finish here?" Alia asked. "Ciern, you and Amicu stay with me," she told them.

As soon as the others left, Alia began her examination of Zimpf. Aside from being completely exhausted, he seemed to be okay. At least Alia could find nothing physically wrong with him. She motioned Ciern and Amicu to follow her into the sitting room, where she reported her findings. Then she went through her medical bag and made two cups of calming tea.

"I am going to check on Aistra," she said then. "When Zimpf wakes up, come get me."

She left one cup for Zimpf and carried the second cup across the hall to Aistra's room to examine her. As soon as she stepped into the young woman's bedroom to begin her examination, Aistra opened her eyes.

"Zimpf?" she asked anxiously, trying to get out of bed.

Alia pushed her back down with one hand. "He's asleep," she reported. "You can check on him as soon as I have given you a physical." Then she proceeded to examine Aistra.

"That was very brave," she told the young woman once she had finished.

"Thank you," Aistra answered. "I was so worried."

"Did you *see* what he *saw*?" Alia asked curiously.

"Not really," Aistra told her. "What I did was *sense* his feelings." Then she looked up at Alia, her eyes wide. "I could *feel* his terror, his pain." She blinked tears from her eyes. "It was both horrifying and excruciating."

Alia handed the young woman the cup of calming tea she had carried into the room.

"How does *sensing* him help?" Alia asked curiously.

Aistra was quiet for a moment, thinking of how to explain it. Finally, she answered slowly, "By *sensing* his emotions, I ease the pain associated with them." She looked up at Alia. "I literally pull his pain into me."

"Is it the mental or the physical pain you're talking about?" Alia asked.

"Both, but Zimpf doesn't know that I feel the pain too. I convinced him that it was just my being there that relieved his suffering. Otherwise, he would never allow me to help." Then she looked up, alarmed at what she had confessed to the healer. "Please don't tell Zimpf what I just said," she begged.

"I cannot tell him," Alia explained gently. "Information between a healer and her patient is confidential."

"Zimpf's training in the temple was particularly demanding," Aistra confessed, "Shao's education was primarily physical, but Zimpf's training was mental. Sometimes, after a very difficult session, he would come to me almost broken. Our instructor, Gatara, was especially hard on Zimpf."

"Why?"

"I think she pushed him to excel because of his talent. But you know Zimpf." Aistra looked up. "He wasn't the most tractable of students."

Alia grinned then grew serious.

"It must have been very hard for you to talk to him that night I sent him to your quarters at Temple," Alia said shrewdly. She was thinking about how broken Zimpf had been after the young woman's rejection of him.

Aistra nodded, but she didn't answer. She sat quietly, sipping her tea. After a few moments, she looked at Alia. "I can *feel* the connection between you and Shao," she said simply. "It's very strong."

Alia smiled.

"Can I go see Zimpf now?" Aistra asked.

"Yes," Alia answered. "I want to check on him again anyway."

Chhdar, Sh'ron, and Shao were surprised to see Aistra up. They all walked with her across the hall to Zimpf's room. He was still asleep. They left Aistra to watch him.

The rest of the group followed Alia and Shao to their sitting room, where Amicu deposited the note from Marek onto the table. Then he looked up at them questioningly. "Should we open it?" he asked.

After much discussion, they decided that it would be unfair of them to open it without Zimpf and Aistra.

"Besides," Ciern pointed out, "my father would be so disappointed."

"How long do you think Zimpf will be asleep?" Sh'ron asked.

"It's hard to tell," Alia answered. "I would guess at least until early evening."

"Let's take the afternoon to refresh ourselves, and we can continue the meeting tonight," Ciern decided. "I'll make arrangements for dinner to be served in the meeting room just before sunset."

"Can you also make arrangements for some lunch to be provided, now?" Chhdar asked plaintively.

Everyone laughed.

"I'll have lunch delivered to your rooms." Ciern smiled.

Once everyone had left, Alia leaned wearily against Shao. Smiling, he wrapped one arm around her shoulders. "Are you tired?"

"What I really need is a nice, long bath." She said ruefully as she shook dust from her hair.

"I will arrange for a bath to be drawn for you." He told her, and then, for no particular reason, he tilted her head toward him with his index finger and kissed her seriously.

After they both had bathed, changed clothes, and eaten lunch, they decided to check on Zimpf. Shao quietly opened the door to the diviner's room and they tiptoed through the sitting room. Soundlessly, Shao cracked the door open to peer in on the diviner. Then, smiling, he beckoned to Alia. She peeked inside to see that Aistra had laid down beside Zimpf; they were both sleeping soundly with her head nestled against his chest.

They slipped out of the room and spent the rest of the afternoon in their own room, sitting on the sofa, holding hands, talking, and occasionally kissing. It was the first time they had been alone for quite some time.

It was getting close to the time for the meeting when Shao suddenly held up his hand in a gesture to indicate silence. Listening intensely, Alia could also hear angry whispers coming from Zimpf's room next door. Thinking something was terribly wrong, she and Shao rushed toward the diviner's room. Before they opened the door, however, DaiSur's voice broke through the whispers.

"You will follow my orders!" she demanded harshly.

"No!" Aistra's voice was unyielding. "I will not."

"You will obey me!"

"I was forced into compliance the last time you demanded something of me," Aistra asserted hotly. "I was shattered! Sending Zimpf away nearly killed both of us!"

"But it made you stronger, just like I said," DaiSur insisted proudly.

"Yes, I did grow stronger," Aistra whispered fiercely. "That is why I will no longer heed your orders."

"You will do as I say," DaiSur ordered the young woman in a threatening tone. "You know you must obey my command."

Alia and Shao looked at each other in surprise. DaiSur had been behind Aistra's refusal to leave with Zimpf.

Shao slowly pushed the door open and stepped inside, with Alia alongside him.

"Is there a problem here?" he asked DaiSur in a dreadfully quiet voice.

"No," she answered shortly and then swept from the room.

"Are you okay?" Alia asked the young woman.

Aistra nodded.

"Does Zimpf know that DaiSur forced you to stay behind at Temple?" Shao questioned her intensely.

"I do now," Zimpf answered from the door of his room.

They all turned to look at him as he strode across the room to stand before Aistra.

"Why didn't you tell me what happened?" he asked softly.

"I…I…couldn't," Aistra whispered.

"Couldn't or wouldn't?" Zimpf wanted to know.

She opened her mouth to answer but instead grew silent.

"Aistra?" Alia said, moving to stand beside the young woman. "Did DaiSur *compel* you to obey her command to remain at the temple?"

Slowly, as though she were fighting an unseen force, she nodded her head once, then again.

"Can you fix this—" Shao started to ask, but Zimpf had already placed his hands on Aistra's temples. They stood together silently for a moment, Zimpf with his eyes closed in concentration and Aistra with her eyes wide and unseeing. When he released her, Aistra fell forward into Zimpf, who caught her and held her steady.

"Have her sit here," Alia indicated the sofa.

Zimpf helped Aistra sit down between Alia and Shao, and then he sat across from her.

"Well?" Shao asked.

"She was mesmerized, much the same way Marek mesmerized Alia and then Airafae," Zimpf confirmed angrily. "It was very subtle and well-hidden, or I would have found it earlier."

"Did you take care of it?" Shao asked.

Zimpf gave him a steady look.

"I mean, did you also put up a block so she can't do it again?"

"Oh please," Zimpf said sarcastically.

Aistra opened her eyes.

"Why did DaiSur want you to stay at Temple?" Zimpf asked her.

"She said I had to finish my training," Aistra said. "She brought someone who…" She hesitated as though she was trying to remember. "…someone to talk to me," she finally said. "I…I can't really remember everything. But I was ordered to remain at Temple, because DaiSur needed me to do something for her."

"Do you know what this something was?" Shao asked intently.

Aistra shook her head, then stared at the floor.

"Zimpf," she finally said when she looked up again. "I don't want to go with her; I want to stay with you."

"What you need," Shao suggested, "is a more permanent way to stay together. Something public that others can be witnesses to."

They were quiet then, thinking.

Alia noticed then that Shao began acting strangely. He kept raking his hair with his left hand. Shao was one of those rare people who could use either hand with equal facility. But she knew he preferred one hand over another for certain things. For example, he wrote with his left hand and threw things with his right hand. He always used his right hand to rake his hair back.

Zimpf knew Shao was trying to tell him something. But he was baffled.

Shao leaned back, crossed his left arm over his right and tapped the third finger of his left hand.

Zimpf frowned and shook his head ever so slightly.

Shao blew his breath on the plain gold ring Alia had given him at their wedding ceremony and buffed it dramatically on the front of his shirt.

Alia tried not to laugh.

Zimpf cocked his head to one side in bewilderment.

Shao leaned back and pretended to stretch while he held up his left hand, pointed to his ring, and then pointed at Alia.

Zimpf squinted, perplexed. His eyebrows drew down into a V. He knew Alia and Shao were married.

Alia had to bite her lips in suppressed mirth.

Shao finally leaned forward casually and, so fast that Alia was sure Aistra hadn't even seen it, popped Zimpf on the side of his head. Then, behind Aistra's back, Shao recreated the pantomime again, only this time, he pointed at Zimpf and Aistra.

Zimpf's eyes grew wide in sudden understanding. Without saying a word, he abruptly jumped from his chair and bolted to the bedroom.

Confused, Aistra stood to follow him. She had barely taken a step when he ran back into the room and skidded to an abrupt stop in front of her.

"Aistra?" he said in a squeaky voice that reached the highest registers of his range. He coughed and tried again. "Aistra," he said then in a comically lowered tone.

She looked at him, confused.

"Did you mean it when you said that you want to stay with me? And did you mean like…forever?"

"Of course," she said, her eyes wide and vulnerable.

"May I please have your hand in marriage?" he asked. Then, almost as an afterthought, he sank to one knee and presented her with a ring.

Aistra smiled with pure joy. "Yes," she whispered nervously. Her hands had begun to shake.

Zimpf stood, placed the ring on her finger, and then leaned in to cup her face with his hands. She returned the gesture. They stood quietly in a moment that was beautiful to see and was at the same time intensely private. Finally, Zimpf kissed her chastely.

"Oh Zimpf," Shao scoffed in disappointment. "That can't be the best you can do."

Marek's family group had grown considerably in the few weeks since he had made it to the wilds. It now boasted between two and three hundred people, a number that was almost unheard of in Vheral society.

By unanimous decision, the mage had been elevated to the position of eldre, which translated to holy man; they addressed him as "master." As such, he was given the largest tent, which was always located in the center of the camp. The idea was that Marek would be meeting with the leaders of the new family groups who joined them, with any ill family member, and with any other man of honor.

The first such dignitary was an old, blind man who entered Marek's tent without knocking, walked confidently to a chair, and sat down without error. It seemed almost as though the man wasn't blind at all.

"Who let you in?" the mage asked brusquely.

"I let myself in," the old man shot back sharply.

Marek stared at the man; his eyes narrowed thoughtfully. Everyone else treated him as they should—reverently, deferentially, obsequiously. Clearly this visitor was someone of importance, otherwise the men who stood guard at his door would not have allowed him to enter.

"Who are you?" Marek asked, trying a different approach.

"My name is not important; what is important is what I have come to tell you."

"Proceed," the mage invited as he sat down opposite of his visitor.

"I know who you are and what you carry."

Marek didn't answer; he merely stared quietly. There was no way this blind, old Vheral man could possibly know about the Aghara. No one in the south had ever heard of it, and only a small handful of mages knew of its existence.

"You think I'm lying; I can sense *it*," the blind man continued.

"You can sense *it* or see *it*?" the mage questioned intensely.

"Does it matter?" the man bandied back.

Marek leaned back and smiled slowly. This was the first time in a very long time that he had met someone worthy of his intellect. "Tell me your story," he invited.

The old man smiled slyly in return.

"I was born in the south, just beyond the Skarsgaard Mountains in a little town called Kuthra."

Marek nodded, then realized that his visitor couldn't see the action.

It didn't seem to matter, because the man continued with his story.

"By the time I was eight, my parents abandoned me, and I was forced to beg in the streets. Before long, people began to avoid me, because I just knew things." The old man paused and seemed to look straight at Marek.

"You're a diviner," the mage said softly.

"If that's what you want to call it," he acknowledged. "But the citizens of Kuthra didn't understand my talent. I frightened them just as I had frightened my parents. Early one morning, I was kidnapped, taken far up into the mountains, and deserted. I would have died except for a small family of Vherals. They found me and took me in as one of their own." The blind man grew quiet.

"You said you came to tell me something," Marek urged.

"Your plan to use the Vherals to attack the south has the potential to succeed," he answered candidly.

"I'm not—" the mage started to lie.

The old man held up his hand for silence, and Marek immediately complied.

"I came to tell you that you are using the Aghara incorrectly. If you wish to utilize its full power, if you really want to succeed, you must involve another. You see, all things in the universe work in pairs—day and night, good and evil, women and men."

"What do you *see* with those blind eyes?" Marek asked, studying the old man intently.

"I see a woman who must agree to help you, willingly and without reservation. She is young and has a tannish complexion, waist-length, dark-brown hair, and big, brown eyes. She smiles when she looks at you, but her heart belongs to another."

Marek caught his breath sharply.

Alia.

Chapter 14 – The Note

Alia and Shao walked down to the meeting room, leaving the newly engaged couple to make their appearance later. The two couples had made a plan to surprise the others, and at the same time, stop DaiSur from ever being able to separate Aistra and Zimpf again.

As expected, everyone was in the conference room when they arrived. The others had just started to fill their plates with a variety of mouthwatering elven food. Alia and Shao joined the queue, made their selections, and then sat on the side of the table nearest King Elator.

"How are Aistra and Zimpf?" he inquired worriedly.

"They are doing much better," Alia replied.

"Will they be joining us?" King Elator wanted to know.

"They should be down in a little while," Shao answered. "They wanted to eat a quiet meal alone first."

Just as everyone had finished dinner and the plates had been removed, the door was flung open, and Zimpf and Aistra entered the room grandly, with their elbows linked together.

"I have returned," Zimpf announced in a lordly manner.

Everyone applauded spontaneously. Zimpf bowed grandly, and as the applause died down, he turned, bowed to Aistra, then turned to the room and announced, "I would like to present my beautiful fiancée!"

"Fiancée?" the king asked in surprise and pleasure. Immediately, the couple was surrounded; everyone wanted to congratulate them, shake their hands, and hug the bride-to-be. Everyone, that was, except for DaiSur. She remained seated with a cold, cunning look on her face.

When things finally settled down and everyone was seated, she offered her congratulations rather stiffly. "I would imagine that it will be some time before the wedding," she said in what Alia thought was a rather calculating tone.

"Actually," Zimpf said to King Elator. "We were hoping that you would perform the marriage ceremony."

"Me? Really?"

"Yes. Will you?" Zimpf asked solemnly.

"I would be honored," the king said, pleased. "When would you like to have the nuptials?"

"Right now," Zimpf stated, looking at Elator sincerely.

"Are…are you serious? Both of you want this now? Right now?" he asked incredulously.

"Yes," Aistra told him. "We are already bonded by our shared past."

"And we have been separated for far too long already," Zimpf chimed in.

Then, as planned, Shao started chanting, "Marry them! Marry

them! Marry them!"

He winked at Ciern and Amicu, and although they didn't know what was going on, they joined in because of the old signal from their school days. "Marry them! Marry them! Marry them!" they chanted in unison.

Alia nodded at Sh'ron and Chhdar, and then the three of also began chanting. "Marry them! Marry them! Marry them!"

Then, both Skala and King Ganayt added their baritone voices to the mantra. "Marry them! Marry them! Marry them!"

Finally, King Elator, laughing in delight, assented. "Let's go out into the throne room and make this official."

As everyone began to file out, DaiSur voiced her objection. "I do not have time for this nonsense," she suddenly announced. "I must be on the road tomorrow, and we have postponed this meeting long enough. I demand, with all of the power at my authority, that this ridiculous ceremony be stopped!"

Alia happened to be looking at King Elator as DaiSur spoke. At first, she thought that the king was going to stop, to call them back into the meeting, to refuse to marry Aistra and Zimpf.

But when DaiSur made her demand, the king's face clouded in anger.

King Elator turned to look at her with eyes as hard as agates. He answered in an indomitable tone. "You presume to command me in my own kingdom?" he asked in a low, threatening voice.

DaiSur didn't answer, but her face looked like it had been chiseled out of stone.

As the king, Zimpf, and Aistra walked toward the front of the throne room, DaiSur strode to intercept them. But Shao stepped directly in front of her, impeding her advancement.

She glowered at him challengingly.

Shao looked directly back at her. His expression was emotionless, bland even. But his body language was that of a tiger—threatening, menacing, intimidating. He exuded stealth and power, which displayed an iron will ready to annihilate her challenge.

DaiSur stepped back in defeat then turned away.

Alia looked at her husband with pride. It was incredibly difficult for her to reconcile this dangerous martial artist with the kind, gentle man who owned her heart.

After the simple wedding ceremony had been performed, King Elator offered a toast, wishing them a long and happy life. Then King Ganayt followed, offering them the dwarven hope for a life filled with health, contentment, and love.

The newlyweds thanked everyone for their support and announced that at some point in the future, they would have a formal ceremony, to which everyone would be invited.

Then, uncharacteristically, Zimpf suggested they continue the meeting.

"After all," he said, "my spellbreaking and Aistra's support is what led to the engagement and wedding. Besides," he said facetiously, "I can't think of a better way to spend my honeymoon than in a long, tedious meeting."

Everyone laughed.

"I can," Amicu muttered.

"I believe Zimpf," Shao teased. "You should have seen the polite peck he bestowed upon Aistra after she accepted his proposal."

They all laughed as they made their way back into the meeting room.

Once everyone was settled, Amicu handed the letter that he had taken earlier to King Elator.

"Are you sure the spell is broken?" he asked Guiden.

The mage removed the protective wrapping and then carefully ran his hand over the top of the letter without touching anything. Nothing happened.

"Zimpf, do you sense anything?" the king asked.

Zimpf leaned forward and ran his hand over the envelope without touching it as well. "No," he answered, "there is nothing." And then he calmly picked up the letter and handed it to the king.

"Here we go then." King Elator broke the wax seal on the outside of the envelope. Carefully, he opened the letter and slid out the note. There was only one page, which was folded neatly in half. Elator unfolded it and began reading:

Alia,

If you are reading this, it means that you and your friends have somehow circumvented my little surprise.

What a pity.

It also means that Medjii failed in her mission. Are you feeling sorry for her? Don't. She received that reward for her attempt to murder me on the slope of the Skarsgaard Mountains. You didn't know that, did you? She sent me back to set the Orb, when, in fact, she had already set it to explode.

I have the Aghara.

Medjii retrieved it for me after she visited me upon her discovery of my survival. She agreed to steal it after we had a nice, long chat over a cup of...let's just call it a well-seasoned tea.

So, what now?

Are you wondering what I plan to do with one of the most powerful magical objects of all time?

Think, Alia. You know me. At least, you think you do.

Do you need a hint?

Ask DaiSur.

Your old friend,
Marek

The room went instantly silent, and every eye turned to DaiSur. Her face had drained of all color.

"DaiSur?" King Elator asked.

"I…I don't know what he's talking about," she asserted forcefully. But then, she looked down. Hesitated. Licked her lips. "I don't know," she said again.

Alia instantly knew she was lying. Before she could say anything, Aistra spoke.

"She's lying," the young woman accused confidently. "I can *sense* it emanating off her in waves."

Zimpf nodded in agreement.

DaiSur stood, her face a mask of indignation and pride. "I will not sit here and be maligned by a child bride," she declared scathingly as she marched to the door.

King Elator of the Elven Kingdom, and King Ganayt of the Dwarven Realm looked at each other, disturbed by the letter. Clearly something was very, very wrong. Something that involved the actions of DaiSur.

"DaiSur," the elven king said, with a hint of steel in his voice. "You do not have our permission to withdraw," he said formally.

"Try to stop me," she challenged him scornfully. "I have ambassadorial status. I politely acceded to your commands earlier, but you do not have the right to hold me here." Then, she angrily flung open the door.

Alia saw King Elator make a motion with his hand. Instantly, the guards at the door drew themselves up while unsheathing their swords. One of them grabbed DaiSur politely but firmly by her arm and promptly escorted her back into the room.

"You have your position because we allow it," King Ganayt told her in a low, threatening tone. "You will answer our questions or you will be charged with treason against all the peoples of the Four Lands."

"And you will answer truthfully," King Elator added. "If not, I will have Zimpf pull the information from your mind. Forcefully if necessary."

DaiSur looked from one angry king to the other, then she glanced at Zimpf, who smiled at her bleakly.

She surrendered. Lowering her head, she stared at the floor, her lips trembled and her eyes filled with unshed tears. Finally, she collected herself and looked at them.

"Talk to us, DaiSur," King Elator said in a low voice. "Your father was one of my best friends, and I do not wish to see you imprisoned or worse."

"My father was a great man," DaiSur began sadly. She looked at the people whom she worked with as an ambassador: King Elator, Ciern, King Ganayt, and Skala. Then she looked at the others in the room: Shao, Alia, Sh'ron, Chhdar, Zimpf, Aistra, Amicu, and Guiden.

"I have tried to live up to Father's towering reputation, but it has all been a deception. He was in the process of finding his replacement when he passed away. He knew I was unfit for this position. But when he died, everyone expected me to take over."

"Up until today you have done a fine job," King Ganayt admitted.

King Elator nodded in agreement. "You received the finest education available; you majored in everything in the Temple of Anaia."

"And you studied with us at the Order of the Mages," Guiden recalled.

"No," DaiSur disagreed. "I failed at all the schools I attended. When I went to Temple, they agreed to test me only because of my father's reputation. The results were clear: 'No discernible talent.'"

Shao, Zimpf, Ciern, and Amicu all gasped in shock.

"How were you even permitted to stay?" Shao asked.

"As a favor to my father," she admitted. "The teachers allowed me to take a few classes to gauge any hidden potential. I failed them all." She looked around the room, addressing each of them in turn. "I cannot fight," she said to Shao. "I cannot divine or sense," she said to Zimpf and Aistra. "I cannot strategize," she said to Ciern. "And I cannot understand tactics," she said to Amicu. "They let me try every course available. I failed every single one. Finally, I was expelled.

"When my father came to escort me home, I was so ashamed that I could barely look at him," DaiSur admitted. "He told me then that he had arranged for the mages to test me. But the results were the same: 'No discernible talent.'"

"But you studied with us," Guiden said.

"No," she shook her head in shame. "I lived at the order for some time only because Father got called away and I had to wait for him. While I was at the Order, one of the mages did spend extra time with me. He believed that anyone with the desire could learn magic but that only people born with talent could be powerful. I had the desire, but not the talent. The most I was able to learn was sleight-of-hand trickery."

"How is any of this tied to Marek?" Ciern wanted to know.

"A few years after I left, just after I accepted this job, the idea came to me that if I couldn't do the things my father excelled at, things this position demands, then maybe I could hire retainers who could. I made an official visit to the Order of the Mages. But mostly, I wanted to speak to my old professor. He agreed to search for a young mage to train for me."

"Marek," Alia whispered.

DaiSur nodded.

"Then, a year or two later, I made another ceremonial visit to the Temple. It was there I first saw Aistra; she was so young. I inquired about her and was told that she was a polyimpano. I decided then that, like it or not, she would become my retainer."

"Wait," Zimpf interrupted. "You mesmerized Aistra to keep her from leaving with me. I know you did because I found it hidden in her mind this afternoon."

The others in the room looked at DaiSur with a mixture of revulsion and loathing.

"How were you able to achieve that?" Zimpf pressed, frowning at her. "You said you had no talent for divination or magic."

"I used Marek," she admitted. "I snuck us in using a secret key to a hidden door, then he mesmerized Aistra to believe that she could not leave the temple until her training was complete."

"So that's why you told us to come get her," Shao said shrewdly. "Because you need her now."

"Yes," she admitted. "I told you to pick up Sorgin first as a ruse."

"Sorgin!" Guiden exclaimed. "He was dying even before the attack."

DaiSur nodded in agreement.

"So how does your story connect to Marek, Medjii, and the Aghara? Do you know what he's planning?" Ciern asked.

"Did you know about the Orb of Ahi?" Amicu asked.

DaiSur looked at the two men. "The answers are connected," she told them. "I knew about the Orb, but it was after the fact. I had been up north trying to broker peace among the Vherals. When I returned, I received an urgent message from Medjii. She is the one who told me about the Orb, Marek's theft, the orcs' plans, and your involvement. I also learned of the death of both Marek and my former teacher." DaiSur hesitated and then plunged ahead with her story.

"Early one morning while I was still at the Order, Medjii came to my room. She said she received a message from Marek asking for help. I was shocked, of course. Medjii said he had died on the slopes of the Skarsgaard Mountains. I immediately sent a healer to his aid. Medjii and I went to his house together. He was recovering. But he had changed. He was…different, quiet, pensive, penitent." She paused for a few minutes to collect her thoughts, then continued.

"Marek apologized to Medjii for the things he had done. He was sincere and remorseful. When he was strong enough to travel, the two of them were supposed to go to the compound of the mages. Medjii promised she would message me upon their arrival."

DaiSur looked up, her face etched with sorrow. "The message never came. When I went to investigate, I discovered the village empty and Marek gone. A few days later, I received intelligence that Medjii had died."

"Aistra?" King Elator interrupted DaiSur. "Is she being honest?"

"She's telling the truth, at least as she knows it."

"Zimpf. Check her story," the king ordered.

"Why?" DaiSur demanded. "Aistra told you that I'm telling the truth."

"The truth as you know it," Zimpf answered as he walked toward her. "Marek could have altered your memories." Then, without waiting for an answer, he placed his hands on either side of her head.

She jerked back in shock and then sat still, her face frozen, her eyes wide and glassy-looking.

After a few moments, Zimpf released her.

"She's telling the truth," he announced. "her memories are unaltered."

"Guiden," Amicu started, "do you know anything about how the Aghara works?"

"The first thing I want to know is, what can be done with the Aghara?" Ciern asked at almost the same time.

"If the rogue mage has unlocked its power, he can unleash the greed, hate, and evil contained within," Guiden answered. "I'm sure of that."

"Once released, can the evil be returned to the Aghara?" Amicu questioned intently.

"I don't know," Guiden responded. "I suppose it's possible if one knows how."

Ciern and Amicu exchanged a long look, indicating that they were considering the same idea—an idea beyond the imagination of the others.

"What would the mage gain by opening the Aghara?" King Ganayt asked.

Chhdar, who was normally quiet during meetings, answered, "He wants to start a war."

"But to what end? Why?" the dwarven king questioned.

"Power," Alia said simply. "He craves power."

"DaiSur?" Amicu asked. "Does Marek know about the discordant nature of the Vherals?"

"Yes. Marek, Medjii, and I spent long hours discussing the issues and how to solve them. It seems like the people of the north are always on the verge of war…" She trailed off.

Alia gasped in sudden understanding. Marek wanted to start a war, and DaiSur had inadvertently shown him how to do it.

The old, blind diviner gave Marek one final piece of information.

"The woman you seek is on her way to confer with the elves."

The nameless man left shortly after their conversation; nearly a month passed before Marek saw him again. Occasionally, he wondered what had happened, but wasn't interested enough to find out. Instead, the mage spent what free time he had mulling over the information he had received.

So, he needed Alia's help in order to be successful. The question then became how to possess her again. He had her once, but he didn't think he could drug her with thallum or mesmerize her a second time. Plus, there was the added problem of her marriage to a loutish Temple graduate, who seemed to think of her as his property.

On the positive side, the old diviner had told him where to find Alia.

Julie H. Peralta

Marek sighed with the stress of trying to formulate a new plan. Two days later, the answer walked into his tent.

Chapter 15–The Morning

"I don't understand," DaiSur admitted when everyone else in the room grew quiet and thoughtful. "What am I missing?"

Ciern turned to her and began talking slowly, as though he was speaking to a child. "Marek is going to go up north to the Vherals. He will open the Aghara to sow discord and unrest among them, resulting in warfare. Then he can seal the device to negotiate peace. He will be revered. With this device and his talent for mesmerizing, it will be a simple matter for him to control the Vherals. He will easily be able to create his own private army."

"So?" DaiSur asked.

"An army that he can lead south to conquer the entirety of the Four Lands."

She gasped in sudden understanding as the rest of the room went deadly silent.

"How do we stop him?" Alia asked. But no one had the answer.

"I think you should all retire for the night," King Elator suddenly suggested. "We are all exhausted, and tired people don't think well. Besides, King Ganayt and I still have some business to discuss. Ciern, Skala," he said to them. "We would like for you two to stay for this matter. The rest of you are free to go. Except for you, DaiSur. You will remain as well."

The rest of them filed out through the throne room and walked silently toward the hallway leading up to their rooms. When they reached the stairwell, the fussy, old elf was waiting for them.

"Mr. and Mrs." he said politely to Zimpf and Aistra. "His majesty has requested that I escort you to your new room. You will be housed in the cottage just outside of the castle. Follow me, please." With that, he turned down a separate hallway and led the newlyweds, who were holding hands, toward the honeymoon cottage.

Shao suddenly laughed. "I hope he kisses her better than he did after his proposal. You would think that as many times as he interrupted us, he would have been better at kissing," he said, looking fondly at Alia and winking.

Alia blushed but laughed good-naturedly.

"That's it," Sh'ron said. "We are all coming to your room so you can tell us everything that happened earlier tonight."

Everyone followed Alia and Shao to their suite, where they lounged comfortably on the sofas in the sitting room. They were all laughing hysterically over the description of Zimpf's confusion at Shao trying to encourage him to propose when someone knocked at the door.

It was Ciern.

"I sure wish I had been up here with you all," he complained as he let himself in, walked over, and plopped down on the sofa beside Sh'ron. "It sounds like you all are having a great time."

Shao repeated the engagement story to him.

"I love Zimpf, I do," Ciern laughed. "But he can be impossibly dense sometimes." The elven prince shook his head. "So, whose idea was it to have them get married tonight?"

"Mine," Alia admitted. "I thought that if they were married immediately, DaiSur wouldn't be able to separate them again without it looking suspicious."

"Clever," Ciern grinned admiringly. Then he continued, "But DaiSur will no longer be a problem."

"What happened in the meeting?" Amicu asked.

"DaiSur has been relieved of her duties," Ciern informed them seriously. "My father and King Ganayt were very upset with her for her unscrupulous practices. Apparently, she violated several bylaws, any of which could have ended with her execution."

"What will happen to her now?" Sh'ron wanted to know.

"She will be allowed to return to her home, where she must remain in perpetuity. It was Skala's suggestion," he informed them.

"I like Skala," Chhdar said softly. "He doesn't feel the need to fill up quiet times with senseless chatter."

"Her punishment should have been more severe!" Alia announced vehemently. Everyone turned to look at her. "DaiSur did some truly abhorrent things."

Shao smiled and leaned over to hug her. "I think we all agree with you on that," he whispered.

"When is the next meeting?" Amicu wanted to know.

"Tomorrow after lunch. You all have the morning off," Ciern told them.

Everyone stayed until it had grown quite late, just talking over old times and laughing. But finally, the evening together ended, and they all retired for the night.

When Alia woke up the next morning, Shao had wrapped one arm around her and pulled her close. She was nestled comfortably with her head on his chest. He was wide awake and had apparently been watching her sleep. She smiled up at him, feeling comfortable, loved, and rested. It was nice to be able to lounge in bed and not have to get up early to go somewhere. Alia felt like they had been running hard since they left the Temple of Anaia.

"Did you sleep well?" Shao asked.

"I did," she smiled. "Did you?"

"I slept very well," he answered. "We have a while before the meeting. What would you like to do?" he asked.

Alia had learned that when Shao asked what she wanted to do, that meant he already had something in mind. And it was usually something fun that involved just the two of them.

"I don't know," she answered shyly. "Do you have any suggestions?"

"Get dressed!" he said excitedly. "I want to take you somewhere."

Alia rushed to get dressed and braid her long, dark hair. Then she met Shao in the sitting room.

Taking her hand, he led her into the stunning hallway with its carved granite floors and arched stained-glass walls. The glass depicted pastoral scenes of lush fields, blue skies, and brilliant wildflowers. Interspersed down the hallway were marble statues of hundreds of years of elven kings.

The hallway opened into the Music Room, which was an enormous, open-windowed room with dark wooden buttresses holding up a ceiling several stories tall. The floor was also made of carved granite, and there were comfortable chairs lining the rectangular room. Four massive candelabras hung suspended from the ceiling, creating a sense of peace and beauty. Musicians were warming up their instruments on the dais at the front of the room.

Alia and Shao slid in quietly and took seats on the chairs lining the walls. Then the musicians began playing the most beautiful song that Alia had ever heard. It was soft, natural, and melodious. The tempo was that of a beating heart, representing life itself; the music was soothing and relaxing. Then the tempo gradually built up in a crescendo, echoing strength and power that Alia found exhilarating. Finally, it moderated to a slow, steady decrescendo, which served to heal the soul. Alia was enchanted.

When the song ended, Shao and Alia softly tiptoed out of the room.

"That…that…" Alia stammered, her eyes wide in admiration, "was amazing!"

"I thought you needed a distraction from the stress of the last few days," Shao said, raising her hand to his lips and kissing it.

"How did I get so lucky?" she asked him.

Shao laughed. "Let's have an early lunch, then afterward, if you would like, we can visit the library before we go to the meeting," he suggested.

When they walked in the library, Alia was in for another surprise. Sh'ron and Chhdar were lounging in a couple of deeply cushioned armchairs. Sh'ron was reading a book, and Chhdar was thumbing through an ancient volume depicting various weapons.

The twins, who were also best friends, were soon sitting across from each other, their heads close together while they whispered and giggled.

Shao looked at Alia talking with her sister and smiled at the bond between the sisters. He glanced over at Chhdar and saw him watching the two women with a fond expression.

Then Chhdar glanced up and saw Shao looking at him.

"Hey, Shao," Chhdar said casually, "I saw a huge reference book with some unusual weapons pictured in it that I couldn't identify. Would you come take a look at them with me?" he asked. "Maybe you can tell me something about them."

Shao smiled at the ruse to give the twins some privacy, "I'll be right back," he told Alia. Then the two men walked together to the back of the library, leaving the girls alone to chat.

Alia was in the middle of telling Sh'ron in detail about Aistra and Zimpf and how their connection worked when the door to the library opened softly and a middle-aged human man slid in quietly. He smiled at Alia, and she nodded politely in return.

Alia thought it was unusual for a human to be in the library, but she didn't really pay that much attention to him. After all, she and her sister were here with their husbands. The library is open to everyone, she thought, not just elves.

The twins continued their conversation in whispers and quiet giggles so as not to disturb the new patron.

Alia had just leaned toward Sh'ron to describe Zimpf's proposal in detail when the man walked close behind her. Without warning, he grabbed Alia's hair, pulled her bodily from her chair, tilted her head back, and placed a sharp knife against her throat. One hand held the knife, while the other snaked tightly around her waist.

"Don't move!" he warned both girls in an evil, sibilant voice, "or I will slit Alia's throat right here and now."

Alia froze.

Sh'ron backed up a step and held up both hands. "Don't hurt

my sister," she said in a voice loud enough to carry to the back of the room.

"Alia," the attacker said, "you're coming quietly with me. If you make any attempt to escape or signal for help, you will be dead before the spit has dried on your lips."

Alia could feel the man tighten his arm around her waist, and the edge of the knife was pushed harder against her skin.

"She won't resist, will you, Alia?" Sh'ron said loudly. "Please don't cut her throat."

The thug began pulling Alia backward toward the door. Alia tripped slightly, and in an apparent attempt to regain her balance, automatically it seemed, she grabbed at the man's knife hand. Then, several things happened all at once.

Alia seized the man's thumb with her right hand and pulled it down, quickly twisting it to the right while stepping to the side and rotating away from the man's grip. The sharp crack of the man's thumb breaking reverberated throughout the library. At the same time, she stomped down hard with her right heel, crushing his foot. He stumbled backward. Almost simultaneously, Shao appeared from out of nowhere. He smoothly grabbed the man's arm, twisting it at the same time that Alia broke his thumb. The counter-twist applied by Shao at the same moment caused the man's elbow to shatter, and he screamed in agony. Then with a seamless side kick, Shao's foot connected solidly with his knee. The attacker hit the floor hard, his lower leg angled in the wrong direction.

Chhdar, almost too big to be believed, had also appeared, and stood looking down at the man threateningly. The attacker tried to slyly reach his knife. But Chhdar's foot came down with a hard crunching sound on the man's wrist.

"No, you don't," Chhdar growled as he bent to pick up the knife.

"Who are you, and why did you attack my wife?" Shao asked in a soft, dangerous voice while looming over the assailant menacingly.

The man didn't answer.

"Are you working alone?" Sh'ron asked, taking the knife from Chhdar and testing the edge in a threatening manner.

The attacker stared at her but remained silent.

"I'll get the guards," Shao said. "You all wait here." Then, moving stealthily, he cracked open the door and peered quickly into the hallway. Everything seemed perfectly normal. He signaled one of the guards and spoke to him quietly. Then he stepped back into the room and closed the door firmly. Within moments, their friends began to arrive.

King Elator and Ciern were the first to enter the room. The king was livid.

"How dare you!" he roared at the attacker. "You have tried to forcefully kidnap a royal guest, and your life is forfeit!" Then he looked at Ciern. "Call the executioner. I want this man's head on a pike within the hour."

For the first time, the attacker reacted. All the color in his face slowly drained away until he was as white as the marble floor.

Ciern stepped to the door and spoke to the guard, who sprinted away.

Amicu was the next to arrive, followed by King Ganayt and Skala.

"What happened?" Amicu asked of the badly injured man on the floor.

"I'll explain in a minute," Shao said. "Did anyone send for Zimpf and Aistra?"

"Please," Zimpf said, walking into the library with Aistra holding his hand. "Did you really think I wouldn't have *seen* something like this?" He looked at the badly wounded man. "Did you do all of that to him?" Zimpf asked Shao.

"Some of it," Shao admitted. "Alia did the rest of it."

Everyone turned to look at Alia, who had seated herself in one of the chairs.

"She's going to give you a run for your money, if you keep training her," Zimpf teased.

Aistra suddenly released Zimpf's hand and moved to kneel in front of Alia, talking to her softly.

Shao watched, angry at himself for not seeing how upset Alia had become. He suddenly realized how pale and shaky she was, and he could clearly see a small amount of blood trickling down her throat from where the attacker had pressed the knife against her skin.

He turned a baleful eye at the man, and for the first time, the attacker flinched away from Shao's malevolent glare.

"Check him, Zimpf," Shao ordered, "and don't be gentle either."

Then Shao went to sit on the arm of Alia's chair and wrapped his arm around her shoulders. She leaned into him gratefully.

"I am so sorry," he apologized sincerely. "I should have seen that you were upset."

Alia was a swordswoman, and Shao had been training her for a year on how to defend herself. Fighting was nothing new to her. What scared her was the sudden, vicious attack on her in a place where she had felt safe.

Zimpf stood looking down at the fallen assailant. "You really should answer their questions, you know," he said conversationally. "If not, I'm just going to rip the answers forcefully out of your head."

The man looked away.

"Alrighty. But I tried to warn you," Zimpf told him sadly. Then he squatted down and placed his hands on either side of the attacker's head.

The man screamed an agonizing cry of pure pain. His eyes grew fixed and glassy, and he flung his head from side to side. Tears streamed down his face. After a few minutes, Zimpf released him. The man immediately lost consciousness.

Zimpf looked at King Elator. "Let's discuss this in the conference room."

The king nodded. He signaled to Ciern, who opened the door and called in a guard. "Get some help and take this man to a holding cell," the prince ordered. "Put double guards on him. I will send a message later as to his fate."

Once the attacker was removed, everyone followed King Elator to the meeting chamber.

"How are you feeling?" the king asked Alia kindly.

"I'm a little shaken up," Alia admitted. "I could use a cup of tea," she said hopefully.

King Elator arranged for a variety of beverages to be delivered. Once the servants had departed, he started the meeting.

"Let's begin with the attack. Will you tell us what happened?" he asked Alia and Sh'ron.

Sh'ron told the story while Alia quietly sipped her tea. It was clear that she was still very upset by the attack.

Shao watched her closely and from time to time leaned over to speak to her softly.

"Okay, Zimpf," the king turned to the diviner. "What can you tell us?"

"It's odd," Zimpf answered. "The death threat was one thing, but the things in his head were completely different."

"What do you mean?" Shao demanded.

"He was obsessed with Alia. Like, head-over-heels, swept-off-your-feet, puppy-dog in love."

"Wait, what?" Alia stammered.

"I know!" Zimpf exclaimed. "He thought you were the most beautiful woman he had ever seen. It was crazy."

"Hey!" Alia protested.

"I haven't seen that level of obsession since…" Zimpf hesitated, looking sideways at Shao and smirking.

"Shut up, Zimpf," Shao growled.

"Could it have been a ploy? Could he have been pretending to be unreasonably obsessed with her?" Amicu asked.

Zimpf chuckled.

Amicu looked over at her. "Sorry Alia, that came out all wrong."

Zimpf continued to giggle.

"Shut up, Zimpf," Amicu echoed Shao.

"Are you sure you didn't get it wrong?" Ciern asked the diviner.

"Hey!" Zimpf complained. "I am the best diviner in the Four Lands."

Aistra nodded, and Zimpf smiled at her.

"I meant," Ciern qualified. "Is it possible that someone planted the notion of being in love with Alia into his head?"

"I couldn't find anything," Zimpf said seriously.

"Could he have been drugged with thallum?" King Ganayt asked. "I remember how the rogue mage used it to control both Alia and Airafae."

Shao and Zimpf exchanged a long look.

"It's possible," Zimpf admitted thoughtfully. "But I didn't sense any trace of the drug."

"I would feel better if you checked the man again," Shao told him.

Zimpf opened his mouth to complain, but both King Elator and King Ganayt agreed with Shao.

"We need to make absolutely sure that the rogue mage isn't behind this," King Elator said.

"You are all going to insist, I take it?" Zimpf asked.

"Yes, we are," Elator told him firmly.

"I don't know why people don't trust me," Zimpf lamented in feigned sadness. Then he rose to his feet and held his hand out to Aistra. "Coming, dear?" he invited.

"I'm coming too," Ciern announced.

The three left the meeting hall together. They were gone for nearly an hour.

"Just like I said," Zimpf announced when the three of them returned to the conference room. "He's just a crazy man who thinks Alia is the most beautiful woman alive." He giggled, the dimples boring into his cheeks. Shao glowered at him.

"Shut up, Zimpf!" Shao warned. Then the martial artist turned to Aistra. "Did you go along on Zimpf's little *trip*?" he asked.

"Yes," she answered. "It is as Zimpf said; he's just a deranged man who for some reason thinks Alia is the most beautiful woman in the world." Then she looked up at Alia, suddenly realizing what she had said. "I'm sorry Alia," Aistra apologized, blushing. "I didn't mean for it to sound like he's crazy for thinking you're beautiful."

Zimpf laughed again.

"Shut up, Zimpf!" Shao, Ciern, and Amicu said in unison.

"So, what should his fate be?" the king asked.

Everyone was silent.

"Ciern? What do you think?"

"I am not comfortable with executing someone who is disturbed," Ciern answered. "However, he certainly can't be allowed to roam free for fear he'll harm someone else." He looked straight at his father. "Imprison him."

The king nodded. "Tell the guards to have him treated by a healer and then confined."

Ciern went to the door, spoke to the guard, then resumed his seat at the table.

King Elator looked around the room. "Speaking of executing disturbed men, that is exactly what will happen when that rogue mage is caught," he promised. "Marek will pay with his life for his crimes."

"Master?" Kamet began. *The servant was the only ruffian he had hired in Kuthra to survive the perilous trip over the Skarsgaard Mountains.* "With your permission, I would like to go hunting with the Vherals this morning."

Marek looked up sharply as an idea clicked rapidly into place.

"Go," he waved magnanimously. "But report back to me as soon as you return."

Kamet bowed deeply and left the tent.

The mage stared after his servant; his eyes narrowed slyly. The sudden notion of using the man to hunt his quarry in the elven kingdom for him was brilliant.

Kamet was totally under his control, but Marek needed his henchman to follow directions perfectly without the constant reinforcement that had so dominated the man's independent thinking. And the idea of forcing the man to ingest the contents of the Aghara directly, along with implanting a post-mesmerization suggestion to kidnap Alia, was a stroke of genius.

Marek grinned maliciously. Somehow, he knew it would work.

Chapter 16 – Plans

"Before we start discussing Marek and his possible connection to the attack on Alia, can I ask a question first?" Sh'ron inquired.

"Certainly," King Elator answered patiently.

"Who are the Vherals you all were talking about last night?"

"The Vherals are the people who live on the other side of the Skarsgaard Mountains," the dwarven king answered. "They are mostly nomadic groups consisting of hundreds of small tribes. Each tribe is led by an elder and is mostly made up of his children, their spouses, and their children. The number of each tribe varies from as few as twenty to as many as a hundred. The tribes will sometimes work together to bring down large amounts of game or to fight an outside threat. But generally, they fight among themselves for resources. They have long wanted to expand to this side of the mountains because of the milder climate and abundant food supply. But the individual tribes are too small, and there has never been a leader strong enough to meld them together into a significant fighting force."

"Until now," Amicu said. "If Marek is successful, we're in for a real war. The Vherals have a nasty reputation as fearsome fighters."

Ciern nodded. "We studied them extensively at Temple," he explained. "The instructors there were all in agreement that if the Vherals were ever united enough to mount an attack to the south, we would all be in serious trouble."

"So how do we stop Marek from melding them together?" Chhdar asked.

"King Ganayt, Skala, Ciern, and I had a long discussion about it last night," King Elator answered. "Our first thought was to try to stop Marek from making it over the mountains. But we suspect he has a nearly impossible lead. If he headed into the mountains after the attack on the Order of the Mages, he has probably already started to put his plan into action."

"Where is the mage who was here earlier?" Zimpf suddenly asked. "Where is Guiden?"

"Observant, isn't he?" Amicu muttered under his breath.

Shao laughed; Zimpf scowled.

"Guiden escorted DaiSur home," King Ganayt answered. "Why?"

"Can Marek use the Aghara for destructive purposes?" Zimpf wanted to know.

"Yes," Aistra answered. Zimpf looked at her in surprise. "How do you know that?" he asked, pleased at his new wife's knowledge.

"Did you forget that I studied magic at Temple?" she grinned.

"And another example of Zimpf's observational skills," Amicu teased.

"Keep it up, Tactics Man, and I'll delve your brain while you sleep and reveal your worst secret to everyone," Zimpf threatened.

Amicu howled with laughter.

Aistra smiled tolerantly at their bantering, then continued. "The Aghara can be used as a weapon, although its primary purpose is to…" she trailed off, her eyes suddenly growing very wide. "Alia!" she gasped.

"No," the diviner quipped. "I'm Zimpf, your husband, remember?" he teased.

Aistra looked straight at him. "Zimpf!" she gasped. "The attack on Alia! I think the man was under the spell of the Aghara! It makes sense. One of the purposes of the Aghara is to influence emotion."

The smile fell off Zimpf's face. Before anyone could say anything, the diviner was up and running out the door with Aistra right behind him. Ciern jumped up to follow them. "Stay here!" he commanded the others.

Alia glanced at King Elator. One of his eyebrows had shot straight up at being told what to do by his son. He saw Alia looking at him, then winked.

They sat, waiting impatiently.

"I have a question," Chhdar asked curiously into the silence. "Why did Marek have this man obsess over Alia so much that he tried to kidnap her?"

"My guess is to delay us," Shao answered. "Marek knows that if Alia is taken, I would stop at nothing to find her."

"Me too," Sh'ron said, looking at her twin.

"And where you go, I will follow." Chhdar smiled at his wife.

Finally, after almost an hour, Zimpf, Aistra, and Ciern returned to the meeting room, their faces somber.

"Alia's attacker is dead," Zimpf reported.

"What?" Alia asked.

"How?" Skala wanted to know.

"I have never seen anything like it," Zimpf answered uneasily. He sounded shaken. Alia noticed that he and Aistra were sitting very close together and holding hands. As he spoke, Aistra occasionally reached up to touch his face.

"The attacker was still unconscious," Zimpf told them. "But he should have been awake by now. I didn't put him out for that long. I tried several different ways to wake him up, but he didn't respond." He looked around at them, his eyes wide and sincere. "Usually, I can call someone back easily, but…" Zimpf trailed off, shaking his head. "I tried to examine his memories. I thought maybe I could find a hint of Marek or at least a strange figure who approached him, but there was nothing there. Not even images of Alia. Just…nothing. It was like his brain had melted. I have never seen anything like it." Zimpf looked down at the floor, clearly upset.

"What kind of weapon melts a man's brain?" Skala asked.

"More importantly, what kind of a person would use such a weapon?" King Ganayt asked, his voice tinged with horror.

But Alia knew. She was aware that Marek would stop at nothing in his single-minded drive for power. And she understood that he would have to answer for his crimes. She looked up at Shao to see him looking back at her. He nodded. They were going to have to stop the monster that Marek had become.

Amicu, clearly upset, looked at Aistra. "You were saying that Marek could use the Aghara as a weapon," he stated. "How so?"

Aistra looked around. "It's only a theory, because nearly all of the information about the Aghara has been lost in antiquity. But, based on what you all told me about the destruction of the mage's compound, I suspect that he drew some of the…" She hesitated, thinking of what to call the contents of the Aghara. "…evil from the device and then used it to make himself more powerful. I was told that the reason Marek wasn't invited to study with the mages was because his talent was geared for destruction. The mages won't accept such students because they view such aptitudes as belonging to agents of chaos."

"Well, they got that right," Zimpf said dryly.

Ciern nodded his agreement. "So how do we stop him?" he asked everyone.

"We obviously can't prevent him from reaching the Vherals. But what if we talk to them first?" Amicu asked. "You said they are scattered all over the lands north of the Skarsgaard Mountains. Based on the route he followed, he would have started in the east. What if we go to the leaders in the west? Would they be willing to accept a peaceful envoy?"

The king was quiet for a moment. "They might," he answered thoughtfully. "Especially if King Ganayt and I both send representatives."

"I think we should give it a try," Ciern said. "The first rule of strategy is to avoid military confrontation."

"That's the first rule in tactics as well," Amicu agreed.

King Elator and King Ganayt looked at each other. Finally, King Ganayt nodded. "I think sending an envoy might be our best chance to avoid this war," he said.

"I will be the representative for the dwarves," Skala told his father.

King Ganayt turned to stare at his son. "Are you making demands of me?" he questioned sternly.

"I am best qualified to do this task" He replied confidently.

"Your cub has grown teeth," King Elator said to the dwarven king.

"It would appear so," King Ganayt replied. Then he turned to Skala, "I will consider your request."

"We should also send emissaries to the leaders of all of the settlements, hamlets, and villages north of our position here," Amicu told them. "Just as a precaution, they should be warned to prepare for the potential for trouble."

"We should warn the villages and hamlets south of here as well," Ciern said thoughtfully.

"I still have some concerns about Marek and the Aghara," Shao spoke quietly to Zimpf. "How do we protect our minds from a weapon that can melt a person's brain?"

Zimpf looked at Aistra. "A block?" he asked.

She shook her head. "I don't think that would be strong enough. I think you would have to place a shield," she told him seriously.

Zimpf clenched his teeth together, pulling down the sides of his lips and frowning at the same time.

"What's that face?" Amicu said. "I don't like that face Zimpf's making at all."

"It doesn't exactly fill me with confidence either," Shao admitted dryly.

Zimpf looked at them. "A shield won't hurt you," he informed them.

"Then why are you making faces?" Ciern demanded.

"Because it will be hard on me," Zimpf answered ruefully. "It takes an enormous amount of effort to shield someone's mind." He was quiet for a moment, thinking, then he continued. "But I think Aistra's right; a shield is more of an extensive safeguard than a block."

"The question is, how many people will Zimpf have to place shields into?" Aistra wanted to know.

Alia could see how worried Aistra was about her new husband. It didn't give her any confidence about needing to be shielded. Zimpf had *visioned* her three times and placed blocks in her twice; each incursion had been unpleasant. She dreaded having to endure the insertion of the more intrusive shield.

"Who is going to go north as an envoy?" King Elator asked.

"Me," said Alia, looking into Shao's eyes. "If we encounter Marek, I will be the best person to confront him."

"Me," Shao echoed, while returning Alia's stare. "I will not be separated from Alia."

"I agree with that," Zimpf muttered under his breath with a sideways look at Shao.

In the end it was decided that Alia, Shao, Sh'ron, Chhdar, Ciern, Amicu, Zimpf, Aistra, and, after a nod from King Ganayt, Skala would go to the Vherals as envoys. Meanwhile, warning messages would be sent to all the settlements, hamlets, and villages informing them of a possible invasion. King Ganayt would alert the people located to the north and King Elator would caution the people located to the south.

"When do you all want to get started?" King Elator asked.

"I will need some time to shield eight people," Zimpf said apprehensively.

"What about you?" Amicu asked,

"Please," Zimpf scoffed. "I had a shield put in ages ago."

"So, how long do you think you'll need?" Ciern asked.

"Let's be ready to leave in three days," Zimpf answered.

"Three!" Aistra exclaimed. "You can't insert that many shields in three days. You will need time to rest between each insertion."

Zimpf held up his hand. "Let's be ready in three days. But, be aware that it could possibly take me longer. Aistra's right, I will need to rest after each insertion because shielding takes an enormous amount of energy. Plus, you all could potentially be disoriented for a few hours afterward. "

"This sounds like so much fun," Ciern said sarcastically.

"I just know it's a bad idea to let Zimpf poke around in my head," Amicu complained.

"Hey!" Zimpf protested.

"You just threatened to delve my mind and then reveal my worst secret to everyone," Amicu protested.

Zimpf smirked as everyone else laughed.

"I have arranged a dinner for us this evening," King Elator said, dismissing them. "We will have another meeting the evening before you all leave to go over any final plans. Meanwhile, you should prepare for your trip. I will inform the kitchen and laundry to provide you with whatever supplies you may need, and I will have the grooms check your horses."

With that, the meeting adjourned to give everyone time to get dressed for the dinner party.

When Alia and Shao made it to their room, Shao took Alia by the hand and pulled her onto the sofa with him.

"I want to talk to you," he told her gravely.

Alia nodded. He was so serious that she thought something must be horribly wrong. *Have I somehow offended him?* she thought.

"How are you?"

That wasn't what Alia had expected at all. When she hesitated, Shao rushed on. "I understand if you are upset with me. And I am so sorry," he apologized.

"What?" Alia finally managed to murmur.

"I should have known," he professed. "I should have been watching."

"Wait." Alia held up both hands. Shao opened his mouth to continue, but Alia placed her index finger on Shao's lips while she raised one eyebrow questioningly. "What are you talking about?" she asked, confused.

"You were upset after that madman attacked you in the library; I didn't notice until I saw Aistra attending to you," Shao confessed.

"Oh," Alia muttered. "No, I'm fine. I was a little upset at first," she admitted. "But mostly because of the suddenness of the attack. It was unexpected, and I just wasn't prepared for it."

Shao looked at her in disbelief.

"I thought you were angry with me," she told him in relief. Then she smiled at him, leaned in, and gave him a rather serious kiss.

"I could never be angry at you." He smiled.

"Don't make promises you can't keep," she teased.

"Let me take a look at your neck," he demanded. "I want to see how badly he cut you."

Alia leaned her head on the back of the sofa and stretched her neck out. Shao carefully looked at the small nick. It was actually just a tiny scratch. "Let me put something on that for you," he insisted. Then he got her medical bag and pulled out the container of healing salve. Sitting back down, he leaned in and kissed her neck. Alia giggled.

"Is that better?" he said jokingly.

"Actually, it is better," she acknowledged with a smile.

They sat talking for a few minutes then finally decided that they needed to get dressed for the dinner party. Once they were ready, they went to Sh'ron and Chhdar's room, and then the two couples stopped to invite Amicu to go with them.

The group sat with Aistra and Zimpf at one of the large, round tables while King Elator, Ciern, King Ganayt, and Skala sat at the head table. As always, the food was delicious. After dinner they were invited to a concert in the Music Room. The musicians performed flawlessly; Alia was spellbound by their talent. She thought she had never heard such inspiring music.

At one point Shao leaned over to her and whispered softly, "Breathe, Alia."

She smiled at him.

At the end of the concert, the music began to change and evolve until the guests began to move to the middle of the floor in a soundless celebration of dance.

Shao took Alia's hand and escorted her to the dance floor, where they joined the other couples in a joyous tribute to music and those who make it. Alia never wanted the evening to end.

She was still enthralled the next morning when she woke up with her head nestled against Shao's shoulder. She smiled to herself in memory of the evening before.

"I hope you're smiling because you're happy with me," Shao commented.

"I am very happy to be with you," she said.

Just then there was a knock at the door.

"Who could be here so early?" Alia wondered aloud.

"You mean late," Shao laughed. "Half the morning drifted by while I watched you sleep."

The knock came again, more insistently this time.

"We'd better answer that," Shao said. "You get dressed and I'll see who our unrelenting visitor is."

"Hey!" They heard Zimpf's voice from the hallway, yelling at the top of his lungs. "Stop smooching and open up!" Then he began hammering on the door with sharp, loud, staccato blows.

Shao rolled his eyes comically. "I'm going to let him in, all right," he grumbled as the shouting and banging continued.

Dressing quickly, they hurried into the sitting room.

"Stand back," Shao warned. Then, all in one smooth motion, he threw open the door, grabbed Zimpf's fist, which was still in the act of knocking on the door, and pulled him bodily into the room with a quick downward motion. Zimpf, thrown completely off balance, did a quick forward flip and, unable to arrest his momentum, landed face-first into the back of the sofa.

"Ow," he complained, sitting up and rubbing his nose.

Then Aistra stepped into the room. "They haven't changed at all," she remarked, shaking her head sadly.

"At least you didn't break my nose this time," Zimpf remarked.

"You broke his nose?" Aistra said disapprovingly to Shao.

"It was an accident," Shao protested. "Besides, Zimpf deserved it," he muttered under his breath.

Alia laughed while Aistra simply shook her head in long-suffering silence.

"So, why are you here before we've even had breakfast?" Shao asked.

"If you didn't spend so much time smooching, you would have had time for breakfast," Zimpf retorted.

"Well, maybe if you knew how to do it right, you would spend more time smooching," Shao snapped back.

"We've come so Zimpf can implant the shields against the Aghara," Aistra interrupted. Then she looked at Alia. "I ordered a light breakfast. You both should probably eat a little something first."

Breakfast was delivered almost immediately. Alia could hardly eat anything because of her nervousness. Zimpf had already worked on her mind several times, and it was never pleasant.

"So," Zimpf asked in a challenging voice. "Who gets to go first?"

Alia and Shao looked at each other. "I can go first since you're nervous," he offered. "That way you can see that it's not that bad."

"Has Zimpf done this to you before?" Alia questioned.

"Of course," Shao replied casually. "Who do you think he practiced on when we were at Temple?"

"If you've already been shielded, then why do you have to do it again? Does it fade over time?" Alia asked curiously. Zimpf inserted a block into her mind after Marek had stolen the Orb of Ahi from her, but shielding was something new.

"It's like she thinks I can't do anything right," Zimpf complained in an aside to Aistra.

"Be nice," Aistra murmured before turning to Alia. "Shields and blocks don't fade. At Temple, Zimpf had to practice inserting and removing both."

"Taking that last block out of Shao was especially grueling," Zimpf complained. "For a while, I thought I had caused permanent brain damage."

Alia stared, first at Shao and then at Zimpf. Finally, unable to say anything, she just sank her face into her hands.

"Hey," Shao said softly, wrapping his arms around her. "Don't be afraid."

"I'm not afraid," Alia said. "I'm appalled. It's a wonder Zimpf didn't mutilate both of your brains."

"He didn't damage my brain," Shao assured her. "I'm not sure about his though," he said, smirking at the diviner.

"I'm standing right here," Zimpf protested.

"I want to go first," Alia suddenly insisted.

"This will be easier if you're reclining," Zimpf told her, suddenly very businesslike. "Let's have both of you lay down on your bed."

With that, they moved to the bedroom, where Alia and Shao lay down side-by-side.

Zimpf carried a chair into the room and placed it at the foot of the bed for Aistra.

Then he sat on the bed beside Alia. Immediately, she reached out to take Shao's comforting hand.

"Okay," Zimpf told her. "Just close your eyes."

Alia immediately did as she was told. She could *feel* Zimpf's presence in her mind. He was searching for something, penetrating the nooks and folds of her brain. It was an invasive, frightening siege of her consciousness. She began to panic, and in her terror, she began to fight, trying to expel the invader, the destroyer. But the intruder became more aggressive, stronger, inflexible in his single-minded determination to vanquish her completely.

"Help me!" she cried aloud.

Then Shao was there with her. She could feel his mouth very close to her ear, whispering, comforting, soothing. Alia couldn't understand his words, but she clung to his presence, to his voice, to his feelings. Not even realizing it, Alia fell asleep.

When she woke up, it was late afternoon. Shao lay asleep beside her. Aistra was still sitting in the chair at the foot of their bed.

"How do you feel?" she asked.

"A little confused and sort of dizzy," Alia told her. "What happened to us?"

"Zimpf implanted the shields," Aistra answered.

The memory of that morning came flooding back. "Shao?" she suddenly asked, turning toward her husband.

"He's fine," Aistra told her. "He's been through it before, so his surrender to Zimpf made the implantation easy. Would you like a cup of tea?" she suddenly asked.

"Yes. That sounds delicious!" Alia told her. Then, almost as an afterthought, she asked, "How is Zimpf?"

Aistra smiled. "He's fine. He's napping on the sofa in the sitting room."

Aistra left and returned quickly with two cups of tea. She sat one on the bedside table by Shao, and she handed the other one to Alia. Just as she was finishing the tea, Alia felt Shao stir. When she turned to him, he was looking at her with concern.

"Are you okay?" he asked worriedly.

"I'm perfectly fine," she answered. "How are you feeling?"

"I'm as sound as ever." He smiled at her.

Forgetting that they had company, Alia leaned down and gave Shao a long kiss.

"See, I told you," she heard Zimpf's voice from the doorway.

Alia blushed in embarrassment.

"If her face can turn red like that, it must mean that she's feeling okay," he said laconically.

Dinner was brought to their room shortly after that. The four of them moved to the sitting room to eat, although Alia still felt slightly weak and rather clumsy.

Aistra and Zimpf left shortly after they ate; Alia and Shao retired for the evening as soon as they had gone.

The next day, they began preparing for their trip north in their quest to stop Marek.

It was not quite a month later when Marek was visited by the old, blind diviner. He had been dispensing herbs to the Vherals for their various complaints when the old diviner walked into his tent unannounced and took a seat.

"Your plan failed," he announced without preamble.

Marek stared at him, his eyes narrowing dangerously.

"How do you—" he started.

The diviner raised his right hand for silence, and Marek immediately grew quiet.

"The servant you dispatched was unsuccessful with the abduction and was immediately imprisoned. It seems that his failed mission, in combination with the amount of the potion from the Aghara, caused a catastrophic episode to occur within Kamet's mind."

"Explain," Marek barked.

"His brain liquefied."

The mage was quiet for a few minutes, thinking over this new information. He didn't lament the loss of life; his only concern was how to adjust the dose so it didn't happen again. Finally, he looked at the old diviner.

"Nabii," he called the old man, using the Vheral name for someone who could divine. "What else can you tell me?"

"You no longer need to send someone after this woman. She and her friends will come here looking for you." Nabii answered directly.

"Will I be successful in coercing her cooperation in order to achieve my goal?" Marek asked cautiously.

Nabii was quiet for a few minutes as his eyes glazed over and he saw for the future. Finally, he focused on the diviner.

"The future is fluid; it cannot be determined," he replied. "My advice to you is to find a way to lure her to you. I believe that if she comes of her own accord, you will be able to use her any way you want."

Marek's eyes narrowed as a new plan coalesced in his mind.

Chapter 17 – Departure

Alia and Shao spent the next day getting outfitted for their trip to the mountains. The day after that was spent meeting with their friends, King Elator, and King Ganayt, as they made final preparations and planned their route. The fourth day was a day for Zimpf to finish shielding the remaining members of their group, so when they got up that morning, Alia and Shao had a free day. Although Alia already had something planned.

For once, she was already awake and watching Shao when he woke up.

"Good morning," he said. "You're awake early." He smiled.

"We have a free day," she answered. "What would you like to do?"

Shao looked at her with one eyebrow raised thoughtfully. "Well, I would tell you, but I suspect that you already have something planned."

"Get dressed," she told him excitedly. "Then come to the sitting room."

When Shao came out of the bedroom, he was surprised to see what Alia had arranged. On the small table that sat in between the two sofas was a basket overflowing with food.

"How would you like to go for a nice picnic?" she invited him, indicating the basket.

Shao nodded and flashed a surprisingly boyish grin.

"Let's go," said Alia. "Quickly, before someone wants to join us."

Shao picked up the basket and took Alia's hand. Together, they left the castle by a side door. Shao steered them toward the back of the castle, out through a field, and toward a small rise. Once they reached the top, they could see for miles toward the west. There were forests and a huge, shimmering, blue lake. Alia laid out a large blanket for them to sit on, and they spent the remainder of the afternoon enjoying peace, sunshine, and each other's company. The sun was beginning to set before they walked back to the castle. They crept quietly to their room and retired early.

The next morning, they were up and waiting by the stables for their friends before the sun had even risen. The group left quietly out a back door, following the same route that Marek and Airafae had followed more than a year before. It would take them five days to reach the city of Kuthra, where they would meet Skala and continue with their journey.

The trip to Kuthra was long, boring, and dusty. There was nothing to look at except for barren hillsides and the brown, dusty ribbon of a road, which turned and twisted in endless S-curves. Finally, as the fifth day of travel ended, they emerged from the tunnel-like exit close to where the gates of Kuthra stood open. Skala, sitting astride a small, powerful-looking horse, awaited them in the shade of a nearby tree. He rode to meet them when they were about halfway to the city.

"Let's avoid Kuthra," he told them. "Unless someone has a reason to stop."

When no one answered, he urged his horse into a canter and led them toward the northeast.

They rode until the sun was just barely peeking over the edge of the horizon and their shadows had grown long and spidery-looking. He suddenly turned his mount onto a nearly concealed trail and led them to a cave that was covered by overgrown vines.

"Follow me," the taciturn dwarf said, dismounting, pushing the foliage aside, and leading his horse inside.

When the others entered, they discovered the cave opened out into a large room. The back of the cavern was walled off as a stable for the horses. The walls were lined with bunks, and there was a fireplace nestled in the corner. Wood was stacked neatly along one wall.

"Clever," Amicu said admiringly as he entered, leading his horse.

"It's a shelter that the dwarves built many, many years ago," Skala informed them. "Dwarven shelters like this are hidden all around the Four Lands."

"I hope we find one every night," Zimpf said, stretching out comfortably on one of the bunks.

Alia agreed; this was the best camping spot she had ever seen.

Everyone pitched in, and soon the horses were bedded, dinner was eaten, and everyone except for Alia and Shao, was asleep. They had first watch and sat quietly by the cave entrance, holding hands and whispering. They were relieved at midnight by Amicu and Ciern.

The next morning, they discussed their route as they ate breakfast. It had been decided that they would continue traveling northeast following a series of valleys leading to the lower peaks. From there, they would be able to descend the northern slope to the base of the Skarsgaard Mountains. The way would lead them into the foothills, which would flatten into a series of plains where they hoped to make contact with the Vheral people.

"We're a pretty diverse group," Ciern said. "Hopefully that will give them reason enough to convene with us."

"And if not?" Shao asked.

"You could always beat them up." Zimpf grinned impishly.

Shao gave him a stern look.

"I have gold coins to entice them," Ciern laughed. "They value gold, so I should be able to get their attention well enough that we'll be able to talk to them." He paused, then continued in a bantering tone. "If that doesn't work, then Shao can beat them up."

"Keep it up," Shao threatened with a sidelong wink at Alia, "and I'll beat up both of you."

"He could, you know," Ciern agreed, looking at Zimpf.

Zimpf nodded glumly.

They packed and left immediately after they had eaten. Unlike the other trips Alia had been on, the road did not gradually dwindle from street to road to trail. This time, they simply turned off a street, rode through a field, and then wound their way up into the foothills of the mountains. Skala and Ciern led the way. Zimpf and Aistra followed. Behind them were Sh'ron and Chhdar, then Alia, Shao, and Amicu rode rearguard. For the first week and a half, the travel was easy, and the weather held fair.

In the early morning hours of the tenth day, they had their first conflict. Alia and Shao were both asleep when, a couple of hours before dawn, they were awakened by Sh'ron's whistle. Immediately, Alia was up, her hand on her sword. As swiftly as she moved toward the tent flap, Shao was quicker. He had already untied the flaps and was stepping outside with a handful of shuriken that he always kept close by. The others also came boiling out of their tents with an array of weapons.

Sh'ron and Chhdar were both standing on either side of the fire with their backs to each other. Alia looked quickly and saw that the entire camp was surrounded by wolves. They were creeping forward with their yellow eyes unblinking and their bellies close to the ground. Alia, holding her sword with the point low and dangerous, quickly stepped beside her twin. She felt Shao move to her right. The rest of the group joined the circle, everyone facing outward and with their backs to the fire.

The wolves drew closer. Finally, one larger than the rest made the first move. He charged into the group, growling horribly with the fur on the back of his neck raised in warning. Ciern loosened an arrow into its chest, and it fell twitching to the ground. Rather than frightening the other wolves away, this seemed to anger them, and several attacked at once. Ciern, Amicu, and Zimpf unleashed a volley of arrows into the pack and brought them down one after another. Shao threw shuriken with unerring accuracy so quickly his hands blurred. No wolf survived his deadly barrage. Aistra stood next to Zimpf with a dart gun in her hands. She was blowing poisoned barbs into the animals' hides with such force that they pierced the thick fur. The animals she hit would pause, shake their heads, and then fall over dead. Skala stood on the very edge of the fray, slicing the heads off the hounds with a wicked-looking battle ax. Alia, Sh'ron, and Chhdar slashed and stabbed and eviscerated any animal that somehow managed to escape the deadly onslaught.

Wolves died in droves. Finally, one by one, the survivors began to slink away into the darkness. Just as it seemed like they could relax their position, one lone wolf managed to evade the volley, tore through their defenses, and attacked Chhdar, hitting the big man so hard that he fell backward toward the fire. But Shao was there, grabbing the warrior by the shirt and pulling him forward with the wolf still clinging on to the man's forearm. Alia and Sh'ron both stabbed the animal, and it fell dead at their feet.

Chhdar screamed, his arm pointed in the wrong direction. Alia saw him pull it up to his chest then take the hilt in his uninjured hand; he held his sword steadily as though his right arm wasn't broken.

But the battle was almost over. Ciern and Amicu fired arrows at the few remaining wolves, who fled into the night. Aistra darted the last two wolves, and then it was over.

Sh'ron ran to her husband, and together, she and Shao helped him to sit on a nearby log.

Alia immediately began barking orders in a crisp, calm voice as she knelt to exam Chhdar's arm. "Amicu, get my medical bag. Aistra, you and Zimpf get the pans and get some water boiling. Shao, I need your knife."

Shao handed her his knife and quietly watched her work.

Gently, she cut the sleeve off Chhdar's shirt so she could examine his broken arm.

"Don't move," she said to him.

"Can you fix it?" Sh'ron asked worriedly.

"Yes," Alia replied shortly as she began pulling items out of her bag.

Aistra handed her a cup of hot water, and Alia mixed up a medical tea, measuring the ingredients carefully.

"Drink this," she told the big man. "It'll take away the pain and make you sleepy so I can set your arm."

Chhdar nodded and then drank the potion down in one long gulp.

"That was vile," he complained, drawing his lips together tightly and shaking his head.

After several moments, he began to drowse and finally laid his head on Sh'ron's shoulder, snoring lightly.

Alia had Shao hold the warrior's arm just below the elbow while she tugged and finally wrenched the bone back into position with a loud popping sound. Then she carefully stitched up the larger cuts, applied a healing salve, and splinted the arm. After that, she had Shao and Amicu carry him to his tent.

Sh'ron turned to go with them then stopped to hug her sister. "Thank you, Alia," she said sincerely as tears filled her eyes. "Thank you." Then she turned to follow her husband into their tent.

By then, it was nearly dawn, so they decided to stir up the fire and wait for the sun to rise.

After the sun had risen, Skala, Ciern, and Amicu left to scout after the wolves and make sure they had left the area.

Sh'ron and Chhdar still slept.

Aistra and Zimpf went to collect more wood and to refill the water bags.

That left Alia and Shao alone by the fire.

"I was watching you care for Chhdar earlier," Shao told her.

Alia leaned tiredly on his shoulder. "You were?" she asked, yawning. "Why?"

Shao smiled down at her and kissed the top of her head. "Because I am amazed by you," he said proudly, wrapping one arm around her shoulders and pulling her close.

"I swear, if you all start smooching again, I'm going to dump this water over your heads to cool you off," Zimpf's voice echoed from across the campsite.

Shao picked up a dirt clod and sent it twisting and turning to hit Zimpf full in the chest, where it exploded, sending pieces of dirt into the diviner's open mouth.

"Ugh! Blech!" he complained, spitting out pieces of mud.

Shao roared with laughter.

Alia chuckled and then looked at Aistra. "Have they always been like this?" She smiled.

Aistra nodded. "You have no idea," she complained ruefully. Then she laughed.

Just then, Ciern, Skala, and Amicu came around the side of the tents.

"How long do you think we'll need to be here?" Ciern asked Alia.

"Maybe a day or so," she answered. "Why?"

"I'm not convinced those wolves are gone for good," he admitted. "I would like to move on from here as soon as Chhdar is capable of traveling."

"I would rather not move him today," Alia stated. "But if you think this site isn't safe, then…" she trailed off.

Ciern, Amicu, and Skala all looked at each other, considering.

"I think we should move," Ciern told her. "Even a few miles would put a buffer between us and the pack."

Alia took a deep breath. "Okay," she agreed reluctantly. "Let's go ahead and strike camp. We can move once Chhdar wakes up."

By noon, they were on the move again. They traveled at a slow, cautious pace, and by that evening, they were several miles away from the attack site.

Chhdar held up well initially, but by the time they stopped, he was pale, and his face was drawn with pain.

As soon as they found their campsite, Alia had Shao and Amicu help the big warrior off his horse and to the base of a large tree, where he could sit with his back supported against the trunk. Without being asked, Shao immediately got Alia her medical bag while Zimpf and Aistra started a fire with which to boil water.

Alia unwrapped Chhdar's arm carefully, leaving the splints in place. She was very concerned about infection setting in from the wolf's bite, but the wound looked good. She reapplied the salve, which served to lessen the pain and prevent infection. Then she mixed Chhdar some tea to help him relax.

"Thank you," he told her sincerely as he sipped the tea.

Alia smiled. "You're going to be good as new," she assured him. "But," she said, looking sternly at the members of the group, "we should camp here for at least another day to give that arm a chance to start mending."

Ciern nodded. "We'll scout around tomorrow. We've reached the apex of our route. It's all downhill from here."

The next day was spent doing a variety of routine tasks. Skala and Ciern left early to scout the trail ahead for any dangers. Alia treated Chhdar again and then Sh'ron took over the care of her husband. Zimpf, Aistra, and Amicu checked the horses' shoes for stones and their coats for burrs or sores. Alia watched them work for a minute, then Shao slid silently up behind her. He was so quiet, she never heard him. It seemed like he would suddenly appear out of nowhere. He gently took her hand and then turned her around.

"Would you like to go foraging with me?" he invited. "It might be nice to be able to expand on the menu tonight. Ciern promised to shoot a couple of rabbits, and I thought a nice rabbit stew would be delicious."

"What if he can't hit any rabbits?" Alia asked curiously.

Shao didn't answer. He just grinned at her with one eyebrow raised.

"Never mind," she laughed, her face tinted with an embarrassed red. She knew how good Ciern was with his bow. "Let's go find some veggies for that stew."

That night was the most relaxing night the group had enjoyed in a while. They had been traveling hard for nearly two weeks and surviving mostly on travel rations. Then there was the frightening wolf attack and Chhdar's injuries. But this was one night where they were able to sit around the campfire and enjoy a hot meal of rabbit stew and bread heated by the fire. It was nice to be warm and well-fed and with friends while telling stories and laughing.

The next morning, Chhdar was feeling better, and the color had come back into his face. After Alia examined him, she declared that they could continue their journey, but only at a slow pace.

Everyone pitched in to strike camp, and they were soon over the lower peaks and were riding slowly through the series of valleys which descended into the northern foothills of the Skarsgaard Mountains.

They rode along what seemed to be an old animal trail until about midday. Then, in the distance, Alia could see that the pathway forked. The main trail angled to the left and downward into a broad valley, but a narrow footpath veered upward and to the right of an enormous oak tree. Standing in the shade of the tree, Alia could see an old man with flowing white hair and a long beard. He watched them curiously but made no movement or sound.

Ciern and Skala rode past the fork and continued following the trail, veering to the left and moving downhill. They took no notice of the old man. Then, Zimpf and Aistra, followed by Sh'ron and Chhdar, passed him without notice.

Alia looked at Shao and Amicu. Amicu's eyes were riveted on the road ahead. Shao was gazing at the old man with a mysterious smile on his face. He glanced at Alia and nodded. He had seen the old man too.

When they reached the tree, Alia and Shao drew in their horses; Amicu continued as though nothing out of the ordinary was happening.

Both Alia and Shao dismounted and bowed before the strange old man.

"Greetings, YeYe," Shao said with respect.

The old man nodded politely. "I came to warn you," he said without preamble. "You and your friends are riding into danger."

"Can you explain the difficulty yet to come?" Shao asked formally.

"You are in grave peril. The Vherals have become dangerous and unpredictable. They are controlled by a malevolent mage who has begun to gain dominion over their civilization."

"We were sent to parley with the western clans. We seek to stop a war," Shao told him. "Is there no hope?"

The old man was quiet for a moment, his eyes lost and far away. Finally, he looked at the two of them. "Seek Sabio Omu Olori."

"Can you tell us where to find him, please?" Alia asked respectfully.

The old man held up his hand. "My time grows short. Find Sabio Omu Olori. Give him this token," he said, handing Alia a clear blue stone slightly larger than a child's shooter marble. "Tell him it will neutralize the evil that descends."

Alia looked up into the brown eyes of the wise old man as she clutched the one object that could destroy her old friend.

"*You should also watch out for a fledgling diviner named Sabio Omu Olori,*" Nabii warned him. "*I don't know how he may become involved in any of this. But I can see his face surrounded by images that haven't coalesced into a readable vision.*"

Marek nodded. "*Thank you. I will find some way to make contact with this young man.*"

Nabii started to leave but then stopped with his back still turned to Marek as the mage called to him.

"*Why are you helping me?*" Marek purred cajolingly.

The old, blind diviner froze, then turned slowly, looking directly at the mage as though he could see. "*That won't work on me,*" he sneered scathingly before walking confidently out of the tent.

It was some time before Marek saw him again.

Chapter 18–First Contact

Alia and Shao both gazed at the stone in her hand, then they looked up at each other.

"Can you tell us whe—" Alia started to ask, then trailed off, her eyes wide in astonishment. The old man had vanished completely. She turned to Shao in surprise.

"We have been blessed beyond measure," he said in awe. "That is our second visit by a Zduhac."

"It's just like the one who aided us with the taotie on the way to Temple," she agreed, then she paused and looked up at Shao. "Unless it was the same one," she mused.

"It could well have been the same one," he agreed. "He did the same things he did last time—he appeared as a human, warned us, and provided magic to aid us."

"Then he disappeared. Just like Sifu explained when we were at the Temple," Alia finished.

They stood for a moment, staring at the clear blue stone the

Zduhac had handed Alia. It looked like a solid piece of the sky.

"I guess our task has changed," Shao stated. "It looks like we're going to go find Sabio Omu Olori. We'd better go tell the others."

They remounted and started to follow their friends down the main trail that angled downward into the valley.

They rounded a curve and saw that the trail descended steeply. Alia hadn't made it to the edge when Shao suddenly yanked her reins from her hands, whipped their mounts around, and cantered silently toward the footpath from which they had just emerged.

Alia found herself suddenly hanging on to her saddle bow with her hands while her legs clutched her stallion's sides as they fled. Her first instinct would have been to scream, but Shao had spent more than a year training her to maintain silence in all situations. So, she clenched her jaws shut and endured the jarring ride.

Shao moved them noiselessly up the trail, onto the footpath, and past the giant oak tree. Several yards in, he located a tangled depression, where he led their lathered mounts.

Alia looked at him in uncertainty, her eyes wide. Shao pressed his index finger to his lips and gestured for her to follow him. They dismounted then ghosted their way through the underbrush on a track parallel to the trail until they reached the top of the hill the others had descended only moments before. Shao peeled back the undergrowth, and Alia peered through the tangle of brush to see what had so alarmed the martial artist.

At the bottom of the descent lay a broad valley. Their friends had reached the bottom and were standing in a tight circle, their weapons tossed casually several feet away in the tall grass. Surrounding them, spears pointing at them dangerously, were perhaps fifty wild-looking men. As they watched, the horses were led away by some of the savages. Alia could see Ciern gesturing as he talked. But the chieftain shook his head and signaled his men. Quickly, several savages stepped forward, tied the hands of Alia and Shao's friends, and led them toward the east. As they began walking, Alia saw Zimpf look back quickly. Then, as though he was only entertaining himself, he began to whistle; it was a lost, mournful sound.

Shao listened intently to that sound, his eyes narrowing dangerously.

Within minutes, the horde rounded the edge of the valley where some trees grew, and were lost to Alia's sight. Even after they were gone, she could still hear the haunting melody of Zimpf's whistled song. She started to speak, but Shao held up his hand and she fell silent.

Finally, the tune faded away, and Shao looked at her. "Let's go get them," he said firmly.

As they walked back to the place where they tied the horses, Alia looked up at her husband. "Why was Zimpf whistling as they led him away?" she asked curiously.

"It was a signal for me."

"I have known the two of you for a while now, and I'm still surprised at how little I know," she complained ruefully.

Shao gave her a tight smile but didn't answer.

"Are they in danger?" Alia wanted to know.

Shao was silent for a minute. "Zimpf didn't think so."

Alia stopped. "What exactly was Zimpf telling you?"

Shao looked at her, puzzled. "I'm still trying to understand the message. It didn't make sense. Either that, or Zimpf didn't get it right," Shao said with a frown.

"Could you have misinterpreted it?" Alia questioned.

"No," Shao answered simply. His eyebrows pulled down into a V in concentration.

"Let's go over it," she suggested. "How exactly was the tune encoded?"

"Each note has a specific meaning," he explained. "In the notes he whistled, he said, 'I'm going home, we are safe, save us,'" Shao looked at Alia. "He repeated it several times. But it doesn't make sense."

Alia was quiet for a minute. Then, very softly, she whistled the same song, mimicking Zimpf's tune exactly—the notes, the tone, the tempo.

Shao looked at her in complete awe. "Wow!" he finally uttered. "Talk about being surprised by someone. How are you able to so perfectly imitate Zimpf's melody?"

"My father taught us music," Alia answered sadly.

It was obvious to Shao that this connection to her father was painful for her. He decided not to pursue the omission of her musical knowledge.

"I wish I had known him," Shao told her instead.

"He would have liked you." Alia smiled.

"Can you whistle that tune again?" he asked.

Alia repeated the performance.

Again, Shao shook his head. "The message is the same; it doesn't make sense. It repeats over and over that they are going home, they're safe, they don't need help. Then it's followed by a desperate cry for rescue."

"Maybe he's *seeing* something," Alia suggested worriedly.

"Perhaps," Shao answered. But he didn't sound convinced. "I think the best thing we can do for now is to follow them at a distance.

Zimpf will be looking for us and will be able to *see* that we're close by. Maybe he can send us another signal that will make more sense."

The two of them retrieved their horses and led them down the trail they had been following. Before they reached the top of the hill, Shao stopped them. They tied the horses to a nearby tree and proceeded the rest of the way on foot, crawling the last few feet to the ridgeline leading down.

Shao studied the field below them so intently, Alia began to think something was wrong. She started to ask if he was okay, but he held up his hand to indicate silence. It was only a few moments later that he nodded his head at the valley. Rising from the tall grass were at least a dozen savages that had lain concealed in the field below. Alia could see them gesturing to each other. Finally, they turned as a group and jogged in the direction the others had gone. Once they were out of sight, Shao rose and helped Alia stand.

"Are you ready for this?" he asked.

Alia looked up at his face, which was etched with worry.

"We can do this," she assured him.

"This could be incredibly dangerous," he warned her. "So, I want—no, I need your promise that you will follow my orders exactly."

Alia was surprised at Shao's intensity.

"I will not risk your life," he stated adamantly. "So, while I would normally never tell you what to do, this time, you must obey me without question."

Alia stepped back, slightly unnerved by his forceful demeanor.

"This is war," he continued, still staring across the valley floor, unaware of Alia's trepidation. "In war, there can only be one leader." He turned to make sure she would acquiesce and was surprised to see that she had backed away, her eyes reflecting her alarm.

Reaching for her, he pulled her close then hugged her tightly. He could feel her tenseness. "You are well trained," he said. "But you must promise to follow my command."

"I was trained by the best," she whispered.

Shao quietly waited.

"I promise to follow your lead," Alia told him seriously.

"Let's go get our friends," Shao commanded.

They rode cautiously down the hill and then made their way into a tree line that bordered the valley floor.

They traveled for hours, fighting their way through the brush and undergrowth. It was almost impenetrable, and they were forced to dismount and literally push their way through the vegetation in places. It was swelteringly hot. The underbrush was so thick, it stifled any chance of a breeze, and they were attacked by swarms of biting insects. It grew late, then shadowy, then dark. And still, they continued. Alia began to stumble with weariness. Finally, Shao stopped, and Alia, overcome with exhaustion, plowed right into the back of him and would have fallen had he not caught her.

Shao held his forefinger to his lips and pointed ahead. The cloudy sky hid any chance of moonlight, and the darkness felt palpable. Alia could clearly see a fire ahead, surrounded by several tents. She could make out figures sitting around the fire, but she couldn't make out the faces.

Again, Shao touched his lips with his forefinger and then, placing his mouth against her ear, he whispered, "You are to wait right here. Do not move from this spot. No matter what happens; no matter what you hear. Remember, you promised me."

The next thing she knew, he was gone. He moved so swiftly

and silently that she couldn't even see him making his way toward the encampment. She suddenly remembered something Ciern had told them when they came in search of Airafae and herself after the ogre abduction: "He could sneak up on a destruction of cats in broad daylight wearing bells around his neck." Alia sat down to wait alone in the dark.

Shao moved step by cautious step toward the tents. He walked on silent cat feet, imitating the breeze that moved the tall grass. He stopped and looked and studied the landscape and the people in the camp. He searched for guards, found them, and avoided them. He placed each foot carefully, sometimes moving only inches at a time. The night wore on, but Shao paid no attention to time. His only focus was on the camp and his friends held within.

As he knew it would happen, once he reached the outer ring of tents, he heard Zimpf's low, cautious whistle. Making absolutely no sound, Shao artfully ghosted his way around the camp, blending in cautiously with the sights and sounds. No one saw him. No one knew that the potential for awful violence moved treacherously between their shelters.

Shao reached the tent where the captives were being held. Soundlessly, he withdrew the evil-looking knife he always carried, inserted it in a seam in the back of the tent, and sawed it open one stitch at a time. One by one, his friends emerged from the opening, each stopping so Shao could cut the ropes tying their hands together. The last to leave was Ciern. Shao pointed at the direction where he had left Alia, and they began to make their slow way out of the encampment. Just as they passed the last tent, a savage came around the corner. Before he could say anything, Shao grabbed the man on either side of his head and, with a quick twist, snapped his neck.

The man fell silently to the ground. Shao took the body with them and deposited it some distance away.

The sky to the east was starting to lighten up ever so slightly when they finally made it back to the horses. "Alia?" Shao whispered anxiously. There was no answer. He looked all around the area his search growing more and more frantic as he failed to locate her. "Zimpf," he hissed, but the diviner's eyes had already gone blank as he tried to *see* where she went. When he looked back up, his eyes met Shao's, he shook his head and then slid quietly behind Ciern

"Shao!" Skala hissed in a low, commanding tone. He could see how alarmed Shao had become, and he remembered how the martial artist had so casually tossed him aside when Alia was missing the last time.

"Look!" The tracker pointed at an almost indiscernible set of Alia's footprints, which moved further into the tree line. "Come with me," he ordered as he followed the young woman's tracks. Shao followed so closely behind him that the tracker could feel the man's breath on his neck.

They went several hundred yards before they encountered her walking casually back to the horses.

Shao, moving like quicksilver, ran to her and hugged her fiercely. Then he released her and stepped back. The expression on his face was one Alia had never seen before. She wasn't sure if he was angry with her or happy to find her. Alia held her forefinger to her lips for silence, then she motioned everyone to stay where they were while she walked back to retrieve the horses. Shao followed her closely.

He didn't say a word while Alia untied their mounts. He didn't say a word while she led everyone deep into the woods, angling to the southwest and upward. He didn't say a word as she reached the edge of a steep cliff wall, towering several hundred feet upward. He didn't say a word as she walked around the perimeter and disappeared into the wall itself; he simply tailed her. As the others got closer, they discovered Alia had pushed aside a profusion of vines and entered a hidden cavern. Inside, they were delighted to find their horses, backpacks, and weapons.

Alia had also started a well-shielded fire in the very back of the cave and had a stew bubbling merrily over the flames.

Nervously, she turned to face Shao, who looked at her sternly. "You promised to obey me without question," he said hard-heartedly.

Alia looked up, stricken at his harsh demeanor.

"Please, Shao," she said, looking at the ground while taking his sleeve in her hand and twisting it gently. "Please forgive me. I was told to do this."

"By whom?" Shao said, frowning down at her and tapping his foot impatiently.

"The Zduhac."

Marek had sent his servants away and sat quietly, alone in his tent. Between his hands, he held the vase-like container known as the Aghara. The mage had closed his eyes and was focusing all of the magic he held within on the vessel, which had begun to glow an eerie green.

Chapter 19–A New Plan

"The Zduhac?" Shao asked incredulously.

"He came to me about an hour after you left," Alia explained. "I was sitting on the ground trying to watch you make your way toward the camp. I happened to look over at the horses, and he was standing there gazing at me. I walked over to him and bowed."

Looking up at Shao, she continued. "It was the same being we saw earlier. He bade me to follow him, and that's when he showed me this cave. He promised that if we hid here, the Vherals would be unable to find us, that we would be safe."

Alia scanned the group and then carried on with her story. "Then he told me I had to steal the horses back from your captors. He promised it would be safe because he would protect me." Alia looked over at Shao. "I trusted him. We walked to where the horses were picketed on the edge of their camp, untied them, collected the weapons and backpacks, and then simply returned here. No one saw us."

"Once we were inside, he started a fire. He's the one who provided the food. The Zduhac was walking me back to meet you when he said, 'You no longer need my protection; they have returned.' I turned to answer him, but he had disappeared."

"Well, you can't fault her for that," Ciern said.

"If a Zduhac appeared to me, I would do whatever he said," Amicu admitted.

"Me too," Zimpf chimed in, "even if it did make you mad. And I remember making you mad one time…" he trailed off as Shao turned to look at him sternly. "It was really scary," he said earnestly to Aistra.

"I would like to speak with you outside," Shao said to Alia. Then he turned and led the way through the vines covering the cavern entrance.

Alia followed slowly. Like a scolded puppy, she walked with her head down and her footsteps dragging.

As she left the cave, she heard Zimpf whisper loudly, "Do you think we should follow? I would hate to see what would happen if he got *really* mad."

Outside, Alia saw that Shao had walked several feet away and was standing with his back to her. He was staring at the sky.

"Shao?" she said nervously. She was nearly in tears, because in all the time she had known him, they had never fought. Not once. At no time had he ever been angry with her.

"Will you sit?" He indicated a nearby boulder.

Alia sat down uneasily. Her hands had gone ice cold, and she kept twisting them in her lap.

Shao, refusing to look at her, finally walked over and sat down, his head bowed.

"Alia," he whispered in a voice so soft that she had to lean her head near his face to hear. "Alia." This time he choked on her name.

Alia turned her head slightly and was startled to see his eyes were filled with tears that had begun to spill over and run down his cheeks. She turned toward him, cupping his face with her hands and using her thumbs to wipe them away.

He reached up and covered her cold hands with his warm hands.

"I'm an idiot," he said, still not looking directly at her. "I am so sorr—" he started.

But Alia interrupted him. "You couldn't possibly have known what happened while you were gone," she comforted him. "And I did break my promise to you."

"I should have asked what happened before reacting," Shao admitted.

"Except that before you could ask, I signaled for silence," Alia reminded him. Then she plowed on. "It was a simple misunderstanding," she insisted, leaning her forehead onto his.

"You forgive me too easily," he protested.

"Do you want me to be angry with you?" she teased in confusion, pulling away and looking at him. "Or would you rather be angry with me?"

Shao finally looked up at her. "I never want us to be angry with each other. I couldn't bear it."

"I never want us to be angry with each other," Alia echoed, laying her head on Shao's shoulder and taking his hands in hers. "Shao," she said softly. "I love you."

He didn't answer. Alia looked up to see him staring at her, his heart in his eyes. "You are my world," he said simply.

They sat quietly then, holding hands.

After several minutes, Sh'ron called from the cave mouth, "breakfast is ready."

They stood to walk back to the cavern, but before they got there, Alia paused.

"Shao," she said, grabbing his arm to stop him. "We have a visitor."

"Who?" He froze, immediately moving in front of Alia and assuming a defensive stance.

"Look," Alia answered. She bowed respectfully.

Shao stepped back to look at her in confusion, his eyebrows drawn together. He had been trained by the best and had become the best. His powers of observation were unequaled. Yet, he still didn't see anything.

He glanced at Alia. She was staring to her right. Shao followed her gaze.

There, in front of the boulder they had just left, was a filmy, fog-like vapor that coalesced into the image of a man. The semblance was vague and nearly transparent.

Taking her hand, Shao led Alia to stand in front of the apparition. Then he too bowed. "How may we serve you, YeYe?" he asked politely.

"I have come to bind you together," the Zduhac answered. "Will you accept my offer?"

"You…" Shao hesitated. "You want to…" He trailed off, not really understanding what the old man was proposing.

But Alia immediately understood the old man's unusual request.

"You want us to make a vow to each other?"

The Zduhac nodded his head.

"With you presiding?"

"Yes," he continued. "I want to bless your union."

Alia and Shao looked at each other in surprise. It was an unusual request.

"This is important," the Zduhac told them solemnly.

Shao nodded.

Turning to face Alia, Shao took her hands in his, the same way he did when they made their marriage vows.

"Alia," he said in his soft voice. "You are my world, and I love you more than life itself. I vow to you today before the Zduhac and before all the stars of the heavens to listen to you and learn from you. I vow to discuss our problems calmly and rationally and to resolve our issues peacefully. I vow to respect and honor you and to grow with you in mind and spirit. I vow to always love you."

Alia, touched to the heart, repeated the vows, her voice shaking with emotion.

Once she had finished, the Zduhac laid his ethereal hand on the top of their hands. "Love and be at peace, one with the other," he whispered. "Thus, are you united with a bond that cannot be broken." Then, with a gentle smile, he quietly faded away.

Shao pulled Alia toward him and kissed her seriously. They stayed locked together for several moments. Finally, Shao pulled away. "I wish we could be alone," he whispered gently. "I feel like I did when we exchanged vows on our wedding night."

Alia looked up at him through her thick lashes, a blush staining her cheeks. "Somehow I think tonight may have been even more profound," she murmured. Then she leaned up to kiss her husband again.

"There they go again!" Zimpf's mocking voice came from the cave entrance. "If I had known that a little bit of smooching would calm Shao down that well, I might have tried it myself."

"I'm going to smooch you, all right," Shao growled at him. "I'm going to smooch Mama's wooden spoon with your bottom." Then he jumped at Zimpf.

Zimpf made a high-pitched squeaking sound and scurried back inside.

Laughing, Alia and Shao went to join the others.

Inside, everyone was sitting around the fire, and Sh'ron was dishing out the stew. She glanced up at Alia questioningly. Alia, holding Shao's hand, smiled and nodded. Sh'ron winked in return. The others ignored the couple as they began eating—everyone, that is, except for Aistra. She was staring at both Shao and Alia with a look of profound respect. When Alia looked back at her, Aistra mothed the word, "Zduhac?" then moved her index finger back and forth between Alia and Shao. Alia nodded. Then, so imperceptibly that no one else saw, she bowed slightly in reverence.

After they had eaten, Alia asked for everyone's attention. "The Zduhac asked me to tell everyone that we are not to step foot outside this cavern until tomorrow morning. He has put an enchantment on it so that the Vherals cannot locate us. The spell will last from sunup to sunup. He said that by tomorrow morning, this band of Vherals will have moved far to the east."

"Looks like we'll be staying here then," Ciern said. Then he looked at Alia. "Do you think we need to set a watch?"

"No," she answered. "The Zduhac was insistent that we would be absolutely safe here."

"I don't know about you all, but I could use some sleep," Amicu told them. "It was a long day marching yesterday and an even longer night waiting for Shao."

"I agree," Zimpf complained. "It took Shao forever to rescue us. I mean, we were in terrible danger, and he was just lollygagging behind us, taking his own sweet time." He looked at Shao. "I'm bitterly disappointed in you, my old friend," he said, shaking his head sadly.

Shao looked up. "Then why did you signal me that you were going home and that you were safe? Actually, your message didn't really make any sense at all."

"You didn't translate it right," Zimpf accused him. "I clearly signaled that we were going to their camp, that we were in terrible danger, and that we needed you to rescue us immediately. You need to go back to Temple and learn your lessons properly."

"Alia?" Shao looked at her while tilting his head toward Zimpf.

She smiled, then whistled the exact same tune that Zimpf had whistled earlier. Almost as soon as she started, Sh'ron joined her, humming the piece note for note.

Chhdar looked at Sh'ron in surprise.

"Our father taught us music," Sh'ron stated quietly.

Amicu looked over at Ciern. "I told you he did it wrong."

Ciern glared at Zimpf. "You are no longer allowed to send rescue messages," he stated, pointing an angry finger at the diviner. Then, he glanced quickly at Shao and winked, before looking back at the diviner. "And why didn't you *see* to warn us about the attack?"

"You know that I can't *see* the future unless it's set," he protested.

"Sure," Ciern said flatly.

Everyone laughed.

"Well, if you're going to be *that* way about it," Zimpf objected, standing up.

Zimpf was clearly upset. He didn't like for anyone to question his talent, not even jokingly. But Aistra pulled him back down to sit beside her. Then she placed her hands on either side of his face and began speaking in a low tone. Finally, he began to laugh sheepishly.

"It was a very long night for everyone," Shao said as he stretched and yawned. "Why don't we get a few hours' rest? Then we can discuss what to do next."

They bedded down and were soon sound asleep.

It was the middle of the afternoon before they began to awaken. Skala was the first to rise. He quietly started a fire and had a good campfire going by the time the others started to stir. Alia and Shao got out the provisions and started cooking a meal. While they worked, Sh'ron, Chhdar, and Amicu checked the horses. Zimpf, Aistra, and Ciern checked their gear.

Then they gathered around the fire to eat.

Alia and Shao told them about their first encounter with the Zduhac and Alia showed them the round, blue stone.

"Clearly that changes our mission," Shao said seriously.

"So how are we supposed to go about finding this man, Sabio Omu Olori?" Chhdar asked. "If the rest of the Vherals are as friendly as the first group, we're in trouble."

Sh'ron nodded her head in agreement.

"Ciern, when you were talking to the leader, were you able to learn anything useful?" Amicu asked.

He nodded. "This particular tribe was very excited about the 'big chief' to the west. They were planning on turning us over to him. I can only assume they were talking about Marek."

"Were they looking for us?" Amicu asked.

"I'm not sure," Ciern answered.

"If the tribes in the area are looking for us, we're going to have to be extra careful," Amicu told them.

Everyone nodded.

"Alia?" Sh'ron asked. "When you were with the Zduhac, did he give you any hints about where to find Sabio Omu Olori?"

"Not really. I asked, but he just said that we needed to go west."

"You two are the great tactician and the mighty strategist," Zimpf bantered. "What do you recommend?"

"First," Ciern told them, "I think we need to change our traveling order. I don't want to risk getting captured by unfriendly natives again. Shao, you will lead the group. Keep your eyes and ears open." Shao nodded. "Zimpf, you and Aistra will ride with him. You will keep your minds open." Then he turned to Skala. "You will be next in line. I want you to look for any signs of previous travelers." Skala nodded. "Sh'ron and Chhdar, you will ride with Skala in case we need your swordsmanship. Amicu, Alia, and I will take rearguard." Alia started to nod in acquiescence, but Shao was already shaking his head.

"No," he said firmly to Ciern. "I want Alia to ride with me."

"Shao," Ciern said in a commanding tone, his eyebrows pulling downward into a frown. "I gave my orders."

"No," Shao disagreed. "Alia will ride beside me."

"I said—" Ciern started again.

But Shao was already shaking his head. "I will not be separated from her," the martial artist said adamantly.

"I am your commander," Ciern said in an authoritative voice. "You will obey me without question."

"No," Shao said, in a dangerously low tone. "I won't. Not this time."

The two men were staring angrily at each other across the fire, neither willing to back down from the confrontation.

"Ciern? Shao?" Aistra called the two men in a quiet voice. "Look at me," she whispered.

Alia glanced at her and then looked quickly at Zimpf. He winked at her conspiratorially.

Both Ciern and Shao turned to gaze at Aistra. She didn't say anything more. She merely stared first at the man and then at the elf.

Alia could literally feel the tension being pulled out of the atmosphere. This was clearly one of the talents Aistra possessed. Alia had a funny feeling that Shao didn't really need to rescue the group. Somehow, she thought that Aistra could have talked them out of their captivity. She saw Zimpf look at her and nod.

"I'm sorry," Ciern suddenly apologized to Shao. "Of course, you're right. Alia and Skala will follow behind you, then Sh'ron and Chhdar will come next. Amicu and I will take rearguard."

"Thank you," Shao said in his soft voice.

After some discussion, the group decided to continue traveling west and attempt to make cautious contact only with small groups of Vherals while they searched for Sabio Omu Olori.

Because they decided not to leave until midmorning, they stayed up late that night talking and laughing.

Alia smiled inwardly at the sudden alteration in the group's mood and the reason for it. Occasionally, she glanced over at Aistra, impressed by the young woman's talent.

Later, as she slept, Alia was having the most wonderful dream. It was the night of their wedding, and she and Shao were in the living room of their house in town. Shao had pushed all the furniture against the wall, and they were slow dancing. She could feel his arms around her, along with the long, slow kisses as they moved with music playing softly in the background. The light was faded, subdued, like the sun just before it sets. It was a single, perfect moment in time.

There was a sudden peal of thunder, and the light faded to dark. Alia found herself alone. She turned. A figure wearing a dark cloak stood outside the window. The hood was pulled down low to hide its features. From Alia's viewpoint, the apparition looked faceless, and she stepped backward in horror, her hand rising involuntarily to cover her mouth. The specter reached up with a long-fingered hand to push the hood back, and that is when Alia jerked out of her slumber, a scream of terror caught in her throat.

For a moment, she was disoriented, confused, lost.

"Alia?" Shao asked, reaching out to comfort her. "Are you okay?"

"Shao!" she gasped.

"What happened? Do you want to talk about it?" he invited.

"It was just a dream," she muttered in a voice already heavy with sleep.

Shao pulled her close, wrapping his arms around her while she nestled her head against his shoulder.

The next morning, she had forgotten all about the dream and the phantom who had invaded it.

Marek grinned the crooked smile that everyone seemed to find so charming. And, at the same time, the Aghara had begun bathing his face with its eerie green glow, making him look foreign, alien, otherworldly, turning his grin into a rictus of evil.

He had succeeded in unlocking the secrets of breaking into another person's dreams and inserting an illusion of his own. This was completely different from what he had done to Medjii in order to save his life. That time, he had managed, through a series of lucky tries, to send a quick message. This time, he had interrupted a dream to modify it, weaving his own indistinguishable visions in with hers. He knew that in order to be successful, he needed only to continue adding to his nefarious message.

Alia would come to him willingly, happily, eagerly.

Chapter 20–Going West

The next morning after sunrise, Shao quietly stole out to scout around their camp. He returned a few minutes later and slid into the cave, as quiet as a cat.

"There are tracks all around the area," he reported. "But they didn't come anywhere near this cave. The Vherals are nowhere to be found."

While the others packed up their belongings and saddled the horses, Shao went back out with Skala to follow the tracks. They returned just as Alia finished cooking breakfast. Everyone sat down to eat while Skala described what they had found.

"It's the strangest thing I have ever seen," he told them with a puzzled look. "Our tracks are completely gone. There is no evidence that we were ever in the area. It looks like the Vherals searched everywhere for us, found no signs anywhere, then moved on to the east. Their tracks are at least a day old."

"So, you think we're safe to continue traveling?" Amicu questioned intently.

Skala nodded. "This part of the forest is completely empty of our Vheral pursuers."

"Let's go," Ciern announced, standing up as soon as everyone had finished eating.

Alia was the last to leave the cave. She looked back just as she reached the curtain of vines covering the cave's mouth. Standing in front of the cold fire pit was the Zduhac. The old man held one finger in front of his pursed lips, then he pointed to the west. Alia nodded, mouthed "thank you," and bowed politely.

When she stepped outside, the others had already mounted and had turned their horses to the northwest, heading in the same direction they had come in the early morning hours the day before.

"Where are you all going?" Alia asked. "The Zduhac told us to travel due west."

"We will," Ciern told her. "We're going back to the valley where traveling will be easier, and then we'll turn west from there."

"No," Alia insisted. "The Zduhac said that we are to travel west from here."

"It's going to take an awfully long time if we have to fight our way through all that vegetation," Amicu countered, frowning.

The others exchanged quick glances as Alia mounted her horse and turned it directly toward the west.

"I think…" Zimpf said thoughtfully as he looked toward the cave, then his eyes widened suddenly, and he nodded.

"Ciern, Amicu," he commanded, turning his horse to follow Alia. "We are going this way." Then, without waiting for a response, he rode away from them.

The others had no choice but to follow.

Alia had learned long ago that, although they liked to aggravate Zimpf and he could sometimes be a bit unpredictable with his light-hearted teasing, no one would cross him when he took command. They had too much respect for his talent.

So, they rode through the weeds and briars down a hill toward the west, and then they struggled back up a gentle rise. Before they reached the top, Shao signaled for them to stop. He and Zimpf slid easily off their horses and crept to the apex, where they lay quietly studying the terrain ahead. After several minutes, the two men stood up and walked back to their horses.

"You all have to see this," Shao told them, his eyes wide in wonder as he mounted his horse and led the way up the hill.

They rode to the top, and there in the next valley was a road running directly west. It was old and slightly overgrown, but it was straight and clear of obstacles.

"Wow!" Chhdar exclaimed. "I wonder who built this?"

No one answered because no one knew.

"This will make things easier," Sh'ron remarked as she studied the unexpected trail.

They still had to struggle through the brush and brambles to make their way to the valley floor, but once there, they were pleased to see that the trail was smooth.

Alia had expected to find that such an old road would be crumbling, full of holes, and difficult for the horses to traverse. But this pathway was as smooth and solid as any town street.

They were able to pick up the pace, although Shao, Zimpf, and Aistra continued to survey the land ahead as they approached the top of each hill.

At the end of the first day, they found a clearing at the side of the road, which seemed to have been made for camping. While Shao, Zimpf, Aistra, and Skala surveyed the area for Vherals, Sh'ron and Chhdar picketed the horses, Amicu and Ciern set up the tents, and Alia started a fire. Just as she was starting to heat up some water, the scouts returned. Shao brought some vegetables he had foraged, and Zimpf carried two fat rabbits. So that night, they had a nice, hot meal.

As they ate, Shao reported that he could find no trace of people, Skala found no tracks, Aistra couldn't *sense* anybody, and Zimpf couldn't *see* any danger.

"There is no one here," Zimpf said sincerely. "Nothing but peace and serenity. It feels like this part of the forest has been blessed."

"I have never felt such a sense of tranquility," Aistra agreed.

Alia could feel it too. She looked at Shao, and he nodded his agreement.

"I too feel harmony among all things here," Ciern admitted. "Still, we must be vigilant."

So, when the others went to their tents, Alia and Shao stayed up for the first two hours of guard duty. The couple did a perimeter check and then settled in front of the fire. It was the first time they had been alone since making their vows in front of the Zduhac.

"You know," Shao told her, "I realize this will sound irrational, but I feel even more connected to you since the Zduhac bound us. It's almost like I can sense what you are feeling and where you are."

Alia looked at him in astonishment. "I feel the same way," she admitted. "I have a much stronger perception of you."

They stared at each other for a moment in awe. Then Shao wrapped his arm around her, and they sat quietly together until Amicu and Ciern took their turn at watch.

That night, Alia had another dream. She was tending to a patient, and Shao was helping her. The patient was on his stomach and was badly burned. They turned him over gently so Alia could assess him. As she was looking at his wounds, he suddenly grabbed her wrist and hissed, "You left me to die!" Alia screamed and tried to pull away, but she was trapped. She turned to Shao for help, but a faceless stranger had taken his place.

The next morning, Alia had no memory of the nightmare.

It was another four days before they emerged from the forest and made contact with a second group of Vherals.

This group was a small band of only nine adults and several children.

Shao saw the Vherals well before the others caught up to him. By then, Zimpf and Aistra had already assessed the small group and declared them to be peaceful. After a quick consultation, it was decided that Amicu, Ciern, and Skala would approach them as emissaries of the peoples of the Four Lands. If all went well, they would signal the others to join them.

"If all goes well?" Zimpf complained as soon as the emissaries left. "Like I didn't just tell him that we would all be welcome."

Aistra smiled at her husband.

Within a quarter of an hour, they heard Ciern's whistled signal.

"Told you so," Zimpf snapped spitefully.

The group emerged slowly, leading their horses and holding their right hands up, palms facing the Vherals in a gesture of peace, as Ciern had instructed them.

This family group was very welcoming. They invited everyone into their camp and offered to share their food. As dinner was being prepared, Ciern spoke with their leader while the others listened quietly.

"I am Ciern, son of Elator Kristoris, King of the Elven Nation," he introduced himself. Then he introduced each member of his group. "We come as emissaries of the people south of the mountain. We have heard some disturbing rumors of war, and we came to investigate and perhaps offer our aid," he said formally.

"I am Ghan," said their leader. "We are honored to have emissaries from the peoples who live south of the mountain come to visit us." Then he introduced the adult members of his tribe. He was the eldest of the three brothers who led the group. The other adults were their three wives, two grown nephews, and the eldest nephew's wife.

"We too have heard troubling news from the east concerning war. That is why we are traveling west."

He and Ciern continued discussing what caused the threat of war and what could be done to stop it. The group sat silently and listened politely. It was clear that Ciern was a master at negotiations. His questions were subtle and designed to glean information from the tribe's leader. His offer of help was restrained and vague and served to learn more about the Vherals' combat techniques. His proposal of friendship was genuine but couched in vague generalities.

Just as the two leaders concluded their business by shaking hands, dinner was served. They were given roasted deer, potatoes, and bread. The deer was lightly seasoned, tender, and delicious. The children joined the adults for the meal, and it was obvious how treasured they were. All in all, this group of Vherals seemed to be a happy, close-knit family.

After dinner, the children ran off to play. Alia watched in concern as they wandered over to a huge tree that she couldn't identify and climbed onto its broad branches. Some of the more adventurous children were climbing to the very top. Alia looked around at the adults, but no one seemed worried. She turned her attention back to Ciern and Ghan as they began discussing how best to locate other bands of Vherals.

Without warning, there was a horrifying scream coming from the children. Alia looked over in sudden terror as she saw one of the smaller children plummet to the earth from the tallest branch of the tree. Without thinking, she ran to the child with the adult members of the Vheral community following behind her. Shao immediately grabbed her medical bag and ran, his long legs easily outpacing everyone.

Alia reached the child and fell to her knees. Gently, she turned the young boy over. His mother, who was right behind the healer, screamed in grief and horror. It was clear that the child was dead.

But Alia wouldn't give up. She ordered for the mother to be restrained from snatching the child up into her arms. So decisive was she that the father obeyed her commands immediately. Alia laid the child flat out on the ground and examined him in a professional manner. Then, using the heel of her hand, she began pressing down in a rhythmic pattern on the child's chest, intermittently stopping to blow air into his mouth. She stopped occasionally to listen to his heart. After several minutes, the child gasped and coughed as his lips slowly faded from a pale purple to a healthy pink.

The boy's parents dropped to the ground beside their son, crying in relief and thanking her profusely. Alia then checked the child over again. She discovered that he had several broken ribs, which she bound tightly to stabilize them. He also had dislocated his shoulder. Alia had Shao hold the unconscious little boy while she popped the shoulder back into its socket. Then she tied the child's arm against his chest to brace it. Finally, she had someone bring her a blanket; she gently rolled the boy onto it and had him carried back to the campsite.

Once the child had been placed in his own tent with his mother hovering anxiously over him, Alia took her bag from Shao and mixed up several herbs. Sh'ron had already heated water over the fire and handed Alia a cup of hot water for tea. She carried it into the tent and gave instructions to the mother.

When she finally rejoined the others at the campfire, all the Vheral children as well as adults stood up and bowed in respect.

Alia looked down in embarrassment.

Everyone sat down; Ghan looked at Alia in awe.

"That was truly a miracle," he told her. "I have never witnessed someone being brought back to life."

"I was—" Alia started, but Ciern shushed her with a look and a shake of his head.

"We would like to thank you by giving you this," he continued, handing her a funny-shaped rock that had the impression of a fish embedded on its surface. "This is a token which is very rare and highly valued. It proclaims you as a friend to all the peoples of this land. As long as you and your group carry this, you cannot be harmed."

Alia looked up at Ghan in surprise, touched by the value of the gift.

"Thank you," she said simply. "Thank you."

"Is there anything else we can do for you?" he asked.

Alia looked at Ciern for advice, and he nodded.

"As a part of our emissary duties," Alia stated politely, "we were instructed to find Sabio Omu Olori. Do you know of him or where we might find him?"

Ghan looked at her in surprise. "The young man is rumored to have the potential to be the greatest holy man that has ever lived. Others say that he cannot be found but that he will appear to those in need. My advice is for you to continue traveling west. Tell all families you meet that you are in search of him. Perhaps he will come to you."

Everyone went to bed shortly after that. Everyone except for Alia. She was up and down at least a dozen times during the night to check on her young patient. The next morning, he was sitting up watching Alia with a bashful smile on his young face. By that afternoon, she had befriended him enough that he shyly climbed into her lap so she could examine him. Afterward, he wrapped his little arm around her neck, laid his head on her shoulder, and promptly fell asleep.

The group stayed one more day until Alia was sure that the child was past any danger. On the final evening of their visit, the Vherals prepared a feast and played music. Alia noticed that the two adult nephews were missing.

"I have sent my nephews as runners to the other Vherals in this area to be on the lookout for you. They will render you any aid you may need," Ghan told them. Then he provided them with food for their journey.

In return, Ciern gave each of the brothers a gold coin.

That night, Alia had another dream about the strange hooded figure. She jerked out of sleep in terror, and again Shao was there to comfort her. Once more, she had no memory of the dream when she awoke.

They left early the next morning, following their shadows as the sun rose behind them.

The first day, they only traveled until noon before encountering another family of Vherals. This was a much larger family group; Alia would guess it consisted of as many as sixty or seventy people. Shao saw the warriors first. As soon as the Vherals saw them, they dismounted and walked forward with their right hands held upward. Aistra immediately proclaimed their peaceful intent, and Zimpf announced that he could *see* no problems.

The group accompanied the Vherals to their camp. Apparently Ghan had spread the word about Alia's talent as a healer, because as soon as they arrived, she was inundated with requests for help. She set up a triage area and, together with Shao, Sh'ron, Aistra, and Zimpf, she began treating the sick and injured. Ciern, Amicu, and Skala spent their time conferencing with the leaders. Chhdar befriended the warriors, even going out on a hunt with them.

The next two weeks turned into a whirlwind of activity as their reputation spread. They were stopped sometimes two or three times a day to help, to confer, and to advise. Every leader of every family they met promised to support the effort to stop Marek's war.

And every place they stopped, they asked about Sabio Omu Olori.

Finally, at the beginning of the third week, they traveled almost half a day without being stopped. They had just passed through a copse of tall oak trees that ended in an almost park-like setting. As usual, Shao, Zimpf, and Aistra led the way, scouting for Vherals. Before they emerged from the tree line, Shao returned from scouting and reported seeing no one in the area.

As soon as they all had entered the clearing, however, a young man was suddenly standing in the center of their path. He was only a teenager and had the stereotypical dark hair, skin, and eyes of the Vherals. The horses whinnied at the appearance of the man and then refused to walk toward the stranger.

"I have been told you are looking for me," he said. "I am Sabio Omu Olori, and I have a message for you from the mage, Marek."

Marek continued the dream revisions he had discovered. He plagued Alia every evening with nightmare after nightmare. He planned to gradually alter himself from the terror she experienced each night into a kind, compassionate, benevolent power who had come to aid her. At the same time, he would implant the idea that her nightly terrors were caused by evil enemies who had stolen her away from her true friend.

Meanwhile, he sent message after message to the boy diviner, Sabio Omu Olori, as a ruse to his true intentions.

The young diviner swallowed his lies as truth.

Chapter 21–Dreams

They exchanged surprised glances. Shao was the first to dismount; Alia was the second. The others followed their example, climbing down from their horses and walking slowly toward the stranger with their hands up and palms held outward in the Vherals' gesture of peace.

Alia saw Shao glance back at Zimpf, who was staring wide-eyed at the man.

Then she and Shao stopped several feet in front of Sabio Omu Olori and bowed politely.

"I am—" Shao started, but the strange man stopped him.

"I know who you are. I know who you all are," he said sharply, looking around at the group. Then he continued. "Follow me to my shelter, and there we will talk." Then he abruptly turned his back on them and walked further into the woods, clearly expecting them to follow.

Alia looked at Zimpf then suddenly realized that everyone else was also looking at him for instruction.

Zimpf was frowning in concentration.

"Stop that, stranger!" Sabio Omu Olori barked angrily.

Zimpf reeled back as though he had been slapped. He turned to look at Aistra, who grinned in confirmation and then nodded.

They all followed the young man to his solitary camp. In front of his tent, there were three logs arranged in a U shape. In the middle of the logs was a campfire, and at the hollow of the U was a lone stump. Sabio Omu Olori sat on the stump and gestured for the rest of them to be seated on the logs.

"I know why you are looking for me," he announced without preamble.

"I am Ciern of the Elven Nation," the elven prince began. "We come as emissaries—"

"Save it, elf," Sabio Omu Olori rudely interrupted Ciern's rehearsed speech. "I know you are here to stop the mage, Marek."

Then he looked over at Zimpf. "Will you stop doing that?" he demanded.

"I'm sorry," Zimpf apologized. "Can I just *see* you?" Zimpf practically begged, holding his index finger aloft.

"Fine," Sabio relented. "I will let you *see* if it will stop you from poking into my brain."

Zimpf practically ran toward Sabio Omu Olori. Skidding to an excited stop before the young man, he laid his right hand gently on the man's forehead and stood silently, frowning. Then he placed his palm over the man's temple. Finally, closing his eyes in concentration, Zimpf placed both hands on either side of the strange young man's head.

After several moments, Zimpf let his hands fall while his head bowed down in weariness. "I have never encountered anything like it," he whispered in awe. Looking over at Aistra, he continued. "There is so much untrained talent, so much untapped power."

Zimpf looked back at the young man, who was staring at him. "How did you do that?" he whispered, looking at Zimpf in astonishment.

"Sabio." He hesitated. "May we call you Sabio?"

Sabio Omu Olori nodded.

"Did someone teach you how to use your gift?" Zimpf asked.

"I could always do some things without trying," he answered. "But I have never met anyone who could do what I can do. At least, not until now."

"You need training," Zimpf told him. "I know where you can receive instruction, and I am willing to take you there, if you will consent."

At first, Sabio shook his head, but Zimpf continued talking to the young man. "I can start training you myself," he offered. "I can show you how to do what I just did."

Sabio looked at Zimpf gratefully. "You can? Really?"

"Absolutely!" Zimpf smiled excitedly at him. "My wife here"—he nodded at Aistra—"is also talented. She can help teach you too."

Sabio seemed to have lost most of the belligerence with which he had greeted them. He smiled at Zimpf. "There really are places that can help me learn how to use this…?"

"Talent," Zimpf supplied. "Yes, when we are finished with our mission, I would like to take you to such a school."

Sabio's face fell. "It's a school? I heard that schools cost money, and I don't have any money."

Zimpf looked at Aistra, who nodded. "That's okay. My wife and I will help."

Shao and Alia looked at each other and nodded. "As will we," Shao said to the young man.

"Us too," Chhdar and Sh'ron said together.

"As will I," Ciern offered.

"And I," both Amicu and Skala spoke at the same time.

Sabio looked around at his new friends in wonder. "Thank you," he said in a shaky voice. "Thank you. I would like to learn more. How can I ever repay you?"

"Can you answer some questions for us?" Ciern asked.

"I have a question that needs answering first," Zimpf said, looking at Sabio.

"You have a block. Who put it there? I can sense that you didn't do it yourself."

"I have a friend who helps me sometimes," Sabio admitted. "He's an old man who lives in the mountains. When I need help, I go to him."

Everyone looked around at each other.

"The Zduhac," Alia whispered.

"The what?" Sabio asked.

"It's not an old man who has been helping you," Zimpf explained. "It's a Zduhac—a mountain spirit."

By then, Alia had retrieved the blue, marble-like stone the Zduhac had given her.

"Here," she told him, handing the stone to the young man. "The Zduhac gave me this and told me to find you and give it to you."

"What is this?" he asked in confusion, studying the stone.

"We don't have any idea," Shao answered. "We were hoping you would know."

Sabio examined the blue stone carefully. "There is something…

familiar about this," he mused. Then he looked at Zimpf. "Let me sleep on it tonight," he said. "Sometimes the old man comes to me in my dreams and tells me what to do."

Zimpf nodded. "I'm sure he'll explain it to you," he assured the young man.

"You said that you have a message for us from Marek," Shao said politely. "Can you explain how he contacted you and what he had to say?"

Sabio nodded. "He visits me in my dreams," he said. Then he turned to Zimpf. "That's why my friend put in a…what did you call it?"

"A block," Zimpf supplied.

"A block," Sabio continued. "Actually, he didn't do it for me, but he helped me, in here," he said, tapping his head. "Since then, I haven't had any more dreams." Then he looked directly at Alia. "That mage is evil; he frightens me."

"Can you tell us what he said?" Alia asked gently.

Sabio nodded. "His message is directed to you, Alia." Sabio caught his breath and then continued. "The words offer friendship and help, but the real message is veiled in evil." The young man paused for a moment then looked back at her, his face reflecting his fear. "He doesn't think I *see*, but I do. My friend, the old man—the one you called the Zduhac—showed me how to *see* into his mind. You must avoid him, Alia. Because if you go to him, he plans on binding you so tightly to him that you will never be able to escape."

He continued staring at her, his face a mask of terror. "The future he plans for you is one of utter horror and enslavement. And it's all the worse, because he plans to rip the will to escape from you."

Alia gasped, her face draining of all color. Shao wrapped one arm around her reassuringly.

"He will have to get through me first," Shao whispered with an iron-hard determination.

"Is it true?" Sabio appealed to Zimpf. "Can the mage really do something like that to someone?"

Zimpf looked at Aistra.

She nodded. "He has the Aghara. As long as he possesses it, then yes, I think it could be possible."

"Even with the shield Zimpf put into Alia's mind?" Shao asked intensely.

Aistra and Zimpf looked at each other. "We don't know, because we don't understand the full power of the Aghara," Aistra admitted.

"The shield will provide protection," Zimpf added. "Marek would have to find a way around it to gain that kind of power over her."

"Sabio," Shao addressed the young man. "You said Marek had been invading your dreams. Can you tell me what he looks like?"

"He wears a long cloak with a hood pulled down low. I have never seen his face," Sabio replied.

"Zimpf," Shao asked with a quick tilt of his head at Alia, which she didn't see. "Is it possible for Marek to invade someone's dreams even with both a block and a shield?"

Zimpf frowned in concentration, thinking over the question. "It's possible," he conceded. "But it would be extremely difficult."

"The mages, at one time, experimented with sending messages to each other through dreams," Aistra offered. "The technique is difficult and often unreliable, so most mages don't attempt it. I believe that the practice has largely fallen into disuse."

"I think—" Shao started, then stopped to consider what he was going to say. Finally, he took Alia's hand and looked at her. "I think he may be invading your dreams."

"He hasn't been in my dreams," Alia protested. "I'm pretty sure I would remember something like that."

"Alia," Shao told her gently. "You have been having nightmares for a couple of weeks now. Ever since the night we left the cave."

"No, I haven't," Alia insisted.

"Alia," Sh'ron spoke to her twin. "You have been having nightmares. From the way you scream in your sleep, they are terrifying. You have woken all of us up on several occasions. At first, it only happened a few times, but lately, the frequency and intensity are getting worse. It's almost every night now."

"But how can I have such horrible dreams and not remember them?" Alia demanded.

"Marek could be 'suggesting' that you forget his visits. The more he invades your mind, the easier it is to access it. The block and shield I put in would remain intact, so I would have no way of knowing what was happening," Zimpf answered.

"How do we stop this?" Shao asked intensely.

"I'm sorry," Zimpf smiled insincerely at Alia. "I know how much you hate this. But I need to *see*."

Alia looked down. She knew Zimpf wasn't sorry at all. She hated for him to "poke around in her brain," as he called it. The whole process was frightening and invasive, and she detested the way it made her feel. She was terrified of what he might find.

But what if Marek has already done something irreparable? she thought to herself. Letting Zimpf *see* is my only way of knowing for sure.

The more she considered what Marek had done, the angrier she became. She had been Marek's only friend through his entire childhood. She had fought his battles with him and for him. And even after he turned his back on her in the orcs' camp, she had still tried to help him. Then she left and started a new life with the man she had fallen head-over-heels in love with. Yet Marek was still trying to cast a shadow over her life. He had killed Medjii and he had tried to kill her family and her.

This will stop, she thought angrily. *I will make it stop.*

Alia looked up at Zimpf, determination etched on her face. "Okay," she said resolutely. "You may *see* me."

"Thank you," he replied simply. "Is it okay if Aistra helps and if Sabio observes?"

Alia nodded. She didn't trust herself to answer. Despite her resolve, she was still frightened.

Shao sat beside her and held her hand while Zimpf arranged things. He went to his backpack and retrieved the red silk scarf that Alia had seen him use when he *visioned* more than one person at the same time.

As soon as he returned with it, Alia saw Aistra's eyes open wide in surprise.

"You still have that?" she whispered quietly to Zimpf. Her voice was so low that Alia was sure no one else was meant to hear her.

"Yes," he answered softly.

"I can't believe you still use that," she said in a soft tone.

Zimpf looked at her with a sad smile. "It was all I had left of you."

Aistra's eyes filled with tears, and she turned away so Zimpf wouldn't see her cry.

He didn't see her cry, but it was clear he could sense her grief. He handed the scarf to Shao and turned to Aistra. Taking her hand, he led her a little way into the woods, where they stood communicating silently with their hands on each other's faces while the others waited in uncomfortable silence. Finally, he kissed her gently.

"I think he's getting better at smooching," Shao observed clinically.

Everyone burst into sudden laughter.

Zimpf looked over suspiciously then returned to the camp, leading Aistra by the hand.

He sat beside Alia. "Are you ready?" Zimpf asked.

"No," she replied. "But I'm willing to do this."

Shao sat to Alia's right, and Zimpf sat to her left. Behind Zimpf stood Aistra, and to Aistra's left, his hand tied to hers with the red silk scarf, stood Sabio. Aistra's right hand was touching Zimpf's face.

"Are you ready?" he asked Alia again.

She nodded and let go of Shao's hand.

"Are you ready?" he said to Aistra and Sabio. They both nodded their heads. "Remember, Sabio, you are to watch only."

Sabio nodded again.

Alia laid her head back and closed her eyes just as Zimpf placed his hands on her temples. "Relax, Alia," he murmured in a soothing tone.

The next thing Alia knew, she was having the most wonderful dream. She and Shao were in the living room of their house in town, and they were slow dancing. She could feel his arms around her along with the long, slow kisses as they moved with music playing softly in the background. It was a single, perfect moment in time.

There was a sudden peal of thunder, and the light faded to dark. Alia found herself alone. She turned. A figure wearing a dark cloak stood outside the window. The hood was pulled down low to hide its features. From Alia's viewpoint, the apparition looked faceless, and she stepped backward in horror, her hand rising involuntarily to cover her mouth. The specter reached up with a long-fingered hand to push the hood back. Alia screamed.

Then she relived scene after nightmarish scene, each more appalling than the last, until she felt as though her sanity would be ripped away by the terrors that descended upon her. It seemed, for a moment, like she would be released, but as her mind struggled to free itself, she found herself surrounded by evil strangers who sought her destruction. There was a martial arts master, a tall woman with short, blond hair, and a huge warrior. They all sought to dominate her, bending her to their malevolent purposes. There were other accomplices whose monstrous intentions strove to destroy her utterly—a blond-haired man with dimples, an elf, and a dwarf.

Alia began to struggle. She screamed and scratched and kicked and fought to escape the madness.

She thought she heard someone say, "restrain her!"

She felt herself being pulled backward as iron hands pinioned her arms together and strong legs wrapped tightly around her legs, trapping her unmercifully.

She threw her head backward and howled a cry of absolute despair, tears streaming down her face.

Then…darkness.

Marek dismissed all of the Vheral leaders with sharp words and angry vituperations. He had given strict orders that he not be disturbed this evening. But the larger his Vheral family group had become, the more they ignored his requests, insisting that the urgency of their problems

needed his immediate attention.

But tonight was different. Tonight, he would need all of his concentration, all of his destructive talent, all of his evil intent. Tonight, he would implement his insidious scheme to control Alia's will, driving her to escape her family and friends and flee toward the rogue mage who would dominate her mind and smother her freedom.

Marek's brain raced with excitement.

He was unstoppable.

Chapter 22 – The Blue Stone

When Alia awoke, it was early afternoon. She was lying on one of her blankets with her back to a log and her head resting comfortably in Shao's lap. He was stroking her hair gently. She looked up at him and smiled. He leaned down and kissed her softly.

"How are you feeling?" he asked.

"I'm fine," she answered, sitting up. "What happened? What time is it?" It was then that Alia noticed that Shao's face was etched with exhaustion, and he had a huge knot on his forehead. "What happened?" she asked again, confused.

"You're awake." Zimpf yawned from where he was lying on the other side of the fire. He sat up, and Alia saw three huge scratches running down the left side of his face. "How are you feeling?" he asked her, echoing Shao's question.

"What happened?" Alia asked for the third time. It was then she realized that the tents had not been erected. Instead, everyone was sleeping on blankets around the campsite.

Zimpf came around the fire, stopping long enough to pour a cup of tea from the kettle on the campfire. He sat down beside Alia and handed her the cup.

"Drink," he told her. "And then I'll explain everything to you."

Alia took the cup with shaking hands and began sipping the tea while looking back and forth between Shao and Zimpf. Finally, she handed the empty cup to Zimpf.

"I know that was a calming potion," she stated. "So, what do I need to be calm about?" She looked at Shao. "Remember that we vowed to always be honest with each other."

Shao nodded and looked at Zimpf.

"Alia," Zimpf asked. "Do you remember why I had to *see* you earlier?"

Alia frowned, thinking hard. Suddenly, she gasped as she remembered what Sabio had said about Marek.

"Yes," she answered nervously as she reached down to grasp Shao's hand for support.

"That mage," Zimpf spat out the words as though they were a curse, "has been invading your mind for weeks now. Had I not *seen*..." he paused, thinking for a moment. "Let's just say that things would have been bad. Really bad."

"Did...did he break the shield you put in?" Alia asked in a frightened voice.

"No, he was too clever for that. If it had been broken, I would have known, and I think he understood that. Instead, he found a way to mesmerize you without my being able to *sense* it."

"Wait," Alia said. "How could I have been mesmerized by him? How was he able to do it? How did I not know?"

"I hate to admit it," Zimpf acknowledged, "but he's good. Very good. I suspect that he used the Aghara to gain access to a small part of your brain and has been slowly and subtly poisoning your mind."

Alia looked at Zimpf in horror. "Did…can you stop him?"

"Of course I can stop him," Zimpf sounded offended. "The question is, do you want me to?"

"Why wouldn't I want you to stop him?" Alia almost shouted. Then she realized that she was clutching Shao's hand so tightly that he was wincing in pain.

"Oh, Shao!" she said in concern. "Am I hurting you?" She kissed his hand in apology.

"You should be more concerned about the damage you did to us yesterday," Zimpf muttered.

"Yesterday!" Alia exclaimed. "I've been asleep since yesterday?"

"I had to make you sleep," Zimpf protested. "You were starting to get out of control."

"What did I do?" Alia demanded in a voice edging near hysteria.

"Shh, shh," Shao said soothingly, wrapping his arm around her and pulling her close.

Then he looked up at Zimpf, who was sitting upright, one forefinger extended toward Alia's head. "Don't you dare put her to sleep again!" Shao growled at him. "She just woke up."

Shao then turned to Alia. "It's not what you did; it's what Marek did. Apparently, he embedded into your mind the notion that we are your enemies, that you need to escape from us, and that you must find your way to him. It was so deeply entrenched that when Zimpf broke the implant you sort of…fought."

Alia pulled back to look at the two men, horrified by what she had done. Gently, she reached up to touch the knot on Shao's forehead, then she turned to examine the scratches on Zimpf's cheek.

"Somebody hand me my medical bag," she ordered.

Sh'ron, who was sitting on the other side of Shao, reached behind the log and handed it to her with a smile. "I knew you would want it," she told her twin. "So I took the liberty of having it ready for you."

Alia checked Zimpf's injuries first since they seemed worse. She cleaned up the scratches, applied a healing salve, and bandaged the scrapes, apologizing the entire time.

Zimpf accepted her apologies graciously, although Alia was sure she was never going to hear the end of it.

Then she turned her attention to Shao. His knot was superficial. Alia sent Sh'ron and Chhdar to a nearby creek for cold water and applied a cool compress to his head. She also made him some tea to alleviate the pain.

"I am so sorry—" she started to apologize again, but Shao placed his index finger to her lips.

"No," he told her. "Do not say that you're sorry for something that wasn't your fault. We're going to fix this. Marek has no concept of the people he has chosen to antagonize," he said in a low, dangerous voice, his eyes glittering with anger. Then he took the cold compress she was holding and placed it onto a knot on the back of her own head.

"Ow," she winced. "How did you know that was there?"

"What do you think you hit me with?" Shao smiled. He sounded amused.

"So, what do we do about Marek?" Alia asked.

"I didn't do anything to stop him, because I wanted to talk to you first," Zimpf answered seriously.

"Go on," Alia encouraged him.

"He was able to invade your mind through your feelings for

him," the diviner explained.

"What?!" Alia was horrified. "I don't have any feelings for him," she spat, her eyes flashing dangerously. Then she looked at Shao. "I only love you," she told him, her heart in her eyes.

"I didn't say 'love.'" Zimpf chuckled at Alia's outburst. "I said 'feelings.' Search your heart, Alia. What feelings do you have for the mage?"

"Pity," Alia supplied promptly. "I feel sorry for him because he had such a bad start in life."

"Alia," Zimpf told her quietly, "I can expel him for you, and I can put up a different block to keep him from reentering, but then he will know I interfered, and he will continue to chip away until he finds another weakness." Alia looked up; her face fearful.

"Don't worry," Zimpf told her. "I know another way to stop Marek, and it's a fairly easy procedure. But it is something you will have to do yourself." Then he chuckled quietly. "Do you remember what I did with the last block? Back when we were trying to retrieve the Orb of Ahi from him?"

Shao chuckled. "Clever," he said admiringly.

Zimpf shot him a quick grin.

Alia looked back and forth between the two men, confused.

"One of the things I attached to your block was Shao. Each time Marek tried to mesmerize you," Zimpf told her, "you could only picture Shao, think of Shao, imagine Shao."

"You can do that?" Alia was surprised.

"Actually, it wasn't Shao himself," Zimpf admitted, laughing. "The 'suggestion' was for you to see the man you had fallen in love with."

"Did you know this?" Alia asked, looking at Shao.

Smiling, he nodded.

Alia looked down, covering her face with her hands as she turned a rosy shade of red.

"Don't be embarrassed," Shao smiled gently.

Finally, Alia looked up at Zimpf. "So, all I have to do is think of Shao the next time I have a nightmare? Is that what you're saying?"

Zimpf nodded. "Just think about smooching. I'm sure it'll annoy him as much as it annoys the rest of us," he complained.

Shao leaned quickly behind Alia and popped Zimpf sharply on the back of his head.

"Ow!" Zimpf protested, rubbing his head and glaring at Shao.

"But how can I do that if I can't remember the nightmares?" Alia protested.

"I fixed it so that you will know when he invades your dreams," the diviner told her.

"In my dreams, can I do anything I want to stop him?" Alia asked. "Or do I just need to think of Shao?"

Zimpf was silent for a moment, thinking. "You should be able to do anything you want to him. Why?"

Alia looked at Zimpf and then Shao. "I'm going to teach him a lesson he won't soon forget," she threatened in an angry tone. "I am done with his attacks on me!"

Shao chuckled and shook his head. "You were right, Zimpf," he bragged proudly. "Alia and I are a perfect match."

"I'm leaving you two alone before the smooch fest starts," Zimpf grumbled.

By then, it had started to grow late. Alia and Shao went to forage for plants to supplement their dinner, then came back and started cooking. The simple chores of domesticity helped to calm

Alia's nerves more than any medicine ever would.

Sh'ron and Chhdar checked the horses and Amicu and Ciern set up the tents and collected firewood. Zimpf and Aistra sat in a triangle with Sabio. Each had their hands touching the faces of the two people beside them. They were talking half in words and half in images.

Finally, everyone gathered to eat and talk. The mood was somber after the events of the previous night. Sabio's message to Alia and Alia's break with reality caused by Marek's possession of her was particularly frightening.

But Zimpf easily lightened the mood by recalling some antics that he and Shao had been involved in while at Temple, which involved a lot of sneaking around and running.

Then Sh'ron told everyone how she and Alia had gotten in trouble while they were still schoolgirls by playing a prank that went horribly awry. They had put ink in the teacher's tea to stain her teeth blue, but somehow managed to get it confused with their own drink. "We spent a week with bright blue teeth," Sh'ron giggled.

Everyone laughed.

They continued trading stories of pranks and mishaps until well after midnight. By the time it grew late enough for bed, everyone was in a jovial mood.

That night, Alia slept well. There was no invasion from Marek.

The next morning, they learned that one member of their party had received a visitor.

"The old man came to see me last night," Sabio said at breakfast. "I know the purpose of the blue stone."

Everyone turned to stare at him.

"What did the Zduhac say?" Ciern asked.

"The blue stone is called a zafiir—" Sabio started.

"A zafiir?" Aistra gasped.

"Are you familiar with it?" Ciern wanted to know.

Aistra nodded. "It's one of the most powerful magical objects ever created. I didn't think there were any left," she answered, wide-eyed.

"Did the Zduhac say why he sent this gift?" Amicu asked Sabio.

"Yes," Sabio whispered. "I am to use it to stop Marek. And I will need your help in order to be successful. Otherwise, he will plunge the world into war."

"Sabio?" Aistra asked in a soft voice. "Can you tell us exactly what the Zduhac said to you?"

Sabio sat quietly, thinking. "Can you help me?" he appealed to Zimpf. "I want to get this exactly right."

"Of course," Zimpf replied. Then he moved to sit in front of Sabio. He placed his right palm on Sabio's forehead and began speaking to him in a tone so low that Alia couldn't hear the words.

Suddenly, Zimpf began to speak in a voice that was clearly not his own.

"The travelers have brought you a powerful talisman," Zimpf intoned. "You must use the zafiir to neutralize the magic of the Aghara the rogue mage possesses, lest he destroy the world."

Then Zimpf looked around at the entire group. "I charge you all with a task of great consequence. You must divide in order to conquer. Some of you will accompany Sabio in his quest to defuse the power the mage has stolen. The rest of you are to unite the families of the west in the event Marek prevails."

Zimpf fell silent, dropping his hand from Sabio's forehead and lowering his own head in weariness.

Just as he was ready to start, Marek jerked, suddenly realizing that he was not alone. His eyes narrowed dangerously as an obliteration spell suddenly sprang to his lips. He would destroy whoever dared to enter his tent uninvited.

It took several moments before he finally spied his unwelcome visitor. Nabii, the old, blind diviner, sat unobtrusively in a corner. The man was studying Marek intensely.

"What do you want?" Marek sneered.

"I came to warn you," Nabii replied in a voice so low that Marek had to lean in to hear him.

"Warn me? About what?" the mage hissed.

"Do not dream-alter," the diviner warned. "The outcome you plan is beyond your reach."

Marek froze, his brows drawing down into a V as he thought about the warning. On one hand, the old man had helped him on several occasions. But this time was different. This time, he was trying to prevent Marek from fulfilling a plan that had been weeks in the making, a plan that had reached its culmination.

"I can see your decision wavering, and I warn you again: abandon this dream-alteration. There are other ways."

"What do you see with those blind eyes?" Marek demanded.

"I cannot see a face, but I sense a shift in the woman's persona," Nabii whispered. Then he repeated himself once again, "Do not dream-alter."

With that, he stood and made his way unerringly to the front of the tent.

"And what happens if I do?" the mage challenged.

"Then your life may be forfeit," the old man said over his shoulder as he walked outside.

"I did not give you leave to go," Marek growled as he darted after Nabii.

But when he opened the tent flap, the old man was gone.

"Which way did he go?" Marek barked at the two men standing guard. "Don't just stand there! Go get him and bring him back to face me. Immediately!"

"Who?" one guard answered in confusion.

"No one left your tent, Master," the second man echoed.

Chapter 23–To Divide

They sat thinking quietly for several moments. Finally, Ciern addressed them. "It looks like we have some decisions to make. First, are we in agreement that we need to separate?"

"Like I said a while back," Amicu reiterated, "if a Zduhac appeared to me. I would do whatever he said. He told us to separate, so I say we separate."

Everyone else nodded their agreement.

"So," Ciern continued, "who is going to go where?"

No one answered him at first. Finally, Amicu spoke up.

"From a tactical point of view, we have two tasks to perform. One mission is to deactivate the Aghara, thus diminishing, and maybe even destroying, Marek's power. The second mission is to warn the western Vherals to prepare for an invasion from Marek's eastern forces."

"I agree with your assessment," Ciern acceded. "I see the first mission as more of an undercover operation; the second mission is more diplomatic and perhaps militaristic." He sat for a moment, carefully considering the best course for a successful outcome. Finally, he cleared his throat and spoke. "I think that in order to increase our chances for success, those of us who fight mentally should go after Marek and those of us who fight physically should advise the Vherals."

Alia saw Ciern glance quickly at Shao and then at the ground.

"But that only leaves three of us to go after Marek," Zimpf objected. "Aistra, Sabio, and me."

"Four," Ciern responded shortly, still not looking at Shao. "Alia will be going with you."

Shao turned to stare at Ciern. "Five," he said in his quiet voice, standing up as though to emphasize his point.

"No," Ciern said, standing also and facing Shao. "Alia will go with Zimpf, and you will come with me."

"Either Alia goes with me, or I go with Alia," Shao responded in a low, dangerous tone.

"You're suddenly very popular," Zimpf quipped lightly to Alia.

"Shut up, Zimpf!" both Shao and Ciern said at the same time while staring at each other angrily.

Zimpf swallowed hard, his eyes wide. Then he did something Alia had never seen him do. He stood up, walked to the two men, and placed one arm around Ciern's shoulders and the other around Shao's, drawing them close to him. He began to speak to them in low, urgent whispers.

Alia, who was sitting closest, could barely hear Zimpf's quiet words.

"Shao will come with us, Ciern," he told the elven prince. "I can *see* it."

Ciern shook his head.

Shao stared at Ciern, his face set and his eyes hard.

"You don't get to separate them just because you want to win this time," Zimpf said politely. "Don't bother to deny it. I can feel it rolling off you in waves."

Ciern turned to stare at the diviner, his face tight.

"That is not why I—"

"Think of it like this," Zimpf interrupted in a reasonable tone of voice. "We're going after Marek. Shao is, by far, the best person in this group to sneak us in and out of his encampment."

Alia saw Ciern cut his eyes at Shao.

Shao nodded once, quick and sharp, his eyes boring into Ciern's face.

"That's right," Zimpf encouraged Ciern. Then he continued. "Besides, do you really want to take a chance of him blaming you if something were to happen to Alia? Do you remember what happened when he blamed me?"

Ciern flinched.

Shao looked at the ground.

Amicu wormed his way into their huddle. "I am second in command," he declared loud enough for everyone to hear. "When you two had a disagreement at Temple, it was my responsibility to act as an intermediary and arbitrator. I am asserting that authority now. Shao and Alia will go with Zimpf's group."

Ciern shook his head. "No," he disagreed adamantly. "We need all of the warriors with us."

Unexpectedly, Aistra marched over to stand in front of the four graduates of the Temple of Anaia. She carried with her an uncharacteristic air of complete and total authority.

"This will end now," she demanded in a soft, firm tone. Her eyebrows were raised in the certain expectation that she would be obeyed. Immediately.

"I have heard both of your arguments," she said sternly, looking back and forth between Shao and Ciern. "I have made my decision. We will split up evenly. Zimpf, Shao, Alia, Sabio, and I will seek Marek and the deactivation of the Aghara. Ciern, Skala, Sh'ron, Chhdar, and Amicu will continue as emissaries and encourage the western Vherals to begin organizing."

Almost as one, they bowed to the young woman.

She ignored them. Instead, she walked back to her seat calmly as though she had not just pulled rank over the four men.

"What was that all about?" Sh'ron whispered in a low tone to Alia.

Alia shook her head.

"It must be a Temple thing," Chhdar suggested softly.

"We will take today to get organized and to split up the food supplies," Ciern announced, as though he was suddenly in control again. "Meet with your group to make plans this afternoon and we will discuss everything at dinner tonight. We leave in the morning." With that, he walked into his tent and shut the flap.

Shao started after Ciern, but Zimpf stopped him. "Let me," he said. Then he nodded at Aistra, and the two of them walked into Ciern's tent without gaining permission.

Everyone else moved to their own tents and began packing.

Once they were alone, Alia walked over to Shao and wrapped her arms around him, laying her head on his chest.

"Are you okay?" she whispered.

Shao wrapped his arms around her in return, leaning his cheek against the top of her head. "I'm always okay when I'm with you," he replied.

"Just okay?" she teased.

He laughed. "Much, much more than just okay," he said, then he kissed her.

"Shao?"

He looked at her, one eyebrow raised curiously.

"What was that with Aistra? Why did you all obey her?"

"She outranks Ciern," he answered simply. Then he grinned. "In this case I'm glad too."

"Outranks? How?" Alia questioned.

"At Temple, Ciern was the dorm captain; he was in charge of our building. But Aistra was the quadrant commander. She held rank over all of the dorm captains. Actually, the only people who outranked her were the instructors."

"And you all still obey her? Even though you're no longer attend the Temple of Anaia?"

"I guess old habits die hard," Shao admitted with a grin.

Alia chuckled.

They spent perhaps an hour organizing their packs. Just as they finished, there was a polite scratching at the tent flap. Alia opened it to find Ciern standing outside.

"May I enter?" he asked politely.

Alia pulled the flap open wider and stepped aside to admit him into the dim interior.

"I'm…uh…I'm going to talk to Sh'ron," Alia announced, excusing herself and leaving quickly.

Alia and Sh'ron spent the remainder of the afternoon together. They talked and laughed and planned and cried. They had never been separated like this, and it was an almost physical pain. But both women agreed that this plan would give them the greatest chance of success.

As the sun began to sink toward the western horizon, Shao and Chhdar came looking for them. The twins had made their way into the nearby forest, ostensibly to forage for fresh edibles to supplement their dinner. In reality though, they just wanted to talk privately.

"Did you two find anything to eat?" Shao asked curiously. Then he noticed that Alia was looking at the ground, her face a rosy red, and he laughed.

"That's okay," he continued, making an excuse for them. "There isn't very much food here to find." Then he reached down and plucked up a plant with several good-sized potatoes dangling from the roots. He also took a couple of steps to the right and tugged quite a few carrots from the ground.

Alia shook her head in defeat, then she chuckled softly.

"We'll all be back together soon," Shao promised. Then he looked at Sh'ron. "I vow to you that I will return Alia to you safely as soon as we have finished our mission."

Then Chhdar took Alia's hands in his and said solemnly, "I vow to protect Sh'ron and return her safely to you as quickly as possible."

"Thank you," the twins said in unison, then laughed.

At dinner that night, they were a solemn group. They did spend some time talking about how to reunite after their missions were completed. They agreed to meet at this same campsite in three weeks, regardless of the outcome of their assignments.

As usual, Alia and Shao had first watch. They were relieved at midnight by Ciern and Amicu. The rift between Ciern and Shao seemed to have been completely mended, and they were as close as ever.

Alia fell asleep almost as soon as her head hit the pillow.

But unlike last night, tonight she had a visitor.

Alia was having another wonderful dream. She and Shao were in the secret garden he had made just for her. They were sitting in the swing holding hands, talking, and occasionally kissing. She felt calm and peaceful, loved and protected, and altogether safe. But there was a subtle difference to this dream. In this dream, she knew she was dreaming. While the others felt real, this one felt like she was a character performing in a play.

After what seemed like an entire afternoon but was probably only a few minutes, the light began to change. At first, it was only diffused, like the setting sun. Then it grew darker, then it was pitch-black, and Alia couldn't see anything. She could no longer even sense Shao beside her. She was all alone. It grew cold, and she began to shiver.

The next thing she knew, she was sitting at their favorite table in the dining room in the big house in Miast. It was the round table they had sat at so often when Marek had been injured and in the hospital. As soon as she thought of Marek, the hooded figure that had haunted her previous dreams suddenly coalesced in the chair across from her. The figure still wore a cloak with the hood pulled so far over its head that it appeared faceless.

Alia stared directly at the figure for several moments before speaking.

"Hello, Marek," she said calmly.

Slowly, Marek pulled his hood back using one long-fingered hand.

"Hello, Alia," he replied conversationally.

He was the same Marek that Alia remembered from their youth. His brown, curly hair touched his shoulders, he grinned his crooked smile, and his warm, brown eyes were creased with amusement. He was never a handsome man, but he was cute and friendly and charming. Unlike when she was young, however, now Alia could sense his malevolence. She could see a sign of his cold, calculating nature hidden carefully in his eyes.

"Why are you here? What do you want from me?" she asked directly.

"So, you understand that this is not just a dream," he said shrewdly.

Alia didn't answer. She just stared at him, waiting for him to respond. Then she began to drum her fingers on the table in a rhythmic pattern. It was a habit she had picked up in her youth when she was impatient. A habit she knew aggravated Marek.

He glanced at her tapping fingers, his eyes narrowing in irritation. Finally, he put his hand atop her hand to stop the redundant noise.

Alia sat emotionless. But inside, her skin recoiled with revulsion. Marek's hand was cold, inhuman, strange.

"What do you want?" she asked again.

"You know what I want," he purred. "I want you." Then he leaned forward and tucked her hair behind her ear as he used to do when they were young.

It was all Alia could do to keep from screaming in disgust.

"No. You don't want me," she said evenly as she wrapped her hand around his forearm and placed his arm firmly on the table.

Marek smiled at her in what he probably thought was a charming way, but Alia knew differently.

"Stop it, Marek. Stop playing games," she said evenly. "What do you *want*?"

Marek leaned back, clearly amused by Alia's demands. He didn't answer; he only stared at her intensely.

"These people you are with are not your friends," he insisted. "You will come with me now," he said as he stood and extended his hand to her. Clearly, he expected her to acquiesce to his demand.

But instead, Alia laughed at him.

She recognized the rapid change in Marek's emotions as his eyes widened in shock, then narrowed in thought, and finally tightened in anger.

"You will obey me," he ordered in an imperious tone.

Then he made a mistake. He grabbed Alia by her arm to force her to accompany him. But he forgot one thing, and he didn't know another.

Alia had a temper. And she had spent more than a year learning to defend herself under the tutoring of the greatest martial artist in the Four Lands.

As soon as Marek grabbed her arm, the anger she had pent up against his evil burst forth from her like water from a dam.

She twisted around, trapped his arm with both of her hands, and threw him bodily on the table, pinning him facedown.

Without even thinking of how it happened, Mama's long-handled wooden spoon appeared in her right hand as she held him firmly against the table with her left. Inexplicably, the spoon itself seemed eager to do the job for which Alia had summoned it. It no longer even looked like a spoon; it looked more like spanking rod.

"Since you are acting like a spoiled child, I am going to treat you like one," she growled in a voice she could scarcely recognize as her own.

Then she began to smack his bottom with the implement in her hand, listing all the wrongs he committed.

"You turned me over to the orcs. You abducted Airafae. You killed Medjii. You tried to kill me, and my husband, and my sister, and her husband. You sent mongers to attack us. You destroyed the compound of the Order of the Mages. You are trying to start a war using innocent people as pawns. And now you have invaded my dreams to try to bend me to your will."

With each offense, she smacked him time and time again—once, twice, a dozen, two dozen.

Only when Marek was crying in pain did she stop.

"I hope you can't sit down for a week!" she shouted.

Marek raised up from the table and turned to face her. She saw his eyes flicker briefly to Mama's wooden spoon; suddenly, it was gone, and she was holding her own sword. She pressed it firmly against his neck.

"The next time you try to control me, I will run my blade all the way through your throat!" she hissed in anger.

She turned then to leave, but Marek clearly had something else planned. He raised his hand, and at the same time, snarled viciously, "is that what you think?"

Alia didn't answer. She merely pulled her arm back quickly and smashed the heel of her hand into Marek's nose. She felt the bone shatter.

He fell backward, screaming in agony as blood spewed down the front of his cloak.

Turning, Alia saw that a door had appeared in front of her, and she strode purposely out of the room and out of the dream.

She sat up in sudden wakefulness in the tent she shared with Shao. Outside, she could hear Zimpf laughing hysterically.

"Zimpf!" she growled as she fought her way out of the blankets.

She jerked on her tunic and hose and was marching angrily from the tent before Shao had managed to rise. He yanked on his pants and followed her, barefoot and shirtless.

Outside, the others had begun stumbling out of their tents with sleep-filled eyes and tousled hair. Like Shao, they were barely dressed.

Meanwhile, Zimpf and Aistra, who had been on guard duty, were convulsing in laughter. Aistra sat on one of the logs, tears streaming down her face as she gasped for air. Zimpf had fallen to the ground and was clutching his stomach with his hands.

Both of them struggled to speak, saw Alia, and roared with uncontained guffaws of laughter.

"You *saw* everything," Alia stated indignantly. Then her face began to bloom bright red as she stared at the ground.

"What the—" Shao started as he looked back and forth between the hysterically laughing couple and Alia's obvious embarrassment.

"She—she—she—" Zimpf stuttered, pointing at Alia and then collapsing in fresh rounds of glee.

"She—Marek—" Aistra managed to utter before looking at Zimpf and snorting through her giggles.

Shao turned to Alia. "Did Marek visit you in your dream?"

Alia nodded, her face still aflame and her eyes downcast.

"Can you tell me what happened?" he asked gently. "Did that mage hurt you?"

The last question sent both Zimpf and Aistra into fresh peals of laughter.

"I—" Alia started. Then she looked at Sh'ron, who had moved to stand beside her twin.

"I lost my temper," she whispered self-consciously.

"Oh! Oh my…" Sh'ron muttered.

"Lost your temper?" Shao asked in confusion. He had known Alia for two years and they had been deliriously, happily married for over a year. He had seen her happy, sad, frightened, exasperated, vexed, and aggravated. But he had never, not even once, seen her lose her temper.

"What did you do to Marek?" Sh'ron asked Alia gently.

"She—" Zimpf tried to speak through his gasping hoots of laughter. Finally, he managed to blurt out two words: "Mama's spoon."

"Oh my," Amicu echoed Sh'ron in sudden understanding. Then turning to Alia, he asked the fatally funny question. "Did you give him a smack bottom?"

Alia, her face still flaming in humiliation, nodded.

The entire camp erupted in uncontrollable laughter.

Even Skala, the normally reticent dwarf, laughed heartily.

Shao, although he was laughing as hard as the rest of them, pulled Alia into a tight hug. "Don't be embarrassed," he tried to console her through his chuckles.

Finally, Zimpf managed to control himself long enough to haltingly tell how Marek had tried to grab Alia, how Alia had flipped him onto the table, and how she had paddled his bottom, yelling at him the entire time. He ended with Alia's quote, "I hope you can't sit down for a week!" which sent them all roaring with laughter again.

By this time, Alia had regained enough of her composure to chuckle with them, although her face was still red with humiliation.

"Don't forget the punch," Aistra chortled. "That was pretty good too."

"Punch?" Shao asked.

"I…uh…I used the heel of my hand to break his nose," Alia admitted, looking at the ground again.

Everyone cheered.

Shao placed his finger under her chin and raised her face to look him in the eye. "That's my wife," he bragged proudly. Then he kissed her in front of everybody.

Finally, the group settled down to breakfast around the fire, still chatting and laughing.

"Zimpf, I have some questions," Alia addressed the diviner.

"Go ahead, slugger," he teased.

"How do you know what happened?" she asked.

Zimpf chuckled. "When I *saw* you the other day, I set it so that you would know when you were dreaming,"

"You told me that," Alia said in exasperation.

"Well," he admitted, "Aistra helped me to arrange the suggestion so that we could *see* your dreams…"

Alia glared at him angrily.

"But only if Marek appeared," he continued. "It was meant to protect you," he explained seriously.

"The…uh…damage I did to him. Will he feel it when he wakes up?"

Zimpf and Aistra exchanged a long look. "I really don't know," he answered, looking over at Aistra, his eyebrows raised questioningly.

Aistra shook her head. "I don't know either. Why?" she asked.

"Because of this," Alia told them, holding up her right palm. There, on the heel of her hand, a bruise had formed at the exact spot she had used to hit Marek.

Shao took her hand and examined it carefully. Then he kissed her sore hand and began to chuckle.

"I hope he does feel it," Shao laughed. "I hope he can't sit down for a week."

"Alia, why did you go back and punch him in the face?" Aistra wondered.

"I wanted to make sure he knew I meant what I was saying," Alia asserted.

"I think you convinced him," Shao chortled drily.

Marek had taken a full day to consider Nabii's warning before deciding to disregard it. Everything was ready; he could not fail.

The light began to change, and the mage made his preparations to enter Alia's dream. Placing his hands on either side of the Aghara, he began chanting in a low, musical voice. The container started to glow an eerie green; at first, it was subtle, diffused, then it coalesced, pulling together the dark inside the tent until everything was pitch-black.

Marek could see Alia; she was all alone, sitting at a table for six in a vaguely familiar dining room.

He grinned evilly. She only needed to think of him.

Suddenly, his conscientiousness was pulled into the dream. It felt real, as though he was actually sitting before her. This was by far the most graphic dream alteration he had experienced.

Marek sat down at the table he had imagined; it was identical to the one that had been in the dining room in Miast. Alia was there, alone and vulnerable. Without hesitation, he began chanting another spell. A spell that would let his semblance materialize.

Alia stared directly at him for several moments before speaking; she seemed unsurprised to see him.

"Hello, Marek," she said calmly.

Slowly, he pulled the hood of his cloak back using one long-fingered hand.

"Hello, Alia," he replied conversationally.

"Why are you here? What do you want from me?" she asked directly.

"So, you understand that this is not just a dream," Marek answered shrewdly. He smiled: he knew he had her. She would do as he ordered.

But she didn't answer; she just stared at him. Then she began to drum her fingers on the table in a rhythmic pattern. It was a habit that he hated.

He glanced at her tapping fingers; his eyes narrowed in irritation. Finally, he put his hand over hers to stop the grating noise.

"What do you want?" she asked again curiously.

"You know what I want," he whispered softly. "I want you."

Then he leaned forward and tucked her hair behind her ear as he used to do when they were young.

"What do you want?" Alia asked for a third time.

He didn't answer; he only stared at her intensely.

"These people you are with are not your friends," he insisted. "You must escape with me now," he said, standing and extending his hand to her. "It's your only chance."

The entire time he had been dream-altering, he had been slowly smothering her will. Now, she had no choice but to acquiesce to his demand.

To his surprise, she laughed at him.

Marek turned to stare at her in shock.. She should not have been able to refuse him.

"You will obey me," he demanded. His anger slipped through the cracks of his friendly façade; he grabbed Alia by her arm and yanked her toward him. He would smother her will with his own and if that didn't work, if she refused to accompany him willingly, he would take her forcefully.

The next thing he knew, she had twisted out of his grip like a snake and had shoved him down on the table, twisting his arms painfully behind him.

Then she began to shout one thing after another as she struck him viciously, repeatedly, agonizingly. He couldn't even comprehend her words because of the unendurable pain she inflicted.

Once, twice, a dozen, two dozen, three dozen times.

He began to sob in agony, the image of his father beating him came suddenly to mind and, for a moment he lost the will to resist the unwarranted punishment.

"I hope you can't sit down for a week!" she shouted, releasing him.

As he began to raise up, he saw that it wasn't his father, it was only Alia. She didn't have the beating stick his father used, she only held a wooden spoon. For a moment, he thought that he could still win. He would rip the implement from her hand and mesmerize her into obedience. It was only a wooden spoon

He took that first demanding step toward her, then froze in stunned incredulity. The spoon began to glow and change and evolve until Alia was holding her own sword. He wondered where she had obtained such a powerful magical object. He didn't have time to react however, because the next thing he knew, she had it pressed firmly against his neck.

"The next time you try to control me, I will run my blade all the way through your throat," she hissed in anger.

"Is that what you think?" Marek snarled malevolently as he turned to wreak vengeance from her for her insolence. He raised one hand, fully intending to perform a spell. But before he could utter a word, Alia pulled her arm back quickly and smashed the heel of her hand into his nose.

Marek fell backward, screaming in agony as he was ejected forcefully *from the dream and into his own tent. He took two quick steps backward and tripped over a chair before falling painfully onto the ground. Blood spewed down the front of his cloak as his hand moved involuntarily to the shattered bones.*

"I told you not to dream-alter," Nabii said, looking at the injured man clinically.

Chapter 24 – The Emissaries

They separated shortly after breakfast. Alia, Shao, Zimpf, Aistra, and Sabio headed east while Ciern, Amicu, Skala, Chhdar, and Sh'ron continued west.

This trip felt all wrong. Sh'ron was used to having Shao and Alia riding rearguard, but now, when she glanced back, all she saw was Amicu riding alone. She missed the others—Zimpf's cutting wit, Aistra's gentle smile, Shao's towering athleticism. But mostly, Sh'ron missed her twin more than she could possibly describe. She kept looking for Alia with whom she could share glances and giggles and secrets. But each time she looked, Alia wasn't there, and she would be reminded again of her sister's absence. Then Sh'ron began to worry. The thought, "What if something happens?" kept popping into her mind like an evil fiend until she became obsessed with the idea.

The others tried to help her. They included her in all their meetings and decisions. But Sh'ron grew more and more despondent. Her despair was so overwhelming that the others began to discuss the idea of turning back.

Finally, on the evening of the fourth day of their separation, Sh'ron had a visitor. She had gone alone to collect water from a stream very close to camp when she saw an old man. She stopped, confused. Why would an old man be standing in the woods all alone this far from civilization? Then he smiled, and she suddenly recognized him.

"Good evening, YeYe," she said, bowing politely.

"I came to ease your mind," he smiled gently.

Sh'ron startled slightly. How does he know how worried I have been? she wondered.

YeYe reached his hand toward her, and without even thinking, she clasped it in her own. Immediately, she saw Alia; her twin was happy and healthy.

Sh'ron smiled sadly. "I miss her so much it hurts, and I am so worried about her safety," she confessed to the old man as her eyes filled with tears.

"Nothing makes a heart hurt more than missing someone," he said gently. "But Alia has a task to perform."

"Will she be okay?" Sh'ron asked.

The old man smiled. "I have given her all of the tools she needs to succeed. She is under my protection, and she alone has the ability to see this through. That is why she was chosen for this assignment."

Sh'ron nodded. "I understand," she whispered. But the tears had begun streaming down her face.

"Don't despair, child," YeYe told her, wiping the tears from her cheeks. "You too have an obligation to perform."

Sh'ron stared at him. "I do?" she asked.

He nodded. "Alia gave you medicines to treat the most common of ailments among these people. You must act in her stead. Your work will win over the hearts of the Vherals, and that is what will help us more than anything the emissaries have to say. Besides," he said with a smile, "I think you will learn something surprising."

Sh'ron glanced down, and when she looked back up, the old man was gone.

"Thank you," she whispered.

She collected the water and walked thoughtfully back to camp.

"I just had a visit from an old friend," she announced. Then she went on to repeat her conversation with the Zduhac.

"That sounds promising," Ciern said encouragingly.

Amicu nodded. "Do you feel like you can perform as the stand-in healer?" he asked gently.

"I do now, especially since YeYe thinks I can handle the job," Sh'ron admitted.

Chhdar smiled at her and squeezed her hand. "Then I know you can do this!" he encouraged her. "I'll even help," he volunteered.

"That's actually a good idea," Amicu told them. "I saw some of the Vherals watching us from a distance just before we camped. I'm pretty sure we'll meet them tomorrow." Then he went on to describe a plan he had formulated to try to persuade them to prepare for the invasion from Marek's army.

Amicu and Ciern continued discussing their ideas for the Vherals with occasional comments from Skala as they ate their dinner.

Later, after everyone else was asleep, Sh'ron and Chhdar sat by the fire together while they were on guard duty.

"I've been worried about you," Chhdar admitted, looking at his wife while he gently held her small hand in his big one.

She squeezed his hand in affection. "Thank you," she said.

"I was on the verge of giving you chamomile tea and sprinkling lavender in our tent to help you relax," he confessed.

Sh'ron looked at him in surprise. "How do you know those plants are calming plants?"

"I guess I never told you." He chuckled. "My father was the apothecary for our little village. After he died, my mother and I moved to your little hamlet to live with her parents."

Sh'ron remembered when Chhdar and his mother moved to town. She was young, maybe twelve or so. But even then, she had been fascinated by him.

"I don't think I ever knew that," she admitted. "Why didn't you tell me this before?"

"It was so long ago that I didn't even think about it," he answered.

He talked on then, telling her about his father and the man's work and the town in which they had lived. Sh'ron curled up beside him, listening intently, not even realizing when she fell asleep.

The next day around midmorning, they made their first contact with the Vherals. Amicu, Ciern, and Skala walked in front, each leading their horse and holding their palms forward in a gesture of peace. Sh'ron walked behind and to the left of Amicu, and Chhdar walked behind and to the right of Skala.

The Vherals were cautious but friendly.

"Hello," said the leader. "My name is Bheri. Are you the travelers with the healer?"

"We are," Ciern replied. "In truth though, our healer was called by the mountain spirit to perform a task. However, we do have her sister, who has some training." He indicated Sh'ron.

She nodded politely. "How may I serve you?" Sh'ron asked.

"Several of our children are ill. Will you see them?" he pleaded.

"Of course," she assented. "Will you take us to your camp?"

Once in camp, Ciern, Amicu, and Skala went to meet with the elders while Sh'ron and Chhdar set up a treatment area. The first patient was brought to them, and Sh'ron examined the young girl as Alia had taught her. Then Chhdar checked her as well. Thankfully, it was one of the illnesses that Alia had discussed with them, so they knew how to treat the child. One by one, other families lined up to have their children examined and to receive the proper medication. By the next day, all of their young patients were feeling better.

Sh'ron was relieved. She didn't like working in medicine; she was a teacher, and she missed her students. But this was her task.

Chhdar, however, was a natural. He entertained the children and talked to the parents. His questions were clever and revealing and served to diagnose each individual's malady. Sh'ron knew that the others thought the big warrior to be unintelligent, but they were wrong. Chhdar was just cautious. He studied problems and situations from every angle before making decisions with a clear, rational mind. And his familiarity with his father's work gave him a certain insight into his patient's needs.

By that evening, the people of the tribe had welcomed the small group as members of the family, and the elders agreed to Ciern, Amicu, and Skala's plan to call a gathering of as many of the western families as they could.

The next morning, Sh'ron's group continued their westward trek. Meanwhile, Bheri had agreed to send runners east to invite families that Ciern, Amicu, and Skala had already spoken with to attend the gathering. They all agreed to meet in two weeks.

Sh'ron's group had only traveled for about half a day when they were once again approached by another band of Vherals asking for help. This time, it was the elderly leader who had broken his arm and needed aid.

"We are not the true healer," Chhdar spoke for them. "Our healer was called to a task by the mountain spirit. But we will look at your elder and do what we can," he promised.

Sh'ron looked at him in surprise. She had no idea how to set a broken bone.

Once they were in camp, Chhdar and Sh'ron brewed a tea to ease the old man's pain and to induce sleep. Then, Chhdar pulled the arm hard while Sh'ron braced the old man. She clearly heard a pop as the bone snapped back into place. Then together, they splinted the arm and fixed a concoction of tea leaves to ease pain. Afterward, the man's family, with many thanks, carried him to his tent.

Once again, Ciern, Amicu, and Skala were able to persuade the tribe to attend the upcoming gathering.

That night, when they were alone in their tent, Sh'ron leaned up on her elbow as she stared at her husband in admiration.

"How did you know what to do with the elder's broken bone?" she marveled.

"I had some instruction in basic healing techniques when I trained to be a warrior," he admitted. "To be honest, I never thought it would be something I needed, so I was at best an indifferent student." He smiled, remembering the courses he had been forced to take.

"Why would a warrior need to take healer classes?" Sh'ron wondered.

"They wanted us to know how to field dress wounds so we could help our fallen comrades," he explained.

Sh'ron leaned over and kissed her husband. "You constantly surprise me..." She trailed off, her eyes growing wide.

"What?" Chhdar asked.

Sh'ron chuckled. "I think I know what the Zduhac meant when he said, 'I think you will learn something surprising.'"

"Well, I hope that I can continue to surprise you," Chhdar told her fondly.

"You do." She smiled. "Every day."

The next few days continued much the same way as their reputation and word of their mission spread. By the end of the week, larger and larger groups of Vherals came to greet them, had their ailing tribe members treated, and then traveled on to attend the meeting.

By the time they had to turn back for the gathering, they had convinced, what Ciern estimated to be, at least half of the remaining tribes to join them. As a nation, the Vherals did not band together, so the huge number of families that agreed to accompany them was remarkable. And they continued to collect smaller families of Vherals as they returned to the meeting site. The tribes that accompanied them combined with the families that Bheri had invited, resulted in a gathering that contained at least a thousand or more people.

Once everyone was together, they called the head of each family group to listen to the emissaries. There were over fifty leaders gathered around a huge bonfire that Ciern had lit.

Sh'ron and Chhdar stood to the side of the makeshift platform that Skala had quickly constructed and watched intently as Ciern, followed by Amicu and then Skala, walked purposefully before the crowd. Sh'ron was unsurprised to see Ciern step forward while Amicu and Skala stood a few feet back on either side. She had been told that Ciern's talent was the ability to influence people.

"I am Prince Ciern, son of King Elator of the Elven Nation," he began.

"These are my associates, Prince Skala, son of King Ganayt of the Dwarven Realm, and Amicu, commander of the fighting forces of the city of Selo of the Outlands and graduate of the Temple of Anaia." Several Vherals gasped. Apparently even here, people had heard of the Temple. "Traveling with us are Chhdar, warrior of the people of the south, and Sh'ron, teacher, aid-giver, and twin sister of Alia the healer." He stopped as wave after wave of applause rolled over them. Everyone in the group knew of someone who had been treated by Alia, Sh'ron, or Chhdar.

Then Ciern continued. "We have asked you here today to warn of a grave danger that threatens your way of life." Then he went on to tell the story of the evolution of evil. He described how Alia obtained the Orb of Ahi, how Shao and Zimpf escorted her, Sh'ron, Chhdar, and Marek to the elven kingdom. He informed them of Alia's mesmerization, of the theft of the orb and the subsequent abduction of Airafae.

Most of the leaders' eyes narrowed in anger at the story of the abduction. In the far north, kidnapping was considered particularly heinous. It was a crime punished by death.

Ciern, warming to his audience, spoke to them directly, honestly passionately. He disclosed Marek's alliance with the orcs and their grisly plan to enslave mankind. Then he described in exaggerated detail how only eight people—Skala, Sh'ron, Chhdar, Alia, Shao, Zimpf, Medjii, and himself—had destroyed the ghastly threat and defeated the entire orc nation.

By now, the crowd had been stirred to a frenzy, applauding, shaking their spears, and stamping their feet in appreciation for the defeat of the orcs.

Then, just as Sh'ron thought the crowd's excitement had reached its peak, Ciern continued. He described the murder of Medjii and the attack on Sh'ron, Chhdar, Alia, Shao, and Zimpf. The description was so detailed that several leaders demanded to know if the group had survived even though they had met the people involved.

The mass of Vherals grew louder and more angry. They began knocking their spears together—a sign of impending battle. They yelled and cried out and demanded the mage's execution.

Then Ciern, feeding off of the audience's energy, spoke eloquently, fervently, and with an all-consuming belief in his words.

By the time he reached the part where Marek was planning to usurp the Vherals in his evil plan to overthrow the southern nations, the crowd had erupted into a fevered pitch.

Sh'ron thought that there would be no stopping them as they began frantically swarming around each other, their cries escalating and their weapons pivoting dangerously.

She looked wide-eyed at Ciern, afraid of the horde of rioters that had suddenly erupted within their midst. She saw him throw a quick, sidelong wink at Amicu, who grinned in return, and then she understood. The elven prince had planned this.

Ciern let the audience mutiny for several long moments, then, speaking in low, even tones, he brought them down—slowly, calmly, quietly. He began talking and explaining and planning until he once again had them under his control, spellbound, enthralled, captivated.

Nabii, the old blind man who had been trying to advise Marek, sat silently in the audience, listening as Ciern skillfully turned the tide of opinion against the mage. He would have to do something about this.

"I ordered the advance troops to be on the lookout for the woman and her friends," Nabii stated calmly. He was sitting in a chair in a darkened corner of Marek's tent.

The mage looked up quickly from the document he had been reading. He hadn't heard anyone enter.

"Who gave you permission to command my forces?" Marek snarled. He had grown weary of the old man coming and going as he pleased. And now, Nabii was starting to assert authority over Marek's subjects.

Nabii seemed unconcerned with the mage's wrath, the only person in the entire camp to be unafraid of him.

Marek tented his hands until the tip of his left hand lightly touched the tips of his right hand; an elimination spell hovered on his lips. The old man had been useful a time or two, but he had failed to protect Marek the last time the mage dream-altered. The fact the diviner had warned him not to go seemed not to have registered in the mage's fevered mind.

"If you murder me, you will never know why your old friend must be the one to help you augment the power within the Aghara," Nabii commented conversationally.

Marek's eyes narrowed in thought. He had been toying with the idea of selecting a young woman at random and training her to do his bidding rather than struggling to dominate Alia's mind and spirit.

"Why do you seek to advise me?" the mage asked after several moments of silence. "You appear and disappear as easily as smoke, you make no attempt to befriend me, nor do you ask for any type of recompense."

"Does it matter?" the old man shot back. "It seems to me that the most important thing is that I have not led you astray."

Chapter 25 – And Conquer

For Alia, the parting was especially painful. Three weeks was a long time for her to be away from her twin. She rode quietly at the back of the group with Shao beside her. Shao seemed particularly vigilant of any possible danger; he constantly looked around and studied the terrain surrounding them. But he was also aware of Alia, and he could sense her anguish over the separation from her sister.

They rode steadily for most of the day, not even bothering to stop for lunch. Finally, they found an area to camp just inside the tree line they had been following.

They set up their tents quickly. Then Sabio tended the horses while Aistra and Zimpf gathered firewood and Alia and Shao foraged for fresh food and cooked dinner.

After they had eaten, Alia asked a question that had been bothering her.

"How will we find Marek?" she asked. "Are we just going to head east until we find a large encampment and assume he's there?"

"No," Zimpf told her. "When that mage invaded your dream the other night and was busy getting the smack bottom of a lifetime"—Zimpf stopped to giggle, then continued—"Aistra was able to mark him. She can use that mark to trace his location."

"You can do that?" Alia blurted.

Aistra smiled gently as she nodded her head.

"Is there anything the two of you can't do?" Sabio asked in amazement.

"Well, right now we can't figure out how to use the zafiir the Zduhac gave you," Zimpf admitted ruefully.

"It'll be fine," Sabio said, unconcerned. "My friend will visit me when we get close to the mage to tell me what to do."

"I wish I had his faith," Zimpf complained as he tilted his head toward his new protege.

Sabio grinned.

As had become their custom, after dinner, Sabio, Aistra, and Zimpf moved to the other side of the fire to continue Sabio's training. They sat in a triangle, each with their hands on the faces of the people on either side of them. They spoke mostly to each other's minds, although occasionally Zimpf would say something out loud, like, "No, watch me," or, "Try that again."

Shao and Alia watched them, fascinated by the strange three-way conversation, until the three of them finally went to bed. Then, as usual, Alia and Shao, who had first watch, did a perimeter check and then sat together in front of the fire.

"Are you okay?" Shao asked her. "I know you're missing Sh'ron."

Alia looked at him. It seemed like Shao could always understand her. Even when she tried to hide her feelings, he could see through them.

"This separation is almost like a physical pain for you, isn't it?" he stated, taking her hand and kissing it.

"How could you possibly know that?" she asked, raising one eyebrow curiously.

Smiling, Shao held up his right hand. On the heel of his hand, exactly where Alia had bruised her hand when she broke Marek's nose, was a bruise.

Alia held her palm out flat, comparing the bruises. They matched exactly.

"Did—did—" she stuttered in bewilderment. "Did you share my dream?"

"No," Shao answered, shaking his head. "The bruise showed up shortly after you showed me your hand. I talked to Zimpf about it, and he thinks we are somehow linked together spiritually."

"Did he say how?" Alia wanted to know.

"No, but he wants to *vision* us again to learn how this happened," Shao admitted wryly, making a face.

"I hope you told him no." Alia asserted.

"Actually, I told him not now. Anyway," Shao continued, "I can also feel the longing, the almost aching pain you feel for your sister."

Alia stared in astonishment. "You are describing my feelings perfectly."

Shao leaned over and wrapped his arm around Alia's shoulders then pulled her close.

"I didn't tell him about the ceremony with the Zduhac," he whispered softly.

She turned to look at him, suddenly realizing how deeply the mountain spirit had bound them together.

"I'll be glad when this is over," Alia suddenly admitted. "I wonder how long it will take."

"Zimpf said that he, Aistra, and Sabio think this will be over within a couple of weeks. Apparently, Marek is not that far away, and he is marching toward us as we ride toward him."

Alia sighed. "I wish this had never happened. I wish we were still back in Miast living our lives."

"Me too," Shao agreed. "But our lives will be that much sweeter when we return, because rough paths lead to peaceful destinations."

Alia looked at him, surprised by his words. "I love you," she said simply, laying her head on his shoulder.

Two hours later, they were relieved by Zimpf and Aistra. Two hours after that, Sabio, who had insisted that he could keep watch alone, took over.

As they traveled toward the east, they began to encounter bands of Vherals fleeing westward. A few of them were families they had met previously who were delighted to see them again. Alia took time with the families to follow up on her previous patients and treat a few new ones. Afterward, they encouraged each group to go in search of Ciern.

They also met several new bands of Vherals. A few were friendly, having heard of Alia and the help she had been providing. However, many of them were aloof, and a few were even hostile toward them. They would have had a rough time continuing their journey had it not been for Sabio. Apparently, everyone had heard of Sabio Omu Olori; they feared and respected him. The customary reaction to Sabio was to offer him a gift of reverence in the hope that he would bless their family and then depart quickly. Such gifts usually consisted of foodstuffs.

Nearly a week into their journey, they came across Ghan and

his family. Ghan told them that he had just received word of a large meeting being held to prepare the clans of the west in the event of an invasion. The runner who had delivered the news said that an evil shaman had bewitched several of the largest families to the east and had merged them together to form an army. There was a rumor that the army was marching in their direction. Ghan urged Alia and her group to join them.

While they were visiting, Alia, with Aistra's assistance, treated several new patients and visited the little boy whose life Alia had saved during their last stay.

Meanwhile, Shao, Zimpf, and Sabio met with Ghan and his brothers. They explained that they were going east to confront the shaman, and they were hoping to stop the war before it could start.

"Be careful," Ghan warned them. "We had a visitor a week or so after you left. He was fleeing from the groups who had organized under the leadership of the shaman. From what I understand, this leader is searching for a woman that he says belongs to him, and he is offering a reward for her safe return. There is no doubt in my mind that the woman he hunts is Alia."

"Thank you for the warning," Shao said respectfully. "We were recently made aware of the mage's plans. We are taking precautions to protect her."

"But you are taking her to him," Ghan pointed out. "Why?"

"She must be the one to confront him in order to destroy his power," Sabio answered honestly.

Shao looked at him sharply but didn't say anything.

Later, while Alia was treating a patient who had just arrived, Shao pulled Zimpf and Sabio aside.

"What did you mean when you said that Alia has to be the one to confront Marek in order to destroy his power?" Shao demanded of the two diviners.

Sabio and Zimpf looked at each other. Finally, Zimpf heaved a sigh that seemed to come from his feet.

"We actually don't know if she has to face him directly in order to destroy the Aghara," Zimpf explained. "But when we meet each night, Sabio, Aistra, and I, among other things, search the future. The one thing we always see is Alia confronting Marek. Whether she is successful in demolishing his power source has not been decided."

Shao was silent for a few moments, thinking. Then he continued. "Am I with her during this confrontation?" he asked.

"We can't *see* that," Zimpf answered carefully.

"Go on," Shao demanded impatiently.

"We don't *see* anyone with her. And we can't seem to be able to *see* beyond her altercation with him. The future is fluid," Zimpf continued. "So, what happens after Alia's meeting depends entirely on the mage. We do know that the five of us will arrive at the campsite together."

Shao didn't say anything for a moment. "I will not be separated from her," he said adamantly. Then he marched away from them to help Alia tend to her patient.

Sabio and Zimpf silently watched him go.

When they left the next morning, Ghan gave them provisions and offered them shelter, food, and protection any time they met in the future.

"Be safe," he blessed them when they departed.

It was only a few days after that when the Zduhac paid them a visit.

Alia was sound asleep but snapped awake abruptly. Nothing

was wrong; she wasn't dreaming. It felt like she was being called, almost like when she was a little girl and her mother woke her up to come eat breakfast. She lay quietly in her blankets beside Shao and tried to figure out who was calling her. She finally decided to slide quietly out of bed and check outside, but of course, Shao was instantly awake.

"What's wrong?" he muttered.

"I don't know," Alia answered. "I feel like I'm being summoned."

Shao was instantly alert. "Do you think it's Marek again?" he asked.

"No, it's more like a friendly invitation," Alia said, confused.

"Let's check outside," Shao suggested. "If we can't figure this out, then I think we should wake up Zimpf."

As soon as they stepped outside, they found the source of the invitation. The old man was sitting before the fire. He had cooked a large breakfast, and he and Sabio were talking quietly.

"There you are," he said with a smile. "It's nice to see you both again."

"Good morning, YeYe." Shao bowed politely.

"It's nice of you to visit," Alia welcomed him warmly.

"Do you think the others are going to get up soon? Or should I call them again?" YeYe asked.

"We're awake," they heard Zimpf call sleepily from his tent.

Within a few minutes, he and Aistra joined them. Zimpf was yawning widely.

"Thank you for breakfast, YeYe," Zimpf muttered groggily.

They sat quietly eating the food the Zduhac had prepared. He asked them a few questions about their encounters with the Vherals, and he was especially interested in Zimpf and Aistra's tutoring of Sabio. He supported their encouragement of him to attend the Temple of Anaia. He asked about the other members of their party, and he questioned them about their plans.

Finally, he put his plate down. "First, know that you will make contact with the mage and his followers sometime today. So, now has come the time for me to disclose my mind to you," he announced.

"I have met with Sabio, and he understands what he must do and how to utilize the zafiir. Since it is to be used on Vheral territory, the zafiir can only be utilized by a native for the energy to reach its full potential. Therefore, Sabio alone must release the power of the talisman."

Sabio nodded in agreement with the old man. The young Vheral diviner sat holding a staff he didn't have earlier. The zafiir was firmly implanted at the very top.

"You two," YeYe said, indicating Zimpf and Aistra, "are to aid and strengthen Sabio. You must stand on either side of him when he uses the zafiir. You must lend him the combined strength of your minds, which will help to strengthen the power of the talisman. You do it like this," he said, walking to them. Then he placed his palm on the foreheads of the two diviners and stood silently.

Alia could see the concentration on the faces of both Zimpf and Aistra as they absorbed the knowledge the Zduhac implanted directly into their minds. When he finally released them, they stared at him in awe.

"How…" Zimpf hesitated, swallowed hard, then continued. "How is it that I was never taught how to communicate from mind to mind without touch?" he asked in amazement.

YeYe smiled. "Because it is old knowledge, lost knowledge that I am sharing."

Zimpf knelt, took the old man's hand in his, and placed his forehead on it in a sign of respect and gratitude. "Thank you," he said humbly.

"As for you…" The Zduhac turned to face Shao. "What I must ask of you will be the most difficult thing you have ever had to face."

Shao nodded, his face masked in resolve. "I am ready, YeYe."

"You must not fight."

Shao blinked in surprise. The order was clearly not what he was expecting.

"You will want to fight to protect those whom you love and those under your protection. But you cannot fight this battle. If you do, you will die. If you die, Alia will fail, and the world will fall to the malevolence of this rogue mage," the old man said earnestly.

"I understand, YeYe," Shao answered.

"You must suppress all of your instincts and training," the old man continued seriously. "It will be incredibly difficult for you, but I want you to vow before me that you will not do battle against this foe or his minions."

"You have my vow," Shao promised.

"Thank you," the Zduhac replied softly before continuing. "I will give you one exception to this rule. If you are invited to take part in a tournament, then you may participate, and in that case, you must win."

Shao bowed before the old man in acceptance of his commands.

Then the Zduhac turned to Alia. "You have already started on your path, my child." He smiled at her. "Your task will flow naturally out of who you are and who you have become."

Alia gazed at the old man, her eyes wide with fear. "What is my task?" she asked nervously.

"I think you know," YeYe told her, looking directly into her eyes.

"I have to confront Marek," Alia whispered.

The Zduhac nodded. "Yes," he replied quietly.

"I'm afraid of him," she admitted to the old man. "He has used his evil to mesmerize me on several occasions, and now he has the Aghara…" She trailed off, looking at the Zduhac with a mute appeal.

"Know that I have already given you the bond to resist his spells. He cannot mesmerize you, nor can he separate you from those you love," he assured her.

"But—" Shao started to object.

The old man held up his hand for silence, and Shao fell quiet.

"My time grows short," the Zduhac announced. "I have given each of you tasks that must be obeyed without fail. You are the Four Lands' best hope for salvation; you must defeat the rogue mage and his evil power source." Then the kind old man began to dissipate until only his words remained.

The group stood silently for a few minutes, looking back and forth at each other.

"I guess we'd better get started then," Shao said.

They struck the camp and headed east, traveling at a mile-eating canter.

At the top of each hill, Alia was sure that they would see the camp of the enemy below, but each valley was empty and silent.

She grew more anxious with each passing mile until her nerves were stretched as tight as lute strings.

Just after lunch, they descended into a broad valley with hills on all sides. There were woods that sloped gently down each hill, ending in a graceful basin. It was beautiful, quiet, and peaceful. Alia wished they could stop there for a little while and rest.

She looked over at Shao, expecting to see him smiling back at her. Instead, he was quiet, focused. She saw him exchange a hurried glance with Zimpf. She saw Zimpf nod once, quick and sharp. It was then she realized the valley was quiet. Too quiet. No animals moved; no birds sang.

Her stomach did a somersault of fear, and then they were surrounded. Marek's army had found them.

Marek spent several days isolated in his tent with only his pain and his anger as companions. He had amassed a large following, several hundred strong, of Vheral family groups, and he knew that he could show no weakness. So, he suffered alone in silence.

Nabii helped him on that first night. The diviner insisted that he knew nothing about healing. But despite his blindness, the old man administered the right calming tea in the correct amount then proceeded to set Marek's nose properly.

As for the injuries on his thighs, buttocks, and lower back, nothing could really help the mage except time and a deep cushion for his chair.

When Marek was finally alone, he examined the injuries from the wooden spoon and was shocked to find that they were akin to both a beating from a spanking rod, leaving red, sore welts that would certainly bruise, and a lashing from a horse whip, with its long tears and shredded skin. It was as though Alia's weapon had changed form in the middle of her tirade and she hadn't noticed.

Despite his confinement, Marek continued with his scheme to dominate the will of the innocent Vheral people by poisoning their minds with his own. Occasionally, he used small doses of the substance within the Aghara to control those few leaders who questioned his actions.

The mage was pleased with his progress to rule an entire nation, but it wasn't enough. He didn't just want to be the leader of a rag-tag group of natives here at the top of the world. He wanted to rule the entirety of the Four Lands. In order to achieve that goal—at least, according to Nabii—he still had to somehow enlist Alia's unwilling help in order to utilize the full power of the Aghara.

Once he achieved that goal, he would discard her as no more than chattel.

Chapter 26 – The Mage's Army

The group stood perfectly still except for Sabio. He dismounted and walked forward, trailing his horse behind him, while he held both palms up in a gesture of peace. Three men walked toward him.

Alia surmised that they must be the leaders of the Vherals that surrounded them. Nervously, she watched them approach.

Perhaps, she thought, they will react to Sabio the same way all of the other families reacted—with fear and respect.

"Greetings," Sabio said politely, bowing to the three men. "I am Sabio Omu Olori—" he began. But he never finished.

The largest of the leaders slapped Sabio so hard that he immediately spun around and hit the ground hard. As he spun, he swung the strange staff with the zafiir embedded on the top around his head and pointed it toward Alia and her group. Alia got a quick glimpse of the blue stone, but nothing special happened.

"I know who you all are," the big man sneered. "You are Sabio the traitor and his spies. My master has sent us to capture you. You will accompany us to our camp to face justice."

Before anyone could say anything else, Shao was out of his saddle and helping Sabio up and onto his horse.

Shao had an expression on his face that Alia had never seen before—part determination and part rage. He stared at the leader of their captors as though daring him to interfere.

The big man, perhaps sensing his danger, stepped back in fear. Then, looking around at his troops, he seemed to gain courage from their numbers.

"Surround the prisoners," he ordered. "We leave now."

There were perhaps a hundred Vherals who had been hiding in the tall grass. None of them were mounted, but they surrounded Alia and her friends and began walking. The five mounted captives accompanied them docilely.

The captors with their submissive prisoners marched east until well after dark. By the time they stopped, Alia was drooping with weariness, and she could see Sabio swaying dangerously in his saddle. As soon as they were given permission to dismount, she walked quickly to the young man and, together with Shao, helped him to the ground. Sabio's left eye was swollen almost shut, and his lip was split wide open.

Alia went to her saddle, untied her medical bag, then sat beside the young diviner and began treating him. She saw that several of the Vherals were watching her with interest as she applied a numbing salve on the left side of his face and then carefully sewed up his lip with tiny, even stitches. Later, when dinner was brought to them, she took the cup of warm water that was handed to her and used it to make a tea to alleviate pain; she handed it to Sabio.

He thanked her, drank it gratefully, and then fell asleep.

Just as she stretched out on her own blanket, a Vheral approached her.

"Miss?" he asked politely. "Are you a healer?"

"I am in training," she replied.

"Will you please look at my friend?"

"What's wrong?" Alia asked. She knew they were the enemy and, as such, she shouldn't be helping them. She hesitated for a moment, but they were humans – humans who needed help. She was a healer and as such she couldn't turn down anyone in need. She had taken an oath to treat anyone who was injured or sick.

Another Vheral approached, carrying a young man; they laid him near the fire by Alia.

"What happened to him?" she asked as she examined the unconscious man.

"We don't know," his friends said. "When he went to bed, he was fine. Then this morning, we found him like this."

Alia frowned, going over in her mind all the things that could cause such a reaction. She checked the man thoroughly, even pulling off his socks. Finally, on the bottom of his left heel, she found two perfectly round puncture wounds.

"Snake bite," she told his friends in a sinking tone, showing them the marks. There was no treatment available to cure snake venom. All Alia could do was treat his symptoms and hope the man would survive. So, she went to work. She gave him an antidote for his fever and then dosed him with every known concoction to alleviate his remaining reactions to the snake's venom. She worked with the young man all night, and by morning, he was doing better. His breathing was not so labored, and his lips had changed from a dusky purple to a healthy pink.

As they made ready to continue their journey, Alia gave the medicine she had been using to the victim's friends with instructions on how to continue his treatment.

They left shortly after that and continued traveling. Their captors were unfailingly polite after Alia had treated the young man, although she was never sure why they were so respectful. Was it because she had helped, or was it because of Sabio's reputation? Was it the dangerous persona that radiated from Shao's very presence? Or was Aistra carefully controlling the mood with her strange talent? Whatever the reason, the Vherals were kind, courteous, and very distant. As evening fell on the second day of travel, they topped a hill, and below lay a massive encampment of hundreds of Vherals.

Sabio gasped with shock. Alia thought that he had probably never seen so many people together in one place.

They were escorted to the very center of the camp and ushered into a large tent. The flap was closed and tied, and they were told to stay there. Shao peered out.

"We're being very carefully guarded," he announced. "They want to be sure that we don't escape until Marek decides what to do with us."

"So, we just wait then?" Alia asked.

"It's what we came for," Zimpf told them.

"Can you *see* anything, Zimpf?" Shao wanted to know.

Zimpf sat on the ground and covered his eyes with his hands in concentration. After several minutes of silence, Aistra sat beside him and placed her palm on his face. Immediately, he opened his eyes.

"We need to make a plan," he suddenly announced with a smirk.

The five of them plotted quietly.

Shortly after dark, the Vheral man who had slapped Sabio

marched forcefully into their tent and demanded that they follow him.

"You are to be judged," he announced rudely.

They trailed behind the man, who took them to a huge bonfire not far from where they were being held. They were told to sit on the ground on one side of the fire; facing them were perhaps a hundred Vheral men, all staring at them with angry, accusatory eyes. According to Sabio, these men were the heads of their individual families and would act as judges.

Alia felt much the same as she did when she had faced the leader of the orcs when she had been abducted. She swallowed hard in absolute terror.

"These are the spies that our master told us to capture," began the Vheral leader. "They seek to inflame our western brothers against us in their evil plan to sow discord and hatred among our people. I have brought them here to be judged and to see that judgment carried out!"

The men facing them began to chant and rattle their spears in agreement.

"We will end their scheme to destroy our very way of life, and we will end it tonight!" he shouted, waving his spear high in the air.

Their judges began shouting and waving their weapons in return. There were several cries of "Kill them!"

Then the man grabbed Alia, yanking her to her feet, grasping her arm painfully, and shaking her forcefully. "We will punish all but this one," he sneered, putting his face close to her ear. "The master has a special punishment planned for this one."

The men shrieked and bellowed and cheered, laughing raucously.

Alia looked at Shao in terror. He nodded and winked in return.

She immediately felt better.

Shao, with a look of absolute defiance, stood up to face the leader.

"You will not touch her," he ordered in a low, dangerous tone.

The man threw Alia down and immediately swung an angry fist at Shao, clearly planning to knock him forcefully, if not fatally, to the ground.

But Shao calmly stepped to one side and turned slightly so that the man missed his target completely.

Stunned, the leader tried to hit Shao again, but again Shao simply danced out of the way.

Then he tried to grab the martial artist, and once more, Shao slipped easily through the man's hands.

Roaring with anger, the leader pulled out a huge knife and charged at Shao, clearly planning on stabbing his opponent to death. But again, he was thwarted by Shao's skill and pure athleticism. The martial artist slid gracefully out of the charging man's path, and the man, suddenly meeting no resistance, tripped and fell heavily to the ground. His knife flew several feet away, landing at Sabio's feet.

Not once did Shao even touch the man. He had obeyed the Zduhac's absolute command to not fight.

Calmly, Sabio bent to pick up the weapon and then stood to face their accusers.

"I am Sabio Omu Olori," he announced dramatically, holding the knife up in one hand and his staff aloft in the other.

The crowd was instantly silenced. They had all heard of Sabio Omu Olori. He was the Vheral who could *see* the future, the Vheral who *knew* things, the Vheral who could bless and curse with a cruel evenhandedness.

"I am a man of the Vherals. I am a shaman of our people. As is my right, I demand a trial by action."

Then, as though to accentuate his words, he swung the staff he held in his right hand over the heads of the judging crowd. This time, Alia saw what looked like blue sparks being released from the zafiir. She was sure none of the Vherals were able to see it.

First, the men in the front began to nod, until slowly, the entire throng agreed with Sabio's demand.

The big Vheral leader who had already challenged Shao and lost stood up and bellowed, "I will accept this trial, and I will destroy this spy!" he pointed at Shao dramatically. "Clear a spot!" he demanded of the men sitting nearest to the fire. Immediately, several men began ordering the crowd to back up. Then they set up a ring outlined with sticks and rocks. Soon, the Vherals had gathered excitedly around the impromptu trial arena.

The big leader was the first to enter. He was several inches taller than Shao and at least fifty pounds heavier. It was obvious he thought the size difference would give him an advantage. But Alia knew better. Although she was frightened for her husband, she also felt confident in his talent.

Pausing only to take off his shirt, Shao stepped softly into the ring.

The big leader looked at the crowd, laughed, and then began mocking Shao.

"Come on, skinny," he taunted. "Show me what you have."

Shao didn't respond. But Alia saw a slight smile turn up at the corners of his mouth. He stood silently, waiting.

The leader then began dancing around the arena, punching at the air and sidestepping around Shao.

Still, Shao didn't respond.

The crowd began stamping their feet and hitting the butts of their spears on the ground.

The leader laughed in delight at his admirers. Then, without warning, he swung a heavy blow at Shao. He missed.

Shao had moved quickly to the side, and at the same time, trapped the man's arm with his own and delivered a resounding blow to his shoulder. Then Shao let go and stepped back.

The man roared in anger and charged at Shao, who sidestepped him swiftly, threw his arm straight out, and caught the leader with a solid blow to his throat.

Gasping and choking, the man fell to his knees.

Shao stepped back politely and waited for the man to rise again.

The crowd grew quiet.

Alia felt like she was watching a cat play with a mouse.

The leader got up again and walked slowly toward Shao. Clearly, he had decided to try a new method of fighting.

The Vherals cheered encouragingly.

Shao stood very still. When the man was within a couple of feet of him, Shao exploded, jumping toward the man and punching him with a devastating blow to the chest. The leader fell backward, hit the ground hard, and didn't get back up. The contest was over. Shao had won.

The crowd froze in surprise.

Shao bowed politely to the silent group and turned to rejoin his friends. Just before he stepped from the arena, there was the sudden twang from a bowstring, and then there was another. Shao, quick as lightning, caught the first shaft before it could do any harm. But there was a second arrow shot on the heels of the first, and it was suddenly protruding from Shao's right shoulder. He froze, then turned to stare threateningly at the bowman. Without even looking at his injury, he reached up and broke the shaft of the arrow off a few inches from the entry point, leaving the arrowhead buried just beneath his skin.

Alia bolted toward her injured husband, but Shao, his face a thundercloud of deadly anger, prowled toward the young bowman.

"Stop!" Sabio shouted in a resounding voice. Everyone froze. Even Shao stopped his deadly advance.

"We will take our injured man to our tent to be treated," he demanded. "When we return, you," he said, pointing at the bowman, "will meet our champion in the arena as punishment for disobeying the rules of a trial by action. This is our law," he commanded in a ringing tone.

No one said anything for a moment, and then the crowd began to cheer. There was to be a second competition!

The bowman turned pale as Shao smiled bleakly at him.

Once they were in the tent, Alia immediately went to work. Unlike the last time Shao had been hurt, she treated his injury with cool professionalism. She examined the injury, then applied a numbing salve. She wanted to give him a tea to alleviate pain, but he refused.

"That stuff always makes me sleepy," he admitted. "I might need my wits about me."

"This will hurt," she told him. She carefully enlarged the wound using a special knife she kept in her medical bag.

Shao winced but didn't cry out.

With more room, Alia was able to remove the arrowhead carefully, grateful that it didn't pierce his shoulder deeply. Then she checked him for any additional damage and sewed the gash together. Afterward, she applied a healing salve and wrapped the injured shoulder.

After that, she cried.

Shao took her in his arms to comfort her. "I'm fine," he told her. "And once I defeat him in the arena—" he started.

But Alia had pulled back to stare at him incredulously. "What are you saying?" she demanded. "You are not going back into the arena with that injury. I will not allow it!"

Shao looked at her, his eyebrows raised in surprise. "Wait, you… what?" he muttered, confused.

"You heard what I said," she said firmly, placing her hands on her hips.

"I'll be fine," he insisted.

"You can't *know* that," she asserted.

"Zimpf," Shao pleaded to his friend.

Zimpf lowered his head in concentration. After a few moments, he looked at Alia's angry face.

"I'm sorry, Alia," he said. "Shao must return to the arena." Then he grinned. "But he will win," he added nonchalantly.

Alia didn't answer. She turned her back on the two men and looked steadily at the ground. She didn't want anyone to see her cry. After a few minutes, she was able to turn back to Shao, dry-eyed.

"If you rip out those stitches," she threatened, "I'm going to put them back in using a rusty awl and some burlap string."

Shao looked at her in surprise. He had never seen her angry like this, and he had most certainly never seen her angry with him. He glanced at Zimpf and tilted his head quickly at the tent flap.

"Come on," Zimpf said to Aistra and Sabio, "let's step outside." As they were walking to the door, Alia heard Zimpf ask about the blue sparks from Sabio's staff. She didn't hear the answer.

Alia looked at the ground again. She was very upset and was still trying to control her emotions. After a few moments, she calmed herself and looked up. Shao was staring at his feet like an abashed schoolboy.

Her heart melted.

"I'm so scared," she admitted quietly.

"You know that I will always protect you," he promised sincerely, looking directly at her.

"I'm scared for you," she maintained, slapping at his arm playfully.

He smiled gratefully at her. "At least you know that I'll be fine, and if it helps, I'll fight with my arm like this," he said, holding his right arm across his chest. "Then I can't rip the stitches out."

Alia looked at him as he held his arm steady and gazed at her in sincerity and adoration. Finally, she smiled ruefully.

"Okay," she agreed. But as they started to leave the tent together, she muttered, "But I meant what I said about the awl and the burlap."

Shao chuckled.

Then they joined the others outside and were escorted by their guards to the arena.

Shao, holding his injured arm firmly against his chest as he had promised, stepped lethally into the ring. The bowman was pushed forcibly inside by two burly guards. Alia heard one of the men growl, "you have to pay for breaking the law," before throwing the bowman to the ground.

The offender finally rose shakily to his feet, his face etched in fear. He turned toward Shao, and Shao stepped back in surprise. The attacker was a thin, young boy. Alia thought he couldn't have been older than fourteen.

Shaking his head in resignation, Shao began stalking the child as the crowd cheered and screamed and pounded the butts of their spears on the ground.

Finally, in a move of pure desperation, the child charged at Shao. The martial artist turned, dropped to the ground, and swept the child's feet out from under him. Once he was down, Shao stepped neatly on his back, leaned over, and pushed the boy's face directly into the dust, effectively washing his face with the smooth, powdery dirt. Then he pulled the bowman up by one skinny arm, kicked him a solid blow directly on his bottom, and forced him out of the ring.

"The next time you try to assassinate me," Shao threatened, "I will do more than dirty your little face."

The child turned to stare at Shao with both fear and gratitude, nodded, then ran quickly away.

The crowd cheered.

For a moment, Alia thought that maybe they had won the Vherals' hearts. The judges that had surrounded the arena continued to cheer for Shao. They were laughing and friendly. Several approached him and congratulated him on his handling of the situation.

A few of the leaders went to talk to Sabio respectfully.

Aistra and Zimpf stood quietly to one side. An older man stood beside them, gesturing animatedly.

The young man whose snakebite Alia had treated approached her and thanked her for taking care of him. His father, who was an elder, accompanied him and offered Alia a necklace in payment. A handful of others also asked Alia to treat their sick friends or relatives. Just as she turned to get her medical bag, she saw him.

Standing at the edge of the crowd, wearing a dark cloak with the hood pulled low, stood the invader of her nightmares.

Marek.

The Mage

Marek studied his plans, he reread his spells, he revised his strategy. He was ready. The mage stood and made his way easily to the front of the tent. He paused before making his exit, then looked back as he heard a slight noise.

"The woman and her friends will not be easy to defeat," The old man warned. Once again he had suddenly appeared in the tent.

Marek stared at him coldly: then, tired of the insolence, raised his hand to perform a fire spell.

Nabii laughed. It was a heartless, calculating sound devoid of any humor. "Do you seek to annihilate me?" I have guided you without fail. Destroy me and you destroy your own future. Then without another word, he swept imperiously from the tent

Marek didn't respond; he allowed the old man to leave unscathed. It was time to claim Alia.

Chapter 27 – The Rogue Mage

Alia froze. For a moment, it seemed like everything began to move in slow motion.

Shao laughed with one of the Vheral leaders.

Sabio raised his palm to the forehead of another man. Zimpf stepped beside Sabio, his brows creased in concentration and his hand on the young diviner's face.

Aistra smiled at the older man she had been talking to as he stared at Sabio and Zimpf.

No one else saw the man at the edge of the crowd.

Alia saw Marek's pale, long-fingered hand escape from the folds of his black cloak. He crooked his index finger at her in an imperious beckoning gesture. Everything and everyone fell away from her vision. Alia could only see Marek. She shifted her weight from one foot to the other and took that first fatal step toward him, her eyes staring and her mind bemused. She took a second step and then a third.

"Alia!" Aistra screamed in a panicked tone. "No!"

But by then, Alia was unable to focus on anything but the powerful calling of the rogue mage. She took another step and then another.

"Shao!" Aistra shrieked.

The martial artist spun around and quickly assessed the threat, his eyes wide with fear. Then he sprinted toward Alia. Zimpf and Sabio both turned in time to see Shao tackle her to the ground. He rolled up quickly, looking around for danger as blood slowly seeped from the torn stitches in his right shoulder. Seeing nothing, he reached down to help Alia up.

She turned to stare vacantly at Shao; it was as if she was listening to someone else, someone only she could hear.

Zimpf ran to them, but Aistra was already there, her hands on either side of Alia's face.

"He's here!" Aistra announced in a horrified tone. "Marek is here."

Just then, the previously clear night sky suddenly boiled over with black, roiling clouds, and a mournful wind ghosted its way through the camp, picking up speed as it assailed the Vherals. The gale wrapped around the people, encircling them, whispering, instructing, changing.

For a moment, everyone was immobile—hearing, listening, learning.

Everyone but Sabio. Clutching his staff with his right hand, he ran to Zimpf and touched him lightly with the zafiir. Zimpf jerked, suddenly aware of the unnatural wind. The two men ran together to Aistra, Shao, and Alia; Sabio touched each of them with his staff, and they all roused to consciousness.

All except for Alia.

She continued to stare at the spot where Marek had stood only moments before, her hand held out imploringly.

"Alia!" Zimpf shouted, trying to get her attention.

She didn't respond; her eyes were glassy and unfocused as though she was mesmerized.

"What's happening?" Shao yelled, his arm wrapped protectively around his wife.

But before anyone could answer him, the wind suddenly dissipated. Instantly, they were surrounded by most of the Vherals in the camp. There were hundreds. Their faces were flat with anger, and they held their spears pointed threateningly at the small group. The silence was deafening.

Sabio thrust his staff into the ground and stood quietly, one hand firmly grasping the shaft.

"Stop!" Sabio commanded the Vherals.

Strangely, they all paused. Then a tall, thin man in the very back forced his way through the throng.

"Who are you to give orders?" he demanded arrogantly.

"I am Sabio Omu Olori, and I am a member of the Vheral family," he asserted.

The thin man laughed. "No," he declared angrily. "Your group lives west of here. You are nothing but a usurper and a spy. Tie them up," the thin man ordered. "Then we will decide their punishment."

Before anyone could move, however, two large, heavily armed guards pushed their way through the crowd.

"The master will decide her fate," one of them declared, grabbing Alia roughly by the arm. The second guard grasped her other arm, and together, they began pulling Alia through the crowd.

But there was no need for their violent force. She seemed willing, eager even, to accompany them.

Shao, his face a mask of pure fury, shouldered his way past the spear-wielding crowd, snatching weapons from the Vherals and breaking them effortlessly in his furious race to reach Alia.

"I am going with her," he announced quietly to the guards when they turned to stare at him.

The men looked at each other for a moment before one of them finally spoke.

"No," he firmly denied the order. "The master said we were to bring her alone."

"I will not be separated from her," Shao demanded grimly.

One of the guards made a signal, and several Vherals stepped toward Shao, brandishing their spears threateningly.

Shao contemptuously swept the spears from first one, then two, then several of his captors until the entire legion began to descend on him.

"Stop it! Stop it!" Aistra shouted at the men. She looked at Shao, including him in her command.

Shao tried to grab her and pull her behind him, but she stopped him.

"Let Alia do this," she said so intensely that he took a step back. "You all will stay right here!" she commanded, turning to face the group of attackers who had begun inching forward. It was clear she was using her talent to control the emotions of those closest to her.

Then she turned to Shao. "You must let Alia go."

"No," he shook his head emphatically. "I will not be separated from her."

"You must. Otherwise, they will kill you, Shao," she said, looking directly at him. "Remember what YeYe told us," she whispered softly.

"'If you die, Alia will fail, and the world will fall to the malevolence of this mage.'"

Shao froze.

"Besides," she continued, "Zimpf told me what happened when you thought you lost Alia. Do you want her to have to live like that if she loses you?" she asked.

"I…" he groaned.

Then Zimpf and Sabio were suddenly there.

"She's right, Shao," Sabio said. "Alia must confront Marek."

The four of them turned to look at Alia. She was staring intently at a large tent erected in a clearing in the middle of the encampment. Whether it was isolated in order to show its importance or because no one wanted to be near it was unclear.

Zimpf stepped forward, taking Shao's elbow in support. "This is Alia's task," he told his friend.

Shao looked at him. "Can you tell me that she will return unscathed?"

"No," Zimpf answered. "I cannot. The future is uncertain."

Shao shook his head stubbornly. "I will not be separated from Alia," he insisted again.

"Shao. Look at me," Sabio commanded.

Shao looked at him, then his eyes widened suddenly.

"This is Alia's task. Let her go." It was Sabio who spoke, but the voice belonged to the Zduhac.

Shao looked down in defeat, tears streaming down his face.

Then, calling to Alia, Sabio asked in the same distant voice, "Are you ready?"

"Yes," she whispered.

Sabio smiled. "Then go to him."

Alia turned and led the Vheral guards toward the tent. She turned once to look back at Shao without recognition.

He watched her leave, his heart in his eyes.

It was dark inside the tent, and a solitary figure waited within. The man had his back to her, but slowly turned upon her entry. He wore a black cloak and had the hood pulled forward to cover his face. A pale, long-fingered hand emerged from the folds and pushed the hood back.

"Hello, Alia," the mage softly uttered her name

It was Marek.

But it was not the Marek Alia had seen in her dream. This man had been badly burned. The skin on the right side of his face was creased and wrinkled, and his beautiful curly hair was missing on that side of his face.

"Oh Marek!" Alia whispered in shock. She stumbled awkwardly toward him and hugged him fiercely before pulling back to examine skin that was stretched in some places and puckered in others.

He stood still while she surveyed his face. His shoulder and his chest on that side were also burned and scarred. She touched it gently, intently, curiously. Finally, she stepped back.

"What happened to you?" she asked. It was clear she didn't remember.

Marek shrugged as though it didn't matter. "Tea?" he invited.

"No," she refused hesitantly. It was as if she knew not to accept his offer but didn't know why.

"This is just tea," he assured her. Then he sat down gingerly on a cushioned chair, indicating that she should take the chair opposite of him.

But Alia remained standing, her arms dangling loosely at her sides.

"What do you want with me?" she asked softly of her old friend.

Marek chuckled evilly. Then he stood and slowly crossed the distance between them, his face creased in the crooked smile she had once found so charming. He wrapped both arms around her and pulled her in to hug her as he used to when they were children and she was frightened or upset.

"I've missed you," he said softly. "And I need your help." Then he began whispering instructions into her ear, his hand rising to cup one side of her head as he laid his cheek against the other.

Alia stood very still, listening to his voice as a strange lassitude came over her.

Marek stepped back, one hand still cupping her face familiarly. He grinned at her, and Alia smiled back.

"You will do this for me," the mage said. It wasn't a question.

Bemused, Alia nodded.

"Good," Marek purred. "My first two assassins, the big fighter and the bowman, did not succeed in murdering the tall, thin man. But I know you can get close enough to do my bidding."

"Yes, Marek," Alia agreed without question. Her eyes were still glazed and far away as she continued listening to a voice only she could hear.

"I have arranged for the others to be executed. But you must be the one to assassinate the martial artist." Marek dropped his hand, his eyes glittering malevolently.

Alia nodded, her eyes unfocused and lost.

There was an unexpected eruption of chaos outside. People began screaming and running as though the camp had been abruptly and viciously attacked.

Marek ignored the chaos.

At that very moment, a strange blue smoke began to seep into the tent.

And inside Alia's mind, a tiny spark of resistance began to bloom.

"I will instruct one of my guards to escort you to the man you are to kill. Once you are close enough, he will hand you a knife. You will go directly to the martial artist, hug him, then plunge the blade into his unprotected back," Marek instructed as he bent to get the weapon from the folds of his cloak.

He either didn't see or didn't care about the strange blue smoke.

Alia took a deep, cleansing breath of the sapphire-colored fumes, and the glazed look suddenly fell away from her sight as the spark became a flame.

Marek started toward the front of the tent to call the guard.

Just as he passed Alia, she grabbed his arm and spun him around to face her.

"What—" he snarled angrily. But he didn't finish.

Alia was glaring at him, her eyes clear and her face angry. Without warning, her fury exploded in a frenzy of revulsion and hatred.

Without warning, she swung her hand to the side and slapped the mage so hard that he tumbled sideways, tripped over a chair, and fell over the table to land in an unceremonious heap on the floor of the tent.

Alia saw the cushion on Marek's chair fly across the room, and she chuckled silently.

"I told you that the next time you try to control me, I will run my blade all the way through your throat!" she snarled in a harsh voice. Then she reached into her tunic and retrieved Mama's long-handled wooden spoon, which she had tucked into her pocket earlier that day.

Marek's eyes widened then narrowed shrewdly as he saw the implement vacillate between a large wooden spoon, a spanking rod, and Alia's sharpened sword.

It was clear that Alia didn't even notice the strangeness of the object. She merely accepted whatever shape it took. Before he could even think to react, Alia took a threatening step forward.

The fluctuating spoon had firmly and fatally settled into one deadly shape.

"Who did this to you?" Marek whispered in astonishment as one hand rose to touch the red handprint forming on his cheek. "How did you break the bond?"

Suddenly, Alia remembered the words the Zduhac had said when he visited them just before they were captured: "Know that I have already given you the bond to resist his spells. He cannot separate you from those you love." And she knew then that the vows she and Shao had shared before the mountain spirit were wonderfully binding and that Marek could never—would never—be able to separate her from the man she loved.

"No one did this to me," Alia snarled hatefully at Marek.

She held her sword with a steady hand, its newly sharpened edge glistening lethally.

The mage stared at her in shock, unable to process the sudden turn of events.

Out of habit, he cut his eyes quickly toward the back of the tent. Alia followed his fleeting look.

Sitting inconspicuously atop the small table in the very corner was a small, black vase.

She strode purposefully across the tent, her weapon still pointed dangerously toward the mage.

Marek started to rise.

Alia whirled around and pushed her weapon against his exposed throat with a slow, steady pressure stopping just short of executing the villain.

"Sit down!" she hissed.

The mage sank back to the ground.

A bright spot of blood slowly seeped from the wound.

Alia lowered her weapon. Almost immediately, it resumed the shape of the wooden spoon. She tucked it back into her pocket and picked up the artifact.

"So, this is the Aghara," she mused, holding the plain-looking vase lightly. It felt alternately hot, then very cold. "This is the magical object you used to force innocent people to obey your will. And it was all in the name of what…power?"

She looked at him steadily.

Marek didn't answer. He didn't even look at her. Instead, he stared at the object in Alia's hands with a glittering, malicious greed.

Shouts from the camp grew louder. Alia could hear people as they fought and died and fled.

The strange blue smoke that had seeped inside the tent began to shift and glow and writhe in its single-minded mission to find the evil contained within the artifact.

Alia took a deep breath and felt suddenly refreshed, energized, strong.

She felt…ready.

Alia held up the Aghara; the wisps from the zafiir moved to embrace it, caressing the vase with a cool, glowing brilliance. The vase responded with a warm radiance of its own.

It was that radiance that allowed Alia to see the thousands of tiny cracks that permeated the surface of the relic.

The Aghara was brittle, fragile, breakable.

Alia gasped in a blinding flash of insight as the Zduhac's task for her coalesced in her mind. She wasn't here to confront the mage. Her task was with the Aghara.

Then, Marek made a fatal mistake.

He slowly began to rise, as though Alia's words were of no importance.

Then he made a sudden, leaping lunge in an attempt to wrest the Aghara from her.

Alia reacted with that instant of trained violence that Shao had instilled in her.

She defended herself with the weapon in her hands.

Without even considering the consequences of her actions, she raised it up, and, using all her strength, smashed it down on Marek's unprotected head.

It made hard contact.

The mage fell backward with a cry of pain. His hands rose to cover the blood which spewed from his head.

The Aghara crashed to the ground.

Alia watched as it shattered irreparably.

There was a moment of shocked silence. Then, what was left of the vase began to boil and steam, emitting a noxious green substance that instantly filled the tent.

The mage wailed an almost inhuman cry of loss and horror. "NO!" he shrieked.

Alia fled, her task completed.

The explosive pandemonium that had erupted outside intensified uncontrollably as the green mist from within the rogue mage's tent began to permeate the area.

Marek's soldiers collapsed by the dozens.

The few Vherals untouched by the noxious substance dispersed in a frenzy as they escaped in all directions.

"Alia!" She heard Shao screaming her name, but she couldn't find him. The thick green fog which swirled with the chaos of fleeing Vherals left her blinded to an escape route.

"Shao!" she screamed as she coughed and choked.

Then she heard Aistra. "Shao! Here!" And the two of them materialized out of the melee of panicked people.

Shao picked up Alia, cradled her against his chest as though she were a small child, and sprinted with her back to the others, Aistra followed closely.

"Let's get out of here!" Zimpf ordered. "Before that weird green smoke catches us."

Sabio emerged out of nowhere, leading the horses. Shao lifted Alia onto her horse, the rest of them mounted, and together, they galloped toward the west.

Marek awoke suddenly, confused.

"What happened?" he wondered.

The tent he was in was filled with noxious green smoke. He could barely see through the fog. His chest hurt, and when he coughed—a deep racking sound—blood splattered across the room.

I'm dying, he thought. This is what it feels like to die.

His head throbbed with pain, and he reached up to feel the injury. His hand came away from his hair covered in blood. He tried to sit up, but instead, he sprawled weakly back onto the floor, where he lay lost.

"Get control!" *he heard a voice say harshly. He raised his head weakly and looked around, blinking owlishly.*

"Who spoke to me?" *he asked aloud.*

"Get up!" *an inhuman voice snarled.*

Marek thought it sounded like Nabii, but no one was in the tent with him.

The mage rolled to his side and finally managed to leverage himself onto his feet by pushing himself up with his hands like a small child. His legs shook, uncertain if they could bear his weight. Like a toddler, he lurched his way step-by-step across the floor, holding on to first a chair and then a table to keep from stumbling clumsily.

His hands were trembling so hard that he could barely open the tent flaps.

Outside, chaos reigned.

People ran.

Screams rang out.

Women wailed.

Men fought.

Children cried.

Bodies lay prone.

Green smoke ran in and around the people like long-fingered tendrils of evil.

Marek threw his head back and laughed malevolently.

Chapter 28 – The Strategy

It had grown late, and Sh'ron sat quietly by the dying fire, listening as Chhdar, Amicu, Ciern, and Skala discussed the meeting with the western Vherals.

Ciern had ended the meeting by suggesting that one person from each tribe volunteer to act as the liaison for the rest of them. Since most Vheral groups were made of families who had branched off, it was easily arranged. Then, in the event of an attack, they could communicate quickly. He also suggested that a series of runners be organized so that messages could be sent swiftly and efficiently.

At the close of the meeting, the leaders cheered Ciern, many hailing him as a hero. It seemed like almost everyone in attendance wanted to talk to him alone, and Ciern had acquiesced to each request for a private conference. Amicu, of course, stood quietly in the background of each meeting, occasionally offering advice or suggestions.

Skala, as usual, stomped over and sat unobtrusively by the fire, listening, observing, and learning.

Sh'ron and Chhdar were approached almost immediately to tend to the sick and injured.

It grew late, and the day drew to a close. All Sh'ron wanted to do was sleep. Just then, an old friend approached them; it was Ghan.

"I'm sorry to bother you so late," he said. "But I wanted to wait until things quieted down before I came to speak with you." Then, without hesitation, he announced, "I have seen your friends."

"You saw Alia!" Sh'ron exclaimed.

He nodded solemnly.

"What's wrong?" Amicu questioned shrewdly.

Ghan hesitated as though he had to deliver bad news.

Sh'ron's heart began to race and her face turned pale.

"They were traveling with Sabio Omu Olori, and they were going to meet that rogue mage. They said that Alia had to be the one to confront him to destroy his power." Ghan paused for a moment to think about how to say what he needed to tell them.

"I told them about a visitor we had a week or so after you all had left. This man was fleeing from the groups who had organized under the leadership of the evil shaman. From what I understand, this mage was looking for a woman. She and anyone with her was to be taken before the mage to be executed for an unnamed crime. There is no doubt that the woman he hunted was Alia."

Sh'ron drew in a sharp breath. Everyone else was silent.

"Thank you for telling us," Ciern said respectfully.

"Were you aware of the mage's plan?" Ghan asked directly.

"No," Sh'ron replied in a worried tone. Then she looked at the others in consternation. "Should we go after them?"

Everyone was quiet for several minutes, thinking. Finally, Chhdar spoke directly to Sh'ron.

"No, Sh'ron," he said. "It's too late to help them. If they were successful, they are already on the way to meet us. We should finish our task here first. Then we will leave for the meeting spot in one more day. If they do not meet us, then we can formulate a new plan."

Sh'ron stared at her husband, her lower lip quivering with emotion. Chhdar never countered her wishes. He wrapped one big arm around waist and pulled her close. "It would be a bad idea to go running all over the Wilds searching for them. The quickest way to find them will be to stick to the original plan. Don't you agree?"

"I guess you're right," she muttered through her tears.

"But know this," he said in a threatening tone. "If that mage has harmed my sister-in-law in any way whatsoever, I will hunt him down and give him a smack bottom he will never recover from!"

Despite her tears, Sh'ron burst out laughing, and everyone, including Ghan, laughed with her.

They spent the next day much the same way they had spent the last two weeks. Amicu, Ciern, and Skala attended meetings with the liaisons elected from the Vheral leaders while Sh'ron and Chhdar treated patients.

When they first started acting as healers, Sh'ron had been in charge. She examined each person, asked questions, and then dispensed tonics based on their answers. Her decisions were based solely on what Alia had reviewed with her. But now Chhdar was suddenly in charge, he seemed to know by intuition, knowledge, or just plain sense how to treat each ailment. Sh'ron was awed by Chhdar's gift for medicine, and she fully intended to speak to Alia and then to Sairima about furthering his education.

The following day, the gathering broke up, and everyone began to go their own way. Sh'ron's group traveled for a couple of days with Ghan and his small family. They rode cautiously southeast, always on the lookout for Vherals who were under Marek's spell. On the morning of the third day, however, they split up. Ghan's family continued northeast while Sh'ron and her friends turned southeast toward Sabio's original camp.

They picked up the pace and journeyed toward the designated meeting spot at a mile-eating canter. They rode cautiously up each hill, but then Ciern insisted that they stop so Skala could scout ahead. Without Zimpf to look for danger, they were forced to rely on stealth.

Sh'ron quickly grew impatient. She wanted to arrive at the rendezvous spot as quickly as possible. She began to worry desperately about her twin, despite the Zduhac's assurance that Alia was under his protection.

On the fifth day, however, Ciern's caution paid off. They had reached the apex of yet another hill. Skala had climbed carefully to the top and laid in the tall grass, alert to anything amiss. Normally, after several minutes, he stood up and waved them forward, but this time, he lay flat on the ground, still as a stone. Finally, he looked over his shoulder at them, his forefinger pressed firmly against his lips.

"Wait here," Ciern whispered. He started up the hill toward Skala; Amicu followed him. Ciern looked at his friend, one eyebrow raised questioningly, but didn't say anything. A few moments later, the three of them rejoined Sh'ron and Chhdar.

"There is a group of at least thirty Vherals on the far side of the next valley. They are almost certainly with Marek's army."

"How can you tell?" Sh'ron asked.

"Because they are all men. There are no women or children in their family group. Also, they seem to be travel-worn, and their horses are lathered from hard riding."

"Are they coming this way?" Chhdar asked.

Skala nodded.

"There is no place to take cover. Even the grass isn't tall enough to conceal us," Amicu pointed out.

"So that means a fight," Chhdar said, unsheathing his sword.

Sh'ron nodded, following suit.

Ciern and Amicu looked at each other steadily for a moment. Finally, Amicu spoke. "Funnel strategy?"

Ciern shook his head. "Too much room," he answered. "Snare procedure?"

"We don't have time. Net technique?" Amicu countered.

"We don't have enough people," Ciern replied. "What about a blaze box?"

Amicu shook his head. "That could become uncontrollable in this dry grass."

Ciern nodded glumly. "We don't have time for punjis, do we?" he asked, looking at Amicu hopefully.

Amicu scratched his head. "No. What about a deadfall of some sort?"

Ciern looked around. "We don't have what we need to set it up. How about a camouflage pit?" Ciern proposed hopefully.

Amicu shook his head, then he smiled at Ciern, his eyes glittering maliciously. "Trap bowl," he said. Then he leaned over, untying something from inside the bedroll strapped to the back of his saddle.

"Is that what I think it is?" Ciern asked, looking at Shao's blowgun along with dozens of darts and a small container of poisoned liquid.

Amicu nodded, an evil grin on his face.

"A trap bowl *and* a fusillade of darts." Ciern nodded professionally, "I like it."

Sh'ron, Chhdar, and Skala had listened quietly during the strange discussion.

"What are you talking about?" Sh'ron finally demanded.

"We were discussing various defensive techniques," Amicu answered. Then he went on to explain the system they decided on while Ciern began to set up the trap.

Several minutes later, the soldiers from Marek's army galloped over the hill and almost simultaneously reined their horses to a surprised stop. At the base of the next hill, sitting forlornly atop a roan mare, was a blond woman. She almost looked like she was waiting for them.

The men glanced back and forth at each other, and then in a cluster that resembled a large circle, sprinted toward Sh'ron, each soldier trying to outrace the others. Initially, no one noticed that one, then two, then several men began falling from their horses as Amicu, carefully camouflaged in the grass, skillfully embedded poisoned darts into their faces, necks, and arms. By the time the soldiers realized something was amiss, nearly half of them had succumbed to the deadly fusillade of darts.

In confusion, the remainder of the soldiers did the worst possible maneuver; they banded together in a tight knot, which made them an even easier target for Amicu's lethal barrage. Several more men fell before the remaining troops scattered in all directions.

Sh'ron whistled sharply, and Chhdar, Ciern, and Skala came galloping from around the side of the hill to pursue the fleeing members of Marek's tattered group of fighters. Within a few minutes, the entire troop had been decimated.

Afterward, the five defenders drew together.

"Good strategy," Chhdar complimented them.

"I rather liked it," Amicu said in a vast understatement as he carefully replaced Shao's blowgun, along with the container of poison and the remaining darts, back into his bedroll. Then he climbed back onto his horse, and they continued their journey to the southeast in search of their missing friends.

"At least," Marek sneered, "Alia has no idea why I summoned her."

But she would learn. Oh yes. She would learn. He would find her, and he would teach her.

The lesson would be harsh.

Chapter 29 – Evasion

At first, Alia felt dizzy and disoriented after having inhaled some of the thick green smoke that had spewed forth from the shattered Aghara. As they began to ride, she noticed that Shao stayed close to her, occasionally leaning over to steady her in her saddle, his face a mask of concern. But after several minutes of breathing fresh, clean air, Alia began to feel stronger and more clearheaded. She straightened in her saddle and nodded at Shao, indicating that she was feeling better.

The group galloped quickly down a hill and around a bend without pursuit, and Alia began to think that perhaps they would escape Marek's army. They had found their weapons with their horses, so at least they were all armed. They rode up another hill, and just as they started down the backside of it, she heard a shout.

"There they are!" screamed the tall, thin Vheral man that had wanted them tied up just before Alia went to meet with Marek. He had rounded the hill to their left and was pointing at them with the shaft of his spear. There were perhaps twenty or so men with him.

"Do not harm them!" he shouted at the lead soldier, who had pulled his arm back in preparation for throwing his spear. "The master wants them alive!"

Immediately, the warriors ran to intercept them and were on them before Alia's group could escape. Shao dismounted instantly and charged toward their attackers. He took out two men with well-aimed punches, hitting the first man in the throat with a quick side chop and turning swiftly to punch the second with a powerful blow to the chest. Then Shao dropped, sweeping the feet out from under another three men. He stomped hard on the knee of one man, turned and stabbed the other in the stomach with his wicked-looking knife, and then kicked the third man in the face. He continued his one-man vendetta, giving his group plenty of time to draw their weapons.

Zimpf fired arrow after arrow indiscriminately toward their attackers.

Alia drew her sword just as the tall, thin man reached her and tried to pull her from her saddle. With a violence borne of pure rage, Alia eviscerated the man then contemptuously kicked him to the ground, where he fell, his hands trying to hold on to the loops and coils that boiled out from his belly. Then, swinging her sword hard, she turned quickly, lopping off the head of another man who ran screaming at her. A third dashed upon her left and tried to push her off of her horse using his spear as a pole, but Alia chopped the surprised man's weapon in half and then proceeded to stab him through the chest.

Sabio sat calmly on his horse, using his staff as a baton, alternately striking forward and sideways as his blows generated destruction.

No one he hit got up again.

Aistra had the most unique fighting style. Alia was, at first, frightened for her friend when the first soldier tried to yank Aistra bodily from her mount. Instead of fighting, Aistra merely reached out as though she were going to caress the man's cheek. But, as soon as she laid her hand on his face, he collapsed in a heap onto the ground. She took out two more men in the same fashion.

Their attackers were soundly beaten within minutes. Shao, of course, did the most damage; at least half of the men on the ground were his victims.

Climbing agilely back onto his horse, he looked around, his smile tight with excitement. "Suddenly, I feel a lot better," he announced.

Zimpf laughed. "Let's get out of here before Shao decides to exterminate the entire army," he teased, spurring his horse to the southwest.

The group had two more minor skirmishes; they defeated both groups with that instant violence of trained warriors. By the time the sun finally rose, they were several miles from Marek's campsite. They decided to wend their way into the forest that always bordered the valleys in this part of the world in order to get a few hours' rest before continuing westward.

They set up a simple campsite but lit no fire. Instead, they huddled together to listen to Alia's story of her meeting with Marek.

"As soon as the blue smoke coiled around the Aghara, I could see that it was laced with hundreds and hundreds of cracks," Alia told them. "Then it suddenly occurred to me. My task wasn't with Marek; it was with the Aghara."

Zimpf reached out to touch her forehead, and she instinctively flinched back.

"I'm not going to *vision* you," he said in exasperation.

She relented, letting him touch her forehead softly.

He smiled. "She's right. The Zduhac knew that Alia was the only person Marek would allow close enough to that thing to destroy it."

"It still doesn't answer the question: Why Alia?" Shao wondered with a frown.

"I'll do some research on it when we get back to Asath Tesai," Aistra offered.

"Thank you," Alia told the polyimpano. But she, too, wondered what Marek wanted with her specifically.

"Did you kill him?" Zimpf asked.

"I don't know," she answered.

"It'll be a shame if you didn't," Zimpf commented dryly.

"I didn't take time to inquire after his health," Alia snapped. "I didn't have any weapons other than Mama's spoon, and once the Aghara shattered and that green mist began to fill the tent, I knew I needed to run."

Shao, who hadn't moved more than a few feet from Alia and was now firmly ensconced on her left-hand side, wrapped his right arm around her and pulled her close.

"I think you were amazing," he said, kissing the top of her head while simultaneously glaring at Zimpf.

"I didn't say she failed," Zimpf protested. "But if the mage still lives—"

Before he could continue, Shao interrupted him. "So did you expect Alia, heavily guarded and surrounded by an entire army, to march into the seat of evil alone and assassinate the most wicked mage of our time with only a spoon?" Shao asked in a level tone.

Zimpf looked at Shao, baffled. "No, no," he stuttered. "I was—"

"You were what?" Shao asked, raising his eyebrows threateningly while he surreptitiously slid Mama's big wooden spoon from Alia's tunic pocket and began tapping it thoughtfully into the palm of his left hand.

"I—um…" Zimpf started and then trailed off in confusion, not sure what to say or even do.

"Stop teasing him, Shao," Aistra said in exasperation.

Shao laughed.

Zimpf, finally understanding, raised one eyebrow sardonically. "You two are the perfect couple," he intoned sarcastically. "You are both skilled, brave, vicious, and invincible. Your bravery and fierce nature serve to enhance your reputation, which dashes before you, threatening all in your path. Evil flees from your towering personae."

Sabio looked seriously from one man to the other, his eyes wide and his mouth in a perfect circle. Suddenly, he began to chuckle, quietly at first, and then his laughter intensified until he was howling with glee.

They all laughed with him.

Since they knew they were being pursued, the group decided to travel only at night. They took turns on guard duty throughout the day. When it was Alia's turn, Shao insisted on watching with her.

They did their regular perimeter check and then sat, talking quietly.

"I am so amazed by you," Shao complimented her. Then he chuckled. "I sure would have liked to see that mage when you hauled off and slapped his face."

Alia smiled. "I'm embarrassed to admit that I lost my temper again," she confessed.

Alia looked at the ground.

Shao looked at her curiously, "you told Sh'ron that you lost your temper when Marek invaded your dream. But I have never seen you angry."

She nodded at the ground as though she was embarrassed.

Shao put his forefinger under her chin and raised her head to look at her face. He was smiling fondly. "Do you want to talk about it?"

Alia was quiet for several moments. "When I was a child, I had a vicious temper," she confessed. "I was always getting angry and starting fights. So, my parents sent Sh'ron and me to train in sword fighting."

"You told me about your sword master." He acknowledged.

"One of the reasons Mama and Dada sent us was because of my inability to control my anger. The swordmaster taught me how to remain calm and not succumb to my baser emotions."

Shao nodded. "I'll bet some of those lessons were brutal."

"They were. They were also well deserved."

"Under the circumstances, I'm glad you lost your temper." Then he leaned in and kissed her again and again.

"Alia," he said seriously between kisses. "Can I ask you something?"

"Of course," she assented, kissing him back.

"Did you mean what you said about sewing my shoulder up again with a rusty awl and some burlap string if I ripped out those stitches?"

Alia chuckled. "Of course not."

"Good," he answered, "because I've been hiding something since our escape that I would like you to look at." Then he leaned away and pulled off his shirt. Where Alia had stitched up the arrow wound was a wad of bloodied material that had been crudely stuffed under the dressing.

"Shao!" Alia looked horrified. "Why didn't you tell me?"

"I couldn't." He grimaced in pain. "We were too busy escaping."

By the time he finished his sentence Alia had already grabbed her medical bag and was unwrapping Shao's dressing and pulling out the dirty packing Shao had shoved into the wound. It began to bleed profusely. Alia maintained her professionalism, examining the gash skillfully. She applied a numbing cream, pulled out the pieces of torn and broken stitches, cleaned where the arrow had pierced his shoulder, and stitched the laceration closed using the tiny, even stitches that Sairima had taught her. Afterward, she applied a healing salve and redressed the wound.

Shao sat quietly, watching her work with a look of adoration on his face. By the time she had finished and put her equipment away, Sabio had awoken from the other side of the camp.

"Go to sleep," he told them. "You've both had a rough day, and I'm not sleepy at all."

By the time it was growing dark, everyone was up and ready to leave. Shao returned from where he had been scouting, a worried frown on his face.

"We've got company out there," he said, nodding toward the valley. "It looks like they're organized and are more serious about finding us."

Cautiously, everyone followed Shao to the edge of the forest, where groups of Vherals were riding side by side and back and forth combing the hillside the group had descended earlier. They were clearly working together as they carefully examined the ground for tracks.

"So, what do you think?" Shao asked Zimpf. "Do you think we

should go back into the forest? What do you *see*?"

Zimpf stood quietly for a moment, his eyes far away. Then he looked at Aistra. She nodded, and Zimpf grinned, his dimples springing into his cheeks.

"Well?" Shao said impatiently.

"Aistra has this one," Zimpf reported proudly, smiling at his wife.

Shao's eyes narrowed in thought then grew wide in understanding, then he chuckled. "Can you cover this many of us?" he asked.

She nodded. "I've got this," she told him confidently.

"Got what?" Alia asked.

"Cover us? How? With what?" Sabio asked in confusion.

Zimpf turned to Alia and Sabio. "Aistra has a unique talent," he explained. "She can make herself…imperceptible."

"Like, invisible?" Sabio questioned.

"Not exactly invisible," Zimpf tried to explain. "It's more like she's camouflaged."

Sabio looked at him, confused.

But Alia understood what he meant. She remembered seeing Aistra at the Temple of Anaia as the young woman emerged from her concealed corner in Sifu's quarters. And she recalled Shao's words about Aistra: "She is a polyimpano; she has parts of many talents… she can make herself unnoticeable, for one thing. That's why no one saw her sitting in the corner during the meeting."

"You can hide us too?" Alia asked. "Like you hid in Sifu's quarters?"

Aistra nodded. "I can."

"How will you do it?" Shao asked curiously. "We all can't just hold hands like we did when we were students at Temple sneaking around campus."

Alia looked at him, one eyebrow raised curiously.

"We'll just leave here as a group. Shao, you and Alia will take the lead. I will be in the middle, and Zimpf and Sabio will ride rearguard. We will have to be fairly close." She stopped, thinking for a moment. "Actually, it might be easier if everyone is connected to me somehow."

"Will rope work?" Sabio asked.

"It might," Aistra said thoughtfully, looking at Zimpf.

He stood quietly, staring off into the distance. Finally, he looked up and nodded.

Sabio walked over to his horse, pulled a length of rope from his saddlebag, and silently handed it to Zimpf.

When they emerged from the forest several minutes later, Shao rode on the right and Alia rode to his left, closest to the forest. Both of them wore a rope tied to their wrists, which bound them together loosely. A second rope, which was tied to the center, trailed behind them, connecting their rope to Aistra and then to Zimpf and Sabio.

They quietly slipped unnoticed from the overhanging tree line and stood soundlessly, watching the search. Even though the members of Alia's group could clearly see the Vherals, no one, it appeared, could see them. So the strange parade of friends began their silent walk westward. Shao had cleverly tied some brush to the back of Zimpf and Sabio's horses, which dragged behind them, obliterating their tracks.

To the Vherals, it seemed as though their prisoners had simply vanished.

"What happened?" Marek snarled at the first guard he saw.

"The—the prisoners performed…some kind of—of magic to make us want to—to let them go," the man stammered in fear. "But—but the wind blew the spell away, and we came to our senses," he continued with more confidence. "We knew they deserved to die, but…."

The mage nodded. "But, what?" he demanded.

"They—they just disappeared! Everyone went crazy: some people collapsed, others fled in terror, several guards dropped dead…" He trailed off, looking at Marek with wide eyes.

"Some of whatever it was got into my tent, and my prisoner escaped," the mage said softly. "I want you to—" he started before being rudely interrupted.

"All of the prisoners escaped during the chaos, Master," a second guard reported frantically as he coughed in the green, mist-filled air.

Marek stared at the man, his face etched in anger at the interruption.

"Do…do you want us to recapture them?"

The mage didn't answer. Instead, he stared balefully at the cringing man. After a moment, Marek pointed directly at the Vheral and said one sharp word in the language of magic.

The guard collapsed instantly, blood streaming from his eyes, ears, and mouth.

"That's for wasting my time by asking inane questions," Marek whispered in an uncaring tone.

The third guard, a tall, thin man, stared at his dead friend for only a moment before turning to his fellow countrymen and issuing orders.

"Get your weapons!" he commanded. "We're going after the prisoners! We'll bring them back, dead or alive!" he shouted in a ringing tone.

Then he felt a cold, long fingered hand grab his arm; he turned, his face frozen in fear.

"Bring them back alive, idiot!" Marek hissed.

Swallowing hard, the tall guard nodded. "They are to be brought back alive!" he echoed before turning to muster his troops.

Marek watched them leave, an angry scowl on his face. He had lost almost everything. Alia had destroyed the Aghara, and now he wouldn't even have the pleasure of making her pay for her insolence.

A movement caught his eye, and he glanced over to see Nabii studying him. The old, blind diviner subtly tilted his head toward Marek's tent.

The mage glanced over, caught his breath sharply, then smiled maliciously.

Maybe he hadn't lost everything after all.

Chapter 30–Reunion

Sh'ron's group made it to Sabio's old campground in the middle of the afternoon two days later. She had been pushing the men to travel faster and faster in her eagerness to be with her sister again. But when they arrived, the site was deserted, and the firepit was cold.

"Should we continue traveling east to look for them?" she asked hopefully.

Amicu and Ciern looked at each other. Finally, Ciern gently shook his head.

"No," he said, a trifle regretfully.

Sh'ron looked at the ground, disappointed.

"I'm sorry," Ciern told her. "I know you're anxious; we all are. But the plan was to meet here, and I think we should stick to the plan. There is the possibility they could arrive from a different route than we'll take to search for them. In that case, we would miss them. Then if they decide to come looking for us…"

"He's right," Amicu said, supporting his friend. "We should stay here for now. The others aren't due to arrive for a day and a half. If they're more than a day or so late, then I think a couple of us should scout for them while the others remain here."

Sh'ron nodded reluctantly, although it was obvious she was terribly upset.

The group went to work setting up camp. They cleared some of the ground, erected their tents, and started a fire near the logs that had been previously used as seats. Then, Amicu and Ciern fixed supper for everyone from the stores Ghan had pressed on them before they separated.

They all sat quietly, eating.

"Ciern?" Sh'ron asked, breaking the silence.

The elven prince looked over at her.

"How did you get the Vheral crowd all stirred up like you did the other night? You had them completely under your control. I have never seen anything like that," she marveled.

Ciern smiled. "It's called persuasion. It's the talent they discovered I possess when I was tested for acceptance at the Temple of Anaia.

"I don't really understand," Sh'ron admitted. "How can you get that many people to do what you want them to do, to make them feel what you want them to feel?"

Ciern sat thoughtfully for a few minutes. "I don't know if I can explain it," he confessed. "I have empathy for the crowd as a whole. When we started, they were curious, then interested, then riveted. They became engaged and captivated and angry as I drew them in to become a part of our story. I continued to speak until our story became their story. At that point, their anger boiled over into rage, and that rage ignited action."

Sh'ron and Chhdar listened, fascinated by his explanation.

Finally, Sh'ron pulled herself away from Ciern's spellbinding description.

"I can see that," she said dryly.

Everyone laughed.

"I imagine that talent will come in handy since you will one day be king," Chhdar pointed out.

"I hope that day is many, many years away," the prince said fervently.

Everyone nodded their agreement.

They went to bed shortly after that.

Sh'ron was up early the next morning, even though she and Chhdar had taken first watch and had gone to bed late. She sent Skala to his tent to rest, then she stirred up the fire and started the kettle to boil water for tea. Afterward, she sat alone, hoping that the Zduhac would appear to her and tell her what happened with her twin.

Chhdar found her an hour later, crying, her face buried in her hands.

He sat down by her, then wrapped one huge arm around her shoulders and pulled her close.

"I—I..." she sobbed. "I thought that YeYe would visit me."

Chhdar smiled and held her gently while she cried. "Do you know what I think?" he replied soothingly.

Sh'ron shook her head.

"I think it's a good thing he didn't visit."

Sh'ron looked up suddenly. That was not the answer she expected.

"I think the only reason a Zduhac would visit is if there was trouble. Do you remember when we were at the temple, and you asked Sifu about YeYe?" he asked.

Sh'ron nodded.

Chhdar continued. "Sifu told us that a Zduhac is a spirit creature that lives in the mountains and aids travelers. They appear as humans to give warnings and, if needed, will aid them."

Raising her head up quickly, Sh'ron stared at her husband, surprised; she had stopped crying.

"That's true, isn't it?" she said.

"I think that if YeYe hasn't visited, it's because everything is fine," Chhdar stated confidently.

"Very astute, warrior," Ciern agreed, looking at Chhdar piercingly as he came out of his tent and joined them. "It has long been known that a Zduhac will only appear in times of difficulty or in the event of an emergency."

"I too agree with Chhdar's assessment," Amicu announced as he also joined them. "I think that our friends successfully defeated the rogue mage and are on their way here. Otherwise, our mysterious friend would have visited us by now."

Sh'ron smiled sadly at the three men. "Thank you," she said sincerely.

"So," Chhdar asked, "what are the plans for today? Are we going to go in search of the others?"

Ciern and Amicu looked at each other.

"I say no," Ciern advised. "Today is the first day we can reasonably expect them to return. If they are not here in a couple of days, then we should make plans to search for them. Meanwhile, I think the best thing we can do is to set up this camp to welcome them back."

They spent that day cleaning up the campsite, clearing a spot for three more tents, and gathering extra firewood. Once again, they cooked food from their stores, and then the five of them gathered around the campfire to eat.

Later, after they had been sitting for a while in companionable silence, Sh'ron looked at Amicu.

"Can I ask you a question?" she inquired of him politely.

"What is it?"

"Well…" She hesitated. "I'm curious about something, but it might be impolite to ask."

"Go ahead," Amicu encouraged. "If it's impolite, I won't answer." He grinned.

Sh'ron took a deep breath and then plowed on. "Everyone who was accepted into the Temple of Anaia seems to have a talent of some sort. May I ask about your talent?"

Ciern looked at Amicu quickly and then grinned.

Amicu shot him a quick look, then turned toward Sh'ron. "Let me see if I can explain my talent," he said softly.

Sh'ron noticed that everyone, including Skala, had stopped to listen.

"My talent is vague and was difficult for the instructors to uncover. I have the ability to work with people, to persuade them to follow my orders. It's closely related to what Ciern does, except that while he influences crowds of people, I influence only a few people at a time."

"Is that why you were second in command behind Ciern?" Sh'ron asked shrewdly.

Amicu nodded. "When there are smaller groups of people, like in our dorms, conflicts are almost always between only two and sometimes three people. Because of my talent, I was best suited to mediate those small disagreements."

"Were the small group disagreements mostly between Ciern and one other student?" Chhdar asked shrewdly.

Amicu grinned.

"And was that one other student Zimpf?" the big warrior continued.

"I think we should call it a night," Ciern interrupted stiffly. It was clear that he didn't want to talk about it.

Amicu winked; Sh'ron and Chhdar chuckled.

They went to bed shortly after that, all except for Sh'ron and Chhdar, who had guard duty.

The next day creeped by slowly as they continued waiting for their friends.

On the morning of the fifth day of their arrival in camp, Skala and Amicu left to scout for their companions. They agreed that they would only move eastward for half a day and would then return to camp by nightfall.

While they were gone, Ciern, Sh'ron, and Chhdar went hunting. They thought that it would be nice to have a hot meal waiting in case the others did arrive.

Later that afternoon, the three hunters returned to the camp with five fat rabbits. Ciern had also spent the morning foraging for fresh vegetables. They started a stew and then waited.

But Skala and Amicu returned later that afternoon, disappointed that they had nothing to report.

"Although there was absolutely no sign of them anywhere," Amicu said with a puzzled frown, "I could swear that at one point I thought I could hear Zimpf laughing at me."

Alia found the first few days of their camouflaged trip terrifying. She and Shao, followed by Aistra then Sabio and Zimpf, rode parallel to the tree line but were in plain sight of the hundreds of Vheral soldiers who were looking for them. Some of the troops were across the valley, but several times, the soldiers were only a few yards away. Although they were clearly in plain sight of their pursuers, the Vherals completely ignored them. Alia could see them focus on the trees in front of her, then their eyes would glaze over and slide past the five of them and their horses to suddenly focus on the trees behind them. It was unnerving.

At first, there were hundreds of pursuers, but the farther they traveled from Marek's camp, the fewer soldiers there were. At one point, it seemed like Alia's group passed a certain undefinable line, and suddenly there were no more troops. Even though it seemed like they were no longer being chased, the group, at Zimpf's suggestion, continued to camouflage.

Alia thought that the nearly two weeks it took them to return to Sabio's campsite were the most uncomfortable and frustrating weeks she had ever endured. Her rope tether to Shao was easy, comfortable, and as natural as breathing. They were so in tune with each other that being bound to him was effortless. However, when they camped each night, Alia had to maintain constant contact with her horse so that the mare also remained under Aistra's protection. Every time her mount moved, she would tug on Alia's rope, causing her to awaken; it happened several times each night. Alia was unable to get a good night's rest. She eventually became short-tempered and waspish due to lack of sleep.

To compound the problem, once they seemed to be past detection, Zimpf found it endlessly amusing to yank hard on the ropes at unexpected times, causing almost everyone in the group to have countless mishaps. Alia was mostly protected by Shao, who absorbed the shock of the sudden tug, but poor Sabio nearly fell off of his horse on several occasions. Even gentle, patient Aistra finally got so frustrated with her grinning husband that she asked Alia to sew Zimpf's arms to his sides using the rusty awl and burlap stitches.

Finally, Shao had a short, harsh, whispered conversation with him, and Zimpf stopped altogether. Although she didn't ask what was said, Alia was sure that the conversation included the use of Mama's wooden spoon and a severe smack bottom.

Late one evening, when they had dipped down into yet another valley, Sabio suddenly straightened up in his saddle.

"We're almost home," he announced with a smile on his face.

Alia looked around at the indistinguishable landscape. To her, it looked exactly the same as the rest of the country in which they had been riding.

"We should be at camp by tomorrow night," he continued excitedly.

"I wonder if the others have arrived?" Alia asked no one in particular.

"I wouldn't be surprised," Shao answered. "Ciern is a very punctual person."

"They're waiting for us," Zimpf said confidently.

Alia turned to stare at him.

"What?" he asked, confused.

"Never mind," she answered, wondering why he didn't tell them earlier. "Can we stop camouflaging now?" Alia complained.

"No!" Zimpf said, so harshly and so quickly that Alia immediately suspected subterfuge. "There…there is still danger."

Alia saw the quick look that Aistra shot at him, and she saw the puzzled look on Sabio's face. She looked over at Shao, who had turned around in his saddle to stare at his friend, one eyebrow raised questioningly.

Zimpf stared back, a blank look on his face.

"Okay," Shao finally assented with an amused look. "We'll do it your way."

The next morning, they were up early. According to Sabio, they would be in camp by late that afternoon. They packed quickly and rode out at an extremely uncomfortable canter. It was perhaps early afternoon when they saw two horsemen ahead of them. The riders had halted their mounts and were staring eastward. One of them had his hand shading his eyes in an attempt to see farther.

Zimpf laughed out loud.

Before they got close enough to identify the riders, the unknown men turned and rode westward.

Alia and her friends followed at a distance, but the strangers, who were traveling at a gallop, soon outpaced them.

Finally, Sabio directed them to turn under the canopy of a large tree that led toward his old campsite. The group, still camouflaged and bound together with rope, rode at a sluggish pace through the woods. Their approach was not only unseen, but also unheard.

At last, they broke through the shrubbery surrounding the campsite; sitting on logs around a blazing fire were their friends. No one even glanced up at them.

Alia looked over at Shao and saw that he was staring questioningly at Zimpf. Zimpf held one finger to his lips. When he moved his hand, he mouthed exaggeratedly, "On the count of three…" then he mimed pulling the quick release that they all had on their rope knots.

"One...two...three!" he mouthed. Then, together, the group pulled their knots, letting the ropes fall to the ground.

At first, nothing happened. Then, in a wavelike motion, first one person then the next turned to look at them in astonishment, their eyes wide and their mouths open.

Chhdar even took a moment to rub his eyes as though he couldn't believe what he saw.

Then Sh'ron screamed Alia's name and ran to her. Alia jumped off her horse and rushed to meet her sister. The twins stood hugging each other in the middle of the campsite, alternately crying and laughing in delight. By the time they stepped apart, Alia saw that everyone was hugging everyone else and slapping each other on the back in delight while they all talked at the same time.

Finally, the excitement died down, and the group gathered around the fire. Amicu dished up bowls of rabbit stew and served it to them with warm bread and cheese.

Alia thought that this meal was the best food she had eaten in a month. She was with her sister again, and they were warm and well-fed and (mostly) unhurt. She had destroyed the Aghara and annihilated Marek's spell over the Vherals. Although she knew there were probably more trials to come, she was content to just sit quietly in the crook of Shao's arm with her sister on her other side and her friends surrounding her.

Marek's tent glowed an eerie green from within, and the sides drew in then puffed out alternately, as though it was the breathing of some unimaginably loathsome beast.

Without thought, as though he were mesmerized by the aliveness of the shelter, he walked slowly toward it, oblivious to the chaos still raging through camp.

At one point, one of his guards stepped in front of him to ask a question and, without conscious thought, Marek pointed an imperious finger at the unoffending man, blasting him into oblivion with about as much emotion as someone would use to swat a fly.

After that, no one approached the mage.

Marek opened the tent flap and stepped cautiously inside.

Some of the remainder of the substance that made up the Aghara wafted freely, giving the interior a buoyant, underwater effect. But most of the thick, gaseous vapor had coalesced around the broken vase as though it was eager to return to its dwelling.

Marek, realizing that his dream had not broken with the Aghara, immediately grabbed his bag and began dumping everything in the various containers onto the ground. Moving quickly, he scooped up gobbets and blobs and globules of the thick, noxious miasma and stoppered it into a myriad of flasks and ampoules and phials.

After several moments, Marek realized that the mist-like substance seemed eager to be saved. It flowed quickly, easily into each container, and once inside, it made no attempt to seep back out. He began to think that the cork plugs were probably unnecessary. But he would take no chances, so he continued to work, absorbed, focused, and determined.

Finally, there was no more of the mist to be saved.

Marek looked up in surprise. The interior of his tent was absolutely clear from the green mist of the Aghara. It had gone from late evening to early morning, and the sounds of the dying Vherals had dissipated completely.

Curious, he stood up slowly and stiffly and made his way outside.

Julie H. Peralta

The camp was completely abandoned.
He was alone.

Chapter 31 – Exchanges

Although everyone was anxious to hear the other group's story, they all agreed to wait until the next morning. It was quite late by the time they finished eating, and everyone was exhausted.

As usual, Alia and Shao took the first watch. This time, however, Sh'ron and Chhdar stayed up with them. The four of them talked all the way through not only Alia and Shao's watch, but Sh'ron and Chhdar's watch as well. They talked about everything except the events of the previous three weeks. They had all agreed to wait for morning, when everyone would be together. Instead, the two couples merely chatted about small, unimportant things. The twins especially enjoyed their time together. It was quite late when Amicu and Ciern emerged from their tents to take over guarding the camp.

"What are you all doing up?" Ciern demanded.

Amicu stood slightly behind him, arms crossed as though he too was angry. But Alia could see his good-natured smile.

"Go to bed," Ciern commanded. "We have much to discuss

tomorrow and many decisions to make."

With that, the two couples went to their tents.

Alia slept late the next morning. She had spent most of the last two weeks running short on sleep. So it was relaxing to just doze until well after sunrise, knowing that she didn't have to rise early and face another silent day in the saddle tied to her companions with rope.

Finally, she stretched luxuriously and opened her eyes. Shao was lying beside her, his head propped up on his right hand with his elbow firmly planted on the ground. He was smiling.

Alia smiled back. "Good morning," she told him.

"I thought you were going to sleep until noon," he told her.

"I gave it some thought," she admitted, leaning up to kiss him. Then she suddenly pulled away. "Shao!" she gasped in shock. "You shouldn't be putting pressure on your shoulder like that."

"What?" At first, he was genuinely confused. Then he remembered his injury. "Oh," he said in sudden understanding. "It doesn't hurt at all."

But Alia gently pushed him down and opened his shirt so she could examine his shoulder. "It's just too dark in here for me to see well," she complained. "Let's go outside in the sunshine so I can get a better look." Then she picked up her medical bag and marched outside.

Smiling at her authoritarian attitude, Shao followed quietly.

Once they were outside, Alia directed him to sit on one of the logs. Then she sat by him and examined his wound.

Surprisingly, Chhdar moved to sit on the other side of Shao.

"May I observe?" he asked politely.

Alia nodded as she continued to examine Shao, frowning in concentration.

Finally, she looked up. "I think we can probably go ahead and remove the stitches." She smiled. "But," she warned him sternly, "do not overexert your shoulder."

"Yes, healer-in-training," Shao answered seriously.

Alia carefully removed each suture, then she washed the wound carefully and applied a healing salve.

"Now that everyone is awake and the medical exams are completed…" Ciern paused, looking at Alia for confirmation.

She nodded.

"…then I think we should start this meeting. And we are going to start with your side of the story," he said, looking at Shao.

So, Shao began. He told them of their travels, of their meeting with Ghan and his attempt to dissuade them from continuing. He told them about their visit with the Zduhac and his task for each of them.

"I'll bet his command for you to refrain from fighting was a tough one," Sh'ron teased Shao.

"No," Shao answered. "I always follow orders."

"You never follow orders," Zimpf contradicted.

"That's you, Zimpf," Shao disagreed.

"No, I remember one time at Temple, Sifu told you not to leave the compound, and you left to go with me to pick apples from those trees in the orchard. Don't you remember that?" Zimpf laughed.

"I went because you lied and told me you had talked to Sifu and gotten his permission," Shao shot back. "And I was severely punished." He turned to appeal to Alia. "The next day, Sifu made me run the perimeter of the fence surrounding the compound from the moment the breakfast bell rang until the last dinner bell sounded."

Alia was shocked at the severity of the punishment.

"You got into trouble because Zimpf lied?" she asked, glaring at the diviner.

"No," Shao replied. "I got into trouble for not thinking for myself."

"Temple sounds like such a fun place to have studied," Chhdar said sarcastically to Sh'ron.

She giggled.

"Did Zimpf get into trouble too?" Alia asked.

Ciern, Amicu, and Shao laughed; Aistra smiled compassionately at Zimpf.

"Not...exactly," Shao hedged.

"Go ahead and tell her the rest of the story," Ciern said, chuckling.

"I—I um...sort of...punished Zimpf myself," Shao confessed.

Alia, her eyes wide, turned to look at Zimpf, who was staring intensely at the ground. She thought she could see the hint of a blush on the diviner's face.

"So, what happened?" she asked Shao.

"I glued his hair," Shao admitted.

"To what?" Alia wanted to know.

"To his head," Shao told her.

"Zimpf is bald!" Chhdar blurted.

Ciern and Amicu laughed uproariously. Amicu slapped his knee, and Ciern doubled over, holding his stomach.

Sabio looked back and forth between them and Zimpf.

"He wasn't when I put the glue on his head." Shao had begun to chuckle.

"It wasn't funny!" Zimpf protested. "I got into a lot of trouble for missing class and for not *seeing* what you had planned."

"Can someone please explain exactly what happened?" Alia asked plaintively.

Shao somehow managed to control his laughter enough to finish the story. "When I got back from running laps all day, I was hungry and angry. I missed all three meals because my punishment began before breakfast was served and didn't end until the bell rang to signal that the dinner meal had ended. So, I went back to our dorm, and my brother Zimpf there"—he turned to glower at the diviner—"was sound asleep, having escaped all punishment. So, in retaliation, I poured glue on his head and then went to sleep. When he got up the next morning, the pillow…" Shao paused then continued to struggle with the rest of the story through his laughter. "Well, it… it was stuck…to his hair."

"It wasn't funny!" Zimpf declared. "That thing wouldn't come off my head."

By now, Shao and Aistra were both howling with laughter; Amicu and Ciern had collapsed onto the ground, tears streaming down their faces. Sabio giggled. Even Skala, who was normally stoic, had begun to chortle.

Alia, Sh'ron, and Chhdar laughed in tolerant confusion.

Zimpf looked at the ground, his face a rosy shade of red.

"Zimpf?" Alia finally asked gently. "Will you please tell us the rest of the story?"

Giving Alia a pitiful look, he finally continued. "I couldn't get the pillow off my head, so I tried to cut it off," he confessed. "But it was full of feathers and, well…they sort of…fell out and—and…got…stuck."

Alia's mouth fell open in surprise as the image of Zimpf, with feathers stuck to his head, filled her mind.

Shao, roaring with laughter, pointed at the diviner. "He—he looked like—like…a…chicken!"

Chhdar and Sh'ron both burst out laughing; Skala and Sabio joined them.

Alia wanted to be sympathetic, and she tried, she really did. But the image was just too much, and she also succumbed to helpless gales of laughter.

When she was finally able to control herself, she managed to ask, "How did you get all of that out of your hair?"

"I didn't," Zimpf pouted morosely. "Aistra had to shave my head bald." And with that, the diviner got up and slunk into the woods, his head bowed sadly and his back stooped in defeat.

Aistra, still laughing, got up to follow him, but Shao stopped her despite his chuckles.

"Let me," he said.

By the time they returned, the rest of the group had managed to control themselves, although occasionally, someone would chuckle and then try to hide it so as not to upset Zimpf again.

"Okay, Shao," Ciern told the martial artist while he struggled to keep his face straight. "Finish your story. What happened after YeYe's visit?"

Shao continued by recounting their capture by the western Vherals and their incarceration in camp. He told them about Sabio demanding a trial by action and how the leader had chosen Shao to compete. Then he explained that he'd been shot at by one arrow and hit in the shoulder by another, and how he had to face the child assassin in the ring. "I won the Vheral's respect by not harming the child, but by washing the boy's face in dirt."

"You did that to me enough times when we were kids," Alia

heard Zimpf complain to Shao in a low voice.

She wanted to ask about it, but then thought that the diviner had probably been humiliated enough for one day.

Shao, ignoring Zimpf, went on to tell them about the appearance of Marek and how Alia was forced to face him alone. He trailed off at that point, remembering.

Alia picked up the story then and described in detail her meeting with Marek, the destruction of the Aghara, and her escape.

"Let's stop here for a moment," Ciern said. "I have some questions. First, why did Alia have to face Marek?"

"I think it was because she was the only one who could get close enough to him," Zimpf replied seriously.

Aistra nodded. "Despite all of his actions, he seemed to feel a connection to her."

"The feeling is *not* mutual," Alia spat vehemently.

Shao grinned then reached for her hand.

"What were the four of you doing while Alia was in that tent?" Ciern continued.

Sabio, who was normally reticent, spoke up. "They were with me under the protection of the zafiir."

"Can you tell us about the zafiir, Sabio?" Ciern asked intently.

Sabio nodded. "After Shao won the trial by action then taught the young would-be assassin a lesson, my people were forgiving and ready to let us go on our way. The trial by action alone proved us innocent of all charges. It is the law of the Vherals. But a few moments later, a wind began to blow, and my people changed. The wind was of the Aghara. I could see the vile green tinge, I could smell the fetid evil, I could taste the putrid malevolence, and I could hear its wicked voice." Sabio grew silent, remembering the effects of the Aghara.

"What did it say?" Amicu prompted.

"It wasn't so much the words as it was the feeling it produced." He looked up at them. "I watched as my countrymen's eyes went flat with hate. One moment, they were ready to let us leave, free and unharmed. The next moment, they were overpowered by an uncontrollable compulsion to see us die a slow, agonizing death." Sabio paused for a moment, thinking.

Then he continued. "That was the moment the mountain spirit had told me to wait for. First, I touched each of my friends with the zafiir to protect them from the Aghara. Then, I set my staff firmly on the ground and held it with both hands. I had Zimpf stand to my right, and I had Aistra stand to my left. Aistra held Shao's right hand in her left. This connection served to amplify the power of my staff."

Sabio looked around at his new friends, then resumed his story. "Blue smoke erupted from the top of the zafiir, then expanded and grew until it surrounded the four of us, creating an impenetrable shield of protection. We were not only invisible to our enemies, but we were also shielded from all weapons. They couldn't see us; they couldn't touch us. Chaos exploded as we disappeared from their midst. Then the blue smoke swelled and flourished and swallowed more and more victims of the Aghara wind."

"Did those people die?" Sh'ron asked, her eyes wide in horror.

"Only those who carried evil in their hearts," Sabio explained.

"Did it get into Marek's tent?" Ciern asked. "Is that how Alia knew she could break it?"

"Yes, the small amount of smoke that got into the tent did two things. First, some smoke embedded itself into the Aghara, thus beginning the destruction process, and that was what allowed Alia to see the cracks that permeated its surface. The second thing it did was protect Alia. Unknowingly, she inhaled some of that same smoke, and that is what shielded her from the evil trapped within."

"What about Marek?" Chhdar asked. "Did he die?"

"We don't think so," Shao answered.

"We were too busy trying to escape to ask after the man's health," Zimpf answered sarcastically.

"How did you escape anyway?" Sh'ron asked. "For that matter, I've been very curious to know how the five of you just suddenly appeared in camp last night."

Zimpf took up the story then, explaining Aistra's talent for concealment and recounting the exhausting journey to the camp.

Ciern talked about meeting with several families of Vherals and then went on to describe the summit they called. He recounted his speech to the group and their reaction.

"You could always read a crowd," Shao complimented him.

Then Sh'ron explained how she and her husband had worked to treat the Vheral people for their various illnesses.

Alia was astonished to hear about Chhdar's talent for medicine.

"Will you let me talk to Sairima when we get back to Miast?" she asked Chhdar excitedly. "We can always use more healers if you're interested."

"Let me think about it," he told her gently.

Finally, Amicu described their encounter with members of the eastern Vherals and how they had combined a trap bowl with a fusillade of darts in order to defeat their attackers.

"Clever," Shao said admiringly.

"So, what do we do now?" Amicu asked. "Are we heading home?"

"I think so," Ciern answered. "We have clearly done all that we set out to do. Now I think we should go back to our own homes and prepare our armies in case Marek survived and continues his quest for power. I—"

"Not just yet," Zimpf interrupted sternly. "Our first stop will be at the Temple of Anaia."

"The Temple?" Ciern asked, confused.

"The Temple," Aistra suddenly demanded firmly. "We will be taking Sabio to begin his studies."

Everyone looked at the young man.

"We made a promise," Zimpf said, blowing on his fingernails and buffing them on the front of his shirt. "Besides," he continued, "it might be fun to know someone who is almost as good as I am."

Marek looked around the camp in confusion. He had not given anyone the authorization to leave camp.

"I sent them all home," a soft voice said.

The mage turned. Standing beside his tent, his arms crossed defiantly across his chest, was Nabii.

"I did not give you permission to disperse my troops!" Marek snarled angrily as he conjured a fireball and threw it directly at the blind, old man.

Nabii swung the walking stick he always carried, easily deflecting the evil magic hurling straight at him.

A huge oak tree towering nearby was suddenly engulfed in a massive inferno.

Marek was forced to avert his eyes to protect them from the intense heat as the tree crackled and popped and burned.

When he was finally able to look up, Marek whispered, "you're a mage."

Nabii seemed unaffected by the conflagration that had incinerated everything around him. "I am much more than that," he replied calmly. "And you would do well to listen to me."

Chapter 32–Return to the Temple

The meeting ended after everyone agreed to travel straight to the Temple of Anaia so Sabio could begin his training.

Ciern, Amicu, and Skala left after lunch to do some scouting in order to decide on the quickest route back. Sh'ron and Chhdar decided to go hunting to secure fresh game for dinner. Zimpf, Aistra, and Sabio resumed their strange three-way conversation. After watching them for a few minutes, Shao looked over at Alia.

"I'm feeling stiff and achy from our trip here. I would like to run some forms in order to work out the kinks. Would you like to come watch?" he invited.

"Absolutely!" Alia answered enthusiastically. She loved to watch Shao practice.

The two of them walked hand-in-hand deeper into the woods until Shao found a flat clearing that was perfect for practice. Then he got to work. Alia thought that there were hundreds of forms, and it seemed like Shao knew all of them. He stretched and turned and punched. He jumped and kicked and rolled. His was a systematic technique of attacking and defending using posture, movement, and exquisite rhythm, which he practiced while simultaneously employing all the animal forms at his disposal. As always, Alia was enchanted.

Once he had finished, he was barely sweating, yet he still took the time to bow with his right hand fisted and his left hand covering that fist—the martial artist's salute. Then he bowed to Alia and held out his right hand, inviting her to join him. Together, they reviewed the forms he had taught her.

Afterward, she was amazed to realize that all of the tension and stress she had internalized during the past few weeks had dissipated. The forms served to calm her more than any medicine ever could.

Alia bowed to her husband. Then she wrapped her arms around his waist and laid her head on his chest.

"Thank you for teaching me," she said simply.

Shao looked down at her smiling. Then, for no reason other than he wanted to, he gave her a serious kiss.

On the way back to camp, they took time to forage for fresh food. Alia found a peach tree, which was bursting with ripe peaches. Shao took off his shirt and, using it as a carrying hammock, they loaded it with the delicious, juicy fruit. Shao also found some wild onions, mushrooms, and a variety of greens.

Back at camp, everyone was excited because Sh'ron and Chhdar had shot and butchered a wild pig. Everyone helped cut the meat into strips to smoke over the fire. Meanwhile, Alia and Shao prepared a delicious meal for the group consisting of seared pork in a light peach sauce, which was served with onions and mushrooms on a bed of greens. They even had a dessert of baked peaches. For the first time in a while, they all ate very well.

The next morning, they rose early and left for the next leg of their journey. Alia noticed that Sabio looked back at the camp that had been his home and then sighed sadly as he turned his back to the sunrise. She saw Aistra lean over and touch him gently on his cheek. He smiled at her gratefully.

They only traveled in the valley for half a day before turning into the woods and beginning the long, arduous trek through the undergrowth toward the peak of the Skarsgaard Mountains, where the Temple of Anaia sat.

Just like the previous trip to Temple, they climbed higher and higher, following a series of switchbacks. At each turn it felt like it grew colder until they were all forced to don cloaks, and hats, and gloves. And every night the campfire needed to be built higher to keep them warm.

It was midmorning nearly two weeks later when the Temple of Anaia, perched snugly between the two highest mountain peaks, came suddenly into view on a cold, overcast day.

The alien-looking main building, with its ornate animal statues balanced across the roof, stood silent guard over the mountain. The entire temple exuded a feeling of peace and tranquility.

The five graduates looked at each other and then at the temple.

"It feels like coming home, doesn't it?" Ciern grinned. The others smiled in agreement.

They made their way past the gently splashing fountains and flawless landscaping; they wound through the meandering pathways, perfectly trimmed lawns, and ornately shaped shrubs.

Alia was so enchanted with the grounds that, at first, she didn't notice the eerie silence. Only when she saw Shao frown and exchange a quick look with Ciern did she realize that something was dreadfully wrong. They saw no students or teachers. No grooms came to take their mounts. The temple was eerily deserted.

The group tied their horses in front of the main building with its round front windows and red-painted columns and walked silently inside, their steps echoing in the empty room. Shao, who was leading the group, turned to them, his face etched with worry and his eyes everywhere at the same time. He held his finger to his pursed lips then signaled everyone to halt—everyone except Zimpf. He beckoned the diviner forward. The two men advanced silently toward the kitchen, then stopped. Alia could see them whispering, their heads close together. Then Zimpf stood very still, his eyes unfocused and far away. Finally, he motioned Shao to follow him back. Standing in front of the group, he turned to Shao and announced in a normal tone, "they're waiting for you in the practice arena. Everyone. The whole school."

"Everyone?" Amicu asked in a shocked tone.

"Everyone," Zimpf affirmed in a bantering tone. "They all want to see the indomitable Shao kick some serious butt."

Alia looked at her husband. He looked back at her, his smile tight with excitement. Then he winked.

"I guess we should all head in that direction then," Shao stated calmly.

Just as they started to walk, Zimpf took his friend by the arm. "Be careful," he cautioned. "Some of the students are still angry about the way you handed them their behinds last time. They've been plotting your defeat since we were here months ago."

Shao looked at him and then nodded curtly. "I'll be careful," he replied seriously.

Alia heard Zimpf's warning and immediately began to worry.

They all strode purposefully across the grounds and down to the practice arena. Zimpf was right; of course Zimpf was right. The entire population of The Temple of Anani had swarmed to the field to see Shao compete. There were several seats open at the very front. Apparently, Sifu had arranged for them to have the best spots from which to watch the bout. By now, Alia was nearly sick with apprehension. Her head understood how good Shao was; her heart worried anyway.

Just before she took her seat, Shao took her elbow. She looked up at him. His tense excitement was almost palpable. Very gently, he cupped her cheek with his hand and winked impishly.

Then he turned and walked resolutely to the middle of the field, where Sifu stood waiting for him. The two martial arts masters bowed respectfully as they performed the martial artists' salute. Then, to the awe of the crowd, they began running forms. They were so perfectly synchronized that they looked like mirror images of each other. Even when the routine moved faster and the forms became more aggressive and powerful, they were still perfectly coordinated. They charged forward violently and retreated respectfully, they threw blocks and punches so quickly they were almost invisible to the human eye. The demonstration grew more precise as they executed nearly impossible kicks: whirling side, spinning hook, and slant-thrust. Then they slowed, approaching each other gracefully and powerfully, displaying the litheness and pure athleticism of the two masters. When the demonstration ended, they bowed to each other. There was a moment of awed silence, and the arena exploded with applause and cheers. Then Sifu walked from the field, leaving Shao alone.

At the edge of the arena stood a line of the most advanced of

Sifu's students, anxiously awaiting their turn to challenge the most famous martial artist in the Four Lands. Alia thought that most of them looked terrified after seeing Shao run forms. Bowing to the group, Shao gave them a calculating smile, and, as before, he invited all of them into the field to challenge him.

Alia had been told repeatedly that nobody could fight like Shao. She had personally seen him fight off dozens of ruffians at a time on numerous occasions. Still, it made her nervous to see him compete against so many trained fighters all at once.

Again, her fears proved to be groundless. Shao utilized every form he had displayed earlier and several he had not. He calmly met each attacker with quick explosive movements. He turned sideways, avoiding strikes while dispensing punches that were almost impossible to see. He attacked from above with high-flying roundhouse kicks and from below with quick, low foot-sweeps, causing attackers to fall heavily to the ground.

Shao, elusive, quick, and deadly, could not be touched. Within minutes, all but one of his foes were down. Most of them didn't get up again. The few students that managed to stumble to their feet bowed to Shao and limped their way slowly and brokenly off the field. But one remaining acolyte stood glaring at Shao balefully, his face a mask of hatred. He ran forcefully at Shao then dropped to the ground just before reaching him. The attacker rolled, came up quickly, and threw a handful of sand directly into Shao's eyes. Suddenly blinded, Shao stepped back as the audience booed at the illegal maneuver. Alia half rose out of her chair to run to her husband, but Amicu managed to grab her arm and pull her back down.

"Wait!" he hissed.

Shao stepped back, shook his head quickly, and then stood perfectly still, his eyes closed, his head bowed, and his arms dangling loosely at his sides.

Sensing his advantage, the assailant made his move at the blinded martial artist. He ran at Shao from behind, dropped down, and swept Shao's legs out from under him. The martial arts master fell.

Alia screamed in horror as the acolyte's foot came down hard, directly toward Shao's unprotected back.

By the time the man's foot had made its descent, Shao was gone. He had rolled nimbly to the side, sprang to his feet, and chopped the attacker on either side of his neck. Shao's foe dropped like a sack of potatoes. Swiftly, the martial arts master flipped the man onto his belly, and, just as he had done with the young Vheral assassin, he smeared the man's face roughly into the ground. Then he yanked the semiconscious man to his feet and kicked him solidly and repeatedly on his behind, forcing him to stagger toward Sifu.

Sifu, with a face like a thundercloud, administered his chastisement for cheating in a sparring contest. He grabbed his acolyte by the arm, trapping it painfully behind the man's back, and then leaned forward to whisper something into his pupil's ear. What little color was left in his face drained immediately, and the man collapsed in a heap on the ground.

Alia was pretty sure that the attacker was going to have some difficult days ahead of him.

There was a vast silence.

Then people began to cheer. Shao turned to the crowd, his eyes still closed from the irritating sand, and bowed politely, offering the martial artists' salute.

Alia broke away from Amicu and ran to her husband. Just as she got to him, he reached out, grabbed her, lifted her up, and swung her around high in the air, even though his eyes were still closed.

Then Sifu was beside them. "Let's go to my quarters," he said, looking around at the group of friends. "I already sent for the healer; he'll meet us there."

Alia took Shao's elbow to guide him, but he immediately dropped his arm to take her hand. Then he led her confidently straight to Sifu's quarters, even though his eyes were tightly shut the whole way. They had only just arrived and sat down when there was a polite knock at the door. Sifu opened it and admitted the healer they had seen last time. He asked Shao to lean his head back, then the healer had Alia assist him as he carefully rinsed the sand and dirt out of Shao's right eye. Next, he asked Alia to treat Shao's left eye while he assisted. Afterward, he gave Alia some healing drops to administer.

"Now, Shao," he said as he tied a cloth around the martial artist's head, completely covering his eyes. "I know how you are, but please keep your eyes covered at least until dinner to allow time for the drops to work. Alia, when his eyes are no longer red with irritation, then he may remove the cloth binding. In Shao's case, that will probably take a couple of hours," the healer advised, looking at Shao and shaking his head with exasperation. "I also want you to administer two drops in each eye before bedtime and as soon as he gets up in the morning for the next three days."

"Yes, Healer," Alia said respectfully.

He turned to leave and then looked back at Alia with a smile. "You are a natural," he told her. "Please visit me before you leave, and I will share with you the components in the healing eye drops I gave you." Then he was gone before Alia could even respond.

"Let's get started," Sifu said. "I have taken the liberty of having lunch delivered to us. I thought we could chat while we ate."

They all took their places around the conference table.

"So, who are you?" Sifu demanded of Sabio.

"I am Sabio Omu Olori of the Vheral Tribes of the North," he introduced himself. "Zimpf and Aistra brought me."

Sifu looked at Zimpf, one eyebrow raised.

"He's a new candidate for recruitment," Zimpf explained.

"His talent?"

"Divination," Zimpf responded proudly.

"Are you sure?" Sifu pressed.

For one of the few times in his life, Zimpf answered seriously. "I personally nominate Sabio Omu Olori as a learner in admittance to the Temple of Anaia. I swear to support, sponsor, and reinforce his training."

Sifu looked at Zimpf, his eyebrows raised in surprise. "Well, I guess we had better send for Gatara."

Zimpf paled suddenly and subconsciously reached for Aistra's hand.

Just then, there was a knock at the door, and attendants entered, served lunch, and quickly withdrew.

While the group ate, they took turns telling Sifu all that had happened since they last visited. He listened intently and asked a myriad of questions. Finally, he looked around shrewdly.

"I would like for most of you to meet with me tomorrow and perhaps the day after so we can form a strategy in case of an invasion. It would be all-encompassing and would include plans to protect all the citizens of the Four Lands. I would like to include some of the teachers here at the temple who specialize in both strategy and tactics. To that end, I would like Ciern, Amicu, and Skala to attend these meetings. I would also like you two"—he indicated Sh'ron and Chhdar—"to attend as representatives of the southern people."

"What about us?" Zimpf asked, indicating himself and Aistra.

"You and Aistra will be working with Gatara on testing Sabio and helping him to adjust to life here at the temple."

Zimpf nodded.

"And us?" Shao asked.

"I have a special project for you and Alia," Sifu answered with a wink. Just then, there was a timid knock at the door.

"Enter," Sifu ordered in a voice bristling with authority.

It was the young martial artist who had thrown sand into Shao's eyes. Alia glared at him menacingly.

"It is time for you to receive your punishment for fighting without honor in the sparring ring," Sifu declared ominously.

"I'm sorry—" the young man tried to apologize.

Sifu held up his hand for silence, and the man immediately stopped talking.

"For the remainder of today, and for the next two days, Shao will be your laoshi. You will obey his every command, or you will leave this temple," Sifu threatened ominously.

"Yes, Sifu," the student said, bowing almost all the way to the floor.

Then Sifu looked at Shao. "This is Feil."

Shao, his face stern and unforgiving, seemed to stare menacingly at the pale young man, even though his eyes were still completely covered.

"Feil," he said in a low, dangerous tone. "Your penance for cheating during a sparring session is to run the perimeter of the inner fence of this temple. You will run continuously without ceasing until after the last bell has sounded."

"Yes, Laoshi," Feil agreed quietly as he looked down at the floor.

"You will report to me at first bell in the morning," Shao demanded of the young man.

"Yes, Laoshi."

"I gave you your orders. Why are you still standing here?" Shao suddenly barked at him.

Feil turned quickly, nearly tripped over his own feet, and darted out the door.

Once he was gone, Sifu smiled. "It seems to me that I gave you that punishment once," he said to Shao.

"Yes, Sifu," Shao said politely. "It was a lesson well learned."

Sifu nodded.

Before the door even closed, a middle-aged woman with her graying hair pulled back into a severe-looking bun marched into the room without waiting for an invitation. She stood imperiously in the doorway, glaring at Zimpf with obvious dislike.

"I *saw* you here!" she growled at him. "You came back despite my order that you were never to enter this temple again!"

"It's wonderful to see you too, Gatara," Zimpf answered with a mocking smile.

"You'd better wipe that smile off of your face before I do it for you," she threatened.

Zimpf continued to grin impishly.

Sabio looked at the intimidating woman, his eyes wide.

"This is Sabio Omu Olori of the Vheral Tribes of the North," Sifu made the introduction. "Zimpf and Aistra brought him. He is a candidate for admission to your program."

"Please stop poking into my brain," Sabio requested politely.

Gatara's head abruptly snapped back as though she had been

slapped. Her eyes widened in surprise. Slowly, she turned to glare at Zimpf.

"Did you teach him that?" she demanded.

Zimpf, grinning mischievously, nodded.

"I might have known," Gatara sighed. "Okay, you three come with me," she muttered, giving up.

Zimpf, laughing, followed her from the room. Sabio and Aistra followed quietly.

"Let's call it quits for today," Sifu suggested. "You are all clearly exhausted from your travels, and I have a class to teach this afternoon." Then he turned to Shao. "Before you ask, the answer is no. You may not help. Go to your quarters and take care of your eyes."

With that, the meeting ended.

Marek's eyes narrowed as he thought rapidly. He should annihilate this usurper for his arrogance. He made his own decisions; no one told him what to do. But after a few seconds, the mage shrugged his shoulders noncommittally. He decided to hear what Nabii had to say. After all, he could always murder the old man later.

"I sent the Vherals home while you were collecting the essence of the Aghara because information arrived that you were not aware of."

"Go on."

"Interlopers met with the western Vherals and stirred them to rebel against you," Nabii continued in a soft voice.

"Alia was here!" Marek snapped.

"It was not Alia, nor was it those who traveled with her. My informants said it was an elven prince, a dwarven prince, a leader of one of the southern towns, a tall, blond-haired woman, and a huge warrior."

Marek spat bitterly on the ground; he should have seen this! Alia never went anywhere without her twin. And where Sh'ron went, Chhdar was sure to follow.

"You were leading your troops directly into the very teeth of a vicious civil war," Nabii pointed out.

Marek didn't answer.

"You would do well to get your head out of the Aghara and learn to think for yourself, apprentice," he snapped viciously, using the word to degrade Marek.

The mage flinched. His old master used to call him that when he made a mistake.

"I—" Marek started

"Don't!" Nabii warned, holding up his hand. "You sat in your tent for nearly three days trying to save every single drop of that vapor while I was forced to take command of your army in order to clean up the mess you made of things!"

"Three days?" Marek questioned in a stunned tone.

"Silence!" the old man roared, his anger suddenly palpable.

Marek's mouth fell open in surprise. He could sense the power emanating from the being who pretended to be a blind, old man.

"If you want to take over the southland, you will listen to me and listen well."

The mage closed his mouth and nodded subserviently.

Chapter 33–The Diviners and the Martial Artists

Zimpf, Aistra, and Sabio followed Gatara out of Sifu's quarters, across the compound, and into a long, low building, finally stopping in a large office.

Zimpf immediately went over and sat comfortably on the top of the desk.

"Get off my desk," Gatara told him in an exasperated tone, which indicated that she had said that phrase hundreds of times.

Zimpf smirked at her, but he slid quietly off the desk and went to sit instead on a nearby table.

Gatara glared at him, but she didn't say anything. Instead, she turned her attention to Sabio.

"How long have you been able to discern things?" she asked.

"All my life. I guess I was maybe five or so when I learned that others couldn't understand things like I could."

"What kind of things could you understand?" Gatara continued.

"Everything, I guess," Sabio muttered, looking at the floor.

"Sabio," Aistra said gently. "Can you be more specific? There are different types of divination, and we're trying to understand where your talent is strongest."

Sabio thought carefully. "I *know* things about people—if they're good or evil, happy or sad, guilty or innocent. Some people have such a strong…" He hesitated, trying to find the right word. "…*pull* that I can predict their future. Also," he continued, "if I wish for it, good things will happen to someone, but if I curse them, bad things happen."

Gatara thought for a minute before continuing. "That last talent," she grilled him. "Can you give me an example?"

Sabio continued talking to the floor. "Once, a woman was very kind to me. I was young and on my own, and she took me in and fed me. But she was sad because she couldn't have children of her own. So, I placed my hand on her belly and wished for her to have children. Nearly a year later, she had three babies at the same time." He smiled as he remembered her joy.

Then he continued. "Another time, I visited a village and asked for food. But they were mean and drove me away. I wished for them to fail. Later, I heard that the entire village had caught fire. The people survived, but they had to start all over, establishing a new community because their old one had failed."

Sabio looked up into the shocked faces around him. Even Zimpf seemed surprised.

"That isn't possible," Gatara said vehemently.

"That is the greatest talent I've ever heard of!" Zimpf exclaimed.

Aistra smiled at Sabio then took his hand and held it gently.

"I would like to delve into your mind," Gatara told him. "Will you allow me?"

Sabio looked at her for a moment, then he nodded. "Can Aistra come too?"

"Yes," Gatara assented. Then she placed one hand on Sabio's face and the other on Aistra's face. Sabio and Aistra closed the circle by touching the others' faces. The three of them sat silently, their unfocused eyes open and far away. Zimpf watched them closely.

Gatara dropped her hands first and looked penetratingly at Sabio.

"Put that down, Zimpf!" she suddenly ordered without looking up.

Zimpf dropped the scrying implement with which he had been playing.

"You have an enormous amount of talent," she said to Sabio. "But you need training, and you need it now. Therefore," she continued, "I am going to utilize my status as master to bypass the requirement of fall semester applicants only."

Aistra, who had reached out to hold Sabio's hand, squeezed it gently. "What Gatara means is that you've been accepted," she told him. "You will start immediately."

He turned to look at her, his eyebrows raised in surprise.

"Zimpf!" Gatara said in annoyance. "If you keep trying to delve into my mind, I will put up a shock block."

"You can do that?" Zimpf exclaimed. "Show me!" he demanded excitedly.

Gatara scowled angrily at the diviner. "Didn't you make my life miserable enough while you were here?" she asked sharply. "Do you really think I'm going to teach you how to annoy me even more? The answer is no," she stated emphatically.

Zimpf looked down the floor. "That's too bad," he grumbled. "Then I guess I won't be able to teach you the technique the Zduhac showed me," he said sadly, looking at her surprised face. Then he grinned mischievously.

"You…you…met a Zduhac?" Gatara stammered. "You? Why would the most mystical of mountain spirits visit you?"

"He didn't only visit me once; he visited me three times. He sort of likes me," Zimpf bragged as he blew his breath onto his fingernails and polished them on the front of his shirt. "He even taught me a new technique. He said it was 'old knowledge, lost knowledge,' and then he shared it with me," Zimpf announced pompously.

Gatara stared at her former student in dismay. Then she buried her face in her hands. "Why me?" she moaned.

Aistra looked at Zimpf.

He grinned wickedly, then winked.

Sabio chuckled.

"Let me delve your mind before I agree to anything," Gatara told him.

Zimpf came over and sat in front of her, his face a mask of innocence.

She laid her hand on his forehead and stared blankly at him. Finally, she pulled away. "Let me think about it," she informed him.

"Think fast," he mocked. "We're leaving in two days."

She stood up and walked to the door then turned before she exited. "I'll get the paperwork for Sabio. He'll be housed in your old quarters. You two can stay in the adjoining guest room." Then, just as she stepped outside, she looked back at Aistra and shook her head sadly. "I can't believe you married him."

Zimpf laughed.

The three of them went to collect their things, and then Aistra and Zimpf showed Sabio his quarters and helped him to get settled. As they were working, it seemed like every divination student in school came to introduce themselves. New students were rare and very much welcomed at the Department of Divination in the Temple of Anaia.

Of course, Zimpf's reputation not only as a great diviner but also as the best prankster ever to attend Temple made him practically royalty. Aistra was also warmly welcomed back. She had only been gone from Temple for a few months, and she had returned married to the man she had loved and lost. All in all, it was quite a celebration that night.

The next day, Zimpf and Aistra were left to themselves while Gatara processed Sabio into Temple as a student. She also did more testing of his divination skills to determine his exact talent. The couple ate breakfast and then wandered down to the practice arena to watch Shao torment the student who had thrown sand in his face. By the time they left, both of them were laughing at the young man's misery.

"That acolyte is getting what he deserves," Zimpf observed to Aistra.

She laughed.

Later, they returned to their quarters to spend some time alone. They sat close together "talking" with their hands on each other's faces.

After lunch, Sabio came looking for them. He was very excited at his acceptance and at the variety of classes he would be able to take.

Then he looked at Zimpf, worried. "Gatara wants to see you. Alone," he announced somberly.

"Great," Zimpf complained.

But he got up immediately and went to her office.

"Sit down, Zimpf," Gatara ordered seriously. "I gave some thought to our conversation yesterday. And I might be willing to teach you how to shock an interloper who attempts to delve into your mind without your permission."

Zimpf's eyes lit up.

"I said I *might*," she continued, holding up her hand. "But first, you will have to explain to me what the Zduhac taught you."

Zimpf nodded. "He showed me how to link minds," he said gravely.

Gatara rolled her eyes at him in disgust. "We know how to do that," she said scathingly. "*You* know how to do that. It's the first thing I taught you! We have always known how to share thoughts with touch! I can't believe I almost fell for another one of your tricks, you insolent little—"

But Zimpf interrupted her tirade. "I can share my mind with another diviner without touch," he stated calmly.

Gatara immediately fell silent.

"He said it was called 'telepathy.' I suspect that with some practice, I will be able to work out a way to link two, three, maybe even dozens of minds together at the same time. I believe that with enough practice, diviners will be able to communicate across distances as well," Zimpf bragged, his eyebrows raised in emphasis.

"That can't be done," Gatara whispered in disbelief.

"Think of it, Gatara," Zimpf pressed. "Think of the potential."

She looked at Zimpf, her eyes suddenly hungry. "You must teach this to me," she demanded. "This needs to be studied. If war is indeed coming as Sifu believes, this knowledge could be devastating to our enemies. We would be able to reach out to other diviners, to share information across great distances. It would be invaluable! Even the mages have been unable to accomplish this feat, and they have tried for hundreds of years." She began to get excited at the very idea.

Zimpf nodded. "Give me what I ask for then," he bargained. "Show me how to shock an interloper."

The two of them spent the remainder of the afternoon together. By the time he left, Zimpf felt as he had when he was in school—mentally drained and physically exhausted.

Afterward, he refused to share his new knowledge with his former instructor, claiming he was too tired.

"You better not double-cross me," she warned.

"Would I do that?" he replied, his face a mask of innocence as he turned his back on her and walked toward the door. He could feel her anger wash over him in waves as he giggled impishly.

The next day, Gatara sent for him at dawn. Zimpf refused her summons, pleading dissipated energy, a common ailment among the divination students. But he promised to meet with her in the evening of the third day of their stay to share the Zduhac's knowledge with her.

As soon as they returned from dinner on the third day, Zimpf, as promised, sent for Gatara. She practically ran to his quarters. When she arrived, she noticed that Zimpf looked particularly tired. She thought it was odd, because it was a fairly easy trick to shock an interloper.

But then, she thought, he has probably been practicing linking minds with Aistra and Sabio.

"Sit down," Zimpf invited. Then he proceeded to teach her what the Zduhac had taught him: he linked her with Aistra, Sabio, and himself. The three of them practiced with each other for the remainder of the evening.

Gatara was elated with the new technique, although she knew it would take months, maybe even years of study to utilize it effectively. Maybe, she thought, Zimpf isn't such an annoyance after all.

She was wrong.

After the meeting Shao, even though his eyes were completely covered, unerringly led Alia to their room.

As before, Alia and Shao's room was plain but meticulously clean. It consisted of one room with a bed, table, and two chairs, and it had an attached bathroom.

"It's still plain, I'm afraid," Shao teased.

Alia sat on the bed and patted the spot beside her. "It's fine, as long as you're with me." She smiled.

Shao sat beside her and then leaned back, stretching his long frame on the bed and pulled Alia down beside him.

"How do your eyes feel?" she asked worriedly.

"Actually, they feel fine," he told her, reaching up to untie the cloth covering them.

Alia caught his hands in her own. "Oh, no you don't," she ordered. "We are going to take it easy for a little while. And by we, I mean you."

Shao smiled at her, and she snuggled up beside him, her head resting comfortably on his shoulder. He wrapped both arms around her and pulled her close.

"Can I ask you a question?" Alia inquired.

"You can ask me anything."

"How did you do that? How did you defeat that man and then walk us to Sifu's quarters and then lead us here while you were essentially blind?"

"That's more than one question," Shao teased.

Alia didn't answer.

Shao kissed the top of her head. "As for the acolyte," he began, "I knew what he was going to do. I could see in his face that he wanted to win even if he had to cheat to do it. So, I let him throw sand in my face. I knew, even blinded, that I would crush him. The fact that he couldn't even defeat a blind man would diminish his standing both in his own eyes and in the eyes of his classmates."

Alia quickly raised her head to stare at her husband.

"I also knew that Sifu would give him to me so that I could teach him a lesson," Shao asserted.

"Shao!" Alia gasped.

"The martial arts give a person great power, but students must learn the wisdom to control that power. It's important." He looked down at Alia, who was staring thoughtfully at nothing. "Do you understand?"

She nodded.

Shao grinned. "I can't hear you when you nod while my eyes are covered."

"I understand what you mean," Alia said softly. "Wait! How did you know I nodded?"

Shao just grinned and pulled her closer.

"By appointing me as laoshi to Feil for the next two days, there is hope I can save him. Otherwise, he would be expelled from Temple, and word would go out to bar him from all martial arts training. The young man is talented, and it would be a pity for such talent to be wasted."

Alia leaned up and kissed her husband. "You are the most amazing man I have ever met," she said in admiration.

"As for the remainder of your question…" He smiled. "I was trained to use all of my senses equally. I could feel the attacker approach, and I could hear the direction from which he came. I could even smell the sweat on his body. As for moving around the grounds, it was just part of my training."

Once again, Alia was overwhelmed by the complexity of Shao's education. "How did I get so lucky?" she asked, leaning over to kiss him seriously.

"It is I who was lucky," he murmured.

They continued talking and laughing and kissing until gradually, they both fell asleep.

Alia woke up later that afternoon with Shao still beside her. She stretched luxuriously, then smiled at him.

"You had a nice nap," he observed, smiling at her.

"We've been traveling so hard for the past few weeks that I guess it just all caught up to me," Alia admitted. "What time is dinner?" she asked. "I'm starting to get hungry."

"We should hear the dinner bell anytime now," he answered, then he winked at her, which Alia found odd. Normally he only winked if he was teasing or was trying to tell her something.

Then she realized what was wrong.

"Shao!" she admonished. "You took off your eye covering!"

"I did," he admitted. "My eyes didn't hurt at all, and that blindfold was giving me a headache."

"You should have woken me up so I could examine them," she said, pushing him down gently with her hand on his chest and then carefully looking into each eye.

As usual, he was right. Both of his eyes were completely normal with no redness at all.

"The next time something happens, you are not to treat yourself," she scolded.

"The next time?" Shao asked, one eyebrow raised quizzically. "Are you expecting me to get hurt again?" he teased.

Alia wanted to be angry, but Shao gave her such a roguish look that she laughed in spite of herself. She kissed him instead.

Just then, the dinner bell rang, and they walked outside to find Sh'ron and Chhdar walking toward them.

"Would you two like to eat dinner with us?" Sh'ron asked.

"We would love to!" Alia said enthusiastically. Then she linked her elbow with her twin's elbow, and they whispered and giggled as Shao led them to the dining room.

Shortly after they sat down, the others began to join them. Zimpf, Aistra, and Sabio appeared last; Zimpf was giggling.

"What's so funny?" Shao asked.

"I—" Zimpf started, but just then, Gatara walked into the dining room, her face set in stone and her eyes angry. She sat a few tables away, facing Zimpf, and scowled darkly at him. Her food sat untouched on her plate.

"Zimpf, why is Gatara angry with you again? Or is she angry with you about something old?" Shao asked curiously, noting Gatara's glare.

"I sort of blackmailed her into giving me something I wanted." Zimpf smirked, looking over at the divination instructor with an impudent grin.

Sifu came in last and sat down with them.

"What did you do to Gatara?" he questioned Zimpf sternly.

"I…nothing," Zimpf answered, his face a mask of innocence.

"I don't believe you," Sifu replied bluntly before turning toward Shao.

"Have you checked on your pupil?" he asked Shao.

"Yes, Sifu," Shao nodded.

Alia looked at her husband. She didn't know that he had left their quarters.

"He's looking pretty rough," Sifu observed.

"Yes, Sifu," Shao acknowledged as he calmly continued eating.

Sifu nodded and then began eating his own dinner. "Tomorrow," he announced, looking at Amicu, Ciern, and Skala and then including Sh'ron and Chhdar, "we will begin our meeting when the breakfast bell rings. The meal will be served in my quarters."

"Yes, Sifu," they responded.

Everyone retired right after dinner; they all had early meetings the next morning.

Shao woke Alia up just before the sun peeped over the horizon.

"I'm going to meet my student," he told her. "Would you like to come watch? You can participate in some of the exercises and forms if you want to."

"Sure!" Alia exclaimed.

Together, they walked through the predawn dimness to the practice arena. Standing in the center of the field waiting for them was Feil. He was an average-built, blond young man with a pointed nose. Now that Alia got a good look at him, she realized that he was young. She estimated that he couldn't have been much older than seventeen.

He looked up in fear as Shao approached and then in surprise as he saw Alia.

When Shao was closer, Feil bowed almost to the ground, his hands extended in the ritual martial artists' salute.

"Get up!" Shao growled harshly at the man. "We will start this morning's session with exercises. And you will address me properly!" he hissed in a low, dangerous tone, glaring threateningly at the student.

"Yes, Laoshi," Feil whispered, his eyes wide.

Alia joined them, but she soon learned that Shao had been holding back on her. A lot.

They started with simple calisthenics, then they moved on to more and more difficult exercises. Finally, Shao gave Alia a break. But he made Feil squat beside him with their backs against a wall and their arms extended out in front of them. Within a few minutes, Feil was nearly crying in pain. Shao made it look effortless.

Feil's morning went from bad to worse as the workout became more and more difficult. Shao made him practice simple kicks—front, back, side, roundhouse. They did low kicks, high kicks, and flying kicks. And each time Feil didn't perform perfectly, Shao made him do the move over and over again until it was flawless. At first, Shao demonstrated the move, then he critiqued Feil's style, then he used a long wooden staff to smack the offending body part.

Finally, the lunch bell rang.

"You have thirty minutes," Shao informed him curtly. "Then we're going to quit playing and get to work."

"Yes, Laoshi," Feil said. Then he collapsed.

They spent the afternoon running forms. The first few, Alia was familiar with, and she practiced with them. Shao continued his criticism of Feil and at the same time complimented Alia's forms as shining examples of perfection. Finally, he excused Alia and directed Feil into more and more difficult routines while he continued to harangue, berate, and admonish the student for his failure to perform adequately. Shao kept his staff handy and used it liberally.

At last, the dinner bell rang.

"You may be excused for the evening," Shao said brusquely. "But if I were in your position, I would stay right here and practice until I at least obtained some level of competence."

"Yes, Laoshi," Feil whispered, his voice quivering.

With that, Shao left the field not even looking back at his student, who had bowed, his head touching the ground.

Once they were beyond Feil's line of view, Shao stopped. He turned Alia to face him and took both of her hands. Looking at the ground, he muttered, "Do you think I was too hard on him? I don't want you to think I'm being deliberately mean to get even with him."

Alia was quiet for a moment, thinking. She had never seen Shao be so brusque and hateful and downright vicious with anyone. It was hard to meld the two different sides of him together.

"I think," she said slowly, "that you are doing what must be done to save the young man. I trust you unconditionally."

Shao looked up at her gratefully, a huge smile on his face. "Thank you," he whispered, and then he kissed her.

The next day was equally grueling for Feil as the exercises, routines, and forms increased in intensity and complexity. The more difficult the forms became, the more Shao demanded of his student. By the time the lunch bell rang, Feil was nearly in tears.

"Pull yourself together!" Shao ordered scornfully at the trembling young man. "You have thirty minutes!" Then he turned to escort Alia to the cafeteria.

Alia looked back once at Feil; he was wiping tears from his eyes. Then he stood slowly and began to practice forms again.

"I wish I had another day with him," Shao fretted at lunch. "I think I've nearly broken through." He looked up at Alia. "Do you think the others will consent to stay an extra day?"

But he need not have worried. Ciern came looking for them just as they finished eating.

"Can we extend our stay one more day?" he asked. "Amicu and I want to meet with our old teachers for an extra session."

Shao smiled. "I was hoping for that as well."

Feil's face went an alarming shade of white when he was informed that he would have to spend another day training with Shao.

"Yes, Laoshi," was the only thing he said.

At the end of the second day, Shao once again reprimanded the young man harshly. "You still have not learned your lessons properly," he admonished, his face stern and unforgiving, his eyebrows drawn down into a V, and his voice low and dangerous.

Feil nodded.

Shao's face, if possible, went even darker.

"Yes, Laoshi," Feil whispered.

Shao didn't respond. He glared at the young man callously, then turned and walked away.

The third and final day of Feil's training began much the same way. Shao was as severe and unforgiving as the previous two days. Then, just before lunch, he showed Feil an extremely complex flip maneuver, which Feil copied. Shao, who normally found a plethora of things wrong with everything Feil performed, only nodded and moved on to the next lesson.

The look on Feil's face was one of absolute relief.

After lunch, Feil received his first positive comment. He flawlessly repeated a form Shao had been teaching him. When he finished, he bowed politely. Shao had watched every move without criticism. "Okay," he said.

As the afternoon progressed, Shao became less and less harsh, and Feil redoubled his efforts to please his laoshi. Every time he did something correctly and Shao nodded with a scarce smile, Feil nearly crowed with delight.

Alia was astonished to see how the young man's attitude changed. By the time the dinner bell rang, Feil was following Shao around like a puppy and begging him to meet after dinner for one last training session.

The fourth day dawned bright and clear—a perfect day for traveling. Alia and Shao went to the dining room as soon as the morning bell rang. Alia was surprised to find that Zimpf, Aistra, and Sabio were already there and were halfway through breakfast. Zimpf was normally the last member of their group to show up for anything.

"Why are you here so early?" Shao asked.

"I'm getting anxious to get home," Zimpf answered.

Alia immediately suspected deceit. She also noticed anytime the dining room door opened, Zimpf jumped nervously. It looked to her as though he had done something devious.

Within a few minutes, everyone from their group was there. They ate quickly; Zimpf's anxiousness to get on the road seemed to have infected them all.

Just as they finished, Sifu, followed by Feil, joined them.

"I want to wish you all safe travels and to extend the hospitality of the Temple of Anaia to you. Know that the doors of the temple always stand open to you and will provide a safe haven in the event of any strife, be it physical or emotional."

"Thank you, Sifu." Shao stood and bowed, offering the martial artists' salute.

"Now," he continued. "I would like to make a proposal to each of you. Shao, should you and Alia ever wish to reside here, I would like to offer you positions, Shao as laoshi and Alia as healer. Sh'ron and Chhdar," he said then, "we here at the Temple of Anaia are pleased with the formation of your school. We would be honored to have you establish a training routine for younger students here with us." Then Sifu looked at Zimpf and Aistra. "There will come a time when we will need new teachers for the divination students. The position is yours if you want it."

Aistra looked pleased; Zimpf looked stunned.

"Thank you, Sifu," Shao told him, his face shining with excitement. "I'm sure we would like to take some time to discuss your offer. We will let you know."

They all filed out. Alia and Shao took time to say goodbye to Sabio and then Feil. And then Zimpf and Aistra said their goodbyes to Sabio. Both of the students were saddened at their departure until Shao invited the two of them to visit Miast when the term ended. The two young men looked at each other excitedly.

Shao smiled, remembering his years there with Zimpf. He glanced over at his friend, and Zimpf nodded. Apparently these two were destined to be lifelong friends.

Once everyone was mounted, Zimpf, followed by Aistra, galloped their horses through the gardens and past the gate.

Alia found it peculiar that Zimpf took the lead, hustling them out of the temple in such a hurry.

Just as Alia and Shao made the last turn toward the road below, they heard Gatara screaming.

"Bring him back now!" she screeched in an infuriated tone. "This time he will answer to me alone, and the severity of his punishment shall serve as testimony to the burden and affliction I intend to make of his life!"

But they were too far away to be caught.

Alia and Shao exchanged curious glances as Zimpf's infectious laughter echoed up to them from below.

Marek sat alone in the abandoned campground, thinking over everything that had happened. He had tried to dominate the Vherals into obedience through fear, anger, and intimidation. But even before Alia's capture, he could see that his control was starting to crumble.

He didn't want to admit it, not even to himself, but Nabii was right. He would have been overthrown even if a civil war had not been developing.

Marek knew he needed to think—clearly, rationally, logically, and without the enhancement of the Aghara. The fact that he had sat in his tent for three days under the influence of the strange mist-like substance scared him badly. So, he had spent the last twenty-four hours outside in the fresh air.

"I need to figure things out," the mage said aloud to himself. "I need to devise a new strategy."

He grew quiet. "And who or what was Nabii?" he wondered.

After the old man, with a great deal of effort, had regained his composure, he had ordered Marek to abandon his original plan.

"You must win these people to your cause, not bully them into obe-

dience," he had warned sternly. Then, moving faster than any old man should have been able to, he darted behind the burning tree. Marek followed, but Nabii had disappeared.

All the mage saw was a strange distortion that quickly winked out.

Marek sighed bitterly. Of one thing, he was certain: he would not take orders. Not from anyone.

He could walk away, give up this whole plan, disappear. He had more than enough of the Aghara's contents to move south and ensconce himself in a small village, where he could live like an anonymous prince for the remainder of his life.

But he didn't want to be the prince of a rag-tag group of people in an unimportant settlement somewhere at the bottom of the Four Lands.

He wanted to rule the world.

Chapter 34 – Explanations

Zimpf pushed the group to travel hard for the remainder of the day, insisting that they only take a quick break for lunch. When Ciern asked what he had done to anger Gatara, he smirked.

"I'll tell you when we stop for the night." He giggled. "But only if we are far enough away from Temple that she can't catch me," Zimpf said fervently.

So, out of curiosity more than anything else, the others let him set the pace toward the elven kingdom.

Alia remembered how mountainous and rough the first couple of days were from their last trip. The terrain was steep, and they frequently had to climb off their horses and lead them along narrow trails, whose edges dropped off into nothingness far below. When Zimpf judged that they were far enough away from Temple and from Gatara, he allowed them all a few hours' rest. But that evening, there was no funny story around a warm campfire. They merely set up their tents, ate a cold meal, climbed into their blankets, and fell asleep. All except those on guard duty.

It was the end of the second day from Temple before they finally stopped traveling at a breakneck speed. They descended into a wooded valley teeming with deer, who gazed at them with curious, wide-eyed wonder. A clear, blue stream meandered its way lazily through the center.

It was extremely late when they finally stopped to set up camp. As was their custom, Sh'ron and Chhdar took care of the horses, Ciern, Amicu, and Skala gathered firewood and started a fire, and Zimpf and Aistra erected the tents. Alia and Shao foraged and then cooked their meal.

Once dinner was served and everyone had eaten, Shao looked at Zimpf, one eyebrow raised questioningly.

"So," he started curiously. "Do you want to tell us exactly why we are fleeing in terror from Gatara?"

Zimpf chuckled. "Well," he said, stretching out the word. "She might be slightly vexed with me."

"Slightly?" Amicu questioned. "She was ready to peel off your skin and use it to make shoes."

Zimpf giggled wickedly.

"Out with it!" Ciern ordered. "I don't want her finding you and demanding your head on a plate at a crucial moment."

"Oh, she won't do that," Zimpf stated confidently while looking at them with a face full of feigned innocence. "She'll be much too busy."

"Do you want me to have Shao force this story out of you?" Ciern threatened.

Shao winked at Zimpf. Then he nodded in the direction of Ciern's exasperated face.

"Okay, okay," Zimpf relented. "When Gatara was testing Sabio, she mentioned a new mental technique called a shock block. It's really great, because if an interloper—someone you don't want—pokes around in your brain or tries something, they'll receive a nasty shock. Actually," he suggested, "I should put it in all of you, especially you, Alia," he said as he looked at her seriously. "Then if Marek did survive and he—"

"That is enough!" Ciern interjected forcefully. "Stop prattling and tell us what you did."

Zimpf gave him a hurt expression but continued with the story. "Anyway, Gatara told me she wouldn't teach it to me. So, I—I sort of…blackmailed her by telling her if she would teach me how to shock block, then I would share the knowledge from the Zduhac about a new way to communication with other diviners."

"Zimpf!" Amicu blurted in a shocked tone. "That is vital knowledge! Gatara must be able to study that technique in case we need to use it as a defense."

"I was going to give it to her anyway," Zimpf protested. "I'm not an imbecile."

"So, she is angry because you tricked her into teaching you a new block?" Shao asked, his brows pulled down into a puzzled frown. "Her level of anger seems awfully disproportionate."

"That's not it exactly," Zimpf hedged.

"So, what exactly is it?" Ciern probed.

"I…um…well, I sort of used her shock block technique against her," Zimpf admitted.

Aistra, her eyes wide in sudden understanding, gasped out a single, surprised word: "Zimpf!"

Whatever he had done, this was clearly the first time she had heard about it.

"What?" Sh'ron asked Aistra, who had begun to giggle.

Then Sh'ron turned to Zimpf. "What did you do?"

Zimpf looked at the rest of them, his eyes glinting mischievously. "I put a shock block in the minds of all the divination students so that Gatara couldn't poke too far into their brains without getting a nasty surprise." Then he began to chuckle.

By now, Aistra was laughing so hard that tears were streaming down her cheeks.

The group looked back and forth at each other with stunned faces.

"You…wait…you…what?" Ciern asked, flabbergasted.

"I used the new knowledge she gave me to insert shock blocks in all of her students. Every single one of them." By now, Zimpf was laughing hysterically. "Can't you just see Gatara's face when she starts poking around in someone's brain?" he said through his laughter, then held up a hand as though he was going to *see* and mimicked a sudden, surprised scream while at the same time yanking his arm back comically.

Alia and Shao exchanged amused glances, and then they began to chuckle; Sh'ron and Chhdar joined them. Before long, everyone, even Skala, was laughing hysterically.

They stayed up late that night, talking and laughing and continuing to revisit Zimpf's latest shenanigan.

"Can the students take the block out by themselves?" Alia asked.

"Nope," Zimpf giggled. "That's one of the things I did. I made it so complicated that the students don't have the skill to remove it."

Aistra was still chuckling. "That's what's so funny. Only Gatara has the ability to remove those blocks, and every time she tries…"

Aistra trailed off in laughter.

"Well, he's clever, if nothing else," Ciern admitted, shaking his head.

"Thank you," Zimpf acknowledged grandly.

The next morning, they got up early and rode hard, stopping only long enough to eat a quick lunch and to allow the horses to rest briefly. Just as the sun was beginning to set, Ciern stood up in his saddle and pointed. They had reached the elven outpost.

Riding toward them was their old friend, Meyta.

They spent the night in the guest rooms of the Elven Stables. Then they were up early the next morning to finish their journey to the elven capital. It took them two days of fast walking to reach the palace at Asath Tesai. Their horses would arrive in a few days by a longer, less treacherous route.

As soon as they entered the palace, they were greeted by the same fussy, old elf, who announced that a meeting had been arranged that evening in the king's conference room. Then he led them to their quarters—all except for Ciern and Skala. The two princes went immediately to talk to their fathers.

The old elf took Alia and Shao to a room identical to the one they had stayed in before. It had a huge sitting room, a large bedroom, and an attached bathroom with a massive tub, filled to the brim with hot, soapy water.

Alia, her eyes dreamy, walked straight to the tub. Then she suddenly turned, and in a gesture of pure selflessness, asked Shao, "Do you want to bathe first?"

Shao smiled fondly at her. "No, you go ahead."

Although she would have liked to soak for hours, Alia took a quick bath so Shao could also have plenty of time to bathe. Later, when he walked into the sitting room, he found Alia visiting with Sh'ron and Chhdar. Servants had delivered snacks, and everyone was waiting politely for him.

He sat down beside Alia, his skin freshly scrubbed and his hair damp and clean smelling, and they chatted as they ate.

"So," Shao began, "what did you all think of Sifu's offer of employment?"

Alia looked over at him. "Were you listening at the door?" she teased.

Shao looked at her, one eyebrow raised questioningly.

Alia smiled at him. "We were just talking about that."

"And?" he asked anxiously. It was clear to Alia that Shao wanted to teach at the Temple of Anaia.

"The three of us," she said, indicating herself, Sh'ron, and Chhdar, "have agreed on two things."

Shao looked at Alia, his eyes wide in anticipation.

"Chhdar and I must first finish training with Sairima," Alia announced. Then she laughed at the look of surprise on Shao's face.

"You and Chhdar?" he asked, looking over at the big warrior.

Chhdar nodded. "I intend to ask Sairima to train me when we return to Miast. Not as a healer," he stated, holding up his hand, "but as an apothecary and a healer's helper."

Shao, like Alia, had been stunned at the story of Chhdar's natural talent with the healing arts.

"And the second agreement?" Shao asked.

"That we all stay together," Sh'ron said almost defiantly. "I do not want to be separated from Alia again."

"I can understand that," Shao muttered with a sidelong look at his wife. "So, does that mean we may be moving?" he asked hopefully.

"That means it is a serious possibility." Alia smiled.

"What about us?" Zimpf asked, a worried frown on his face as he and Aistra walked unannounced into the room. "I'm pretty sure Gatara won't hire me now," he fretted sadly.

"Don't worry about that," Shao said with a grin. "She doesn't even know that Sifu offered you the position."

"She doesn't?" Zimpf's mouth fell open, making a perfect O, while his eyebrows shot up at the new information. Because he was a diviner, it was almost impossible to keep things from Zimpf.

Shao burst out laughing at the surprised look on his friend's face.

"Gatara is considering retiring soon. But nothing has been decided yet. That's why you couldn't *see* it." Shao chuckled. "Don't worry; Gatara will be long gone by the time we make any decisions."

Zimpf sighed with relief. He looked at Aistra, who smiled and nodded. Then his whole face lit up with excitement.

Just then, there was a polite tap at the door, and Zimpf, his face still stunned at the unexpected news, opened it.

It was Amicu. "The king says he is ready for us now," he announced.

The seven of them walked down to the conference room behind the throne on the main floor. The door sat open, and King Elator and Ciern were waiting for them.

They filed into the room and sat around the big conference table.

"Ciern and Skala filled us in on what happened," King Elator informed them. "King Ganayt and I have had a long talk, and we decided there really isn't much for us to do at this point."

"Where are King Ganayt and Skala?" Amicu asked.

"They were anxious to get back home," Ciern answered. "They left for the dwarven kingdom about an hour ago."

"What do you mean by saying that there isn't much for you to do?" Amicu asked seriously.

"Ciern gave us a copy of the tactics you all developed when you met with your teachers at Temple. King Ganayt and I agree that those plans are the most comprehensive and ingenious piece of strategy we have ever seen. There is nothing more we can do to prepare." The king continued, "we have already set up a series of fast runners to warn us in case of an invasion. They will give us ample warning of an attack. Meanwhile, we will both prepare our armies for war, and we will advise the peoples in the outlands and in the south to begin preparations as well."

It was clear to Alia that Amicu wanted to say more. But she saw Ciern give him a quick shake of his head; Amicu remained silent.

The king looked at him kindly. "Don't worry, Amicu. If war does come, you and Ciern will be the first people I call to refine the strategy."

"Thank you," Amicu answered softly.

"Now, let's go to the banquet I ordered in your honor," King Elator bade them, smiling.

Alia was absolutely exhausted after her weeks in the saddle, and the last thing she wanted to do was attend a formal banquet. Shao reached for her hand, and she smiled up at him. She could see on his face that he felt the same way. But they politely followed the king down the hallway.

As soon as they walked into the banquet hall, Alia stopped in surprise. The room was empty except for the nine of them. A huge buffet of delicious, exotic elven food sat in warming trays along the wall. Seated at a large, round table in the middle of the room was Airafae. As soon as they entered, she jumped up excitedly and flew to both Alia and Sh'ron, hugging them exuberantly and talking excitedly.

The meal was perfect. Alia didn't know how he did it, but King Elator seemed to have a talent for graciously entertaining his guests. They ate and talked and laughed and ate some more. Once they were finished with their meal, musicians came in and played the most beautiful music.

After several minutes, Shao stood before Alia and bowed formally. "May I have this dance?" he invited. Then he took her hand and led her onto the floor, where they danced alone.

Early the next morning, their horses arrived from the outpost, and the seven travelers left for Miast.

"Are you glad to be going home?" Alia overheard Zimpf ask Aistra.

His wife was silent for a moment, and then she looked at him with absolute adoration. "Home," she said, trying out the word. "I don't really remember ever having a home."

Zimpf looked at her rather sadly. After a moment, he smiled gently. "You will always have a home with me," he promised.

The group rode quickly out of the city and into the foothills of the mountains. They traveled at a quick canter before stopping late and setting up their camp. As usual, Chhdar and Sh'ron took care of the horses and set up the camp, Amicu started a fire and collected firewood, Zimpf and Aistra erected the tents, and Alia and Shao foraged for plants to supplement the food the elves had given them. Once they had gathered some roots and berries, Shao stopped.

"I want to do something," he said, taking the food and setting it aside. Then he pulled Alia into his arms and kissed her. Within seconds, they heard Zimpf.

"Stop smooching!" he ordered. "We're hungry, and you're supposed to be cooking dinner, not playing kissy face."

Alia and Shao began to laugh.

"How does he always know?" Alia wondered aloud.

Shao looked at her, one eyebrow raised sardonically.

"Oh, yeah," Alia said, slightly embarrassed. "He's a diviner."

They went back then and prepared dinner for everyone.

The trip home was uneventful; the weather was clear, their horses were healthy, and they made good time. In just a couple of weeks, they had gone from trails to roads to streets. There were houses and hamlets and small villages. Finally, at the tag-end of another long day of travel, they topped a hill, and below them lay the large village of Miast. The houses had lights in the windows, beckoning them invitingly.

Marek had packed his things and was getting ready to mount his horse when a young girl came barreling toward him on a horse much too big for her. She slid awkwardly off the stallion's bare back, took two unbalanced steps, and fell to the ground hard. Sobbing uncontrollably, she managed to get to her feet and run directly to the mage, where she flung her arms around him, her skinny little body shaking in fear.

A quick image popped into his mind of himself at approximately the same age. Without permission, he had taken his father's horse to do a chore. Something had spooked the mare, and she had bucked, throwing him to the ground and bolting. As though it had only happened yesterday, he sharply remembered the pain from the fall and the fear he had felt as he watched the animal race swiftly away. But a kind adult saw what happened and rushed to his aid. That was how he met

S'rone, who, sensing he needed friends, later introduced him to his own daughters, Alia and Sh'ron.

Marek shook himself out of his reverie and stood looking down at the little girl.

"What is wrong, child?"

"It—it's Mama," she snuffled. "She's—she's very sick and—and I was sent to—to find the big camp where—where a healer lives. But—but I can't find it," she wailed desperately.

Uncharacteristically, he felt a sudden surge of pity for the child. "There is no big camp," Marek whispered softly. "And I am not a healer. But I do know a few things about plants. I will come with you to see what may be done."

Chapter 35 – Family

Once they made it into the city, they walked their horses directly toward the big house. Alia smiled as Amicu moved his horse to the front and encouraged it into a quick trot. The rest of them walked sedately behind, because once again, a crowd of townspeople had begun to gather around them, calling their names in excitement. Zimpf rode at the head of the column, waving grandly, with Aistra at his side, looking bewildered. Shao and Alia followed with Sh'ron and Chhdar close behind.

They got to the big house just in time to see Sairima run down the stairs toward them. Amicu darted to her, lifted her in the air, and swung her around in a circle while she laughed girlishly. When he finally put her down, she turned and walked with as much dignity as she could muster to greet the rest of them. She hugged each person and then kissed them on the cheek.

Meanwhile, Mama had emerged from the house and hurried directly toward them.

"Amicu!" she shouted, grabbing her son and hugging him tightly. Then she saw Shao and Zimpf.

"My boys!" she screamed in delight and hugged them as well. Afterward, she hugged Alia, Sh'ron, and Chhdar, babbling excitedly the entire time. Finally, she turned to Aistra just as Zimpf took her hand and pulled her toward the two women.

"This is Aistra, my wife," he announced dramatically.

Both Sairima and Mama stared back and forth between the two of them. Their faces lit up with happiness for their friend. It was obvious that both women had been aware of Zimpf's private tragedy, so they were delighted to welcome Aistra into the family.

"Aistra," Zimpf said respectfully, "this is Sairima the Healer, Shao's sister." Aistra bowed respectfully. It was obvious that even she had heard of Sairima. "And this charming lady is—"

But Mama interrupted. "Never mind." She stopped him, then she turned to Aistra. "I am Amicu's mother, but all of these young men are my boys. Even that rascal you married." She laughed. "You will call me Mama."

Aistra's face lit up. She didn't have a good memory of her own mother, and the prospect of having someone to assume that role filled her with joy.

"Come in, come in," Sairima invited. "Let's get you all fed, then you can go home to rest for a while. Later, I want to examine each of you."

So the group trudged tiredly up the staircase and through the entryway to the dining room, where they sat at the large, round table that seemed to be reserved for them. They talked and laughed and traded stories while they ate, although no one discussed their latest adventure. Shao had taken Sairima aside and suggested that they wait until they were in private to explain the outcome of the mission.

As dinner was winding down, Amicu, who had only turned loose of Sairima's hand long enough to eat, once again took her hand and kissed it gently. Then he got down on one knee and looked up at her earnestly.

"I asked you before I left if you would be my bride."

For only the second time since she had met the woman, Alia saw Sairima blush shyly.

"Will you still marry me?" he asked for the second time, his heart in his eyes.

"Yes! Of course I still want to be your wife!" Sairima answered with a gentle smile.

"How soon can we get married?" he entreated. "Tomorrow?"

Sairima laughed in delight. "I did as we discussed before you left, and I planned the whole wedding. How about the day after tomorrow?" She beamed excitedly. "And you three," she said to Alia, Sh'ron, and Aistra, "will be my bridesmaids. Shao, Zimpf, and Chhdar will be the groomsmen."

"But we don't even have dresses," Alia protested.

"Yes, you do," Sairima insisted. "All three of you. They are upstairs in the suite, and they should fit to perfection."

"But…but how could you possibly know about me?" Aistra blurted in confusion.

Sairima smiled at her. "I received a message from Elator telling me that you all were on your way."

"It's late," Shao suddenly announced. "Why don't we retire tonight and then meet back here for breakfast tomorrow?" He looked over at Sairima. "Can you arrange for us to have breakfast in the conference room in the morning? We can have a nice, long talk, then afterward you can give us all physicals, and we'll spend the remainder of the day getting ready for a wedding."

"Before we split up," Zimpf suddenly declared, "I have something I want to say."

They all turned to him expectantly, but he was looking at Aistra. "When King Elator married us, I promised you a real wedding."

Aistra's face flushed with color.

"Will you marry me again?" he asked rather stiffly.

Leaning forward, Shao quickly slapped him on the back of his head.

"Ow!" Zimpf complained, his hand raised to his head as he turned to Shao in confusion.

"You can do better than that!" Shao hissed.

Zimpf looked around at the shocked faces of his friends. "What—" he started. "Oh. Oh!" he said. Then he got down on one knee, took Aistra's hand in both of his, and in a flat tone, he repeated Amicu's proposal word for word. "Will you still marry me?"

Aistra smiled and nodded shyly.

"With a romantic proposal like that, it's no wonder her acceptance wasn't more enthusiastic," Shao muttered sarcastically.

Everyone burst into laughter except for Zimpf. Alia thought he looked a little wounded.

Yawning, Shao stretched his long frame theatrically and then stood up, holding his hand out to Alia. "Coming?" he invited.

"Your house has been repaired," Sairima said to the couple. Then she looked around the table at everyone. "Go home and get some sleep." With that, she stood and shooed everyone out the door.

Alia and Shao walked home quickly, holding hands and talking softly.

"I am so happy to be going home, alone, with you," Alia told her husband.

Shao smiled and squeezed her hand gently. "I'm happy anytime I'm with you," he replied simply.

They climbed the stairs into their home. Everything was just the same as it was when they moved in. There was no sign of the fire. It was nice to be alone again. It reminded Alia of their first blissful days together after their wedding. Tiredly, they moved through the house to the bedroom, where they slept soundly in their own bed for the first time in a long time.

They rose early the next morning and walked back to the big house much earlier than they were expected. It was Alia's idea to get there early. She thought they could go ahead and get their physicals and then maybe she could help Sairima with some of the work. She also wanted to talk to the healer about training Chhdar.

But when she got there, Sh'ron and Chhdar were already there, so she and Shao had to wait their turn.

Alia's twin and her husband came out of Sairima's office smiling and holding hands.

"What's going on?" Alia asked. "Why did you all come here so early?" She knew that Sh'ron liked to sleep late.

"No reason; we just woke up early and decided to come on up here." But Alia noticed that Sh'ron seemed unusually happy for so early in the morning and that Chhdar seemed slightly startled.

"Shao! Alia!" Sairima suddenly ordered. "Go to exam room one. You all can chat later."

Within minutes, Sairima had joined them. "Up on the table, Shao," she commanded. Then she began her examination of him while questioning Alia about Amicu's injuries in the monger attack.

Clearly, he had already had his exam. When Sairima got to Shao's shoulder, she frowned.

"Did you do this?" She indicated the rather large, uneven scar that remained from Shao's arrow strike.

"Yes, Healer," Alia replied softly.

"Why does his scar look like this?" she demanded, clipping her words in a disapproving tone and turning to stare angrily at Alia.

"Don't be hard on her," Shao ordered. "I ripped out my stitches and then didn't tell her for several hours. She did the best she could with the mess I made of my shoulder."

"You what?" Sairima stepped back to look Shao in the face, her arms crossed over her chest and her eyes narrowing dangerously.

"I said," Shao began, speaking slowly and clearly as though he was talking to a child, "I. Ripped. Out. My. Stitches. And. Then. I. Didn't. Tell. Her. For. Several. Hours."

"Why?" Sairima had begun tapping her foot on the ground impatiently.

"Do you want the whole story now, or do you want to wait until the breakfast meeting?" Shao grinned impudently.

"You've been spending too much time with Zimpf," Sairima complained, giving up.

Shao winked at Alia.

After Sairima gave Alia her physical and grilled her on the health of the others, the three of them walked together to the conference room. Everyone else had already arrived, and the food was just being served as they entered.

The meeting began as soon as they all started eating. There was a lot to tell, and Sairima and Mama had many questions, but finally, they had said all that could be said.

"Now," Mama declared, "it's time to move on to more urgent things." Everyone looked at her. "The wedding," she said. "I have a list of tasks for each of you to do." She stood and started handing out assignments to each of the men. "All of the women will come with me to the suite upstairs so we can do the dress fittings. You gentlemen will get every single thing done on your list before we meet for dinner at seven o'clock to discuss final details."

"But," Zimpf started, "what if I..." He trailed off, because Mama had picked up her wooden serving spoon that Alia had returned earlier and was lightly tapping the palm of her hand with it.

She looked at Zimpf, her eyebrows raised. "What?" she asked in a dangerous tone.

"Nothing," he muttered, looking over his extensive list of chores.

"I guess you'd better get started then," Mama said, clapping her hands at them.

Then she turned to the young women. "Let's go," she ordered as she led the way to the staircase. Obediently, the ladies followed her to the upstairs suite, where the dressmakers waited. By the time they were finished, it was late afternoon. Mama took Sh'ron and Aistra with her to finalize the details with the florist, and Alia went with Sairima to check on the patients.

Once they finished their rounds, Sairima asked Alia to stop by her office. Alia was sure she was going to say something about how badly Shao's shoulder was scarred, so she walked into the office reluctantly.

"Sit down," Sairima told her.

Alia obeyed nervously. Normally, when Sairima invited someone into her office, they left in tears.

Sairima sat in the chair behind her desk, a sheaf of papers stacked carefully in front of her.

"These are letters written to me from dozens of healers who all witnessed your work or the aftermath of your work in the field." She indicated the papers on her desk.

Alia nodded, swallowing hard. She thought she had done a good job, but if people were writing to Sairima…

"With one exception, which we will discuss shortly," Sairima said, speaking firmly, "I must officially end your status as a healer-in-training."

Alia looked at the floor, fighting tears. She had failed. This was what she had wanted her whole life, and she had failed. Then she thought of Shao and how disappointed he would be, how she had let him down as well.

"Alia!" Sairima snapped sharply. "Did you hear what I said?"

Alia nodded but refused to look up. She didn't want Sairima to see her cry.

"Take this," the healer demanded, handing Alia a piece of paper.

Alia took it with numb, shaking hands and forced herself to look at the document. What she saw caused her eyes to widen in surprise and her mouth to fall open. There, in large, stenciled letters, was her name followed by the word "Healer." She looked up in surprise.

"I…I… how?" she stuttered in confusion.

"These letters"—Sairima indicated the pile of papers in front of her—"are documents from healers all over the Four Lands who witnessed your skill in the art of healing and who demand that I release you from your training status. After reading these documents and carefully considering the requests, I have concluded that, with one exception, I have nothing else to teach you. As I suspected when you first came here, you have a true talent for healing."

Alia, completely stunned into silence, finally said the only thing that came to her mind.

"What exception?" she blurted.

"You must still do a surgery rotation with me in order to complete the full course of study," Sairima asserted.

Just then, there was a knock on the door, and Shao stuck his head inside. "You wanted to see me?" he asked his sister.

"I believe Alia does," she said with a smile on her face.

Alia, however, was still staring at the document in her hand, as tears began sliding down her cheeks.

"What is it?" Shao whispered in concern. "Are you okay? Why is she crying?" he demanded sternly of his sister. "What is that?" He reached for the document in Alia's trembling hand. Then he read it carefully. His eyes widened in surprise.

Suddenly, Alia was in his arms, being swung around in a circle as she laughed and cried with excitement.

Later, they all met for the most wonderful dinner. Everyone congratulated her, and then they all discussed Amicu and Sairima's wedding, scheduled for the next day. Everything was done, and the arrangements were completed.

"Just remember," Shao said, "that I forbid you to do that binding ceremony. Amicu was in my class at the Temple, so I know how good he is at untying knots."

"I don't know why it should matter." Sairima smirked. "I know you were bound in Alia's room two nights before your wedding."

Shao laughed.

Alia blushed a bright red.

"Wait, what?" Zimpf turned to stare at first Shao, then Alia, and then at Shao again. "You were together? You yelled at me, and then threatened me. I was scared. And you." He turned to Alia. "You made me feel like a rascal. You accused me of staring at you while you slept."

Zimpf's face vacillated between anger and righteous indignation.

Alia wanted to apologize for the deception, but she just couldn't. Instead, she giggled, then chuckled, and finally roared with laughter, tears pouring down her face, causing everyone at the table to join her—even Zimpf.

The next morning dawned bright and clear. Alia and Shao walked to the big house early, where Shao helped Alia make her hospital rounds. They had both insisted that Sairima take off the day of her wedding. By the time Alia finished, they barely had time to get dressed. Alia rushed to the suite upstairs while Shao joined the men in one of the guest rooms that had been reserved for them.

All too soon, it was time for the ceremony. Outside, Amicu, Shao, and Chhdar stood together at the right side of the altar while Zimpf waited at the podium. One by one, the bridesmaids, each wearing a different pastel color, walked gracefully to their position at the left side of the altar. There were scores of guests seated in chairs at either side of the aisle, waiting for the appearance of the bride.

After a very dramatic pause, a cascade of harps played a waterfall of music, and Sairima, accompanied by Mama, made her way regally down the aisle. Sairima's dress was fitted to the hips and then flared out dramatically in yards of old-fashioned lace. She was beautiful.

Per Sairima's instructions, the ceremony was short and direct. Alia knew that Zimpf liked to draw these things out, so she was sure that Sairima had threatened him to keep his sermon brief. There was a full meal and a dance afterward. While Sairima and Amicu danced with everyone, Shao and Alia danced only with each other.

The festivities ended when the newlyweds left for their honeymoon trip shortly after midnight.

The next morning, Alia and Shao were up early. They were going to walk to the big house, eat breakfast in the dining room, and then work at the hospital. But before they could leave, Sh'ron and Chhdar knocked at the back door.

"Come in," Alia invited them warmly. "I'm sorry I don't have breakfast cooked. Do you two want to walk to the big house with us to eat?"

"No, thank you," Sh'ron muttered as she sat down weakly. "I don't think I could eat anything this morning."

"Are you ill?" Alia asked. Now that she looked at her twin, Sh'ron did look pale and rather shaky. "I think you should let me examine you."

"I had Sairima check me out three days ago."

"But you're still sick," Alia pointed out.

"Yes," Sh'ron agreed. "And I'm likely to be sick every morning for the next couple of months, maybe as many as nine," she announced with a huge smile on her face. Chhdar was also grinning from ear to ear.

"That's a really specific time to expect to be sick," Shao pondered in confusion.

But Alia leapt out of her chair and screamed with excitement as she ran to hug her sister.

"What?" Shao asked, his brows drawn together in confusion. Then his eyes grew wide, and he also jumped up to hug both Sh'ron and Chhdar.

"A baby!" he exclaimed.

Within a few weeks, life in Miast had returned to normal.

Sairima and Amicu had returned from their honeymoon. Sairima had resumed her work at the hospital, and Amicu and Mama had moved permanently to Miast. Mama now managed the big house, and Amicu worked with Shao and Zimpf, keeping the hospital and the town running smoothly. Sh'ron was teaching at the school she and Chhdar had founded, but Chhdar had begun his course in apothecary studies under Sairima.

Alia excelled at her surgery rotation at the hospital, although the work was often difficult and demanding. There were some days when she worked for many hours nonstop, and she was frequently too tired to stay awake once she returned home. She began going to bed shortly after dinner and sleeping soundly through the night only to get up exhausted the next day.

Shao began to worry about Alia's health, and finally asked Sairima to give her a thorough physical.

Alia objected. "I'm just tired from all of the work," she insisted. "I'll feel better when this rotation is over."

Sairima, after listening to Shao's concerns and observing Alia for a few days, intervened. She made the couple come to her office for an appointment, where she questioned first Shao on his concerns and then Alia on her health. Finally, she left Shao alone in her office and escorted Alia to an exam room. They rejoined Shao several minutes later.

"Sit down, Alia," Sairima ordered seriously. "I have news for both of you."

Shao, the blood draining from his face in fear, reached over and took Alia's hand.

Alia had seen Sairima give other people bad news in this same manner. She lifted her head bravely and nodded. "Go ahead."

But Sairima only smiled at the couple.
"You're going to be parents."

Marek knew what herbs would help the child's mother, so he treated her quickly and without comment. Then he spoke to the woman's husband, giving him the ingredients for the healing tea he had administered.

Afterward, as he ate dinner with the Vheral family, he listened quietly as the members of the small group discussed an evil mage who had attempted to start a civil war, failed, and then fled south.

"Those people from the southland are always coming up here trying to cause trouble," the leader of the family group stated angrily.

The others nodded their heads in agreement.

"One of these days, we're going to get tired of it," he continued. "Then we'll teach them a lesson they will never forget!"

Marek nodded with the rest of them as though he agreed.

"What we need to do," another man suggested, "is organize ourselves. Maybe if we're ready to fight, like some of those southern groups, they'll leave us alone."

Everyone began talking excitedly at the same time.

"That's actually a good idea," the leader agreed loudly.

Everyone grew quiet as he continued to speak.

"What is needed is for someone to carry our message to as many of the other families as possible. Then our people can form our own army!"

The group grew quiet again, thinking over the alien idea.

"Who could we send though?" one of the younger men asked. "No one here can leave our wives and children to go traveling all over the Wilds."

Marek suddenly realized how much the Vheral people wanted to extract revenge from the people of the south for wrongs that were both justified and imagined.

Nabii's advice rang abruptly in his mind: "You must win these people, not bully them into obedience."

The Vheral people of the Wilds were like a dry prairie that only needed a single spark to ignite an inferno.

Marek suddenly knew how to light that spark.

"I will carry your message," he answered softly.

The End

Epilogue

Zimpf and Aistra finally had their formal wedding. The day after they returned from their honeymoon, everyone met in Alia and Shao's house for a breakfast buffet and to watch the couple open the gifts they had received.

The diviner was in his element as he teased and laughed and bragged about the quantity and quality of his gifts.

"People must like us more than they like you," he aggravated Alia and Shao. "And people definitely like me more than they like Sairima," he continued in a bantering tone. "Our presents are way better than what either of you got when you wed."

Sairima glared threateningly at him.

Zimpf continued to smirk.

Amicu picked up a crystal vase that Aistra had recently unwrapped and, with unerring accuracy, threw it directly at his new brother-in-law.

He knew that the diviner would *see* it coming and would catch it, so he wasn't worried about it breaking.

He was wrong.

Zimpf looked up just then, his face frozen and his eyes glazed and far away. He made no attempt to catch the vase hurling directly at his face.

It was only Shao's agility that saved both Zimpf's nose and the flying projectile.

"Zimpf? Brother?" Shao asked, just as Aistra leaned over to gently touch her husband's face.

But the diviner, *seeing* the past, didn't respond.

In Zimpf's mind, he was still a student at the Temple of Anania and Gatara had called him to her office.

"Do you understand what I need?"

"Yes, Gatara," he replied softly.

"And you understand how dangerous this is?" she pressed.

"I do." For once in his life, Zimpf was quiet, stoic, and thoughtful.

"This creature we are going to confront is incredibly powerful," she continued.

"Isn't that the nature of a diablerie? That is what you taught us," he acknowledged.

"What else do you remember about that lesson?" she quizzed. "As I recall, you spent that entire class humming under your breath, throwing wet paper wads at Aistra, and making rude noises by pursing your lips together and blowing."

"Yeah," he said earnestly, not even trying to deny it. "But that doesn't mean I wasn't listening."

Gatara shook her head in defeat.

"I will be your intensifier," Zimpf agreed seriously.

The next day, the divination master and her most talented student furtively left the Temple of Anaia to confront an ancient enemy.

As they journeyed to the very peak of the Skarsgaard Mountains, Gatara explained how she had visioned the diablerie, and had marked his location. Then she proceeded to teach Zimpf how to perform such a feat.

The sun had begun to lower into the west when they found the creature.

At first, Zimpf thought he was just an old man. It was hard for him to reconcile the stories of wicked persuasion, of stolen magic, and of unspeakable deeds with the frail-looking, elderly graybeard.

But when the diablerie turned to face them, Zimpf flinched against the wave of pure evil that emanated from the very core of the creature.

"What are you doing here, diablerie?" Gatara demanded.

To Zimpf, it seemed as though the divination master had grown as she stood facing evil, her face etched in abhorrent resolve.

The diablerie glanced once at Zimpf and seemed to dismiss him as inconsequential.

"I do not answer to you," the creature sneered.

Zimpf stepped forward and placed his hand on Gatara's shoulder as he had been instructed.

"You are banished from here, never to return," Gatara demanded.

The diablerie laughed, a high-pitched, mocking sound. Then, with barely a breath, he hurled a fireball directly at the diviners.

Gatara, brandishing a walking stick she had carried from the

Temple, swept the conflagration away contemptuously.

"For your impertinence, you are exiled to the Desolation." This time, Gatara spoke in a strangely choral voice.

The diablerie stepped back in surprise.

"How are you able to do this?" he questioned.

"We have enclosed our magic into the diviner; she encompasses all of our power. We are giving you a choice. Go east and live, or stay and die!"

With the last sentence, Gatara held out her staff. It glowed blue and began to emit bright purple sparks as she swung it over her head then pointed it directly toward the old man.

The diablerie recoiled in fear then spoke one word in the spidery language of magic.

"Tethio!"

There was a loud boom, followed by a sudden gust of wind.

Zimpf and Gatara were hurled to the ground. When they got up again, the diablerie was gone.

The scene wavered and shifted and finally shattered.

"Why did you come back?" Marek asked.

"I came to advise you once more," a mysterious cloaked figure replied as he pushed the hood back, revealing his face.

Marek saw the evil smile; it was the same malevolent smile he had seen when he possessed the Aghara.

He caught his breath sharply.

About the Author

Julie Peralta is a fiction writer and the author of *The Mage: Book Two of The Acacia Chronicles and The Crystal Orb: Book One of the Acacia Chronicles*. She holds a BS in English education and an MA in education. She is currently editing books three and four of the *Acacia Chronicles* series and has begun to write a prequel. She lives in northwestern Kentucky.

MEDIA CONTACT:
Webpage: www.juliehperalta.com
Facebook: https://www.facebook.com/profile.php?id=100083307760547
The Crystal Orb – Book 1 of The Acacia Chronicles
X: @TheCrystalOrb
Instagram: @the_crystal_orb
Tiktok: @thecrystalorb
Snapchat: @thecrystalorb

Milton Keynes UK
Ingram Content Group UK Ltd.
UKHW021941281024
450365UK00018B/1202